The Shaman's Apprentice

Book 1

Jovai

The Vohee Song

BY

B. Muze

For information contact Wittily Writ Publishing,
https://www.WittilyWrit.com
2AMayze@WittilyWrit.com

Second Edition

First paperback edition: January, 2018,
by Wittily Writ Publishing.
Originally entitled "The Shaman's Apprentice"
book 1 of the Jovai series

Cover Design by David Gardias
- www.bestselling-covers.com
- contact@bestselling-covers.com

Printed in the United States of America
ISBN-13: 978-0-9995836-3-0

Visit www.WittilyWrit.com

This book is dedicated to my Creator
with soul-trembling awe and gratitude
for my life,
for my love,
for my sustainance,
for inspiring me with
the abundant wonders
of all your creations,
for answering my prayers,
for blessing me with this work
for teaching and growing me through it.
Through all the years of my life,
Your patience with me is the greatest miracle of all.
Thank You!

And to my beloved readers.
I could not have done this without God,
but I would not have done this without you.

Book 1

THE SHAMAN'S APPRENTICE

THE VOHEE SONG

BY

B. MUZE

CONTENTS

Chapter 1

First Curse

Yaku Shaman, whose giant body time had shaped and worn, forced himself awake to icy silence. A sense of yearning, the last breath of his dreams, was shattered in an instant as he saw the faint glow of morning slipping around the hide door that shielded his entry and falling through the smoke hole in his roof. He was late. Never had this happened — and it could not happen now. The lives of his people depended on him. So important was it that he could almost believe time would stop and wait for him to catch up.

This day was the Trintoa — the first hour of the first day of the first season of the year. A hard winter had frosted but not frozen him. He had been granted another spring of life. Now was the hour to call the sun to warm his people, to call the plants to grow, to call the babies forth from their mother's wombs, and to call the spirits to strengthen and nourish his people. This year he would also call for another holy one to guide his people when he should be unable. In his pride, he feared, he had waited too long. Strong and indestructible he had always thought himself. This Trintoa he discovered an old man dying where the young one had lived for so long.

The konis was difficult to mix. His hands trembled as he measured the herbs. The amount had to be perfect. His success, even his life, depended on it. It seemed slow to heat, which fed his agitation. This delayed his call, but he could not go without it. He poured the thick,

1

bitter liquid down his throat and gulped it, then paused as it filled his body with energy and his mind with awareness. He felt his spirit raised and hints of the unseeable played at the edge of his sight. He was ready to talk to gods.

His people watched from doors and windows of their round, clay-coated homes as their shaman strode through the village, softly singing the first chant. The sky was already brightening. His people knew he was late. He imagined he could see the silent reproach in the eyes of some, but they would say nothing. The Trintoa was the prayer for their lives. No one would risk an ill word to curse it.

Yaku suppressed a stab of anger that he should so harshly be judged by these people for whom he had sacrificed so much. He pushed that unholy thought away. Not only must his actions be perfect now, but also his soul.

His gaze turned toward the snow-draped mountains surrounding their village beyond their fields and woods. The people trusted them as guards, but Yaku knew how easily breached they truly were. The mountains would keep no dangers away. Only the spirits could protect them...if they would. It all depended on him.

He climbed the eastern hill, his body groaning under its own weight. Even the strength of the konis could no longer carry him. He should take the women's path, he realized, but his pride would not allow that. He would climb to Trintoa still like a man and hope the sun would wait for him. He was now in a race against the sky's light and all his people would suffer should he lose.

Where his song should have grown stronger it failed. He had no breath to raise it. He gasped as he climbed and mouthed the words. "The spirits will hear," he told himself. "They will understand." In the distance, he imagined, he could hear them singing back to him, gently, encouragingly, with a child's voice. It grew louder as he gained the top.

He mounted the hill and looked to the East. Already the sun had broken the horizon. He had missed the moment! Still the singing continued. A spirit, perhaps, had flown before to play his part until he arrived. He stepped forward wonderingly and followed the voice.

2

To the god's tree he went, the tree that grew in twining fingers around itself, ever widening, which the Mother/Father had planted and in whose gnarled hands, it was said, the new world lay, waiting to be born. Nestled in its upper branches was the spirit singer, child's face raised to the sun, calling it gently to fill the world. As if her voice were the string that pulled it, the sun came. Its warm touch caressed the girl's face, making her dark hair and large, brown eyes glisten and her fair skin glow. She looked as though she were made of shadow-edged light. She reached out her hand to greet the first spring blossom on the sacred tree. It opened to her touch. Around her the day birds were waking — not with their usual chittering, but in silent reverence. They stretched their wings and floated upon the morning breeze. One circled Yaku Shaman's head and landed at his feet, watching him curiously as the old man watched the child. A squirrel flowed up the tree, and from between two roots emerged a painted skunk, her newborn in her jaw, to introduce him to the world.

"I am here now," Yaku wanted to say. "I can sing for myself and my people..." but he could not find his voice.

The girl sang their Trintoa. She used no words that the shaman could recognize, only sound, yet the meaning was clear. She gave to the spirits a natural gift. She shared with them the beauty of her spirit, its joy in its life, and asked nothing in return but that they feel welcomed and happy. They came. Yaku Shaman could feel them dancing around her, competing to please her. The sun rose higher, shone brighter, the day was warmer, the blossoms breathed sweeter scents. The holy tree had never bloomed before, he suddenly realized. Had it bloomed just to please her? The grass grew higher to tickle her bare feet and the wind bent the blades into dancing patterns swirling around the tree.

"You have them listening," Yaku tried to cry. "Ask for protection, ask for abundance, ask that they keep our people healthy and happy!"

The girl did not hear. She did not ask. She simply gave, and the spirits gave back to her with all their power to please. They promised her the safety of her people and joy for them all, good hunting, abundant crops, a year of all the blessings they could bestow. She had made them happy and they would stay.

The Trintoa proper was sung. Soon his people would follow, dressed in vividly dyed wool and hides, ornamented with painted images of flowers and symbols of life and the spring that would soon awaken. The women would bring what could be spared from winter rations in hopes that they soon would be replenished. The men would come, helping the sick and dying so their spirits might find renewed health in this festival of life. The children who were old enough would kneel to the shaman to receive their first names. Those in love, some who had waited all year, would join their lives. He would assure them all that the spirits had listened and promised them a good year. But what would he tell them about the singer?

She climbed down out of the tree — not a spirit, he realized, but a human child — one of his own people. He recognized her as Polisa's youngest — too young to have a name. She had barely seen five years. Her first name would not come for another two. She was not even considered a person yet. Why was she here, alone? Where were her parents? Why had they let her interfere in what she was too young to understand?

———————◆—◆———————

The little girl swung down, dropped from the lowest branch and started running toward the village. Only then did she see Yaku Shaman. Her joy vanished and her eyes went wide in fright. He was a huge man, like a bear, and holy with the power of the spirits flowing through him. His face, as he watched her, looked stern and angry. She had not known he would come to her hill today. Now he would tell her parents and they would beat her and never let her come again.

She did not speak, but stood before the holy man, eyes lowered, trembling.

He stepped to her and lifted her chin. His touch was cold and firm. Briefly her eyes met his. She dropped her gaze quickly, afraid.

4

The holy man could curse her with his eyes alone. He could change her into something different, an animal or a plant or a cloud. His powers were unlimited.

He released her chin and stepped back, out of her way.

"Go home," he ordered.

She ran all the way.

CHAPTER 2

GHOSTLY MESSAGES

Spring bloomed, summer ripened, and fall filled the people's storerooms — portions of deep caves that had already been mined of the silver, the iron and copper, coal and the blue tearstone that they had held. The storerooms were carefully hidden in the hills' depleted mines, dug deep and wide enough to hide ten of their villages — with all their livestock, horses, and supplies, should enemies threaten.

War had been common in their history. They had been a warrior people before the spirits led them through the earth tunnels during the destruction of the last world to this luscious valley. The spirits had taught them to harness the rivers, cultivate crops, domesticate animals, dig and shape metals and beautiful colored stones. Now, protected by the steep mountains that surrounded them on all sides, they were able to put aside their weapons and work the land and give back to the spirits full measure of thanks for the abundance granted them.

Only one nomadic tribe, the Gicoks, still threatened them with deadly regularity, but they had not come yet this year. The valley people saved enough hiding space in their well-stocked storage, just in case, and the rest was filled with supplies enough to see them through three winters. Babies had been born, the sick had healed, and only the oldest and most tired of life had died. It had been a better year than any could remember and thanks to the spirits were given generously.

In bad years it would now be the time to pack and follow the sun south and east — a long and dangerous trek to easier climes where hunting was good even in winter. This year the people rejoiced that they could rest where they were, safe from hunger.

Massern, the Summer Leader, the elected head of the council of elders during the warm, long days, felt at ease to devote more of his time to the simple matters of day-to-day life. Pens for the animals were mended, village records updated, new land cleared and prepared for planting, pipes made and mended for irrigating the lands from the lakes and rivers, new homes of wood and clay allotted space and built for newlyweds, and family homes expanded as children were born or apprentices added. Matters of families were addressed and the town's well-being in general discussed.

"Have you thought of your successor?" he asked Yaku Shaman while they walked through the grain and fruit rich valley. His manner, as he asked, was good-humored but cautious. He had spoken the question before several times in several years and Yaku had always been offended. The great bear still stood tall and proud and did not like to think of his decline. This year, however, Yaku did not growl in response but nodded slowly.

"Fanthsen would have you consider his son Ganju, a quiet boy who might serve well," suggested Massern.

"Ganju is a tiny boy whom Fanthsen thinks will serve for nothing else. He is wrong about that one. He will be a warrior of the mind, a designer, a planner perhaps — not for the spirits."

"Is there another boy you prefer?"

Yaku raised his eyes to the eastern hill, to the holy tree growing there with a new world in its trunk.

"There is a child, two years before naming."

Massern swept the babies of the village with his mind, but could find no boy of that age who would do.

"Harkon's eldest is their only boy so far..." he started.

"No," said Yaku Shaman. "The spirits themselves have chosen another. Polisa's youngest."

"But Polisa has only girls!" objected the village leader.

Yaku nodded and walked on.

"A girl cannot be a holy one!" insisted the leader, following. His shaman's suggestion shocked him into unusual rudeness.

"The spirits, themselves, have chosen her," Yaku said.

"It is a mistake. It is unnatural. Our people will not follow a female, will not let her sit in our counsels. It is not possible, Yaku. Choose another. Choose a boy."

Yaku Shaman shook his head.

"I will offer her family gifts for her at the next Trintoa. It is early, but I am...I have waited long enough."

"It will shame them," warned the leader.

"They have six others — too many for the farmer Takan's liking. Polisa will accept. The child will serve her family better for being turned into gifts."

"But how can a female be shaman?" demanded the leader. "Our men will not follow a woman!"

"Our wise men will."

"It is for the shaman to be wise, not for us."

Yaku Shaman turned on him, a scowl on his face.

"Then listen to my wisdom. A shaman leads the spirit of the people. The spirit is not male or female but whole and perfect. A man's spirit — a woman's spirit — there is no difference. My shaman spirit, this child's shaman spirit — both can lead, both can be followed. I have seen the great spirits come to her and dress her in light. This is significant. They have chosen to follow her, therefore you can."

"Yaku Shaman," answered Massern Leader gently, "there is time.

You are still strong. Think on this some more."

Polisa's youngest had survived her fright from the Trintoa morning. She had not known it was a holy day but had simply sneaked out of her family's house, as she had every morning for almost a year, and had gone to her favorite place in the world.

Her first time there she had gone to listen to the world growing in the trunk. Her father told glowing stories of the Great God's words to their people, promising them this sheltered valley until the new world should be ready to be born of the sacred tree. The people of the valley were to be the midwives to the baby's birth and guardians of this strange new life. Polisa's youngest, curious about the baby world, had listened intently at the growing trunk until she thought she could hear the tree breathe and a baby cry softly within.

"He must be scared in there, so dark and alone," she had thought, and she sang to him to comfort him. It made him happy. When she came again she brought her sweet root bread from dinner and found a hole in the trunk of the tree to drop it. She sang again to the baby, telling him of simple things — her day, the way the blue flowers bloomed between the budding cunarul grass plants, the wild ducklings that swam upon the lakes, her mother's silly frown that made her face look like a squished squash, her father's fabulous stories — all the things she found beautiful and fascinating.

Sometimes she sang to the baby at sunset, telling him of the stars, one by one, as they opened their eyes and the shape of the moon as it rose. At sunset she was often missed, however. That was the time of many chores and stories from their father as they worked inside their house. Sunrise was an easier adventure, and a more beautiful song — for she loved the colors the morning spirits painted in the sky. She could be back in time to gather the goytew's eggs and feathers or sweep the house while her sisters did their chores. When she was late, she could say she had been relieving herself. It was always believed. Everyone was too busy in the mornings to watch her closely.

It took her many days after the Trintoa to get the courage to go back alone. In her mind, the shaman waited for her there, his face fierce and angry. He had not told her parents, but he watched her sometimes when she wandered the village or played with her friends. Had he cursed her, she wondered. How would she know if he had? She asked Silvai, her next older sister as they pounded cooked beans into a paste. The girl laughed.

"You can't be cursed. You don't have a name. You're not even a person yet."

"So, if I never have a name, I can't ever be cursed?"

Silvai nodded.

"Then why would I ever want a name?"

Silvai shook her head in disbelief.

"Because you're no one without a name. You have no voice, no meaning, no rights, no power, nothing. You're just silly."

The shaman still frightened her when she saw him, but that was not often. He did not go onto her hill again and soon she felt safe to resume visiting her tree.

Her parents were glad not to have to leave after the harvest festival. They always preferred to stay through the heavy rains and snow, since it meant less threat to their livestock from wild animals. Now, they had two new calves, twins, and a kid. Everyone agreed it had been an uncommonly good year.

The winter came softly, with much loved rains and enough snow to bleach the world of color and leave it black and white for the solemn and beautiful ceremony of the dead on the northern plain.

Polisa's youngest watched as her named sisters danced with their people, reenacting all the activities of daily life, and making them beautiful,. It was an act for the spirits of their ancestors and for the moon goddess whose power was strongest this night. They sang the ritual songs of simple poetry to which each named person, even the young, could contribute a verse. They carried candle lamps lit at the holy flame of life to their ancestor's graves and left them burning through the night to guide their loved ones back from the dark and lonely regions where they might be wandering. They left a fingerstick of bread filled with bite sized sections of fruit preserves and sweetened bean paste to nourish the spirits of their dead when they returned home. The night was alive with a festival feeling and people dressed in their best — fur and elegantly painted hides and woven cloaks of the softest bofimer wool or the more brightly dyed and warmer gathis wool or the goytew feathers woven together in mosaic designs.

The little girl watched in joy as the plain filled with people she had not seen before, dancing with their kin. She looked for her mother's father, already barely a memory in her mind, and saw a young and handsome man with her mother's strong chin and high cheeks standing just behind her aged grandmother.

"Welcome Grandfather!" she greeted him happily and held out to him a fingerstick bread. He took it with a smile.

"To whom are you talking?" demanded her grandmother, irritably.

"Him," said Polisa's youngest, pointing.

The old woman shifted and, peering behind her into the darkness, saw the shaman looking back from several feet away.

"That's disrespectful," said her Grandmother. "You cannot talk to people like that, not until you have a name and something worthy to say."

"I'm sorry," the girl apologized to her grandfather.

"She is missing me tonight," explained her grandfather gently. "It makes her sad. Give her a kiss for me and leave her alone."

The little girl politely kissed her grandmother.

"From Grandfather," she explained. Then she went back to watch the dancers.

For several weeks after the festival many of the dead people stayed, wandering through the village, watching their families and friends at work and play, and occasionally talking to the shaman. Some would smile at her when they saw her, others would frown, but most just ignored her as the living people of her village ignored them.

Her grandfather came to talk with her once, as she was about her chores. He was off to his wanderings and his home in the spirit world, but he wanted to tell her something. His presence caused too much excitement in the goytew aviary, so he waited until she came out, her basket full of eggs with several small sacks full of the brightly colored feathers.

"Your grandmother is not well," he said. "She will die by the next winter."

The girl looked up at him sadly. "I will miss her."

"You should tell your mother and your uncle. They will need to be ready."

The little girl promised she would.

"And tell your mother to be happy. This next one will finally be a boy."

She told her uncle, the tanner, first about her grandmother's death. He was easier to talk to than her mother.

"Who told you this?" he demanded.

"Grandfather."

"Your father's father?"

"No. Your father."

"But he's dead."

"I think that's why he knows."

Her uncle laughed at his niece's imagination and thanked her for the message.

Her mother, on the other hand, was furious with her for making up such lies. She bent her youngest over her knee and spanked her harshly.

"But I'm only telling you what he said!" cried the little girl.

"You do not talk about the dead, and you do not say that someone will die. I'll have your father beat you the next time you come telling any such stories!"

The little girl drew away, afraid, rubbing her stinging bottom. She had promised her grandfather, however, so she had to tell the rest.

"Only one more thing," she said. Her mother lunged at her. She slipped behind the fire, out of reach, and quickly shouted, "He says you should be happy. It's going to be a boy!" Then she ran out of the little house and kept out of her mother's way for the rest of the day.

At dinner that evening her mother watched her oddly but said nothing.

CHAPTER 3

UNNATURAL THINGS

The little girl watched for the Trintoa that spring. They had warned her that the shaman went to the hill every year on that morning and she did not want to meet him again.

Her oldest two sisters lifted the window flap and peaked through as he made his way to her hill. She hid under her blanket on her sleeping mat until she was sure the shaman had passed.

"He's looking at us," whispered Katira, jumping quickly away from the window. She was the oldest, a woman for over two years, and getting her life joined with her lover this day. This was her last morning in their room. Tomorrow she and her husband would wake in a house of their own already built by her mother's family. The girls had been sewing and crafting for months to prepare it and cooking over a week to make as generous a feast today as their modest means could afford.

"You think he's thinking of you," giggled Misa, the second oldest.

"He's thinking of us all, of course," responded Katira properly, but they all knew that, in her heart, Katira hoped the shaman would sing a special prayer for her and her man.

Their mother watched too, still slim in her fourth month of pregnancy. She was thinking about her youngest who had told her it would be a boy even before she was sure that she was carrying. She desperately prayed that her daughter would prove right.

Her husband prayed with her — not only for a son but also for the continued health of his livestock and the hope of good crops. Another such year as last year had been and he might be able to marry off, with honorable celebration, as many as three more of his girls. He might even get an apprentice or two, which would allow him more of the village's cropland to work and therefore more honor.

As the sun finished its rise over their heads, the people climbed the eastern hill to the sacred tree.

Yaku Shaman looked tired and grim.

"The spirits were here," he announced. "They listened, but they were not so pleased. We may still hope for a good year..." but his eyes looked doubtful.

Through the crowd of his people, he sought out Polisa's youngest. She was against the tree, her ear to its trunk, listening as though she could hear something within. One of her older sisters grabbed her arm and pulled her away, scolding her that such a sacred thing was not a toy for babies.

One by one the children to be named knelt before the shaman. He had watched them grow, had discussed them with the spirits of their families and spirits of the village in general, and knew the names that they would carry until they reached adulthood and found their true names themselves. These he shared:

"Tanasai," to one little girl, "for your stitching is as fine as a spider's."

"Bolasu," to a boy, "in honor of your swift running for short times, like a gust of wind."

And on, until all of age were named and honored for the voice they now were granted.

Then the couples came and stood before him, as a group, each pair hand in hand. The men led the women to him. The wives would lead their husbands away, to the feast and back to their homes.

He told them of the sacredness of this joining of life and what it would mean to them — the commitments that would be expected, the freedoms lost, the strengths gained.

The couples, old and young, smiled at him and at each other and did not really hear. It was only words. The old man who spoke them had never married. A holy man lived with the spirits, not a woman. His children were his people. Such simple pleasures as kissing a loving wife good morning or leading a child that was half your life and half your heart into adulthood, such things were too mundane for the shaman — too distracting from his spiritual duties. Had he come before himself, as a young man with a beautiful lover, perhaps one as strong and wise as the renown Katira, with deep brown hair, hazel eyes, and a full, blooming body...he would not have heard his lonely old man's words either. Each couple would find through time what sharing a life was like. He who had never known could not teach them.

As he proclaimed their lives joined in a new beginning and sang for the spirits to bless them and keep away the evil, which threatened all beginnings, a cheer rose from his people. The singing and dancing commenced, and the feasts were set. Takan and his wife, Polisa, congratulated their daughter and their first new son, embraced their growing family, and set their feast grandly for any who would come. All were welcome. Takan made the sacrifice to the spirits at the holy tree, a gift of holy pollen painted on the leaves. His new son followed with a gift of sweet buds laid at the roots.

It was their happy day and Yaku felt ill at ease, knowing he would intrude with an unwelcome request. Had it been a son he wanted, one already named, his choice would bring the family honor. No one was above the shaman of a village, not even the village leaders. To have a son that the spirits themselves had chosen was the highest approval the gods could show — but not for a girl. The spirits were not known to choose females. She could be looked at as a freak going against the intent of nature, especially since he requested her so young — not even a person yet. But how his bones ached this year — ten times what they had the year before. He could not wait. The Trintoa was the day for apprenticing. His request had to be made today.

He presented Takan with his congratulations. They were happily accepted.

"Where is your wife?" he asked with forced casualness, "I have a request to make of her."

"Polisa is talking with Asta," answered Takan nodding in the direction of the women. He eyed the shaman curiously.

"You might wish to listen," warned Yaku.

He waited until Polisa had moved out of her conversation and caught her before she found another.

"Polisa, mother of...your youngest," he greeted her formally.

The woman looked up at him startled, disbelieving any of the options such an address might suggest. She glanced at Takan. He shrugged, confused.

"What has she done?" asked Polisa, worried.

Yaku lifted himself to the full length of his great height.

"I seek an apprentice," he announced, in a low voice to save the parents embarrassment, "and the spirits have chosen...her."

Takan's eyes widened and his jaw dropped in open astonishment. Polisa took it better. She paused only long enough to catch her breath then, glancing around to make sure they had not been overheard, led the shaman away from the crowd to a place they would not be disturbed. Takan meekly followed.

"Shaman what can you mean?" Polisa demanded. "Our youngest is a girl. You cannot want her."

"She is the one I want."

"Then you must be mistaken."

"There is no mistake."

"There must be," insisted Polisa. "Our family is an honorable one. We have done the spirits no harm. There is no reason for them to shame us."

"It is an honor."

"Not for a girl. It is unnatural — unthinkable."

"The spirits have chosen her."

"But not as shaman. No woman can be shaman. If the spirits want her, let her serve them by marrying and having babies as the rest of us do. I can let her be a healer. I can let her tend the shaman, fix his meals, tan and weave his clothes, keep his house but not live in it. That is not how women serve. It would not be pious for her to be your 'apprentice,' Yaku Shaman."

"She is the one the spirits chose," responded Yaku sternly. "Their decision is clear. There is no mistake. She is the one they will listen to and she is the one they will follow. All our village will suffer if you withhold her from me, Polisa."

"The spirits don't even know her, Shaman. She's not a person yet. She hasn't got a name. You cannot ask for an apprentice who hasn't even got a name."

"It is the spirits who give the names. They have already told me hers. I can name her today..."

Polisa shook her head.

"It's unnatural. One unnatural thing pushing up another."

Yaku waited, his face fierce and unmoving, his body fixed like a statue, his eyes watching the mother. It was her decision.

"What would you offer?" asked Takan suddenly.

"Shut up, you!" snapped Polisa.

"But if the offer is high enough..." argued her husband.

"And you care nothing for our honor? But, of course, you can always say she is not your daughter — there is no doubt that I'm her mother. I would be the mother of a monster while you are merely a cuckold."

He answered her quietly.

"Polisa, we have seven daughters, possibly more. That's seven people on a small farmer's take who eat as much as any man but cannot claim the same share of land. It will be many years before she can bring us a husband who might have skill as a farmer. With so many children to raise and marry how can we afford to keep such a young one for whom a reasonable offer might be made?"

"How would we marry the others with such a shame upon our house?"

"They are all pretty and sweet enough, and people's memories are short, especially young men's."

Polisa shook her head.

"And if the price were high enough," continued her husband with a sideways glance at the shaman, "high enough to marry the rest of our daughters with honorable display, high enough to build our farm into something worthy of notice, high enough to possibly earn me position as an elder, then we will gain more honor than we could lose. It is not our fault the spirits chose her. If she were a boy..."

"But she's not!"

"How can having a holy person in our family — even a woman, be shameful?"

Polisa glared at him angrily but had no answer.

"What do you offer?" she asked carefully of the shaman.

In his heart, Yaku smiled. He had his apprentice. Now only the details needed to be confirmed.

Polisa was a hard bargainer. She got every advantage she could for her daughter. Her husband had his seat with the elders — as the father of a holy one, how could they refuse? They had the promise of honorable wedding feasts for all their remaining daughters, to be subsidized by the communal funds as necessary. And when Carken, the childless farmer whose lands bordered theirs, died, his lands and stock, which would normally go to the village common to be allotted to another farmer, would be turned over to Takan and his family to work for the village, with the promise of three boy apprentices to help grow it. Furthermore, her daughter would not be named until her proper time the following year. Polisa tried to insist on keeping the girl until then, but Yaku stood firm on that count. He had to have the child immediately. It was finally agreed that he would take her as a "servant" — perhaps as a charity to a struggling family – and only officially as an apprentice after she had her name.

"Let her be called your servant from now on," begged Polisa lastly, "and not our daughter. The quicker people forget, the better."

It was settled.

When the time came to return to the village, Polisa took her youngest and placed the child's hand in the shaman's.

"Go with him," she ordered. Then she turned her back and walked away from a daughter who no longer existed for her.

The child drew back, terrified, from the great holy man. She looked around, confused.

"Mother," she cried after the disappearing woman. Polisa did not turn or pause. Some of her sisters looked back over their shoulders, as confused as she, but they did not dare come back for her.

The child started to cry.

Yaku stared at her, bewildered. He had not thought beyond obtaining his apprentice. Now that he had her, he did not know what to do. What had his master done? But that had been different. His family had been honored. He had been a middle son in a craftsman's family, paraded through the village and feasted lavishly. He had been much older than this child — nearly nine, which was an appropriate age for an apprentice, yet his mother had come with him, made his bed, prepared his clothes, and returned in the morning to fix him and his master breakfast. For weeks she had served two houses until she was sure he was adjusted. Then, slowly, she had left him alone. Even so, he had been frightened and unsure.

Yaku looked down at the crying child, her tiny hand dwarfed in his huge one, pulling away from him as far as her arm would let her. She was just a baby, he suddenly realized. What would he do with her? What could he tell her that she would understand? Where would she sleep tonight? He only had one sleeping mat. She could not sleep with him. If he rolled over, he might crush her. What would she wear? She came to him with only the bare tanned hide on her back and her woven under-dress and a pair of shoes already too tight. What a fragile, little creature she was! How could her mother have been so foolish to let him take her when he did not know the slightest thing about babies?

"Come," he ordered, tugging at her arm. The child hung back. He started toward the men's path, dragging her. Then, realizing her limitations, he changed directions toward the women's path. It was the first time in all his adulthood he had used that way, especially going down, but it was dark now. Maybe no one would see.

The village was a warm and inviting place that evening, alive with song and chat. Fires glowed merrily from open doors and windows. Crowds gathered around the houses of the newlyweds and caroused loudly, laughing and yelling at the slightest sound from within and telling bawdy tales to distract the lovers or beating drums in the pulse of love to encourage them. Children ran from house to house reciting their new names to any who would listen. Remains from the feasts were parceled and given to friends and elders, with much congratulations and good wishes and pleasant gossip exchanged. The older men made great and glorious, impossible plans over pipes of fragrant herbs, the smoke rising through the air like prayers.

Traditionally the shaman wandered the village, laughing and celebrating with them. He had learned to draw the satisfaction of his life from the happiness of his people. Tonight, however, the terrified child he held in tow distracted him.

For a moment, he thought of taking her back to her family. Let them have her for another year, give him time to prepare. Just one more year — but the spirits had been disappointed this morning when she had not come. They had been angry, blaming him for keeping her away. The Trintoa had not been successful and the upcoming year would be bad. For his people's sake, he would not delay.

"You took her I see," said Massern Leader, nodding toward the child.

"She is my servant for a year," Yaku answered with unyielding pride.

Massern laughed. He and his wife had raised five living children of their own and eight of his grandchildren had already taken their first names.

"Much good may she do you," he wished the shaman. "By the end of the year, I predict, you will be wise enough to choose a boy."

"It is not my choice," replied Yaku Shaman, coldly.

Massern laughed again and left the shaman to his fate.

Yaku pulled back the front door flap from his little house and pushed the child inside. The fire was already lit in its place in the corner, under the high point of the sloping roof where the smoke filtered out through the opening above. His dinner heated slowly beside it in the little hot-box nestled in the ashes, and his sleeping mat was already laid out for him and waiting.

"Are you hungry?" he demanded of the child.

She looked up at him fearfully and did not respond. He took the bowl from the hot-box and set it in front of her, giving her a sitting place in the corner. She looked at it, then back at him and did not move to touch it.

"You may eat it if you'd like," he told her.

She continued to watch him, warily.

"Do you speak yet?" asked Yaku, worry making his face seem sterner. She had sung. He had not considered that she might not speak, but she was young.

To his relief, she nodded, though she still said nothing.

"Then do you want the food, or don't you?"

She shook her head, slightly. Thankfully he grabbed it back and began to eat it himself. She watched him from the corner where she huddled, eyes wide like a frightened animal. It made him uncomfortable to be watched so. Everything about this child made him uneasy.

"You will sleep there tonight," he said, indicating his sleeping mat. "Tomorrow — we shall see."

She crawled to it quietly, carefully keeping as much distance from the holy man as the room would let her.

"When do I go home?" she ventured to ask, pulling the blanket up in front of her as if it were a shield.

"This is your home now," he replied.

She cringed deeper into the blanket.

"Why?" she whispered. It was only one little word, but it seemed to take all her courage to say it.

The holy man frowned at her, his big, stern face twisting into something terrifying.

"You serve me now," he answered.

"You cannot curse me," she said softly, more to herself than to him, "because I haven't got a name."

Yaku Shaman scowled, puzzled by her words. She disappeared under the blankets and softly cried herself to sleep.

CHAPTER 4

BAD BEGINNINGS

When the shaman awoke the next morning, the child was sobbing still. He had slept all night on the ground in front of the door, and she had been so afraid to go out past him that she had wet his sleeping mat instead. The woman who came to bring his breakfast, a good-natured old wife with an ever-wagging tongue, cheerfully cleaned the bed while the shaman took his 'servant' to the baths to wash. When they returned, there were two clean bedrolls, and the woman was dishing another bowl of vegetable and cereal soup, fore young girl.

"Polisa had an extra," she said, laughing, as she nodded to the bedroll. "She should have thought of it herself, but then she has much to think about these days, with Katira married and another baby coming, or so they say. She refuses to talk about it, but she doesn't deny it..." On and on.

The child watched her fascinated. How could anyone talk so freely to the holy man? With so many words one or two might easily be wrong, yet this woman seemed completely unafraid. The shaman ate his breakfast, silently ignoring the chatterer. The child was sorry when the breakfast was over, and the woman left. She wished she could have left with her.

Her education commenced that day. Yaku Shaman led her back

to the eastern hill.

"We start here," he announced, "because this is the place of beginnings."

He closed his eyes and sat still and silent. The child wanted to go to her tree, but she was afraid with the holy man here. It was probably because he had caught her sitting in it before that he was so angry with her now. Instead, she stood next to him, fidgeting.

"Sit down," he ordered, "close your eyes and listen."

"To what?"

"To whatever there is to hear."

She sat down and closed her eyes, but she could not relax to listen. The breeze came up behind her and tickled her neck. He wanted to play. She smiled. She liked her friend, the breeze. When he tickled her neck again, she reached behind to grab him, but of course, he was already far away, laughing.

"Hold still!" demanded the holy man, angrily.

The breeze came back and blew the shaman's long, white hair into his face, covering his eyes. The holy man waved it away, irritated, while the little girl bit her lip to stop her laugh.

"What did you hear?" asked the shaman, sternly.

The little girl shrugged, unable to answer.

"Then listen until you can tell me. This place is full of sounds. You should find one that I haven't noticed yet."

She listened closer. As she heard things she identified them to the shaman, but it seemed he'd heard them all.

"Deeper," he kept saying, "You must listen deeper."

She did not understand what he meant. The game quickly frustrated her.

Sensing this, the holy man shifted his lesson into stories. He told her of the beginning of the first world and all the worlds since, the beginning of the people, the planting of the sacred tree, and the settling of the village.

26

These were stories her father had told them in the evenings, when their work in the fields was finished and he could work on leather strips for the animals or sharpen weapons and tools while she sorted goytew feathers and her sisters wove and sewed and worked on the food for the next day's meals. She had loved to listen to her father's stories, for he always told them well, with a sparkle in his eye, his hands tracing the visions, and many voices in his speech. Yaku Shaman told them straight and solemn, in a manner dry and well-rehearsed. He left out all the more fanciful details her father had added and included many other things she did not understand.

"No," she kept wanting to correct him, but the look in his eyes held her silent.

"You will learn these stories," he told her.

"Then I will tell them better," she quietly promised herself.

They climbed down for their midday meal, served by a taciturn, pinch-faced, little woman who said nothing the whole time she was there. Yaku Shaman ignored her the same way he had ignored the talking woman that morning.

Quietly, the child amused herself by playing the listening game. She was amazed at how many sounds filled the world, even if she wasn't listening "deeply." Her ears stopped at the shouts and laughs of children outside — friends whom she would play with now if she could only get away.

She would tease Coligu about his new name because he was so proud of it. She would tell him it did not fit, even though she knew it did, and he would laugh and say she could not know because she didn't have a name at all. Then next year, when she got hers, he'd tease her and say it did not fit, whatever it was, and make her feel special with the attention.

She would have liked to have teased Rirylia too. She had been her best friend for two years. But Rirylia had warned her, before she got her name, that once she was a real person she'd not have time for non-persons. Secretly, the child hoped her ex-friend would be very lonely without her this year.

She snuck away when she was excused to relieve herself, and tried to join her friends. They were gathered around an old bofimer, taking turns riding her, as many as could get on. They stopped their sport and watched her curiously as she approached.

"Why are you sleeping with the shaman," asked a boy her age.

She shrugged.

"Are you sick?" asked another girl. Those who were sick often stayed with the shaman as he healed them, or helped them die, whatever the spirits allowed.

"I don't think so," answered the child.

"You look okay," said the boy, "but maybe you're sick in here." He tapped his head.

"I am not," the child flared angrily. The other children laughed and started taunting her with rude names for the insane or possessed.

"Spinning Cloud — that's what they'll name you next year," yelled one boy. He gave her a hard shove that sent her landing on her butt.

She jumped up, her fingers curled into fists, but the boy was looking up behind her, backing away frightened. A huge hand caught her arm and the shaman angrily dragged her back to the eastern hill.

"You will no longer play with children," he told her, his voice hard as rock.

She clenched her jaw to keep back the angry words and obediently followed him.

"If anyone's insane it's the holy man," she thought to herself, knowing such words could never be said aloud. She wished they could. The things her friends had said had hurt her deeply and she wanted to hear them contradicted.

The shaman explained the Trintoa and sang its holy chants to her. She barely heard him, still fuming about her friends. Then he ordered her to sing them. She could not. He made her sing them again with him, over and over.

Quickly her anger was forgotten with this new game, but the words were meaningless to her, and her attention soon wandered. She learned the words swiftly and just as swiftly forgot them. By sunset she could sing all the chants. An hour later, her mind had let them go.

"This is useless," growled the shaman to himself. The child cringed at the anger she heard in his voice.

"This is the simplest of things," he told her, frustrated, "why can you not learn? Are you stupid?"

"It makes no sense," she answered defensively.

"It does to the spirits," he said.

"Then let the spirits sing it."

She covered her mouth quickly, in horror, but the impolite words had already escaped. The shaman let them go with only a frown.

They worked deep into the night, until the child's eyes fell closed more than she could keep them open. The shaman tried to work her longer, but it was useless.

———◆◆———

The next morning Yaku awoke to find the child gone.

He searched the toilet areas, the bathing houses, the lake, the places near his house. She was not to be found.

"Have you seen my servant?" he asked the young, pretty wife, whose turn it was to fix them breakfast and straighten his house. She had not.

He walked quickly to Takan's farm and asked Polisa.

"Your servant is not here," answered Polisa angrily, but she sent two of her older daughters to look for her.

"They will bring her to you as soon as she is found," Polisa assured him, her embarrassment thinning her voice.

———◆◆———

Misa found her first, as the girl was coming down from the eastern hill. She grabbed her little sister and shook her, heartily mad.

"How dare you run away from your master — from a shaman?! Do you know how shameful that is?"

"I was coming back," argued the girl, defensively.

"But why did you go?"

The girl shrugged. How could she explain? She had just wanted to see her tree, that was all. It had missed her singing to it. She wanted to hear the baby breathe and know it was happy and safe.

"Aren't you happy with the shaman?"

"No."

"Why not?"

"He's mean and scary."

"Does he beat you?"

"No..."

"Does he starve you?"

The little girl shook her head.

"Then how is he mean?"

"He just is!"

Misa looked at her thoughtfully.

"I think you're mean," she told her little sister.

"I am not!" the girl objected.

"I think you're being mean to him. You run away. You make him think you don't like him."

"I don't like him!"

"But you haven't given him a chance. It's very hard for him to live with someone. He's never had a little girl before. He's never had anyone. He doesn't know what to do."

"He knows everything. He's a shaman."

"He doesn't know you. All he knows is that you are a mean little girl who doesn't like him and who runs away and makes everyone think he's a bad master when he hasn't done anything bad to you at all."

The little girl stared at the ground, confused and ashamed. No one ever won an argument with Misa, not when she wanted to win. She could make up her mind in any ridiculous way, and it always made sense while she explained it. She always sounded right, even when you were sure she had to be wrong.

"Come on," said Misa, leading her back to the shaman's house. The little girl meekly followed.

The shaman watched them approach, his face frowning terribly. The little girl suddenly decided that running away in earnest might be a good idea after all. Misa gave her arm a sharp yank and forced her to follow.

"Where?" demanded the shaman of Misa, with but a single nod for thanks.

"At the foot of the eastern hill."

The shaman took the little girl's hand awkwardly in his own. His eyes narrowed thoughtfully as he stared at her.

"May I speak to you privately, Yaku Shaman?" asked Misa politely. Her younger sister's heart lifted with the hopes that Misa would find a way to free her from this angry giant. Yaku Shaman nodded and sent his servant in to eat her cold breakfast. He walked with Misa south, toward the woods.

"Speak," the Shaman ordered, when they were out of any other's hearing.

"You are a very wise and revered man, Yaku Shaman," Misa, Polisa's second oldest, began carefully. It was her first time speaking to one of his age and position. She was very aware of her youth, just barely a woman. He towered over her, looking down at her face, waiting for her to continue.

"Your spirits tell you things that we cannot know, but perhaps there are things that we know that they do not, or at least do not wish to tell."

"What do you want to say?" prompted Yaku, his hard voice doing little to ease the woman's timidity.

"My sister...your servant, is a very good little girl. She is a little odd, very imaginative, but her heart is strong and generous and kind, and she will love you if you will let her."

Yaku watched Misa silently, his stern expression giving her no encouragement.

"She is only frightened of you," Misa continued. "We have all heard stories of what shamans can do. With some children it is good to frighten them, but with her...if you scare her, she will run away or fight, but if you love her, she will love you back and do what she thinks will please you. And if she ever thinks you need her she'll always try to help you. I was very sick two years ago. You healed me, remember?"

Yaku nodded.

"She would not leave my side. She got in everyone's way and made Polisa furious. But when Polisa would spank her and throw her out, she'd sneak back in and stay by me. She'd make up stories to amuse me, sing to me, and have pretend conversations with invisible people who all told me I was going to get well soon. She held me when I slept, got me water when I needed, and made me feel that she loved me very much. I hadn't really noticed her before that, she was just another baby, but my other sisters didn't do that. They were wiser, not to risk getting sick themselves, not to get in the way of those who could truly heal me. She is not wise, but that she can learn when she is old enough."

The shaman stayed silent, waiting, until Misa bowed her head, indicating she was done speaking.

"Why do you tell me all this?" he then asked.

Misa blushed, embarrassed.

"I just thought you should know," she finally answered.

Yaku Shaman nodded, with an air of solemnity, but Misa had the impression he was laughing at her in his heart.

"Thank you."

His tone dismissed her. Misa stifled a sigh as she left.

The little girl watched hopefully as the shaman approached his house. Perhaps he would tell her to go home now. He stopped before the doorway and stared thoughtfully at her, his face only slightly less stern than usual. She waited eagerly for the dismissal.

"Have you finished your breakfast?" he asked.

She nodded, holding her breath.

"Then come with me to the eastern hill."

Her heart sank. Yaku noticed her disappointment with surprise.

"Don't you like the eastern hill?" he asked as they walked.

The little girl nodded that she did, but still her face looked sad.

"Then why are you unhappy to go?"

She shrugged. It seemed to her that all Misa's talk had accomplished was filling the holy man with it so that he too could argue her out of her feelings and make her think she was wrong.

"I give you permission to speak to me freely when we are alone," said her master.

The child looked up at the old man surprised. Why would he want her to speak? What could a non-person possibly have to say — especially to a holy man who knew everything?

He watched her, waiting. When she did not speak, he did.

"You are with me so that I may teach you and I will need to know how much you know, what you are thinking, so that I can know what you need to learn."

She took the information in silently.

"What are you thinking now?" he asked.

"Questions," she answered.

"What questions?"

She glanced at Yaku, warily.

"Speak," he commanded.

"What do you want to teach me and why? Why have you made me different from the others? Why do you keep me with you and do not let me go home? Why are you always angry with me? What have I done so bad?"

Yaku frowned. The child's courage withered. She knew he would not like her questions!

"I am not always angry with you," he said, clearly annoyed. "You have not done anything too bad so far. You stay with me because I'm your master. I can teach you better when you're with me."

"Then you are not punishing me?"

He scowled at her.

"I am not punishing you."

She watched him, wanting him to answer the rest of her questions.

He waited until they were on top of the hill then he sat down, away from the tree, as he had done the day before, and nodded for her to do the same.

"I teach you of the spirits," he said when she was settled, "because they have made it clear that they want you to know. It is not by my choice. They like you. You can make them do good things for our people when you know how."

That bothered her. She did not feel that she wanted to make anyone do anything.

Yaku watched the child frustrated. Her responses were not what he had hoped. She should be excited, proud. That was how he had felt. He would have understood if she had been scared, that too was natural, but she didn't seem to be. She sat before him, fidgeting with the grass at her feet, her eyes lowered, looking almost as if she were...could she be angry? But why would she be angry?

"Do you understand what I have told you?" he asked.

She nodded.

"What do you think?" he demanded.

"I want to go home."

"You can't," he told her. "You must stay with me and learn."

"If I learn will you let me go home?"

Her child's face rose hopefully toward his, and he was strained to rein his anger. She did not understand. Why could he not make her understand?

"What have I just told you?" he quizzed her.

"That you are not punishing me, but you will not let me go home, and you keep me with you so everyone thinks I am sick or crazy because the spirits like me, even if you do not, and they want you to teach me how to make them do things against their will."

He shook his head and went over it again slowly.

"No one thinks you're sick or insane."

"My friends do."

"Your friends aren't even people yet."

"Some are. And they're the only friends I have, except for my sisters and you won't let me go home."

"I will tell them you are not insane. I will tell them you are better than they are..."

"Oh no," she interrupted, then she cringed in fright for she had interrupted an adult — a holy man even. Yaku stared at her until he was sure her silence would last.

"I will have them honor you. That should make you happy."

She shook her head.

"Why not?"

"Because I'm not better. Because I don't want to be better. It won't make them happy to think that I'm better."

"Then I will not tell them that you are better, but I will tell them you are not insane. Will that please you?"

She nodded.

"Now, part of what I will teach you is how to make spirits do things against their will, but this is very bad magic, and we only do it against very bad spirits. If you are lucky, you will never have to do it. Many spirits want to please us. What I will teach you is how to guide them in ways that they will please us. Other spirits, the greater ones, the ones we call gods, want to be pleased, and if you make them happy they will reward you and our people. I will teach you how to make them happy. Some spirits want to hurt, and I will teach you how to turn them away to hurt things that do not hurt us. In this way, a shaman is a friend to all the spirits and makes them all happy, and he is a friend to his people and makes them happy. The spirits like you. This is what they want you to learn."

"If I learn, can I go home?" she asked again.

"It will take you many years," he warned. "By the time you learn, you will be too old to go home."

"But if I learn very quickly?"

"You learn as quickly as you can," he said, "and when you know all, then we will see."

She grinned, accepting his words as a promise.

CHAPTER 5

THE DYING

Yaku discovered that the child was not as stupid as he had first thought. He realized that she would not learn the chants unless she understood them, so he started her on the old language, which had taken him many years of hard struggle to master. She loved it. The words came easily to her and stayed. The syntax and conjugations were more difficult, but it was not long before she and her master could sustain a reasonable dialogue. The chants followed as a matter of course, for she loved to sing. Yaku soon realized that it was not teaching her to sing the chants, but teaching her when not to sing them that was the challenge, for she would sing them night and day, even during bathing or eating times which was sacrilegious and possibly offensive to the spirits.

"This chant is to be sung on the morning of the Trintoa only. You may sing it with me here because you need to learn it, but you must not sing it all the time and everywhere, and never to the spirits except on the Trintoa morning."

"But you said it was to please the spirits. Isn't it good to always please them?"

"Spirits are pleased by an order of things. Things done within the order are good, but things done outside the order, like singing the Trintoa when it is not the Trintoa, that is bad. It can make them angry."

The concept was hard for the little girl to understand. It was a riddle for her mind: when is something that pleases unpleasant? She searched in every little thing that pleased her to try to find when it would not and found food when you're full, a blanket when you're hot, a pretty fire that burns your skin, and frost that kills the budding tree.

Late frosts plagued the spring, then rains flooded the fields, drowning the crops. Two good mares and a poor man's bofimer died in labor, taking their babies with them. On one farm, the goytew females pecked their males to death. No one would give or even trade the farmer another, for fear of angering the spirits, and his goytews stopped laying. Rats were the only animals that bred well. They infested the town and storeroom caves, fouling much of the abundant stocks the village had saved. Sickness spread through the very old and very young, and the shaman spent more time as a healer than as a teacher. Even so, he kept his apprentice with him, urging her to watch and learn so that she too might one day heal.

He saw the heart her sister had described. Fear of sickness did not trouble her. The stench of illness, of vomit, sweat, and urine, did not keep her away. This child, whose attention flitted like a butterfly, never staying long anywhere, would sit for hours by the sick and dying, comforting them as best she could. It was difficult to pull her away, but there were too many who needed him for them to stay with any one long enough to satisfy her. It was as if each patient were all the world to her. She even came close once to defying him openly.

"Rirylia" she called softly as she bathed the little girl's head. Her friend was dying. The spirits insisted, and nothing the shaman had done could change their decision. At last, he had called her ancestors to guide her. It was time to see to others who might still be saved.

"Come," ordered Yaku Shaman.

His servant softly shook her head, never taking her eyes off her friend. Yaku glanced around, fearful that her defiance might have been noticed, but the family was lost in sorrow now, unaware of the little non-person.

"Come," he repeated again in the old language, his rising anger giving the gentle sounds an unaccustomed edge. "There are others who need us."

"She's afraid," the child answered in the language her master had chosen.

"Her ancestors are called. They will be here soon."

"She doesn't know any of them. Everyone she knows is still alive, and she's afraid to leave them." She took her friend's hand and held it firmly. "I will stay," she announced.

"There is nothing you can do," he told her angrily.

"I can stay," she answered.

Yaku knew that he should not bend to his servant's will. He was the master, not she. He could drag her from the room and hope she would have enough sense to leave the family in peace, but he did not really need her. She had watched him enough for the day and, if fewer had been ill, he would have stayed to give Rirylia's spirit to her ancestors himself. It was what a good shaman did when he could. Since he could not, perhaps it was right if she stayed.

"I am leaving my servant," he told the mother. "Let her sit with Rirylia. It will help her."

The mother nodded.

"Thank you," she said, her voice thick with grief.

That evening, the shaman's servant was spoken of by her people, although she still had no name by which to be called. It was said she had spoken in the old language, the spirit's tongue, to her master. It was said she had sung a soul's ease to Rirylia. It was said that she had seen the ancestors as they arrived and described them accurately to the grieving family, even the father's parents who had passed on many years before she had been born, and she had helped Rirylia to feel how they loved her and welcomed her. It was said that she had promised the family that Rirylia would be happy now as if she had really known it to be true. It was said that she had acted like a shaman, and the people wondered even more what Yaku Shaman's plans for her were.

The sicknesses passed, and the stronger survived. Even Polisa's old mother survived it. She never caught the illness, but she was growing thinner and, day by day, more of her strength slipped away. Her son refused to call the shaman or the healing women for her while others were so much sicker, so her daughter nursed her with traditional herbal remedies. They did not help. When the village sickness had passed, the son finally relented and sought the shaman out himself.

He found him in the southern wood where he was giving lessons to his servant these days. The sight of his niece brought back the memory of what she had told him last winter. She had prophesied his mother's death. It chilled him. His niece was happy to see him. He barely greeted her, his manner cold, and when he asked the shaman to come, he asked him to leave his servant behind.

The shaman spent many days with the grandmother. Her son and daughter would not let him take her to his home, so he nursed her in her own until it became clear to him that she would die before winter. He had done all he could. He told her children to prepare and to call him toward the end.

———◆———

One long summer's afternoon the shaman's servant found him as he was bathing.

"My grandfather is coming," she yelled to him, "did you call?"

At first, he thought of her living grandfather, but the worry on her face didn't fit.

"No," he answered.

She ran ahead to her grandmother's house. The shaman quickly dressed and followed.

"Go back and get your master," her mother was telling her, barring the girl's entrance to the house.

"I am here," said the shaman, entering. He had seen Polisa's father walking from the northern plains toward the house. He knew the time was short.

The shaman's servant sat on the ground outside and waited. She greeted her grandfather when he arrived.

"Why aren't you inside with your grandmother?" he asked, surprised.

"They won't let me," she answered.

"Did you do something bad?"

She shrugged, angry and hurt.

"I told them."

Her grandfather nodded and sat down next to her to wait.

"Rirylia sends her thanks by me," he told her.

"How is she?"

"Very well. She says she is sorry she called you a non-person. She says you helped her very much. There are others who have been saying the same. You are making me very proud."

He smiled. His granddaughter smiled back. She liked her handsome grandfather who had earned his reputation as a superb craftsman in metals — a spiritual calling of great honor. His praise warmed her.

They heard the shaman's call.

"Time to go in now," announced her grandfather, rising.

"Should I go in too?" she asked.

"Not if your mother won't let you. I'll bring Lila out this way so you can say goodbye."

Her grandfather went in. Others were arriving too, she saw, all from the north where the doorway to their plains was. Most she had never seen before, but their faces were reflected by her mother,

her uncle, her cousins and her sisters. They were all of them young, handsome and strong, a family to be proud of. She was glad for her grandmother to have so many come to escort her. They nodded to the child as they went into the house. It quickly filled up, and many had to stand outside. All around her she felt their love.

Her grandfather came out with a woman on his arm, young and beautiful with long golden hair, smooth golden skin, and shining brown eyes. The child almost didn't recognize her.

"Say goodbye now," her grandfather instructed.

The child looked up at the smiling woman.

"Goodbye, grandmother," she said. "I will miss you. I hope you will be happy."

"I'll be fine," she promised. "And you be good. You serve your master well and bring our family honor."

The child promised she would and watched as her grandmother joyously greeted her brothers and sisters and parents and friends. It seemed they all had so much to catch up on as they wandered off toward the northern plains.

Inside the little house, she could hear her mother and sisters and cousins weeping. She wanted to go in to comfort them, but her master stopped her as he came out.

"It's time to leave the family alone," he said quietly.

"But they are my family," said the little girl.

Yaku Shaman looked at her surprised. It seemed almost as if he had forgotten.

"You will help them more by leaving them alone," he told her. He took her by the hand, still dwarfed in his own, but by now it seemed to fit better, and led her away.

Chapter 6

Attack of the Gicoks

The height of summer came with a blazing heat which burned the fragile leaves and fruit of many of the crops. Drought parched the earth. The yield was very small, and it was obvious to everyone that they'd be living off the hunt this winter in the south country.

The Summer Festival was a modest one. Thanks were given to the spirits through plays, but were not as lavish or heartfelt as last year's had been. Two of their young warriors broke legs, and one broke an arm during the various competitions. Seven children passed into adulthood with proper ceremony and proud parents watching. Two boys would try again next year, for the spirits had not judged them ready. It was not a shame, but it was not an honor either. Several young men had elected to leave the village for the lonely and dangerous hunter/trapper life. Their hopes were high, but the parting was sad, for very few of the men who left on such adventures ever returned to enjoy the lavish honors awarded successful heroes.

Less than a week after the Summer Festival, while the shaman's servant was still struggling to "listen deeply," she heard the sound of horses' hooves pounding the ground quickly, growing louder as they approached. Her master heard them too and raised the cry. The Gicoks were attacking.

Men ran in from the fields and the grazing hills. Women and children grabbed what they could of their livestock and their treasures and rushed to the caves. The men armed, older men holding back to defend the village proper and the access to the caves while the younger men rushed forward to attack as the Gicoks forded the western river. Yaku Shaman armed and ran with the younger men. He did not think of his apprentice, but assumed she would follow the other children.

In her confusion, she ran to her mother's home first, to the old goytew house where her mother had always instructed them to meet in case of danger. It was, of course, deserted. Only then did she go to the caves, but her little legs could not climb very fast, and the entrances were sealed by the time she arrived. One by one she pounded on the hidden doors. None opened. Her people hid deep, away from them, in fortified passages dug long ago that connected and went farther than anyone but the miners had ever explored. It was unlikely that they heard her.

She knew she should hide nearby, but the sounds of the battle, now engaged, drew her curiosity. She ran back to the eastern hill and hid in the thick branches of her tree. From there she could see the village and all the lands beyond.

The Gicoks had not yet crossed the river whose floating bridges had been retracted. They were terrifying, on huge, black horses bred for battle with long legs, broad shoulders and high heads. It was said that these animals were the spirits of their fallen warriors, and the little girl was thankful when she saw one fall wounded. It bled. That meant it wasn't a spirit. The horses were shielded with thick woven hides over their backs and around their chests, tied to them under their bellies. The mats were bright and dazzling, painted with visions of demons and hung with shiny tassels that tried to draw the eye away from the rider.

If the horses were impressive, the men were hardly less so. They

44

were a tall race and strong, trained from birth for battle, for the Gicoks were nomads who fed their people with stolen food and goods that could be traded. Their white or golden hair was cut too short for an enemy to grab and their pale eyes, pink, amber or light blue, were hard to watch. They darted around frenziedly, never focusing on anything but seeing everything and hiding their thoughts. They went into battle covered with glistening oils and magic paint to protect their limbs, throats, and heads. Their shields were vests of shaped and hardened reeds and limber leather that covered their backs and chests and moved with them as they moved. They were painted with the visages of demons, like their horses, and with magic symbols of strength and courage that made them look terrifyingly greater than anything human.

They always came from the west when they attacked, for that was the easiest and quickest passage through the surrounding mountains. They always rode swiftly but the valley setting for the village, coursed with rivers and lakes, allowed it adequate warning. If the Gicoks had ever once snuck in during the night, like a cat stalking its prey, they would probably have found the village unprepared and defenseless, but a Gicok was a proud and honorable warrior. They fought with warriors who could fight back, not with farmers in their beds.

Although their village was a peaceful one, Yaku Shaman's people were well prepared for defense. Their young men were strong and trained to run swiftly and fight deadly well by the time they had reached adulthood. Weapons were always near, and even everyday tools were made strong and sharp for combat, just in case. They were not nearly the riders that the Gicoks were. Their horses were strong but slow and too small to ride far. They were more useful for the plow than the battle, but the men knew every step of their valley, every eddy in the rivers, streams, and lakes, and they knew the lives of their families and their people depended on them. They fought with courage and were at least an equal match for their enemy.

The battle began at the river. Yaku Shaman's people had projectile weapons which could send sharp bone and metal pieces and charmed stones to pierce their enemies' hides and shatter their bones. The Gicoks had some arrows, but they were hand to hand fighters. The arrows were merely to get them to their enemy where the real fighting would occur. Even though the summer's heat had lowered the rivers, it was still a difficult cross for one who did not know the way. The floating bridges had been retracted, and many Gicoks fell before they forded it. The wounded retreated to the hills, where, if they could heal, they would meet their returning warriors, if they could not, they would kill themselves. They never allowed themselves to be taken prisoner.

Those who did not fall were met on the other side by valiant warriors led by a giant shaman, the size of a bear, who seemed to wear an armor of pure light. Spirits surrounded him, and no weapon could come close enough to touch him, yet his ax fell with the force of twenty, bringing down man, and sometimes horse as well, with one blow. The Gicoks were strong, however, and the men of the valley were forced back toward their village. There all looked still, but in trees and on roofs and hidden places along the way were silent men, waiting. When the shaman called retreat and fled, the Gicoks chased them into an ambush, which was led by Sirfen Elder's best pupil. The shaman's warriors split and circled back while blades and stones flew at the enemies with deadly aim. Good men on both sides fell.

The Gicoks pushed themselves in far enough to loot while their stronger warriors still fought. They did not bother with farmer's small, sturdy horses, but tried for bofimers and goytews and anything of value that could run beside them or be easily carried on their horses' backs. The hide doors and windows of houses were ripped open and destroyed. They filled the pouches in their horses' battle mats with what they could snatch, then retreated. The men did not pursue past the river. It was useless. The Gicoks left with what they had grabbed. It was not worth enough to risk their lives further. Hopefully, the Gicoks' losses would be enough to keep them away for at least another year, but no one doubted that they would be back.

The wounded were gathered in the center of town with a tent hastily thrown up around them. The dead, both theirs and the Gicoks', were taken to the northern plain. Women and children were given the all-clear signal and quickly emerged to do their share of tending the wounded, preparing the dead and repairing the village.

Although many men were hurt, less than twenty had been killed. They were mostly the younger men, the braver men who had fought beside the shaman. Two of the boys who had only just reached adulthood were killed. Most were only slightly older. The man that gossip said Misa was going to marry next spring was among the dead. Of the husbands and fathers, only four were dead, and they would be deeply mourned. Carken, the farmer bordering Takan's lands, who was childless and whose wife had died of illness several years ago, was now free to follow her. Two of the elders who, like Yaku Shaman, still thought it necessary to fight as younger men, had also been killed.

The shaman's servant was running back toward the village when she noticed, from her view on the eastern hill, that many men were heading toward the northern plain. Her curiosity pulled her that way to investigate.

She stopped her father who was among the northbound men.

"Why are you going this way?" she asked.

He stared down at her, confused, and could not answer. She gently turned him around and sent him back toward the village. He walked like a man in his sleep.

"Go home, Father," she called after him, but she could not tell if he heard.

One by one she stopped the walking men. She tried to turn them around and send them back to the village, but many were too confused and stood and stared at her instead. She wished her master were here to explain why they were walking like this, but she knew he was busy and she was afraid if she went to get him, the sleepwalkers would wander away and get lost.

"Massern Leader," she cried, "wake up! These men are getting lost. You must lead them back."

He stopped walking north but did not wake up. He stood and stared at her, as though waiting for her to do something. She didn't know what to do.

She reached for Carken, but he pulled away. His eyes were not like the others. He was alert and awake.

"Can you tell me what is happening to them?" she begged, pointing toward the men.

"All I know is I am dead," he said with a smile, "and my wife is waiting with our children and my family for me to be free." He nodded toward the men around her. "Good luck with them."

"Good luck to you," she wished him.

While they were talking, Pinden, Katira's husband, wandered by. She ran to catch him. He smiled at her dazedly, as though he almost recognized her.

"Where are you going Pinden?" she asked.

He waved his hand vaguely toward the north and shrugged.

"But Katira is waiting for you in the village. She will be very angry if you leave her, with your baby on its way."

She took his hand. The others, who had followed her as she ran to him, followed her still as she led him back to the village.

She stopped several more men, including her father, who had somehow turned around again, and led them straight to the shaman, who was working in the wounded men's tent.

"Master," she called, as she entered the tent. He did not look up from the surgery he was performing.

"Soak this well," he ordered, handing a small bronze-edged knife to a woman near him, "and bring it back to me as clean as possible."

"More cloth," he demanded of another.

"Come here and watch," he called to his servant.

She came to his side. The men around her followed.

Yaku Shaman raised his head, looked around, and fixed his eyes on her. His face looked angry, but she was beginning to realize that it always did, especially when he was confused or thoughtful.

"Who is here?" he demanded of her.

"Pinden, Massern Leader, Takan, Focuren..." she named them all, one by one. "They were wandering toward the north. They looked confused. I didn't know what to do so I brought them to you."

His frown deepened. He nodded toward the man on whom he was operating. It was Massern Leader. He lay, unconscious, a stitched-up gash on the side of his head and one in his belly, which the shaman was struggling to close.

The little girl looked between the body on the raised bed and the man standing beside her. The man beside her smiled slightly in her general direction but seemed for the most part unaware.

"Will he live?" she asked.

"His body is not too bad. We work to make it a place where the spirit can stay before the spirit goes too far to find its way back. It is good that you brought them here."

The child caught her breath in surprise. Such praise from her master was very rare.

He tried to explain to her what he was doing. It was much about blood and veins and hearts and muscles, far too much for her to understand. He would often stop his explanations suddenly, as his full concentration was demanded for the work, and not bother to resume where he had left off. The little girl didn't even notice. She watched his hands, so uncommonly large they should have been ungainly, but they handled his tools, slim knives, and little needles, with a dexterity that would be the envy of the finest stitcher or craftsman. She had watched him kill today with one mighty blow. Now she saw how many tiny touches it took to heal.

He was not the only healer. Two others, both women, tended the wounded with similar skill. Yaku Shaman himself, his servant found out later, had been taught the healing craft by an old woman of this village whose skill, his master had judged, had been beyond his own.

Slowly the crowd around the little girl thinned as the men slipped back into the beds where their sleeping bodies lay. Several wandered north again, but this time they knew where they were going. Many of the men woke up in pain, with their friends and wives and families near to tend to their needs and comfort them. Those who were judged well enough were taken home. Several had to stay. The shaman and the other healers tended them throughout the night.

———◆—◄———

Yaku gulped a light konis to keep himself awake, but it bent the mind to hallucinations which he found distracting. He caught himself staring stupidly at tiny spirits who flitted here and there, often dancing around him or his apprentice like moths around a fire. These were harmless, useless little ones, whom there was no reason to watch, but he was tired and the day had drained so much of his energy that he had little left with which to guide his mind.

The next day was difficult. There were the dead to deal with. Yaku had let them wait only because the living had priority, but they could not wait too long to be freed, or their spirits would grow restless and angry and cause troubles for the living. All night he had struggled to keep awake. As soon as the living were tended, he saw to the dead before he dared to try to sleep. They would not have let him succeed anyway.

His strength was not what he would have wished. He leaned heavily upon his servant, his weight almost more than she could bear, but he could not have made it to the northern plain without her. No one dared to offer help, for they all knew his pride.

The people, both the living and the dead, waited while he called to the families and sang the Soul's Ease. His servant sang with him, her clear, young voice steadying his and continuing strongly where his failed. Had he been slightly more alert, he might have felt ashamed at his weakness, his dependence on a baby, but all his mind and energy were pushing him to finish his duty so he could finally rest.

When the last chant was sung, the last spirit freed, he sank to the ground where he had stood, found a pillow in his servant's lap, and slept under the sun as the people around him solemnly buried the bodies with their treasures and with herbs and seeds to help them start new life again in the spirit's world.

Yaku Shaman awoke at sunset, stiff and sore and feeling older than he ever yet had. The little girl offered him her strength, but he refused. He was rested now. He would go home unaided.

As he walked beside his servant through the town, people came to their doors and windows, put down their work and watched. They bowed to him silently, their deepest honor to the great warrior, the worthy healer, and their beloved shaman.

Chapter 7

Attack of the Wolf Spirit

Takan's bones were still mending when Polisa had her baby. It was the boy they had been praying for. It was a hard birth, much harder than any of the others, but Polisa was strong and endured it well. When the time came to move to the southern country, she and her husband, their five remaining daughters, and their baby boy were all ready.

Katira had more difficulty. She was heavy with child, and Pinden had been wounded badly, his leg amputated, and he still could not walk alone with his crutches.

The village used a wagon for those who were weak. This year they used three. Wagons were slow and clumsy, dangerous through the mountains, and difficult to hide. They drew attention and might attract the Gicoks, but the alternative was leaving the weak behind in a poorly protected village with only some of the livestock and the shepherds, or everyone staying and possibly starving. The village chose to risk the journey.

When Yaku performed the fall rituals, he sang a special song for protection on their journey and luck in the search of game. In worlds ago, they had been nomads, he reminded his people, and had never stopped wandering in pursuit of their food. Their lives were easier now, for which they should give thanks. But they should also thank the spirits for this occasional reminder of how their ancestors had lived. A tree can grow tall, but its roots should be as deep as its branches are high if it is to live well.

Each home in the village was guarded by a statue or a painting representing the spirit guardian of the house. The village had several statues wrought in silver representing the spirits of the village. All who left on the journey bound their wrist with a slim chain that held the metal charms in the form of faces of their village spirits and their individual home spirit. They would not take these off again until they had returned to their village, and any who died on the way would be buried with their homecoming bracelet still on, so their spirit could find the way home.

Yaku Shaman, himself, made the bracelet for his servant. It was not the one she was used to. It had the village spirits but not her mother's house spirit or even Yaku's house spirit, but one that she had not seen before. It had a double face, half-man, half-woman with no animal nature depicted.

"It is the Mother/Father" Yaku Shaman explained. "The creator of all the worlds and all the other spirits and gods. That is where the shaman goes home. That is the spirit's home."

"This is the one who planted the world's tree?" she asked.

He nodded. The Mother/Father was the creator and destroyer of all the worlds that had ever been, including the one to be.

The people of the village left through the southern woods, a caravan of families dressed in costumes of thick woven wool and pelts for warmth and camouflage. They traveled with leather tents, warm blankets, dried food, and water sacks tied to their backs and to the backs of their horses. Many walked with long staves or several slim, but strong poles lashed tightly together, blunt at one end and blade tipped at the other. Such poles supported the walker in the day, the tent in the night, and could be used for defense or hunting if necessary. All the men were well-armed, and even women and youths carried blades in straps over their shoulders or around their hips and whistles around their necks to call a variety of well-rehearsed alarms.

Some families chose to lead their bofimers for milk and meat if necessary. Many left their stock behind in a hidden valley, under the watchful eyes of two brave, young men and the spirits. It was hoped neither the Gicoks nor the wild predators would find them. It was hoped the winter would be mild enough that they would not freeze or starve.

The mountains out of the valley were steep and difficult to climb. They pulled and pushed the wagons and, through several passages, those of the weak who could walk for short periods did so. Others were carried on stretched mats while the wagons were lifted and turned onto the wheels on their slim sides. These passages took much time, and at the end of a full day's journey, they still had not left the valley behind.

At first, the people sang while they walked and joked in good humor. It lightened the sadness and fear of leaving their homes. They made great plans of what they would do on their return and looked forward to a good Trintoa, which would earn them a better year next year. Their talk grew quiet, however, as they left their valley. Where they were unfamiliar, it felt as if enemies might be everywhere.

The shaman walked ahead, only hours behind the scouts, his servant at his side. He focused more on the healing skills, teaching her of the body, how it worked, the many ways it could be hurt, the few ways it could be mended.

They gathered herbs, sometimes leaves or buds, sometimes roots. He told her their histories and their powers. He showed her how to take them — this one in the full moon only with a cut like so and this chant...this one in the daylight of a waxing moon...this one never in fall or winter or even summer, but only in spring when it flowered if there was no frost...

There were so many things to know! It seemed impossible that anyone, even a man as great and aged as Yaku Shaman, could possibly learn it all. The little girl slowly began to realize what he had meant when he had told her that the study would take many years.

As they crossed the mountains to the other side, her master stopped her and held her still to look out over the endless world that stretched before them. It was bigger than she had ever imagined. The last time they had gone this way she had traveled mostly on her mother's back as her baby brother traveled now. It seemed to her that there was space enough for everything that ever wanted to live.

"Listen deeply," he ordered.

She listened as deeply as she could but did not hear anything that she could understand.

"What do you hear?" he asked her.

"Water," she answered instantly. But she hadn't heard it. She didn't know why she had said it.

Yaku Shaman nodded. Her answer had pleased him.

"It is deep at this place," he pointed to the ground "but it will rise to the surface soon. It flows far out there, over all that land, to a giant lake, wider than all this land before us, that catches it and keeps it."

"Have you seen this giant lake?" asked the little girl in awe.

"No. Our people do not go so far."

"Then how do you know of it?"

He frowned at her.

"I hear it."

They traveled several weeks south, over plains and rivers, around lakes and canyons to forested lands still rich with game. The winters here were warmer, wet but not frozen. Many of the animals who slept through the winter around their village had kin who did not sleep down here, and there were many good plants for eating that were not common in their valley. Game birds, too, were plentiful.

All their people had survived their trip, and only a few of the livestock had fallen to animals. Wolves and large cats followed the caravan, but had, so far, kept their distance. A Gicok camp had been found, long deserted.

They settled in their first lowlands camp. They would have many as they followed the game.

The shorter days did not shorten the shaman's lessons. There was much to learn by the moon and the darkness of night. They walked in the woods long after the rest of the people had retired to their tents. When she listened, the little girl could hear their slumbering and sometimes imagined she could hear their dreams.

As they walked back toward the camp, late one night, a giant, black wolf mounted a rise in their path and blocked their way. At the height of his shoulders, he was as tall as a man. His teeth gleamed white as they reflected no earthly light and his eyes watched them with sharp and evil intelligence.

At first, they did not see him, so like the shadows he was, but the shaman knew he was there, and knew he had not approached like a normal wolf or dog.

"It is a spirit," he spoke softly to his servant, "a very, very bad one. You must stay back and stay quiet. Do nothing to attract its attention."

She obediently drew back, off the path, and hid behind a tree.

Her master went forward, chanting softly, a strange light collecting around him. As he approached, the wolf growled menacingly. The shaman's chant grew louder, but not one step failed to bring him closer. He showed no fear. The light around him grew brighter and reflected in the evil one's red eyes.

The wolf sprang. He did not crouch like an animal first but simply flew through the air and landed on the shaman. Yaku Shaman fell back, under the weight of the beast. His chant fell silent, but the light around him exploded and from where he had fallen a huge brown bear, taller and mightier than any bear could be, rose to battle.

The bear and the wolf fought furiously over the shaman's still body. They dealt each other blows that would have instantly killed normal animals. Gashes opened in their hides and closed with no blood but only a kind of steam escaping.

The bear fell, with the wolf's teeth at his throat, and rolled over to crush the crying dog under him, claws flying at the evil one's eyes. The wolf scrambled away and ran, with the bear at his heels. For a while, there were only growls and snarls, snaps and yelps in the distance.

The little girl listened, afraid to move, afraid to go to her master's body, which lay as if dead, or to run to her people's camp for help. The sounds of the fight grew closer, then more distant, then suddenly stopped altogether, and all she could hear was an animal panting, and a low growl behind her.

She turned and faced the wolf. He towered above her, his legs taller than her whole body. He glared down at her triumphantly, teeth dripping a fluid that hissed through the air as it fell. Then he crumpled to the ground, the brown bear on top of him.

The child darted away, without direction. She stumbled over her master's body and fell beside it. The wolf made a desperate lunge for her or for the inert body, she could not tell, but the bear swatted at him in the air with his giant claw, and the wolf fell, rolling, missing his mark. The bear was instantly on top of him. Again, they struggled, again the bear chased him. This time they did not come back. She heard the black wolf whining in the distance, getting farther and farther away.

The little girl knelt, trembling, by her master's body, waiting for him to return and tell her what to do. She was scared. Yaku Shaman lay on the cold, hard ground before her. He still breathed. She could hear his heart beat, but his spirit was fighting without him. She didn't want to leave his body. She couldn't carry it. She lifted his heavy head into her lap and waited quietly.

Chapter 8

Lost Soul

The morning came and grew into a cold, windy day. Yaku Shaman did not awaken. The little girl listened as hard as she could. She thought she heard the stirring at the distant camp. Not long after, she heard the sound of footsteps fill the area. They had found the shaman missing and were looking. She finally heard them come her way.

"Here," she called. She blew her whistle in the call for help, but the wind whisked the sound away from the searchers.

Finally, a group of three men, including Tapeten, the Winter Leader, called to her as they mounted the rise. She waved to them eagerly as they approached.

"He's alive," announced Tapeten upon close examination. He ordered the men to lift the shaman and take him back to camp.

"His spirit is still away," said the little girl. "If you take away his body from where he left it will he know where to find it again?"

The men glanced at her curiously but did not bother to answer her. They carried the shaman back to his tent and called one of the healers.

"There is nothing wrong with him," she announced. "He seems just asleep."

"But he doesn't wake up," insisted Tapeten Winter Leader.

"Perhaps his spirit is lost. If another shaman were here, he could call him back."

Tapeten Leader frowned, worried. It was a very bad thing for their people to be without a shaman.

They put Yaku in his bed and covered him with blankets, then left him to sleep while his servant watched. She tried to sing for him. She sang him the chant he had taught her to call the spirits of the sick and dying back, but it didn't work. This was different somehow.

Two days went by. He did not return. They could not get his body to eat. It did nothing but sleep deeply.

"He will die soon," warned the healer, "if we cannot get him to eat or drink more."

The hunting game had run short. It was time to move further south.

"But if you move him so far, Yaku Shaman won't know where to find himself," the little girl tried to argue. No one listened, for she was only a non-person. Yaku Shaman might never come back, and it was time to go.

She would not go without her master, she decided. It was wrong. She knew it was wrong. The shaman was lost. If she could not call him to her, then she would go looking for him.

She ran back to where he had left his body first. He was not there. She looked around for any sign showing which way to look. There were no clues. She listened, quietly, deeply. She closed her eyes and concentrated hard. It wasn't that she heard anything, nothing that she could understand, anyway, but she turned northwest and went that way, calling for her master.

Her steps made a rhythm and her calling made a song. She called the shaman, she called the great bear. She called in the old language, and in the one he had known better, and in something that was no language at all, but just a calling. It's time to come home now. I'll show you the way.

An impossibly big, brown bear, awake in winter, came lumbering toward her through the woods. She stopped and waited when she

60

heard him. He approached her like an animal, not a spirit, but he was too big to fool her, and he wore the homecoming bracelet around his thick bear's wrist. She knew him.

"Yaku Shaman," she called to him.

He approached her warily and sniffed her all over, batting her lightly with his paw to turn her around.

"You're acting like a bear," she laughed. "But you're not."

He snorted and shook his head and started wandering away.

"Not that way," she called in the old language. "This way."

He turned around and came back. She reached her hand up as high as she could, but it could not reach his head. He lowered his head and sniffed her palm.

"This way, Great Bear," she told him in the old language. "Follow me."

Her master gruffly obeyed.

As they walked, she told him how worried about him everyone was, how weak his body was getting without enough food or water, and the plans the people had to leave that morning. He hardly listened to her, even when she spoke in the old language, which was all he seemed to understand. He ran ahead and jumped at a bush, scaring some small animal into flight. He would gladly have hunted it down, but the little girl called him back.

"Yaku Shaman. They'll be leaving soon without us. We have to hurry."

He growled at her with annoyance, but stopped his chase and followed.

She paused, just outside the camp. It was almost all packed. Even the shaman's tent was down.

"You should change back now," she told her master.

He seemed not to hear.

"Yaku Shaman," she said. He looked at her curiously. "You will scare everyone if you're a bear. Don't you think it would be better to be your human self now?"

But he did not change. She sighed. He was the master, he must know better. Together they walked into the camp.

People turned to look at them. They were alternately astonished, frightened, and confused. When they'd see the little girl out of the corner of their eyes, it looked as if an impossibly large, brown bear was following her, but when they looked again, there was nothing there. Many quickly made a sign to ward off evil and hurried away.

"Where have they taken Yaku Shaman's body?" asked his servant of the nearest person she could stop. The pinch-faced woman nodded curtly toward the last wagon and bustled on about her business.

She found his sleeping body lying on bed mats, between an injured man and a sickly old woman.

"You're in here," she told the bear. He flopped himself into a sitting position as if to say, "so what?"

"You need to go and get back into your body."

She was speaking the old language, but he didn't seem to understand.

"The healer says you'll die soon if you don't," she tried to argue.

The bear only yawned.

"Yaku Shaman," she pleaded, grabbing him by the fur around his neck and trying to pull him onto the wagon, "please get on this wagon and get into your body."

He raised himself slowly and heaved himself onto the wagon. It lurched with his sudden weight. The people on it looked around, confused. The little girl who had just climbed on could not possibly be that heavy. She walked to the shaman's sleeping body and pointed, saying something in a strange and lovely language that only the shaman ever spoke.

"That is you," she said. "You are Yaku Shaman's spirit, and you must get back in your body now."

The bear approached the sleeping man. He sniffed him curiously, licked his face with his tongue and gently nudged him with his paw.

"This is Yaku Shaman," she explained, "and you are Yaku Shaman. You need to get inside him, Great Bear."

Slowly the bear dissolved through the shape of a man crouching like an animal over the shaman's body, then into nothing. Yaku Shaman sighed deeply in his sleep, stretched his arms and slowly opened his eyes.

"Are you hungry master?" she asked him in their daily language.

He stared at her, as the bear had, with strange eyes, not comprehending.

"Food?" she asked again in the old language.

He nodded slowly, but he looked around him as a dazed man, not knowing where he was or what he was seeing.

His servant hurried to the healer who came running with food and water.

Yaku Shaman sniffed at the bowl of vegetable broth and snarled like an animal.

"Perhaps some meat?" suggested his servant.

"Too heavy," said the healer. "He has not eaten properly in days."

They poured him a cup of water. He held it awkwardly, between his two palms, and tried to lap it with his tongue. The healer watched him closely.

"He's acting like an animal," she said.

"He was wandering as a bear," the little girl told her. The healer looked up at her.

"What do you know of this?"

The child told her the story of the black wolf and the brown bear.

"That is very bad," said the healer, nervously, when she had finished.

"Will he be a man again?" asked the child.

The healer shrugged.

"If it were possible I would say ask the shaman. The best we can do is get him to eat and wait to see."

The shaman's servant faithfully served her master. She walked by the wagon and talked to him all day long in the old language, telling him the old stories, although she did it more like her father than like a shaman. When the stories that she knew ran out, she made up new ones. The shaman didn't seem to notice. He listened, but it was to the sound of her voice more than her words.

At first the shaman did not like to ride the wagon. He tried to walk beside his servant, but his body was weak. It frustrated and angered him, for his spirit was strong. When his servant asked him to please ride, he reluctantly obeyed her like a tamed animal.

She and the healer, with the help of his hunger, managed to get him to drink some meat broth.

"It will make you strong again," his servant told him in the old language. He seemed to understand.

Massern Summer Leader, himself, helped raise the shaman's tent in the new camp.

"We are glad you're back with us," he told Yaku cheerfully. The shaman looked at him blankly.

He slept the night curled like a bear, but woke the next morning able to speak the old language, although he had little to say except to ask for meat instead of broth. They brought him some dried fish and water. He growled but ate hungrily. He slept a good deal throughout the day, and every time he woke he was a little more like a man. The healer was very pleased.

"He will be all right," she said. "He just needs time."

The third night in their new camp, the little girl was shoved awake by her master crouching over her, on all fours.

"I'm confused," he said in the old language. "Help me."

She forced herself awake and revived the dying fire, making it brighter so that they could see each other.

"You are Yaku Shaman," she explained, once again. "A great, holy man for our people. We love and honor you very much."

She sat down beside him and told him the story about the black wolf and the brown bear. He listened. He stopped her several times with questions and made her repeat many parts. Slowly, he started to understand.

"And you," he asked. "Who are you?"

"I am your servant," she answered.

"You are not a shaman?"

"I am not even a person yet. You will name me at the next Trintoa."

"Trintoa," he repeated softly. He seemed to find the word familiar in an unfamiliar way.

"Why is it that you are the only one who can speak?" he asked.

"This is the old language, the spirit's tongue. Everyone else speaks the normal language. You do too, only you've forgotten."

"Why have I forgotten?"

The little girl shrugged.

"I don't know. You'll probably tell me when you remember."

She yawned and stretched. It was hard to stay awake.

The great bear bowed his head, wearily. She stroked his cheek. It was wet.

"Don't worry, master," she said gently, "You are remembering very quickly."

"You must help me," he told her.

She dared to kiss him like a little mother.

"I will help you," she promised.

The next evening, he was improved enough for the healer to allow the elders to see him. They crowded into his tent and sat around him while the child and a helpful wife served them steaming tea.

"You look well again," Massern told the shaman, pleased. "How do you feel?"

The shaman looked to his servant for interpretation. She dutifully complied. The elders watched the exchange puzzled.

"He says he is feeling well," his servant told the reverend men, "but not..." she paused, seeking words where the translation could not be direct, "not all himself...complete...yet."

"Why do you speak to us through your servant?" asked Nobien Elder, a tiny old man with a beaked nose and a whining voice.

The great bear, seeing their faces, was already answering before the question was fully asked. His servant had to struggle to catch all his words through so many others. When she did, it was difficult to interpret. She was not yet perfect in the language. Much of what she understood was inferred through the context, and it made her awkward as an interpreter. She did not want to say the wrong thing.

"He says his mind cannot be shaped in your words yet, so I will help."

They looked at each other, at him and his servant, confused.

"Why can't he talk?" asked Jatoyen Elder, the youngest but perhaps the smartest of the elders.

"He wants to know why you can't talk," she explained to her master. "They don't understand."

"How much do they know?" he asked her.

"I don't know."

"Did you tell them about the bear and the wolf?"

"It was not my place. I told the healer, but I don't know what she said."

"Tell them now," he ordered.

"My master wants me to tell you what happened," she started. The elders nodded. That was why they were here.

"But why can't Yaku Shaman tell us himself?" insisted Massern.

She interpreted his question for her master. He scowled at Massern with a barely suppressed growl and practically shouted his

66

answer. His servant blushed, but her interpretation was polite.

"He says to let me speak, and I will tell you."

She retold her story with her father's dramatic style, holding her arms out wide and pointing to the top of the tent, which could not be as tall as the giant, evil wolf-dog. Her master watched her, not understanding her words, but apparently amused by the way her arms flew around and her voice changed, deep for his words and high for hers. It was not the solemn telling he would have made, she guessed, but the elders watched her, spellbound.

She gloried in describing her master's courage as he walked unfalteringly toward the terrifying spirit. Her audience startled as the beast leapt through her words and brought her master down. Their eyes went wide with wonder as she told of the great brown bear that rose from the shaman's body and towered over the tallest trees.

"No," her master interrupted in the old language. "Not so tall. Tell the truth."

She looked at him, startled and ashamed.

"Perhaps he was not so very tall," she amended, "but he was beyond any real bear, taller than the wolf by half again as much..."

She described the fight in vivid detail, described her fright at being cornered by the beast and the heroic strength of her master who saved her.

"When you found us the next day, you found his body only. He had not returned yet. He did not return until we were about to leave..."

"You called me back," Yaku Shaman corrected. He said it in the normal language. His servant stopped her narrative and smiled at him. He nodded for her to go on. When she hesitated, he flicked his fingers like a push to shoo her.

"Tell the rest," he insisted, in the old language.

"He was still in the form of the bear," she told the elders. "Even after his spirit returned to his body, it has taken time for him to become Yaku Shaman again."

"The bad spirit — will it trouble us again?" asked Jatoyen Elder.

The shaman looked to his servant for interpretation. When she gave it, he shook his head.

"The bear has kept it away for a while," he told them through the little girl. "But it is a strange one to be troubling us. I do not know what it means."

"You are a very great shaman," Tapeten Leader praised him for his people. "We thank you for protecting us."

"But why do you not speak?" asked Nobien Elder again.

"He...his spirit has not come all the way back," his servant translated for him. "The normal language is still difficult."

"Why is it that you can speak to him?" asked Jatoyen Elder. "What language do you use?"

She turned to interpret to her master, but the elder stopped her.

"I'm asking you," he said.

"Forgive me, Elder," she answered, confused, "but I am not a person yet."

The others laughed. The shaman tapped his servant's shoulder to get her explanation. She gave it. Her master very nearly smiled.

"He says to tell you that we use the old language."

"How does your servant come to know it?" asked Jatoyen, now properly addressing the shaman.

"He says he has been teaching me." She paused while her master said more. Then she smiled, blushing slightly. "He says I have learned very quickly and well."

"Why have you been teaching her?" Jatoyen pursued.

Massern stopped the servant before she could interpret.

"That is a question for the shaman when he is fully healed. For now, we should be thankful that we have an interpreter."

"How much longer do you think it'll take for you to be truly yourself?" asked Nobien Elder.

The shaman shrugged.

"So, do we have a shaman again or don't we?" he insisted of the other elders.

"We will let you rest now," Tapeten Leader told the shaman, as answer to Nobien. "If we have strong need of you, we will come. Otherwise, we will leave you alone."

Yaku nodded but did not rise as they left. The interview had obviously wearied him. His body was still not strong. It demanded him to sleep much more than he was used to. His servant was glad he did not begrudge it, for every time he slept he awoke with more of himself returned.

CHAPTER 9

THE STUDENT TEACHES THE TEACHER

Yaku Shaman had his servant start teaching him their language. It was a strange thing for her to serve her master so. She gave him words for everything she saw. He could not retain them and had to be told over and over. When he did have the words, he could not put them together in the right order. The little girl had never thought of her language enough to explain it. She knew it was right when it sounded right, but the shaman had lost the sound.

Slowly, the shaman came to speak again, through his own reviving memory, more than his servant's efforts. The language was the last thing to come fully back to him. By the Winter Festival he was strong enough to honor the spirits of the dead, to welcome them, should they choose to visit their families in such a distant place, but his servant still stood beside him, to help him speak to his people.

She found it distracting duty. She wanted to find her grandfather and grandmother, but many people crowded around the shaman, both the dead and living, wanting the tale of his adventure told over and over. He was telling it mostly himself, with simple and austere style. The only color was in the phrases he let her supply, and often he would correct her to his style.

"Our shaman is the only one who makes a story smaller in the telling, not bigger" some of the people laughed.

If her grandparents came, she did not see them. Perhaps it was too far. There were many others, whom she did not recognize and several who had died in the past year who still reached for the living as the living reached for them. She was happy to see Rirylia, who had made the long trip, but her master gave her almost no time to visit.

"Tell them I'm well," begged Rirylia, pushing herself to her little friend's side. She pointed to her parents, who were still grieving in memory of her. "They won't listen to me."

"I cannot leave my master," she answered, "and they wouldn't believe me anyway." She remembered her mother's and uncle's responses the last time she had carried a message from the dead.

"Perhaps your master could do it?" asked Rirylia, hopefully.

The little girl asked him when the fourth telling of his tale was finished and he had a moment's peace.

"Rirylia asks you to please tell her parents that she is well."

The shaman addressed the distressed young spirit. "I have told them," he said to her. "They do not cry for you, but for themselves because they miss you."

"Can I help them?" asked Rirylia.

"Time will help them," the shaman answered.

The winter festival marked the turning of winter toward spring. It was soon time to turn the people for home. They had to be back in their village by the Trintoa.

Her master once again focused her lessons on the Trintoa ceremony. He quizzed her on the chants and corrected her until she was perfect. He spoke to her of the spirits whom they particularly wanted to please, taught her how she could call them, the ways they might come and how she might know them. There were so many, it seemed impossible to know them all.

One day, Massern interrupted their evening lesson.

"Have you fully recovered now?" he asked Yaku Shaman in his friendly way.

The shaman nodded, sternly, while his servant offered the Summer Leader some drink.

"The elders are hoping you will not need your servant at tomorrow's council."

Yaku Shaman eyed him suspiciously but said nothing. When he went to the council meeting, he left his servant behind. It was the first time since he had fought the evil spirit that he spoke to his people alone.

"Why do you teach your servant the old language?" asked Jatoyen Elder.

Yaku Shaman glanced at Massern, but he waited with the others for the answer.

"At the Trintoa she will get her name, and I will take her as my..." he paused, seeking the forgotten word, it did not come. "I will teach her to be your shaman."

It was startling for the elders to hear. Massern had said nothing, confident that the shaman would change his mind. There had been rumors, but few could believe a woman shaman. It was easier to believe a crazy, old shaman.

"You waste your time with her," said Sirfen Elder, who prided himself that he was still as strong a warrior as a much younger man. "We cannot follow a woman shaman."

"It is unnatural," cried Nobien Elder, "against the proper order of things."

"You must choose a boy," ordered Tapeten Leader. He spoke little, but when he did his words were strong.

Yaku waited until their objections were finished. Only when they were silent did he speak.

"The people do not choose a shaman. Even the shaman does not choose a shaman. Only the spirits choose. She is the one they have chosen. They like her. They will follow her. If you do not, then you go against them, and our people will suffer."

"How can you know the spirits have chosen her?" demanded Tapeten Leader. It was a dangerous question that meant more than its words. It said to all listening that he believed the shaman was not a shaman but only insane.

Yaku measured the Leader silently, coldly, with his eyes before he turned them away and did not deign to answer. That was an insult back. Only foolish children were ignored so.

Nobien Elder nudged Tapeten Leader, urging him to apologize. The tension in the tent was thick. Tapeten stood up proudly and left the council. The elders all frowned. It was a bad business.

"Why would the spirits choose a shaman that our people could not follow?" asked Jatoyen Elder, with soothing tact.

"They do not say," answered Yaku Shaman. "Perhaps they feel it is time that we should change. When our people were warriors, the spirits chose men who could lead in battle and in hunt, but we are farmers now. Our spirits nurture, like women, more often than fight."

Sirfen Elder shook his head angrily.

"When the Gicoks raid or the journey is needed, how can a woman serve us?" he demanded.

"It is not the shaman, himself, who serves the people. The shaman serves the spirits and the spirits aid the people. The spirits follow her already. The spirits of our ancestors recognize and talk to her. The spirits of our wounded came to her." He spoke now to Massern who had no memory with which to understand. "It was because of her that many more were not lost during the Gicoks' last raid. My spirit," he pushed his pride away to say it, "came to her when she called. The evil one had wounded me. I could not become myself again. I could not even remember. I could think no more than an animal. I could not have found my way back, and no one else of our people could have called me. Only a shaman."

"You have taught her, of course," said Jatoyen Elder carefully.

Yaku shook his head.

"I am teaching her," he corrected, "but this much she knows already."

"Could you teach another?" Jatoyen pressed.

"I can teach anyone everything I know, but the spirits will only listen to the ones they choose."

"If you taught a boy, might the spirits then choose him?" asked Nobien Elder.

Yaku Shaman frowned deeply and slowly forced his fists to uncurl.

"No!" he answered, more like a growl than a word.

"So, you will teach your girl," said Massern with a soothing smile, "but if the spirits should favor a boy soon — she has just had a brother, perhaps he too will have the spirit's interest — could you then teach him instead?"

"I will follow the spirits," answered Yaku with a nod.

That satisfied his people. They would humor their aging shaman's whim. They would accept the little girl as Yaku's temporary apprentice until a proper one was found.

The way back was more difficult than the way south had been. The snow had fallen thickly and still iced the higher mountain passages where the more treacherous climbs were. Lower down the melting snow and rains swelled streams and rivers, and turned good hard ground into mud which bogged the wagons and sucked at the people's feet and the animal's hooves. One young bofimer, a fine, healthy breeder, fell with a broken leg and had to be slaughtered. The wolves and hunting cats were bolder now that the long winter had made them hungry. The camp's guards were doubled to keep them away as well as watch for Gicoks. They were lucky. The Gicoks did not come.

They pushed through storms and lengthened their days' marches into night to reach the village by Trintoa. They arrived by nightfall, only two days before the morning of the sacred ceremony.

One of the men who had been left with the livestock met them with bitter news. A giant black wolf, larger than any he had ever seen, had found the hidden valley and killed many healthy animals before he and the other young man had finally chased him away. The other man went in pursuit to try to kill the beast while his partner guarded the remaining animals. The man did not come back. When his partner went looking, he found his body torn apart — shredded as if by a dozen beasts, but not eaten. His face, still mostly intact, was a mask of terror and his dark brown hair had turned pure white.

The body had been packed in snow through the winter, but the snow was melting in the valley, and the body was decaying. The shaman saw to it immediately, before he saw his house again. They carried it to the north plain, and he gave it a very long and special service to appease the wounded spirit who had been trapped between the living and the dead too long, and to protect it from the evil spirit who might hunt it still, even after death.

Every day before an important ceremony the shaman fasted in solitude to prepare his soul. His servant enjoyed such days when she could be free for a while. This one she eagerly looked forward to. She longed to see her tree again on the eastern hill, to listen to the baby in the trunk and reassure herself that he was still happy and safe. Then she planned to visit Katira, who was busy with a new baby boy of her own, to her husband's delight. Pinden, who was not a farmer but a weaver, could only have been happier if it had been a girl as pretty as his wife, which greatly amused his father-in-law, but

76

everyone was still very proud. Her little brother would probably be there too, for Katira often watched him. It was where the shaman's servant liked to go best in her very rare and very precious free time.

The fast day morning, however, the shaman was up even before his servant. He woke her in silence and took her with him to bathe and to pray.

"But don't you have to be alone?" she asked.

"Today you will stay with me," he answered.

They walked the village, then sat in the holy room with the fire burning lightly scented herbs. They sat for hours, the shaman calmly listening deeply, while his servant fidgeted.

"Be still and listen," he would order, and she would try, but she couldn't concentrate as her master did. She would be still for a few minutes, then her feet would start shaking or twitching, and her arms would feel uncomfortable no matter where she put them, and all she could hear were people working and talking and children playing and she wanted to be out there with them. It made her master angry.

"Tomorrow is very important. We must be ready. You must prepare with me, not distract me."

Again she would try and again she would fail.

"Listen deeply," he ordered.

"What am I trying to hear?" she asked.

She had asked this question often before, and the answer was always the same: "Listen for whatever there is to hear. If you listen for something specific, you may hear what you listen for, even if it's not there." Today, however, perhaps because her restlessness was so distracting, her master answered her differently.

"We are reaching for the spirits we will try to call tomorrow."

"But what if they are too far away?" asked his servant.

He frowned.

"Nothing is too far away. If you listen well enough, you can even hear a fish swimming in the giant lake that is farther west than our people have ever gone."

For a while, this intrigued her, and she tried to listen for that. It didn't seem to work. Her mind slipped off and started to wander again, but it was wandering in a listening way now, reaching all over the endless land she had seen, and bringing her back images of tall, steep mountains of stones formed by men in which many people lived and worked. And there were spirits who could be in many places at the same time, and great billowing spirits who could lift whole villages up into the air. She could hear strange music that was full of so many sounds thrown together that it seemed as if every song that ever existed was being sung at the same time. There were loud explosions and screams and laughter and the growls of strange beasts. There was too much to believe, but it was a game she could enjoy, and it kept her relatively still for the rest of the day.

The next morning the shaman woke her up early again. This was the important day, the Trintoa. She knew in all ways what was expected of her, every step and chant, but still, she was nervous.

She watched her master as he heated the konis. He looked ancient beyond words when he was so solemn. He let her have a taste, just a little drop on her finger. It was very bitter, and she did not like it at all. She felt sorry for him having to drink it, but he gulped it down with a look that was almost pleasure.

Then they started, walking through the town together, chanting the first chant softly. People came to their windows and doors to watch them. The little girl wanted to smile and greet them, but her master would not like it. He had warned her that she must act like a shaman today, which to her meant being stern and proud and never smiling. It was very hard for her and took much effort.

Yaku Shaman started for the men's path, then remembering his servant this morning, climbed the woman's path with her instead, their chants growing stronger as they reached the top.

It was the first time in many months that the little girl had been to her hill and seen her tree. Now, at last, she felt as if she'd come home again and the joy of it overwhelmed her, erasing the last struggling shred of solemnity. Instantly forgotten were her master and his stern warnings and suddenly remembered was the baby in the tree.

She could hear him calling, happy to see her again. She ran to her tree and threw her arms around its trunk in a loving embrace. She raised her voice and sang to the child, to greet him and let him know that she was happy to be back. She could hear him, deep inside, laughing with pleasure.

The spirits came to her, surrounded her, danced and gamboled about her. She welcomed them all, happy in her heart. She knew some of them now, from her master's description, and she sang for them too, as she sang for the child. She reached out her voice to share her song, like a loving gift, and she pleased the spirits greatly.

The shaman changed to the last and final chant. Almost completely unaware, the little girl changed with him. This chant told the spirits how the people hoped they would be treated. It was an asking, but the child sang it as a giving, happy to please the spirits who wanted to help them by telling them how they could succeed. The spirits were ecstatic, and the shaman was well satisfied. He declared that it was going to be a very good year.

When the children came to take their first names, Yaku Shaman's servant was among them. He gave her the name the spirits had chosen for her — Jovai, meaning joyful sound or joyful song.

Chapter 10

Torturing

No formal ceremony was needed to make Jovai Yaku Shaman's apprentice. Her parents and the shaman met before the elders that evening and made a simple, public announcement. The parents were given responsibility for Carken's farm and stock with several apprentices and the promise that their other daughters' wedding feasts would be subsidized by the village common funds as necessary.

It was uncomfortable for the elders to welcome Takan as one of them. He was young for an elder and had done nothing outstanding on his own to earn him that position. Tapeten Winter Leader was particularly angry at the addition, but it was well within the shaman's right to give that place to anyone he chose. Takan was a plain man of good sense with a special talent for humor and storytelling. He turned his agile mind to the task of winning acceptance from the elders, and it was not long before he was a favorite in the council, for the people and the elders alike. Takan paid particular deference to Tapeten Leader, and he quickly succeeded in the challenge to win the winter leader as his strongest supporter.

For Jovai it seemed that little had changed. She was a person now. She could be addressed and talked about and praised and cursed and, if she had something worthy to say, she could demand to be listened to, but it didn't feel any different. She had a new status with the shaman, that her people recognized better than she. They expected her to be proud, but she didn't understand why. Her family, especially her mother, seemed ashamed of her. Her friends were more distant. There had been little time to play with them in the last year, but she had still considered them friends once the shaman had explained that she was not insane. Now they looked at her with a kind of awe, and she overheard some called her a freak, though no one said it to her face. There were several people who would make the sign to ward off evil whenever she passed and once she heard the murmured word "witch" that chilled her with fear, but nothing happened. Yaku Shaman treated her just the same. With him, nothing had changed.

Many years went by. They were very good ones in which the crops grew abundantly, the livestock multiplied, the people were healthy and happy.

Jovai's skill as a shaman became much stronger as she grew older. She began to impress even Yaku. She memorized the chants and the histories exactly as he liked. When he wasn't around, she told the histories her own way, however. She learned to listen deeply, which was not so much a listening with the ears but an opening of the spirit — a controlled wandering, and she learned how to wrap herself in silence, which allowed her not to be noticed.

New and wondrous vistas opened up to her. There was more to hear than she believed she would ever understand — much more than she could identify. The collection of single, individual sounds, each sounded in different parts of a world much larger than she could imagine, came together in an ultimate pattern like one beautiful and perfect piece of music. The apprentice shaman learned to sing in harmony to that music.

She learned to read and write. Writing, in their community, was used mostly for record and history keeping and few other than the shaman studied the skill. She learned the old language — both the spoken, which became as natural to her as her normal language, and the written version, which was a collection of limited but very powerful symbols, not really a language, but specifically for magic. She learned the design magic with rocks and stones, leaves and flowers — anything in an order, with a purpose, could be power. The feelings of the colors and the orders of designs pleased her mind.

At the insistence of her master, she studied warfare like a boy. Many of the projectile weapons were light and easy to wield, except for the huge war spears which a strong arm could throw beyond sight. The heavier hand-to-hand weapons were more difficult for her little girl's strength, but the boys would taunt her and tell her she couldn't do it, so she had to prove them wrong. She became adequate but would be no great warrior in battle. She managed to stay astride a horse, but in the training combats, she struggled more to keep her mount safe than to hurt her enemy.

At healing, her talents shone brightly, both for animals and for people, both for the body and the spirit. In only a few years, the people had learned to bring their sick to her instead of her master, for her touch was better. It was said by the charitable that when the real shaman's apprentice should come, Jovai would make a fine healer.

Her best skill was with the spirits, however. She never failed to please them, and they never failed to follow her. There were so many spirits trying to please her, especially after a Trintoa, that they were sometimes a nuisance. The shaman's house would sparkle and glow even late into the night and once, for a week, they were followed constantly by gentle sounds that they finally realized were meant to be a singing.

Jovai learned to be careful of what she said, for an ill-expressed wish would often come true. One summer she watched one of the village girls as she celebrated her adulthood in a beautifully woven, freshly dyed, long tunic, bound with silver flower-shaped pins.

"You look so lovely today," she told the girl. "I wish I could look as pretty as you."

That evening she found the girl's tunic and pins waiting for her on her sleeping mat. She thought it was a generous gift, but when she wore the dress to thank the girl, she was met with angry accusations. The dress, it seemed, had been stolen. Theft was a rare and terrible crime in their community. It took all of Yaku Shaman's influence to save Jovai from shame and punishment which could have been as harsh as banishment.

The dead visited Jovai regularly as they passed through the village, and wanted to gossip late into the night, telling her all kinds of little things they thought those still living should know — about this farmer's bofimer and that man's child and what was wrong with Tisena's bread recipe and how the people who were newly dead were doing. They, who no longer needed to sleep, sometimes forgot that the living did. Jovai always welcomed them until her master finally made her stop. He enjoyed his solitude too much to let every wandering spirit intrude.

Yaku Shaman taught Jovai the great magic too: the ways to bend the wills of the spirits, the ways to fight them, as he had fought the wolf so long ago, the ways to raise spirits, and even to create a kind of spirit if necessary, and the way to go into the land of the dead and to return alive again. Much of this magic was dangerous magic and only for the most desperate of times. Everything had its price in the balance of things, and sometimes the price was very high. Jovai could not imagine any time so desperate that she would use the dangerous magic: the will-bending and the spirit creating and destroying. Even Yaku Shaman never had used most of it, nor had his master before him, but the knowledge was kept, just in case.

There was much magic that only a shaman with a powerful "real" name could do. It was beyond Jovai's ability until her adulthood came, and the spirits, if they willed, gave her a strong enough name. Until that time, she could only do the more limited healing magic and prayer magic on her own. This gentle magic contented Jovai, however, and she hoped, dearly, that her people would never need more from her.

The years were good, but not without struggle. As the harvests brought her people ease and wealth, time for improving their building and crafting skills, it brought more and more raids. The Gicoks came frequently, year after year. Sometimes they took slaves as well as goods and livestock. Other times they left with almost nothing. One raid, when Jovai was barely eleven, her people finally managed to take one of the Gicok warriors prisoner.

He was a youth, just become a man. Although he fought bravely and well, he was knocked unconscious and left for dead. The people of the valley discovered him, still alive, before he could revive and escape or kill himself. The shaman tended his wounds and healed the warrior. Then they kept him bound and guarded until the women of the valley decided what to do with him.

They, who had lost fathers, husbands, brothers, and sons, devised an array of tortures for the young Gicok. Jovai watched as they dragged the young man from the guarded house and bound him between two stakes in the center of the village. Several women with knives, others with pins and others with lit candles decorated his body with bleeding gashes and charred wounds. They were careful not to kill him quickly or let him bleed his consciousness away. They wanted him to suffer as long as possible. The others of the valley stood around and watched, cheering on the women. They made a holiday of it, drinking intoxicating liquid and eating holiday foods that the women had prepared for them. People laughed and joked, and a musician played on the pipe, while another sang a witty, bawdy song that was highly insulting to the parents of this Gicok warrior.

The Gicok bore it well. He raised his voice in defiant song in his own language, which no one understood, and did not let it falter, even as the pain tried to choke his breath.

Jovai was not so strong. She ran crying to Yaku Shaman.

"Master! Master! They're murdering him."

"Who?" he demanded.

"The boy you saved. The Gicok."

The shaman shrugged, unconcerned.

"You may enjoy it if you like. I will come as soon as I finish here." He nodded to the roots he was cleaning.

"You must come now!" she insisted. "You have to stop them."

"Stop them?" He turned his attention on the young girl curiously. "Why?"

"They're killing him!"

He waited calmly for her to continue. She stared at him amazed, tears welling in her eyes.

"Don't you care?" she asked, astonished.

"He is an enemy. We took him as he was trying to kill our people. It is right that he should die."

"But then why did you save his life?" Jovai cried.

"So that our people could take their revenge."

"Do you know what they're doing?" she demanded.

"Something painful," he answered, with the beginnings of a smile.

Jovai described it to her master. He nodded approvingly. His acceptance horrified her.

"You would not let them continue if you could see what they make him endure!" she cried, forgetting her place and her respect for her master in the black horror that was filling her.

Her disrespect displeased him. He turned away, ignoring her angrily, and would not acknowledge her further.

Jovai could not think to apologize. She could not think at all. She ran to her hill, to the safety of her tree and wept. Her tree embraced her and held her, rocking her soothingly in its branches. The wind played a lullaby through its leaves, but as it blew, it carried to her the sounds of the celebrating crowd and the tormented singer/warrior below. She tried to shut her ears, but the sounds would not be blocked.

"I've lied to you," she cried to the baby in the trunk. "I've told you only the beauty, but there is so much ugliness here it might be better not to be born."

"Everything has its place," came an answering voice that did not touch her ears, only her mind. "There must be balance."

"But so much pain..." her tears choked her as she thought of the Gicok. He was younger than her people would have considered a man. It was probably his first battle. The women who tortured him in the name of their loved ones, did they consider the women who might love this boy? Was his mother waiting, hoping he would come home? If she knew what agony the people of the valley were causing her son, would her hatred ever be satisfied? At least their men had died quickly. No one deserved the treatment of this poor boy.

She wept herself into a daze where her mind was still awake and alert, aware of the singer and the cruelty below, but her heart was blanketed with a protective calm of sorrow.

"Please make them stop," she prayed over and over to the spirits. They heard but did nothing. Even the little ones who served her most eagerly hung back from interfering. They hovered around her, concerned, but would not, or could not obey.

"Is there nothing you can do?" she begged.

There was no answer.

The singer sang his death through the pain of her people's torture. His strength and courage awed Jovai, and she found new respect for the enemies she had always hated.

Jovai fell into a light sleep and dreamed. She stood before the Gicok. He was mutilated almost beyond recognition. He was emasculated, his face and genitals particularly shredded, though no part of his body was undamaged. His eyes were torn from their sockets, but when she approached him, he turned his head to her and seemed to see. He sang still, in a language she could not understand, but the singing seemed to be outside of him, where her people were. She and this enemy were not with them but were instead in an emptiness, a darkness — just the two of them.

"I am a warrior and brave," she suddenly understood him to say.

"You are," she agreed. "You are braver than any man I've known."

"What do you want, witch?" he demanded. "Have you come to torture my spirit while they finish my body?"

"I don't want you to suffer," she cried. "I want to help you, but I don't know how."

"Your people do not hurt me. I let them take me, and I must pay for that dishonor. They only help me to do so. By the time I die, I will die a hero and climb the hero's path."

"I will sing you Soul's Ease," she promised.

"I do not need your prayers," he answered.

"I will sing it to honor you. When you meet my people in the spirit world, they will honor you too."

"Your people won't go my way. They are not heroes." His voice was filled with disdain.

"You will find many," she assured him, her words tinged with angry pride. "But then you will be comrades, not enemies."

The youth raised his head proudly.

"I will not be the enemy of your people, only if you will not be the enemy of mine."

"This is an honor I offer you," she tried to explain, frustrated that he did not understand. "I have no fear for my people from you."

"I will not accept honor from an enemy of my people."

In that evening Jovai hated her people more than she ever could have thought possible. Yet, if the Gicoks attacked, she would defend them, for she loved them too. There was not one among them whom she would let fall if she could save him, and she would kill any who threatened them. She would die, if necessary, to keep the people of her valley safe.

"As long as your people threaten mine, I must be their enemy, but still I will honor you, and through you, your people. Accept it or deny it as you will."

"My horse waits for me beyond the river, in the upper flat in the west mountain above your valley," he said, as if answering her. "In his pouch, he has a tube made of reed. In the reed are my powers and my loves. From it take two things, a lock of white hair bound in gold and a piece of bone. The hair put back in the pouch of the horse and send him back to my people. The reed with the rest of the contents bring to me. The bone you keep. If you do this, I will accept your honor and honor you back. If you do not, you will carry my curse forever."

CHAPTER 11

BETRAYAL

Jovai woke. It was sunset already and she shivered in the cooling air. The Gicok still sang, though his voice was weak and she could barely hear it. She did not understand his words.

Her dream puzzled her. She shook her head to bring back clear thought. The tree branch on which she sat was no longer comfortable. Little branches poked at her, prodding her down. She obeyed, still confused.

Only vaguely aware of what she was doing, she climbed down the eastern hill, walked around the village quietly and paused at the edge of the river. The bridge had not been pushed out again, yet. She had not the strength to do it alone, so she had to swim. She left a trail of water along the bank where she emerged, and up the path, as she climbed into the mountains.

She got safely to the clearing the Gicok had described. Six great black horses grazed there, patiently awaiting their riders. Jovai stared in confusion. It had not occurred to her that there would be others. How would she know which was the right one?

She called up a picture of the dying Gicok in her mind. She called it up so strongly that for a moment it seemed real, and she stepped into it and walked forward into the clearing. The horses glanced up at her curiously. One stepped forward, eagerly, then paused confused.

His nostrils quivered, and he danced away. He was the one.

She tried to catch him, but he would not let her near. When she got too close, he reared and struck at her with his hooves. She quickly ducked away and called to him soothingly in the spirit's tongue, but he would not listen. He whinnied loudly, calling his distress.

Then he raised his lip in an expression almost like a human snarl and rushed at her. Jovai turned and ran, frightened. Another horse leapt in front of her, blocking her path, herding her another way, toward a cave in the mountainside sheltered by trees. She did not think of what beast might claim that cave. She merely ran for it as the only place of safety from the frightful demon horses.

A spear flew past her as she entered the cave. It came from within. She ducked and pressed herself toward the wall, but hands from the darkness grabbed her and held a knife to her throat.

"*Focurna yem toxeti,*" hissed a voice nearby, and a figure stepped forward from the other wall into the meager moonlight struggling in from the cave entrance. It was a Gicok, though not tall like his people, but bent, stooping painfully. In his good hand, he held a spear, raised and aimed at her.

"*Mo moretic jahi vo.*" The one who held her answered back, his voice angry. He pushed Jovai away from him, deeper into the cave. His push was weak, as though nothing backed it, but there were two of them, both armed, and she was not.

"*Moreti forca na yem!*" the other ordered. She felt his spear at her back, nudging her on.

The one who had held her followed at a distance, leaning heavily against the wall of the cave, dragging a useless leg behind him. He too had a spear, but he used it as a crutch.

The spear jabbed painfully at her side, forcing her toward the cave wall. Through a crack, a little light fled, and there was just enough space, behind a shielding boulder, for a grown man to squeeze through into an adjoining chamber. The spearman prodded at her, and she silently obeyed, slipping through the crack, although her heart was pounding with fear.

A small fire in the center lit the little cave chamber, it's smoke thickly filling the high ceiling and drifting low to choke the air around the dead men scattered on the floor beneath.

"*Hisnathek ge?*" demanded a weak voice from the crowd of bodies.

The spearman answered angrily. The other man, who had held the knife, then entered the chamber and spoke to the dying one with a tone more reasonable and respectful.

"*Vohee?*" demanded the dying one.

The others nodded and herded her into the light. The spearman laughed when he saw the frightened little girl and turned his back disdainfully. The limping man was more cautious. With knife drawn, he approached her slowly. She backed away.

"He will not kill you...yet," said the dying man from behind her, his accent thick and harsh, but understandable.

Jovai turned to him, astonished that he could speak her language. The limping man lunged at her and pulled her down heavily as he fell on top of her. With his weight and his knife again at her throat to hold her, he searched her clothes for weapons. There was nothing to find. He let her up again, with a short report to the dying leader.

"What do you do here, Vohee?" demanded the dying one.

"I am sent by the warrior we captured," she answered.

"Why?"

"He wants his...his power and his loves. I am here to get them for him."

She approached him cautiously, her eyes struggling through the shadows to see his wounds. The spearman shouted something at her angrily, but the dying one weakly waved him into silence. He let the little girl approach.

"You are here to steal," he accused.

She shook her head. Blood caked with mud over a wound on his temple, but it was a deep gash in his side, a blade which had found its way between the reeds of his vest, that was killing him. This wound too was caked with mud, but the blood leaked through and took his life with it. It had a stench about it. The fever was fighting to get in and winning. She reached for the wound, to examine by touch what the shadows hid, but the spearman was upon her, wildly ordering her back, his spear dividing her from the dying one.

"I am a healer," she announced. "I can help you if you'll let me."

"You are our enemy."

"If you do not trust me you will die."

"I'd rather die than be taken by your people."

Jovai shook her head in frustration. All this talk of enmity seemed silly to her now. This wounded person was not a warrior striking at her people, but a man weak with pain. She knew in his heart he must grieve for those whose dead bodies were scattered around him. She knew some part of him, however hidden, must tremble in fear as he faced his own death. She knew she could help him, if only he would let her. With all her heart, she wanted to ease away his pain and fear, to heal his hurt and lend him her strength. Her mind struggled to find a way to convince him to accept her.

"I am your enemy only if you are mine. If you will go away and threaten my people no more, then I will heal you and let you go. Otherwise, you wait here until you are captured or dead."

"I cannot trust you, Vohee."

"No more than I can trust you, Gicok." She glanced up at the spearman who guarded her still. She was in at least as great a danger here as the dying man. They could kill her easily, at their whim. With a calm expression on her face, masking her fear, she spoke with a soft strength. "Call off your men."

The dying one hesitated, eyeing her suspiciously.

"I am no warrior, just a defenseless, little girl," she said gently. "If my touch were death it would only be quicker than what you now face. What is your fear?"

He spoke slowly to his men. The spearman scowled but withdrew.

Jovai gently felt the warrior's body and found that the gash on his side was not one, but several, very close. He winced at her touch. His body was wet with sweat, though the cave was cool. It was very bad. She shook her head, discouraged.

"I need water, fresh and boiling, and cloths to bind your wounds, and the knives and needles and threads we use and the oils and salves. What do you have?"

The Gicok spoke to his men, assigning tasks. Bundles that lay among the corpses scattered on the floor were opened and emptied of their contents. The limping warrior tossed a cloth bag to her. It was her master's healing bag, which had disappeared this last raid. Lightweight stretches of cloth, woven for summer wear, were pulled forth from other collections. The Gicok spearman quickly put their remaining water in a travel bag over the fire to boil and went to fetch more.

Jovai set to work. The Gicok would take no sleeping draught but endured the pain as bravely as his comrade had endured the tortures of her people. She cleaned and sewed his wounds, stopped the bleeding, and applied all the medicines she could to battle the fever. She prayed as she worked, calling on the spirits to aid her administrations. They came. They helped, but to what end she was not sure. When she had done all she could, it did not seem enough. The fever still raged in him, and he seemed weaker for the pain he had endured.

He did not speak. He seemed barely conscious. She wrapped him in blankets and mixed some boiling water with dried herbs and roots, making a healing, if distasteful, tea. He fought her when she tried to help him drink it. Even in his weak state, he would not be forced before he saw her sip it herself. Every other sip she took herself until he was convinced it was not poison. Then she let him rest and silently he slipped into sleep.

"You next," she said, pointing at the limping one.

He eyed her distrustfully but cautiously approached. She made him stretch out on the ground and gingerly felt his leg. It was broken in two places and the muscles, she suspected, were torn, but there was no open wound, and the bruises did not speak of deep bleeding. She quickly, firmly realigned the bone. He yelped in pain, surprised, and pulled away, forcing her to have to do it again.

She called to the spearman to ask for sticks, but he did not understand. She grabbed at the spear the Gicok had been using as a crutch. The spearman yelled and brandished his own as if for battle. She shook her head, turned away from him and threw the spear with all her strength at the cave wall. It imbedded only slightly, but it was enough to break off its point. She lay it next to the Gicok's hurt leg and pointed at the spearman's spear. He yelled again, angrily. Jovai sighed and started searching the dead ones herself for any spears they might still have. The spearman grew furious and forced her back into the corner, his spear's point at the bottom of her throat.

"*Gena he yem*," came their leader's voice, weakly from where he lay. The yelling had awakened him.

The spearman shouted something again, angrily, the point nicking Jovai's throat.

"*Gena he yem!*" the leader repeated. "*Tokezt.*"

The spearman clenched his jaw in anger but lowered his spear. He ran out of the cave. Jovai turned back to her search for sticks.

"Do not look through our things," the leader weakly ordered.

"Our things," Jovai corrected, as she pulled forth the tools and treasures of her people only recently stolen.

"They are ours now."

The lame one struggled to rise. Jovai turned to him angrily.

"Tell your man to keep still," she ordered the leader. "At least until l can bind his leg."

"Respect our possessions and he will," the leader answered.

She moved away from the bundles.

The spearman returned with many spears, their points all broken. Jovai measured them against the lame one's leg and showed the spearman where to cut them shorter. She bound the sticks to the leg with cloth which she thickened with strong mud. Then it was the spearman's turn.

He would not let her near him. He would not accept her touch. Of all of them, he had seemed the strongest, yet he hunched oddly and used only one arm when wielding his spear. lt worried her as she considered the wound his arm might hide. She appealed to his leader to let her treat it.

"lf he does not want your help l cannot make him take it," the leader answered.

"But why is he afraid?"

"He waits to see if l will live — or if l will be strong enough to take my life before your people take it."

"lf he waits too long with an open wound the fever might get in him."

"Better fever than Vohee."

Through the night she tended the leader. He fought fever from his sleep, shivering with cold while sweat soaked his blankets. He would cry in his language from cruel dreams and thrash, although so weakly that she alone, with her little girl's strength, could control him. She poured the hot tea, as much as she could, into him. At one point, he hid his face in her lap and cried freely. His garbled Gicok words gave her no understanding of the fever dreams he battled, but she held him gently, stroking his face and head, and sang to him in the spirit language a healing, strengthening prayer.

The dawn was coming. The tortured captive had to be dead by now. They would bury his body soon, and she had promised him his reed of tokens. If she did not deliver it, she would carry his curse, but she could not leave her patient yet. The fever still claimed him, and he needed what strength she could lend to win against it.

The spearman also slept, sweating profusely. Fever was slowly taking him too, but there was nothing she could do. The lame warrior watched her from the only entrance to this cave chamber. She knew that he would not let her pass. She could not talk to him to argue.

Her master would be missing her soon. If he searched for her, he would find her. If he found her, all her effort for these men was worse than wasted. All her attempts to help them would instead have brought their worst fears upon them. She felt in her heart the curse of the traitor — those whom she had loved best, she now feared most. But what she did she felt she had to do. It was right. At least, she hoped it was right.

Chapter 12

He Who Walks This Star Among Many Stars

Shortly after the dawn broke, so did the leader's fever. He slipped into an exhausted sleep so deep it seemed a death. She let him rest for several hours, but that was as long as she dared.

"You must leave now," she told him, waking him gently.

He stared up at her, bewildered, not recognizing the child who spoke strange words to him.

"Go back to your people now, before mine find you. They will be looking for me soon."

The light of comprehension slowly filled his flickering eyes.

"The slave who taught me Vohee language, I will free. If my people make war on yours again, I will not be among them," he promised her.

She helped him rise. The spearman rose dizzily to his feet as the lame one pushed him awake. He helped his comrade stand, and they made their way out of the cave, the packs of her people's treasures on their backs.

Jovai filled their flasks with the healing tea and warned the leader to rest as often and as long as he could, for the fever could come back. As a gesture of good-will, the leader led the captive Gicok's horse to her.

"A gift," he announced.

He held him as she searched his sack for the reed. When she found it, she emptied it into her hand. There were many little things, feathers, teeth, stones, jewels, charms of gold and silver and different, beautiful stones. She found the white hair bound with gold and put it back into the horse's sack. She found the bone — a strange and unfamiliar thing from no animal she could identify, shaped like a star with many points of light and with a natural hole in its center. She strung it on a string pulled from her underdress and tied it around her neck. The rest she put back into the reed and tied the hide covering again over the opening.

She bid her patients well and started off.

"Will you not take the horse?" asked the leader in wonder.

She stared at him, surprised that he should offer a prize so rich. His warriors were known to kill their horses rather than to let their enemies take them. This horse was a beautiful stallion, a fine specimen of the breed. There was not one person in her village who would not have given all his possessions in trade for such a stud. Horses with such a sire's strength and courage would make her people rich indeed. But she had promised the captive Gicok. She could not take him.

"His master wanted me to send him back," she explained. "Please lead the horse safely to your people. Tell them that the Vohee honor the courage of their warrior. He is a worthy hero."

"You must at least have this," insisted the Gicok leader. From his own sack, he pulled a hide bag. From the bag, he drew a little cord on which was strung a carved and painted metal disk.

"My people will know you as one of our own with this," he said. "You will be honored and welcomed as a friend, but only if you hold it for them to see like so." He held it up, inverted from the way it was strung, and slowly swerved it to its side, then back. "Remember," he warned, "or they will believe it stolen."

She thanked him and watched as the three Gicoks rode away, out of the reach of the women of the valley.

She swam the river again and made her way around the village toward the northern plains. She expected to find the young warrior's body, but there was no sign of it. Bewildered, she walked back to the village and found the crowd still gathered and the warrior still singing with the last gasps of his breath.

Her master lounged lazily among a group of men. He glanced up at her as she arrived, then looked away. He was still angry at her disrespect and would not recognize her again until she came to him with an apology.

She did not. She went toward the front of the crowd around the captive and looked up into his burned eye sockets. She stood there silently, waiting, until his song finally ended and his life was over.

The crowd cheered. Jovai did not. The women argued about what to do next. Some wanted to leave him hanging there until what was left of his flesh was gone. Others worried about the stench that would cause and voted rather to drag him through the town and leave him to rot, unburied, somewhere in the mountains.

"Master," begged Jovai respectfully of the shaman. "Will we not be cursed by his angry spirit if we trap it here?"

Her master did not acknowledge her.

He let the women argue until it was finally decided to drag him to the mountains, not by horse but by dog, and leave him for the scavengers to pick his bones.

Jovai walked with the crowd to the high point where they had chosen to leave the body. One by one, her people filed by, spitting, urinating, even defecating on the corpse. They kicked it, pierced its cold flesh with blades and pins and called it names. Then, their hatred relieved, they returned to their daily lives. Jovai's master took his turn along with the rest and left without a second glance at his apprentice.

Jovai hung back until the others had gone. She stared at the brave one and grieved for all the men of her village who had left on adventures to possibly meet the same fate. She grieved for the brave Gicok's mother, for all the mothers of the dead, and for his friends and family who would never see him again on this side of life.

When she felt certain the others had left, she took the reed container from under her clothes and pressed it into the corpse's stiffening hands. He seemed to grab it away from her, and he clutched it desperately, as though life were in his body still to treasure these powers and loves. She jumped back in wonder at this last convulsion of the dead, but there was no other hint of movement.

Softly, she sang for him the Soul's Ease. She called to those on the other side of life to welcome and honor him, singing high praise of his bravery and strength. She welcomed any of his ancestors who would come in peace to usher him away. The woods stirred around her, but she saw no one.

It was not their way, she realized with sudden insight. These warrior people walked their first trials of death alone. She prayed for the gods to welcome this spirit and honor him and that was all she could do.

Her song finished, she rose and turned to walk away. The Gicok youth was standing there, strong and whole. His spirit's body was scarred with the tortures her people had inflicted, and these scars he carried proudly.

"You wear it?" he asked in the spirits tongue.

She pulled the bone from beneath her tunic and held it out. The pendant the Gicok leader had given her also fell forth. The Gicok youth nodded approvingly.

"I was led to it in a dream. A giant beast I did not know, met me as I walked the desert beneath the night. He told me he was of the first world that came from the stars, and so his bone is shaped like a star and shines sometimes when it will give me dreams or power. Those dreams must be heeded and the power respected. The guiding beast existed before our first creation of our first world and will continue beyond our last destruction of our last world. He is very wise. At the time he came to me, I was searching for myself and did not understand how little that was to seek. The dream guide gave me a world beyond myself. When I woke, I knew my place, not only among my people, not only in this world but in all the worlds, everywhere. I looked into the sky and saw my guide, beyond body's reach but not beyond touch. I looked into my hand and saw my guide, and knew my place and myself. I am He Who Walks This Star Among Many Stars. I was instructed to carry that sacred bone to my glory. It has given me courage and strength and wisdom beyond my years. Now I pass it to you because you are finding your place not only among your people but beyond, as I did. You are one whose spirit walks this star among many stars and who lives in a world where many worlds are born and die. Now this spirit will guide you as he guided me."

Jovai looked in wonder at the star-shaped bone she held in her hand. It seemed to glow and was warm to her touch. She looked up again at the spirit Gicok but saw only his back as he walked to the north.

"Thank you," she whispered, deeply in awe. The Gicok spirit nodded his head in acknowledgment but did not turn or pause. He had a long journey before him.

CHAPTER 13

SECRETS

It was difficult for Jovai to return to her village. She had to accept the wisdom of her master first, and that was hard. What good had come from making a person suffer so? She knew her master must be right somehow, but she could not understand.

Night came and still she sat where they had left the Gicok warrior. She was tired and lonely and frustrated and afraid of the wild animals, which might be drawn by the scent of his blood, but still, she could not go back.

At last, the shaman came to her. He said nothing, did not even look at her, but calmly gathered wood and lit a small fire in a circle of stones. When the fire was going, he placed the hot-box from his house beside it and sat to wait for the food within to heat.

Jovai watched quietly, holding herself away from the seductive fire. She felt cold, but she did not feel worthy to sit beside her master.

"There is a story," said Yaku Shaman gently, breaking the silence between them, "of a boy who grieved for his dead brother. He would not eat since his brother did not eat and he would not sleep except where his brother slept. When the ancestors came for his brother, they made the natural mistake and took him instead."

"What happened to his brother?" asked Jovai, shocked.

"He had to find his way alone."

"Then his brother's grief did not serve him."

"Grief does not serve any but he who grieves. Foolish grief serves no one at all."

There was silence between them as Jovai struggled to find a way to apply this story to herself.

"I know I am foolish, Master," Jovai admitted at last, "I just don't know how."

"You are thinking of yourself before your people. You are not considering their needs."

"Why did they need to hurt him so badly?"

"His people have been hurting ours for a long time. They kill our men. They steal our livestock, our things that we worked hard for. They destroy what we build. They are our enemies."

"This one was young. If he had been one of us, he would not have fought at all. I don't think he killed any of our people."

"His people did. No man is inseparable from his people. For what his people do, he takes responsibility. For what he does, his people will be judged."

"What if he does things the rest of his people would not?" asked Jovai, thinking of her own recent deeds.

"Your family, your people, they are you. If you work against your people, you work against yourself."

Jovai flushed with sudden guilt. She had healed the enemy of her people. It had seemed right at the time, but she knew she would be punished if any of her own people ever found out. They would call her "traitor." They might even kill her. She trembled with fright and with anger as this realization hit her. The people she loved would kill her for doing what she still felt was right.

"But, Master, if I am not just myself, but my family, and not just my family but my people, can I also be not just my people, but all people?"

"This man was your enemy!" exclaimed Yaku Shaman, losing

patience. "He fought to kill your people."

Jovai wanted to understand. She wanted to feel as her master felt, so that the pain of what had been done to the Gicok boy would disappear, but she could not. She knew she should feel ashamed of her folly since her master called her foolish, but for the first time in her memory, she considered the possibility that she might be right and her master wrong.

"These people have hurt us deeply," Yaku persisted. "Even so young, you have seen the pain they have caused. You have lost friends. Your sisters have lost husbands. Would you forgive them all of that?"

"Until now, the Gicoks have been my enemies, and I have always hated them. I thought that we were good people and always right and they were evil people to attack us and hurt us. It seemed very clear and simple. But I had only seen my people kill for food or for defense. Now I have seen them kill for pleasure, and the pleasure they took in it was worse than any I've seen in my enemy."

"Our people have carried the pain from the Gicoks a long time. It has grown deep and turned into hatred that burns brighter because it is frustrated and has no vent. Such a common hatred can meld a people together stronger, but it can also grow dangerous and turn on itself. The spirits gave us this enemy. They put him into our hands so that we could vent our anger and relieve it. We needed it. The balance is now better for it."

"But he suffered so much!"

"He did his people honor. Someday his death might be part of a foundation for friendship between our peoples. Then, maybe, we will honor him — but not now. We are not ready yet. It is not time."

"I honor him," Jovai confided.

The shaman looked at her coldly.

"Do not put yourself against your people," he warned. "You need us. We need you. If you turn on us, you will destroy yourself."

"I love my people, Master," she assured him quickly.

It was true, and she knew it from the core of her being. But she also knew that there were many among them now whom she would never be able to look at in the same way again. They were not always right. They were not always good, and the trust she had placed in her people from the time of her earliest awareness was now, no longer absolutely theirs. Even her faith in her master was shaken.

Yaku clenched his jaw in fear for his apprentice. The people of the valley still distrusted her. He had seen the signs of protection some habitually made as she passed. To them she was unnatural, and therefore evil, in spite of all the good she had done, all the people and animals she had healed, and all the happy years that her Trintoa singing had welcomed. She still had to prove herself. She had to be better than the other children, wiser, gentler, and more loyal.

He pulled two covered bowls from the hot-box and handed one to Jovai. She took it with a nod of thanks but set it beside her, unopened. As she did so, the two pendants she wore fell forward and caught the moonlight. Jovai was unaware, but her master saw. He caught the strings that held them and, careful not to touch the objects themselves, pulled them deeper into the light. Jovai watched him, startled and afraid.

The bone was nothing the shaman had seen before, and it glowed with a strange light that was not a reflection of the moon. The way it glowed, it seemed to grow and shrink in light, like a twinkling star in the sky. He looked up at them wonderingly, then back down at the bone and pendant.

The pendant he recognized, not in a particular way, but as a piece of Gicok jewelry. Yaku felt a deep rage at the sight of this pendant. He longed to ask the girl where she had gotten it, but a nameless fear held his tongue. He looked away, toward the captive's body. It had been stripped of everything by his people. There had not been even a lock of hair to steal. Of the things they had taken from him, nothing like this pendant had been found. As he looked, however, he saw the reed tube clutched in the Gicok's hands.

Jovai trembled before him. She would not raise her eyes to meet his. Yaku Shaman tucked the pendant and the bone under her tunic top.

"Show no one," he warned her, turning away toward the fire. That was all.

Jovai kept the pieces hidden in a private bag that she wore strapped beneath her clothes. Her master never asked for an explanation. She never offered one. She served him obediently and lovingly and made herself more useful than ever to her people, sharing with them generously, not only of her talents, but of her bright smile, her sweet voice, and her rich heart. For her master, she outdid herself in her lessons, and her devotion and respect for him were well appreciated by many. Quickly, Yaku dismissed his anger for her and did not think on the pendants again.

Chapter 14

First Love

In the spring of her thirteenth year, while she was still a child, Jovai fell in love. It was with a boy on the brink of manhood. He was handsome, with fair skin and brown hair, worn long down his back. They were training together, even though he was much larger. It was the game for the day to try to unseat the others.

She had already been unseated by two boys her size and one of the larger boys. Litazu also toppled her. He jumped off his horse and pinned her to the ground with the wood he used in place of a short blade. Had he been her enemy, she would have been dead. Then he bent over and kissed her, hard and full and firm on the lips.

She gaped up at him astonished, speechless. Deep in her stomach, she felt the excitement, but in her head she only felt confused.

He raised his fist in triumph to the boys who were watching from the side. They all cheered. His blade still pinned her, as long as she accepted it as a knife and not the piece of blunt wood it really was.

"Why did you do that?" she asked, trying to sound angry but only sounding dazed.

Litazu smiled at her. His sharp eyes had noted her response.

"Because you're pretty," he said.

She did not know how to believe him. No one had ever told her that.

"Have you ever been kissed before?" he asked.

She mutely shook her head.

He raised his fist again. His fingers held up the count of two. Again, his fellows cheered.

"Then you've just won me two bets," he announced, laughing at her as he stepped back. She scrambled up and ran away as fast as her legs could carry her. All the boys were laughing loudly. She could hear them as she ran.

She felt angry, humiliated, and something else, unfamiliar, that she couldn't name.

From then on, she could not stop thinking of Litazu. In her listening, she listened not for what was to be heard, but for him, what he was doing, what he was saying, what he might be thinking and feeling. It seemed that he didn't think of her. When he practiced with her again, he smiled with insufferable pride that infuriated her and made her forget everything she'd learned. But when he passed her outside the practice field he didn't seem to notice her at all.

She could not stand it. She sent some spirits to trouble him — just little ones. They would trip him, pull his hair, blow up his tunic, and stare back at him with strange and ugly faces when he looked for his reflection. That got his attention. When things like this happened, he would look around to find her.

At first, his glares were angry, but they softened to an expression of amusement which she found intolerable, and the pranks grew worse. Each time he caught her eyes, she blushed with shame and felt like running away, but pride, or something stronger, held her firmly in place.

Finally, he stopped staring from the distance and approached her. It was what she most wanted, and what she most feared. Could she have run away she would have, but she was trembling so badly she could hardly stand.

He was smiling at her — that same look of triumph as when he had kissed her. She looked around, desperately hoping for someone to whom she could call, in a friendly, casual way, to give herself an escape. No one was around.

Litazu stood next to her, closely — too closely. She could smell the light odor of his body and feel its heat. All she wanted to do was run, but her knees were trembling so badly she couldn't.

"Come with me," he ordered, taking her arm. The touch of his hand was like fire on her burning skin. She pulled back, afraid.

"I could tell your master about your witch's pranks," he threatened. "The shaman would not be pleased."

With horrible guilt, she realized he was right. Her master would be very angry with her. Spirits were not to be played with, he kept saying, and they should never be allowed to hurt someone because they didn't always know when to stop.

Litazu pulled her after him. She didn't resist. He led her south, into the woods.

"Where are we going?" she demanded, afraid.

"Just for a walk," he answered her. "I want to talk to you."

There was a smile on his lips and a light in his eye that made her stop in her tracks. He pulled her harder and forced her to follow him, deeper into the woods.

When they were out of sight of the village, he finally stopped.

"Now tell me why you do such things," he ordered.

She stared at him dumbly. Her mind was blank. She could think of nothing to say.

"Do you hate me?"

She shook her head and blushed.

He smiled.

"Do you like me?"

She dropped her eyes and blushed deeper. She could not deny it.

He raised her chin gently and looked into her eyes.

"You're just a little girl, but you're a pretty little girl." He gave her an appraising look. "It might not be so bad to have a witch on my side."

He leaned forward to kiss her. She did not resist. This time she tasted it and decided that she liked the taste. His hand lightly touched her arm, her back, her neck. He brought it down to stroke her chest, but she pulled away, struggling for breath. He pulled her closer, claiming her body with his strong, sure touch. That was too much. She wasn't ready for that.

"You really are a little girl, aren't you?" he taunted. He tried to pull her to him again, but she pushed him away and ran back toward the village. He was right. She was too young. It was too much for her. Litazu didn't chase her, probably knowing that she'd seek him out again, soon enough.

Yaku Shaman suddenly loomed, tall and angry, in Jovai's path. He startled her. She had not heard him. Of course, she had not been listening...

He caught her in his arms before she could stop her flight. She cringed, terrified at the look he gave her. Long ago she had learned that her master was not as fierce as he seemed. In many ways, he was the gentlest man she knew. At this moment, however, he was more frightening than ever, even as a baby, she could remember imagining him.

He picked her up with a strength much younger than his years and carried her back to where Litazu still lingered.

The boy stumbled backward, frantically, over rocks, around trees, as he saw the giant shaman approach.

"Stay," ordered the shaman, and Litazu froze, instantly.

Yaku Shaman set Jovai on her feet and held her, roughly, by the hair. She winced with the pain.

"This is a shaman," he told the boy. "No one touches a shaman as you have dared!"

He jerked her hair harder. She squeezed her eyes shut and bit her lip to hold back the cry.

"The spirits are very jealous of her. Consider her untouchable in every way from now on, or I will throw you to them. Do you understand?"

The boy mutely nodded, his eyes wide with fear.

"Go!" growled Yaku Shaman.

Swifter than a stone from a sling, the boy ran away.

The shaman dragged his apprentice angrily through the woods and said not another word until they were in the privacy of his house.

"What have you done?" he demanded.

She knew she should tell everything. She knew he knew already, but she didn't know what to say. Shame overwhelmed her.

"You are a shaman," he shouted at her. "A shaman does not touch like that. A shaman does not marry. A shaman does not have children. A shaman belongs to the spirits only!"

"Spirits don't make me feel like that," she said in timid defiance.

"I could call up an evil one who would, but he would drain you and leave you nothing. That's what that boy would do — leave you nothing. He would pull you away from the spirits, fill up your belly with children and your mind with trivial worries and you would be nothing for the spirits — nothing for your people except a breeding bofimer. Our people need a shaman, not another gossiping wife."

"But they'd like me better as a wife!"

"Not when they need a shaman."

"Then let them find a shaman they'd like," she yelled, "Because I'm not a shaman. Do you know what they call me? They call me witch!"

He struck a mighty blow to the side of the head, and she fell to the floor stunned. It was the first time her master had ever hit her. He stood over her like an immovable mountain and waited for her to get up. She shook her head to try to clear the dizziness and pushed herself back to standing. The room was heaving around her.

"You are a shaman," he said, his voice solid and strong like the voice of a prophecy. It allowed no denial. She looked into his eyes and saw the giant brown bear there, with all the other shapes his spirit had stretched into. This was a great shaman, greater than any legend. If he called her a shaman then she was a shaman, whether she wanted to be or not.

She bowed her head and silently wept.

The next eight days she spent in total silent and dark seclusion, fasting on broth and water. It was not only a punishment but also an exercise to help her regain the discipline she had recently lost. She was supposed to be listening, but her concentration had been shattered. She felt like a baby again, unable to sit still. She wanted to think of Litazu, to remember his smile, his kiss, his touch, but every time she did, she also remembered the fear in his eyes and her master's fury. He would never touch her again. She was certain. No one would ever dare go near her after what happened with him. And he was the only one, ever, to have told her she was pretty.

That period felt like a death, but it helped her find some calm again, and her listening came back. By the time she returned to the sunlight and the noise, she was seeing her feelings for Litazu as a feverish confusion, a sweet madness that she could leave behind.

When she saw him again, however, the feelings surged up and made her tremble with shame. He glared at her hatefully. He looked much paler and thinner, and his eyes were shadowed strangely for one so young. The spirits she had set on him to get his attention danced about his head. In horror, she realized that she had forgotten to call them off.

She called them now, and they came, but they wanted to go back to their tricks. They enjoyed tormenting Litazu, especially since he had hurt her so badly. It took all her will, much time and effort, to finally convince them to stop. She felt guilty and would have had them do pleasing things for him if she could, but they would not go so far. They would stop hurting him only because she wanted it so badly, but they hated him for what they thought he had done to her. Every-so-often, even months later, she'd catch them at mean pranks to hurt him when they thought she wasn't aware.

Litazu, for his part, avoided her as completely as possible. He never touched her again, and he never spoke to her when he could help it. He told no one what had happened, although the gossip ran high, and he had nothing to say about her except that he didn't think she was pretty after all.

From then on, her master dressed her like a boy rather than a girl. He gave away the only two woman's tunics she had, made for her by Katira and Misa, and made her wear her hair in a simple boy's style, in a ponytail down her back, instead of the more attractive braids that the girls and women usually wore.

"You're a shaman," he said, "Not a woman. Such things will only make you forget again."

When she complained, he threatened to cut her hair off altogether, like a Gicok. Her hair was long, dense, and fine, flowing in soft, dark waves down her back. She suspected that it was her best feature. She didn't want to lose it, even if a shaman didn't need such things.

CHAPTER 15

THE REAL APPRENTICE

It was deep in the winter of that year when Yaku Shaman and his apprentice were called to attend to a young boy just approaching his naming. The boy was thrashing and writhing, limbs out of control, and gurgling strangely. His parents were frantic.

"He has a spirit inside him," Yaku Shaman explained. "It's trying to talk through him, but he fights it."

They could only wait until the spirit let him go. Then the boy awoke, disoriented and confused. He remembered nothing.

Yaku explained to him what had happened. He gave the child some medicines which relaxed his body and helped his spirit be calm and feel safe. Then the shaman called forth the visiting spirit and helped the little boy to let it speak.

At first, the words were only garbled nonsense. The child was still resisting. Jovai held the child and sang softly, soothingly to both competing spirits within the little body. The child's spirit finally stepped back, and the voice came forward.

"The Gicoks are dying. Many are dying. The disease is coming here. Beware them when they come." It was the little boy's voice, speaking in the old language.

"When do they come again?" asked the shaman.

"They are on their way."

"When will they arrive?"

"In the next living time, during the lengthening days. The loss will be great."

"What should we do?"

The child shuddered in Jovai's arms, and his little boy's spirit came back. He could not remember. Only Yaku Shaman and Jovai had understood the words. Jovai looked to her master to see what he would do.

"He should be well now," the shaman told the parents. "If the spirit comes back, call me immediately."

Then he went directly to Tapeten Leader and called a counsel.

The elders listened to the story and frowned at the spirit's words. Not since the captive Gicok was tortured to death two and a half years ago had they suffered the Gicok raids. Many had hoped that the show of their horrible tortures had frightened the Gicoks away forever.

"What do we care if the Gicoks die?" asked Nobien Elder. "It makes our life easier."

"The warning is that the disease will come here," Yaku explained.

"What kind of disease is it?" asked Takan Elder.

"The spirit did not say. I will try to find out more, but we must be alert and watch carefully for the Gicoks."

"Will you be apprenticing the little boy then?" asked Jatoyen Elder.

Yaku looked at him with surprise. The thought had not occurred to him.

"The spirit did choose to speak through him," said Massern. "Doesn't that mean he is favored?"

"It might mean many things," answered Yaku carefully. "It does not necessarily mean he is a shaman."

"But he might be," said Massern with a grin, "and since we have no other..."

"We have Jovai," Yaku growled. He did not like what they were thinking.

"But this is the only boy to be favored so far," insisted Jatoyen Elder with a triumphant smile.

"I do not know that he is favored," Yaku Shaman all but shouted.

Tapeten Leader looked to the elders.

"I say we pay the apprentice fee to let the shaman teach him. If the child does not serve, he can be returned to his family. If he does serve, we have our new shaman."

The elders all were agreed. Yaku Shaman was furious, but he felt himself trapped. In his mind, he knew that he could probably teach the little boy, but his heart ached to see his other apprentice so quickly and easily dismissed. Jovai was a shaman of worth, better than anyone could have hoped for. He had worked hard for her, and she had done very well, and now that the honor of the position should have soon come to her, as well as the duties and denials which she already bore, they were pushing in another child, completely untried. He felt unwarranted hatred for the little boy usurper. He felt afraid of what might happen to Jovai.

The following Trintoa, the little boy took his name: Kotayu, mouthpiece. He was apprenticed with a lavish show, and all the village rejoiced. They made a huge parade and carried the boy in the center, from the feast, which had been grander than any wedding feast, to the shaman's house. Jovai watched in amazement. Yaku Shaman watched in disgust.

The shaman walked the village late that night, dreading the time when he would return to his house and find the unwanted stranger there. Jovai was curious about the little boy. She returned early to make sure he felt welcomed and happy.

When she arrived, she saw Kotayu's mother busily cooking dinner for her son and his new master. The boy was playing happily with a small lizard at his mother's feet. The house had been cleaned and brightly decorated with toys and objects the little boy might want. He had many changes of clothes, all looking new and neatly sorted. A beautiful bedroll that was thicker than her master's, against which it was laid, was open and waiting. She looked for her own bedroll, but she could not find it. All her few belongings seemed to be missing.

"Where are my things?" Jovai asked Disara, the mother.

"At Polisa's of course," she was answered. "You'll be going home, now that the shaman has a real apprentice."

The words hit Jovai like a blow. It hadn't occurred to her that her master would send her away. She felt suddenly, deeply unhappy. In all the times recently that she had thought she did not want to be a shaman, she had never thought of leaving her master. She loved the old man dearly. She could not imagine what her life would be like without seeing him and talking to him and learning from him every day.

"Did the shaman, himself, say I was to leave?" she asked.

"Of course you are to leave," Disara answered. "Now go home. Your mother is waiting."

She did not go home but sought out Yaku instead. He was not in the village proper but had gone to his favorite thinking place, a fallen boulder by the western river. It was not a place she felt she could intrude, so she waited. Deep into the night, when even the latest revelers had grown weary, her master finally rose and turned toward his house.

"Master," called Jovai softly, intercepting him just before he reached the village.

The shaman frowned at her.

"Why are you here?" he asked. "I thought you went home early."

She shook her head and took a deep breath to push the tears back from her voice.

"Are you dismissing me?" she asked him.

His frown deepened as he gently raised her chin to see if there was a joke in her eyes. He saw the tears and realized her question was serious.

"No," he said, his anger rising, "Who told you this?"

"Disara, Kotayu's mother. All my things are at Polisa's. She says now that you have a real apprentice, I must go back to my mother's house."

Yaku stared at Jovai, amazed at what he heard. How could they dare to dismiss his apprentice without his approval — without even his knowledge? In his anger, he could have grabbed Kotayu and thrown him back at his mother. He could have ripped the elders from their beds, one by one, and wrung their wrinkled necks. He could have torn Polisa's house down, piece by piece until Jovai could walk easily through the rubble to get her things back. How dare they? How dare they?!

"Why do you cry?" he demanded harshly of Jovai. "I didn't dismiss you. Why do you listen to a stupid wife who knows nothing?"

"I was afraid, because of what happened before..." Yaku knew she was thinking of Litazu, who had passed into manhood during the summer and taken the name Berailen, the bold fool, then left the village to go the way of the adventurers. He had been a popular boy, and many people grieved at his leaving. People still said it was Jovai, with witch's evil, who had driven him away. "I was afraid I was no longer good enough. When she said you didn't want me anymore, I thought it might be true."

"It is not true," he said angrily.

"Then why do you take another apprentice?" she asked. It was the first time she had dared to so directly question her Master's action. Yaku accepted the question as right. He had been asking it himself.

"Kotayu may have the approval of the spirits. It seems as if, possibly, they want me to teach him."

"Just because one spirit chose to speak through him?"

Yaku nodded.

"But we don't even know what kind of spirit it was."

"It may have meant nothing, but there is a chance that Kotayu is a holy one. There is a chance that the spirits will want him trained, so I will train him. If I die, then you will train him, until we know if he is really a shaman."

"And if he is," said Jovai, "No village needs two shamen."

"We have worked well together," said Yaku. "If he is a shaman, then you two can work well together."

But in his heart Yaku knew that would not be. If the boy were a shaman, even a weak one, then Jovai would have no place in the village except as a healer, if the people would accept her as such. Kotayu would be her master in the eyes of the people. Jovai's power would be thrown away. The only hope for the village was that Kotayu was a stronger shaman than Jovai or, as Yaku hoped within his heart, no shaman at all.

That night, Yaku gave Jovai his bedroll, beside the sleeping boy, and rested himself on the ground near the door for the few hours before dawn. He would not allow Jovai to protest. He found that it cheered him, for it reminded him of this night so many years ago when a crying baby with no name was pushed into his life. He hadn't wanted her then any more than he wanted this new one now. It had been the spirits' choice, not his. Now he thanked them for choosing her. He hoped he would come to value his new apprentice as much.

Disara was not pleased when she came the next morning to fix her son and his master breakfast. Polisa was not pleased when Jovai came to get her things back. The elders were not pleased when Yaku Shaman announced, absolutely, that Jovai was still his apprentice. His anger was too great to allow him to discuss it calmly. He simply said it and left them to discuss it among themselves.

Yaku had thought to spend his time equally between his two apprentices, but Jovai had very little left to learn that practice and experience couldn't teach. Kotayu knew nothing at all.

It seemed to Yaku that Kotayu was a very poor student. He couldn't sit still. He couldn't listen. He learned the chants slowly and forgot them quickly, protesting that they made no sense.

Jovai laughed when Yaku complained, reminding her master that he had said the same things about her. He knew she was right. One difference he was sure of, however, was that Jovai had learned the old language much faster. Languages, both written and spoken, came as easily as breath to her while this new apprentice seemed even worse at them than Yaku had been.

Kotayu soon got bored with the study of histories, chants, and languages. He wanted to learn magic instead. He wanted to call spirits and make them do things for him.

"That comes later," Yaku tried to explain.

"But my mother told me she was doing it right away!" Kotayu insisted.

"Jovai worked harder and learned quicker," said his master angrily.

It was hard for Yaku Shaman to be patient with this boy. Kotayu made the lengthening days seem longer, and the short time he still got to spend with Jovai, far more precious.

CHAPTER 16

NEW DANGERS

It was many weeks after the Trintoa, when spring was stretching toward summer, that the little village had a strange visitation. Jovai was listening in the southern woods when she heard the sound of Gicok horses walking leisurely over the western mountains. It did not sound like a raid, but she went ahead and raised the call.

Women and children scrambled for the caves. Men grabbed their weapons and took position. Jovai found her master.

"It's not a raid," she said. "There are only five I think."

He too had heard. He had sent Kotayu to the caves, but Jovai he ordered to stay, though at some distance behind the warriors.

The five approached slowly, leaving their horses tied to trees in the hills. They were all men, but only one was Gicok. The rest, in build, looked like her people, only taller, with much darker skin, almost black, and eyes and hair of varying shades of gold or copper brown. They were filthy, hair matted, beards sprouting wildly from their faces. Their clothes looked like layers of rags and hides. It looked as if the spring mud had sucked them whole and spit them out again.

The Gicok was similarly dressed, in cloths instead of hides. He had no battle paint on him and he did not look as frightening as the warriors of his people always had. He moved awkwardly over the land without his horse. The famous pride of the Gicoks seemed to be missing in him.

The group stopped just across the river and eyed the waiting warriors suspiciously.

"What do you want?" shouted Massern Leader, his weapon aimed and ready.

One of the men, medium height, modest build, responded in a language no one knew. He held up his hands to show they were empty. The rest of the men, even the Gicok, followed his lead and did the same. Massern Leader kept his weapon pointed, though some of the other men cautiously lowered theirs.

The shaman and several of the elders came to the leader's side.

"What do you think?" Massern Leader asked Yaku Shaman, never taking his eyes off the strangers.

"The spirit warned us that the Gicoks would bring disease. We should not let these people near."

"Should we kill them?" asked Massern.

"Kill unarmed men?" demanded Sirfen Elder, incredulously. He was a warrior and a warrior trainer. Such things could not be honorable.

"If the Gicoks would bring some, the Gicoks might bring more," Jatoyen Elder said, thoughtfully. "These men do not seem to threaten us, but if we treat them as enemies, we might make them enemies."

"We cannot welcome them as friends," Yaku Shaman insisted. "The spirit has warned us that our loss will be great. We must be cautious."

"What if we meet them in the mountains," suggested Takan Elder. "We can go as a larger group than theirs, with weapons. It will keep them away from the village and let us find out what they want."

"They might have others hidden and waiting," warned Tapeten. Sirfen Elder nodded his agreement, but Yaku shook his head.

128

"It is only these five on this side of the mountain. There are no warrior groups waiting."

"Then they are fools," exclaimed Tapeten. "We could kill them easily."

"But we won't," remarked Jatoyen Elder. "Perhaps they are smarter than we think."

It was decided to meet the strangers in the mountains and talk to them, to find out what they were seeking, why they had intruded where they weren't wanted. A young man, famous for his strong arm and good eye, quickly brought a painted stone. He held it up for the strangers to see. They looked at him confused.

"We will meet where this lands," shouted Massern Leader.

The strangers glanced at each other confused. The Gicok said something with a knowledgeable air, but their confusion persisted.

The strong young man wound his sling and let the painted stone fly into the hills. The shaman asked the stone to fly to a good place, as distant as possible. It was a very fine throw. A day's ride could take a group of men on horses there and back easily, yet it was out of sight of the village, and any approach from that place would be seen quickly enough to prepare.

"Go there," shouted Massern Leader, pointing after the stone. "We will meet you there."

The strangers still stood, their arms over their heads, looking at Massern, looking over their shoulders at the place the rock was thrown, then looking back at the village.

When they did not move, the people got nervous. More weapons were readied. The tension grew tighter.

In a foreign language, the Gicok said something to the strangers. He said it loudly enough for the warriors to hear that he did not speak their language or even the Gicoks', but one they had not heard before.

"Go," Massern repeated, pointing toward the place where the

rock had landed.

The Gicok spoke again to the leader of the strangers. The bushy-faced man slowly nodded. He cautiously turned around and led his people away, into the mountains.

The warriors watched them until they were out of sight. Then a group stayed, still armed and waiting, while the council quickly met. It was decided that Massern Leader would go with Sirfen Elder, Yaku Shaman, and seven strong young warriors of Sirfen's choice. The women and children stayed in hiding, the guard stayed posted, and the group set out immediately. Jovai listened carefully and deeply from her self-appointed post on the eastern hill. There she could see any sudden attack and, if an alarm were needed, she could make everyone hear it.

It was late at night by the time the group of elders and warriors returned. Their faces were dark with frowns, but they called the worried women and children out of the caves and had them all meet in the center of town. They told the people everything they knew. It was not much. No dialogue had been possible since the strangers didn't speak their language. All the warriors had were guesses.

The strangers had made a camp. They planned to stay. No one could discover how long. They had shown them things that no one had ever seen before and whose purpose was unclear. The strangers had carried blades and statues, tools and other things stolen from their people by the Gicoks. But they seemed more interested in the metal and stones that made many of the things than in the things themselves. They had pointed to the stolen blades repeatedly with questions no one could understand. They had seemed friendly and had offered food and drink, but no one had touched it. The shaman reminded everyone once again of the spirit's warning and told them to beware of disease. They must stay as far away from these strangers as possible.

The strangers chose to make that difficult by sending their leader to the village the very next day. The leader, his empty hands in the air, led his horse toward the waiting warriors. He spoke slowly in his strange language and clearly wanted to be welcomed. The village warriors made it as clear, with readied weapons and thrown stones, that he was not.

The man frantically pointed behind him with his thumb. He pointed with his arm toward the place they had met before. Yaku listened. He could still hear no more than the five strangers in the mountains, but he didn't know what point there was to meet with these strangers again. His people needed nothing from them and wanted nothing to do with them. They had no common language and as far as the village was concerned, no need for one. But the man would not go away.

He went to a bag tied onto his horse and pulled forth a tangle of animal fur. This he held up and then held forward as if a gift. One of the warriors, perhaps for a joke, shot a heavy arrow into the mass of pelts. The stranger dropped it and jumped away. He ran to his horse and quickly led him back to the mountains.

The warriors cheered, but the elders were not so pleased. They didn't want to make these strangers enemies. They only wanted them to go away.

The next day the leader and the Gicok came back. They carried an extra horse, one of the Gicoks' magnificent breed. Once again, the leader dismounted. He led the horse to the edge of the river and held the reins forward, in offering. This was a splendid gift. The villagers had long admired these horses but had never been quick enough to capture one during the Gicoks' raids. Now, here was one simply being offered to them.

They did not risk pushing out the bridge. Instead, Tapeten went bravely forward to where the river crossing was shallowest. Three warriors stood by his side. The stranger followed him along the other side, and when the leader stopped, he started to cross.

Immediately, all weapons were pointed at him. The stranger stopped, the water to his knees and stared. Tapeten sent one of his warriors to cross the river and get the horse from the waiting man. When the warrior got there, however, the stranger paused before handing him the horse and pointed back to the place where the elders had met with him before. He yelled something, again in his stranger's tongue. He obviously wanted to meet with them again.

Tapeten looked to Massern Summer Leader, and Massern looked to Yaku Shaman. The shaman did not like it. He did not think a horse, even a Gicok horse, worth the risk. Massern and many of the other elders thought differently, however, and they agreed to go. The warrior returned to the village with a magnificent, strong, young stallion.

Again, the elders and warriors returned to the village discouraged by the meeting.

"They are trying to teach us their language," Massern Elder told the people, "and we tried to teach them ours, but we cannot understand each other. They want us to come back and try again. It seems they have offered us a mare next time, but the shaman does not think it's wise."

"Then the shaman does not have to go," replied Tapeten.

"The spirit gave a warning," Yaku Shaman growled.

"The spirit said to beware," argued Jatoyen Elder. "We are being wary. They do not come into our village, yet we have not made them enemies. But we must talk to them and find out why they stay and what will make them go away. If they will teach us their language, we should try to learn."

"Then Jovai will go," said the shaman impulsively. Jovai looked up at her master, astonished. She could not read in his face what his mind was thinking.

Tapeten turned to him angrily.

"This does not concern a child — especially not a female child."

"Jovai learns languages easily. She can learn to speak to the strangers quicker than I can."

"Are you not worried about the disease?" asked Takan Elder. "It might be dangerous to expose her."

"Jovai is a shaman," Yaku said firmly. "The spirits will protect her."

Objections were quickly dispensed with, and the next day Jovai accompanied her master, Massern Leader, Sirfen Elder and six young warriors.

CHAPTER 17

STUDYING STRANGERS

Yaku dressed Jovai carefully, as much like a boy as possible, in clothes that covered every open space of flesh which disease might penetrate. He would have covered her face with a fiber mask, but she objected. Such things were for the summer and autumn drama ceremonies only. To use them for something other than the spirits would be offensive. She was right, and he let her go with a bare face.

Already Yaku regretted his thoughtless offer of Jovai. It was bad enough that he should risk disease, but if she caught it too, the village would have no shaman at all. What evil spirit had prompted him to give such bad advice?

"Am I sufficiently ugly?" she asked him when he had finished dressing her.

He held her chin up and looked her deeply in her large, brown eyes. The eyes betrayed her. They were too feminine, too perfectly shaped like a doe's or a bofimer's eyes, tilted up slightly at the corners. A man with such eyes would learn to scowl to hide their beauty. She only smiled. He shook his head.

"It is the best I can do," he told her.

"I would not like the strangers anyway," she reassured him.

Yaku Shaman knew that. That was not his fear.

"So, am I to be a boy to the strangers?" she asked.

"No," he replied. "You are much more. You are a shaman. You will show them all."

Jovai looked up at her master worried.

———◆———

They reached the stranger's camp by midday. The camp was disordered, or so it seemed to Jovai's eyes. There were papers, an honored commodity to her people, torn and discarded, along with bones, shells and other offal littering the ground. The tents were placed in no recognizable order. It was not a pattern of power, even for defense.

There were fewer tents than men, so they must share, or some must sleep in the open. The tents were large and not made of leather, but of some kind of shiny cloth which could not be woven from the plants or animals found in the valley. It reflected the sun. They were not afraid of drawing attention to themselves. They must either be exceptionally well defended, exceptionally stupid, or have exceptionally good reason to know they had no enemies.

Their tents had no chimney draw, so they had made a communal fire outside. Used cooking and eating utensils lay hastily discarded in the dirt and ashes next to it. They let the horses stand inside the camp, next to the tents, and their manure made the flies swarm and the camp smell.

There were also two wagons, made to be pulled by horses. They used their magnificent horses to haul. It occurred to Jovai that she had yet to see any of them, even the Gicok, ride for any real distance.

Jovai's people dismounted, leaving one of the warriors to guard their horses, and walked to the group of strangers who waited politely by the ashes of the communal fire.

The men at the camp greeted them with expressions of much pleasure. They talked constantly, Jovai noticed, not only among themselves but to her people whom they knew could not understand them. It reassured her a little, for people who talk so much probably did not listen as well. It was a good measure that gave her people the advantage.

The strangers offered them mats of pelts to sit on, but her people preferred to stand. Jovai took the initiative. She stepped forward, like a man, and greeted the stranger's leader in her language, then in the words she had heard him use. She guessed he had been giving a welcoming, not a greeting, but she wanted to show that she was trying to speak.

He looked at her strangely and bent slightly from the waist in an awkward bow. Then he held out his hand, toward her. She looked at it confused. He called one of his men, a short man with very dark, peeling cheeks, and held his hand out to him. The man grabbed his arm at the elbow. A cloud of dust arose as the cloths around their arms hit and it seemed as if they were both the dirtier for the exchange.

"Shake," the man kept saying in his language.

He held his arm out to her. "Shake," he repeated.

Her arms were covered and her hands gloved. She cautiously copied the movement of the other man and repeated his word, "Shake."

The leader laughed and nodded, looking very pleased. He let her hand go and thumped himself on the chest.

"Bawlner," he said.

She pointed at him to verify "Bawlner?"

He nodded. That was his name. Then he pointed to her.

"Aitouku," she said, pointing to herself. She had meant to say her name but her tongue surprised her and twisted into that — a name for a boy that meant "student," "learner," or "apprentice." Her people looked at her curiously, but she recognized the intervention of a spirit and accepted it. She did not correct herself.

"Aytownko" he tried to imitate. She had to correct him several times before she finally gave up and allowed him to call her "Atty".

He tried to ask her something she could not understand and made many strange movements with his hands and fingers that made no sense to her. Seeing that she didn't understand, he finally gave up. He pulled a blade and pointed to it. The way he held it was as no warrior would have handled a blade. He seemed unaware of it as a weapon.

"Silver," he said in his language.

She repeated the word until she got it right. Now she knew better what he most wanted. She guessed, as the elders before her had, that it was the metal, not the blade itself, which interested him. She pulled out a painted charm of one of the spirits that she had carried that day — a little human-shaped female figure with an overwhelmingly large, open mouth. It was the talking spirit, and she hoped it would help their communication. She handed it to Bawlner to see.

"Silver?" she asked.

He examined it closely, scratched at the paint, then put it in his mouth and bent it with his teeth. Jovai watched him horrified, but he seemed unaware.

"Silver," he confirmed.

He handed it back to her, but she refused to take it. If he had made the spirit angry, he could keep the anger. He accepted it as a gift, much pleased and stuffed it into a pouch at his waist.

Now she would show him something that they wanted. She walked to the nearest horse and put her hand on his neck. Bawlner followed with a string of words that she could not possibly understand. He did not seem angry, merely talkative. He tried to lead her to another horse, but she resisted.

"Horse," she said in her language. Then she pointed to him. He was slow to understand. He shook his head and pointed to one of his men, a dark-eyed, frowning man. She also pointed to the man.

"His horse," she said. Then she pointed back to the horse. "Horse."

He finally understood and gave her the word she wanted. She made very careful note. She pointed to the horse's genitals.

"Mare," she said.

The man laughed and gave her the word.

She found a stallion and got a word for that.

She went to one of the tents and touched the fabric. Again the man came at her with a string of words. She listened, instead, to the sounds within the tents and went to the nearest one with no one else inside.

Bawlner came after her, calling. She motioned for him to follow and went into the tent. It was full of supplies. They had bags of dried meat and fruits, of a kind she couldn't identify, grains, beans, fermented beverages and water. For only five people, it looked like enough to last them through the winter. That was not a good sign.

They had blankets and furs as well. They also had a variety of things that could be used as weapons or tools. Their cutting edges were made of a shiny black stone that was very smooth and sharp and stronger than many of her people's weapons. There were many other things that she could not identify or understand. There was much that was made of metal, though very little looked like silver.

Bawlner was clearly unhappy that she had chosen to enter this tent. He also, clearly, was afraid to ask her to leave. She pulled him to the nearest bag of beans and asked him for the name. Bag by bag she had him widen her vocabulary. It was buying her people, who crowded in behind them, a good look at the supplies. She especially wanted Sirfen Elder to see the weapons. To her, there seemed many more than only five could wield, hand to hand weapons mostly, although there were some spears.

Bawlner offered her a drink of some liquid — strongly fermented, from a smooth, smoky colored, see-through container. She sniffed it but refused. Bawlner took a large swallow himself from the container, then offered it to her people. It was hard to tell if this were some kind of insult, but she didn't think so. Her people refused as she had.

One by one, Jovai went into all the tents. She touched beds, woven mats not much different than their own, blankets, pieces of clothes, lamps of a fluid that was not the oil she knew, collections of colored papers and weapons. Bawlner got more and more nervous. She asked the names of everything she touched, and he dutifully gave them, among many other words that seemed pointed to getting them out of the tents.

She saw where the Gicok slept. He did not sleep with the strangers, but in his own tent, yet it was no different from the stranger's tents except that it was smaller, had less things in it and no weapons. The Gicok was sitting in it at the time they entered. He jumped up angrily but sat down again at a sign from Bawlner and glared as they curiously looked around. The people of the valley touched very little, but their presence made him obviously nervous.

The sun was getting lower. Jovai's people wanted to be well away from the camp by dark.

"We go," she said slowly in her language, pantomiming leaving.

Bawlner said a word in his language that might have been "go" or "leave" or "walk". She didn't know. He brought out the mare. It was a beautiful horse and seemed healthy. When Jovai tried to thank him, he held out his hand as he had in the beginning.

"Shake," she said, to show she remembered, and she shook arms with him again.

He spoke quickly, many more words, and made gestures toward himself and his camp — coming back. He was asking them to come back.

"Will we return?" she asked Massern Leader.

"We will talk about it," he answered.

She turned to Bawlner and shrugged. He seemed to understand the gesture.

"You," he said, pointing. "Atty?" He made the gesture of returning again. Again she shrugged, but with a smile. He seemed to consider her particularly welcome, so she had not gone too far in her investigations.

The council that evening lasted long. The elders were worried about what they had seen.

"It is wise we did not make them enemies," said Jatoyen Elder, "If their weapons are as many as you say. Perhaps there will be more coming or even here, already, in hiding."

Yaku Shaman did not believe there were any here already. He had spied on them the night before in a spirit wandering and had seen no one else.

"They seemed eager to be friendly," noted Massern Leader.

"They want something," Sirfen said.

"They want our metal," Jovai clarified. It was the first time that she had sat in the council as an equal. Yaku Shaman showed no acknowledgment of anything unusual in that, but she knew that the extra sternness on his face hid his feelings of triumph and his pride in her.

"And they will trade good horses for it," said Takan Elder. The silver metal was too soft to stand alone except in ornaments and small statues. They sometimes mixed it with other ore to make it strong, but this was only for small things, like healing tools. In general, the other ore in their caves served them better when they needed. The horses, however, were a grand prize. Their strength could serve a farm well, would lend speed and power to the hunt, and their breeding for war would put them on an equal footing with the Gicoks if they ever attacked again.

"Perhaps they will trade us many more horses if we offer them silver," suggested Nobien Elder.

"Could they be stupid enough to give away their power like that?" asked Sirfen Elder. He directed the question to Jovai.

"They gave away much information about themselves today," Jovai answered, "as well as a horse, and got nothing for it. That does seem stupid."

"But we should be careful," warned Yaku Shaman. "They need not be smart to be dangerous."

It was decided that they would go back, particularly Jovai, who had learned so much today. They would approach the strangers cautiously, but as friends, and learn as much as they could.

Over the weeks, Jovai went back daily. She kept almost every word she heard and had the sound of the language in her ear so quickly, even Yaku Shaman, who had witnessed her skill before, was impressed. Bawlner kept questioning her about their hills, particularly where they mined their silver. Although she understood the questions, Jovai always shook her head as though confused. She would point toward the south and say "We walk, sometimes, for winter hunt. We find people who will trade."

Bawlner clearly had difficulty believing her. He would press for more and get less.

"Why tell them we don't have silver?" asked the council.

"I am hoping they will go away and leave us alone," replied Jovai.

"But do we want that?" asked Tapeten. "They have horses and weapons and things we could use, fabrics we cannot make ourselves, pelts we have never seen before, and they will trade us this for silver."

"I do not trust them," Jovai answered. "The spirits have warned us..."

"Perhaps they warned us so we would not make enemies of friends," interrupted Tapeten.

"It is rather that they warned us so we would not make friends of enemies," insisted Jovai.

"You are only a child. What do you know?" said Tapeten dismissively. Her voice was silenced for the night.

"Why do you let them silence you so?" demanded Yaku Shaman,

angrily, as they returned to his house that evening.

"They are right, I am only a child," Jovai answered.

"You are a shaman," her master argued.

"I am only your apprentice...One of your apprentices," she replied.

"All you lack of a shaman is your adulthood," he told her. "As soon as you get your shaman name, I will put the mark on you myself."

By the time fall was full, Jovai had the strangers' language well, and the strangers had the trust of many in the council. They would have invited the traders into the village itself, had Yaku Shaman not been so insistent against it. Although two seasons had passed without unusual illness, he still worried about the "disease" of which the spirit had warned.

Jovai learned to ask Bawlner many questions, and he answered them all without the slightest hesitation.

He was from a land to the south that was filled with wise and talented people who made many things, built great buildings so high they touched the sky, and the stars had to make special detours around their tops. It was a land filled with strange and wondrous beasts, birds of plumage beautiful beyond belief, and plants which could cure any disease known to man, which could feed a family for months with a single leaf, and which lent their bewildering beauty to women for their dyes and their adornment.

His people were peaceful traders, he told her. They were attracted by many things, but especially the silver, which the Gicoks had stolen from her people. He wanted to know where they got it and how plentiful it was. He would buy it bit by bit, in raw ore if they chose, or he would buy the rights to mine it from their mountains, where he believed it lay. His men had been wandering the hills looking for it. They had not found it yet, but they still believed it might be nearby.

She assured him that it was not. He did not believe her. He promised her people wonders beyond their imagination if they would trade him silver. His greed for it was great, and it frightened Jovai.

He asked her very few questions about her people. He was interested in little more than getting silver. He asked her if she were some kind of leader or the leader's son perhaps. She denied it, which surprised him. After that, he pressed to speak to the leader through her. Massern Leader finally agreed.

To Massern Leader he offered the same riches beyond belief that he had mentioned to Jovai, in exchange for the silver. Jovai was careful in her interpretation to downplay the riches, to make them sound like useless and impossible trash, for Massern's mind was as split on the question of the strangers as the council was. He had always listened to Yaku Shaman with great respect, but since no disease had infected his people from this contact with the strangers, and since so many of the elders were pushing to trade, he was no longer as sure as his shaman that the strangers should be avoided.

He gave the traders hope. They announced that they were leaving, but that they would return next year with greater temptations. Their leaving was a relief to everyone. Their return — a desire to many.

Life once again became as before. Yaku Shaman spent his time with Kotayu, and Jovai split her time with the normal duties of a shaman and teaching her people what she knew of the strangers' language and ways. Languages came too easily to her for her to be able to explain them well to those who were slower. However, she got several of her people to a point where they could talk, in limited ways, to the strangers on their own.

CHAPTER 18

JOURNEY TO THE OLD WOMAN

Jovai's womanhood came upon her late in the winter of that year. She awoke one morning with a sickness in her stomach and her clothes and sleeping mat stained with blood.

Kotayu stared at her as she rose, his eyes wide with alarm.

"Are you hurt?" he asked. "Should I get the healer?"

Jovai could not fully stand. She stooped, her folded arms pressed against the ache deep in her body, and glanced around for Yaku Shaman. He was not there. He was out gathering the Lonik root, she recalled.

"How did you do it?" Kotayu pressed. He peered up at her ashen face and frowned.

"I'm all right," she told him, but he shook his head and started pulling on his winter shoes.

"You look bad."

"It'll pass," she insisted.

"You look like you're dying. I'll get the healer..."

She caught his arm as he rushed toward the door.

"Don't disturb the healer, Kotayu. It's really nothing."

"But..."

"No! And don't tell anyone."

"Not even Master?" he asked her suspiciously.

"I'll tell him...when he gets back. No need to bother him."

"But..."

"I'll just lie in today. If anyone asks, just say I'm tired. That's all, Kotayu. Do you understand?"

The little boy shook his head, bewildered.

"Then say nothing at all," she instructed him, irritably.

A dour, old widow came to tend the shaman's apprentices that morning. She came late, without explanation. Jovai knew her to be one who resented the duty to the shaman, thinking it unnecessary while a female lived with him who could do it. She took one glance around and saw Jovai back in bed and the shaman gone. It was enough to raise her indignation.

"If you will be lazy while your master's away, that is none of my business, but I won't tend to you," she told the girl with an angry sniff.

Jovai intended to ignore her but Kotayu, suddenly as defensive for her as any little brother might be, angrily answered.

"She's not lazy! She's..."

"Kotayu be still!" snapped Jovai. The boy shut his mouth with a guilty look.

"Eh? What is it then?" demanded the widow. She stood over Jovai, squinting down at her, and gave her one or two cautious jabs with her toe. "You sick then?"

"Go to your business," answered Jovai, "and leave me to mine."

"If you don't want my help, I won't offer it," said the widow, almost sounding merry, "Just tell us if you're dying or not."

"Not!" Jovai answered, meaning the conversation to end there.

"Are you sure?" asked the widow.

Jovai rolled over in her blankets and would not respond further.

"Poor thing," the old widow shook her head with a show of sympathy. She turned to the little boy and said sadly. "The dying are always the last to realize it. They lose all sense, you know."

Kotayu looked between Jovai and the widow, his eyes wide with fear.

"Then I should get the healer?" he whispered softly, his expression begging the widow for guidance.

"Ignore her!" Jovai snapped.

"But you're wounded!" argued the boy.

"Eh? What's that?"

"Kotayu!" But it was too late.

"There was blood everywhere," the boy was telling the widow, his hands tracing on his own clothes where he had seen the blood on Jovai's.

"Blood?" The widow's sharp eyes took in Jovai's bundled form. "Ah." She nodded, understanding dawning. "Ah."

Jovai winced but did not look up, did not even open her eyes.

"So, he didn't change you into a boy after all, did he? At least not all the way..." She grunted and nodded, smiling to herself. "Well then, he'll be done with you now, won't he? No choice now. Now you're no good to him...except in ways a shaman doesn't use."

She set about her task in good spirits and even chuckled merrily at some passing thoughts.

A cold chill swam through Jovai. "Ignore her" her rational-self counseled, but her emotions were all jumbled today and out of control. It made sense what the widow said. It shouldn't, but it did. She caught a sob in her throat. Another, behind it, slipped through her defenses. Then another and another until there seemed no point in trying to restrain them. They were not loud, but they shook her.

"What should I do?" asked Kotayu, sitting beside her. He reached out a bowl of food he had brought to her, then pulled it hesitantly away, unsure whether he should offer it to her or not.

She did not answer at first. He sat beside her, confused, waiting.

"Sing to me the Trintoa chants," Jovai said at last. "Let's see how much you remember all alone."

The old widow had been gone for less than half the morning before Jovai heard Misa at the door requesting to enter. Kotayu was working hard to learn the third chant of the Trintoa and had seemed to have forgotten Jovai's bleeding altogether. He paused when he heard Misa at the door, but Jovai waved him to continue. She did not want visitors.

"It's not going to work, sister," said Misa, letting herself into the shaman's house. She was the only one of Jovai's living relatives who still acknowledged her as family. Even Katira, in deference to their mother perhaps, was careful to make her friendliness appear such as anyone of the village might expect.

Jovai trembled before her older sister like a little, unnamed child before its angry mother.

"We were...studying the Trintoa," she fumbled to say. "The third chant. You shouldn't interrupt..."

"This is more important." Misa shot a glance at the little boy who was staring at her, mouth hanging in mid-word. "Go visit your mother, Kotayu."

Jovai grabbed at the little boy, holding him where he was. She moved herself a little behind him, as if he were a shield to defend her against Misa, and held onto him with all her strength, afraid to let him go. He squirmed in pain at her grip.

"The Trintoa isn't that far away," she said. "He has to be ready..."

"That can wait," Misa answered shortly. "What you and I have to do can't."

"But the Trintoa is important!"

"Not as important as this. Really Jovai!" She shook her head angrily at her sister's folly. "Let him go. Can't you see you're hurting him?"

With a surge of shame, Jovai let the child go. Misa quickly caught his arm shooed him out the door.

"Your mother's waiting. Go on."

The boy didn't need more urging. He liked visiting his mother much better than reciting unknown words.

Jovai cowered in her bundle of furs, in anticipation of her sister's scolding.

"One would think I was going to beat you!" exclaimed Misa, laughing.

"What are you going to do?"

"Well, what do you think?" but then she stopped and stared at her frightened little sister, her eyes suddenly watching and wise. "You really don't know, do you?"

"The woman's place?" asked Jovai in a voice of terrified reverence.

"No one has ever explained it to you, have they?"

"My master..."

"Your master is a man," Misa said with a dismissive wave of her hand. "He knows nothing about it."

"But he's a shaman!" exclaimed Jovai.

"He's still only a man."

Jovai had never heard her master called "only a man" before. She could not believe she was hearing it now. It shocked her beyond words.

Her sister stared at her wonderingly, shaking her head.

"You really have been isolated, haven't you? In this place full of people, more than half of them women, no one has ever talked to you about it. Not even me." She dropped her eyes thoughtfully. "I always assumed...but I don't know why I did. I mean, if Mother wouldn't, and I know she hadn't, who else was going to except me?"

She shrugged the wonder away and jumped quickly to her feet.

"No use wasting time," she said. "We're going to have to start at the beginning — right back from when you got your first name. Better get started. Where are your clothes?"

Jovai nodded toward a couple winter tunics and a change of leggings hanging from a peg in the wall above her mat.

"Nothing!" exclaimed Misa angrily as she rifled through the clothes. "Some people say he has been trying to turn you into a boy. Is that true?"

"No!"

"Then why is there not one decent thing for a young woman to wear here?"

Jovai stared at the bundle of clothes, not knowing what to say.

"Come on then," said Misa, tossing off the tunics as though they were rags, "We'll stop by my house on the way and get you one of mine."

"On the way to...to the woman's place?" asked Jovai softly.

"Of course."

"No Misa. I can't."

"What do you mean you can't?"

Jovai swallowed hard. She didn't know how to say what she felt. Misa watched her in angry impatience, quickly building to an explosion. If Jovai wanted a word at all, she had to say it quickly.

"My master..."

"Your master has nothing to do with this!"

"I can't go without his permission."

"Of course you can. You have to."

"But he might not think I'm ready."

Misa grabbed her and pulled her forcibly up from the blood-stained blankets.

"It's time," she said. "It is obviously, undeniably time!"

Misa always had her way, Jovai remembered too late. As she walked through the snow beside Misa, her body freshly washed, wearing Misa's long, beautiful tunic, hair quickly but gracefully braided in the woman's style on her head, she wondered why she had even bothered to try to argue.

They were on their way to the woman's place — a special house in a special grove forbidden absolutely to any man or child. For women only — a place of beauty and mystery and magic deeper and subtler than anything the shaman knew — or so Misa was saying. She talked continuously as they walked.

"The old one, she doesn't come into the village anymore. I never saw her before I was a woman and Polisa, too, can't remember her ever being outside the woman's place. She is immensely holy and wise. She has a book — older than creation, or maybe a part of it. From the labor of creation to birth the first world, and on up to this very moment, then the next, everything that touches the spirits of women is written in it. Our names are all written there, as we come into ourselves. I will introduce you to her, and she will write your name – your true name – there, joined with all the women who have ever lived. She has a place for you, saved. In a way, I guess, she knows you already. She told me I should bring you if Polisa wouldn't."

Misa glanced at her sister. She had not meant to tell her that Polisa had refused to do her mother's duty by Jovai, but surely Jovai understood that already. She was relieved to see no sign from her sister of hurt or resentment. All that showed on Jovai's face was nervousness and wonder. Then, suddenly, fear.

"What's wrong?" demanded Misa.

Jovai did not answer but looked behind her. Misa followed her gaze and saw a figure hurrying along the path, coming toward them. He was far away, but Misa knew by Jovai's expression that it was the shaman.

"Quickly," she told her sister. "We are almost there. He can't follow us there."

"He will..." Jovai gasped.

"He can't." She pulled her sister onward. "The old one will keep him out."

"An old woman," muttered Jovai ruefully, "against the great Yaku Shaman."

"Come on," urged her sister. "It's just over this hill."

The hill was not tall, but the climb was steep and slippery with snow, and the figure behind them steadily drew closer. Every-so-often Jovai would pause and stare at him, as someone transfixed.

"He's angry," she warned her sister.

"We must hurry..."

But Jovai shook her head.

"You go on," she told Misa. "I'll join you when I can."

"We go together," insisted Misa. She took Jovai's arm and pulled her along.

At the top of the hill, the brown bear was waiting. He stood on his hind legs, impossibly tall, and clawed his fury into the air.

"Go away, Shaman. This doesn't concern you!" shouted Misa angrily. Jovai caught her breath at her sister's bravery.

The bear lunged at them, but Misa, her grip firm on Jovai, held her ground. With one great sweep of his paw, the bear sent both the women sprawling. His claws left bloody gashes along Misa's back.

Jovai screamed in horror. Misa screamed in pain. The brown bear shimmered into the shape of the Yaku Shaman and stood glaring at them both.

"You may not take my apprentice!" he growled at Misa.

"She is a woman now," Misa answered him furiously.

"She is a shaman!" he yelled.

"I must go, Master," Jovai told him, pulling herself back to her feet. As she said it she suddenly knew, absolutely, that it was right. It was the order of things.

"Do you defy me?" he demanded of her, incredulously.

"I will come back," she told him, "and accept the life you want for me, but right now, for a little while, I must go."

"No!"

The shaman grew taller, almost the bear again, and towered over her. Jovai pulled herself to her full height and looked up into the burning fury of his eyes.

"Yes," she told him again. "I must."

She looked past him, toward the little house nestled in the snow and tree-filled valley beside the hill on which they stood. There was smoke rising from the chimney flap that promised the warmth of a welcoming fire and a sense of peace and beauty all around the place. Suddenly, more than anything, she wanted to go there — to be welcomed wholly and completely as she knew she would be there, without any mingling of suspicion or fear. It seemed so close. Maybe if she ran...

"You cannot get by me," Yaku growled.

"Will you destroy me to stop me?" she challenged.

He stared down at her and drew all his anger into one terrible focus. She felt her skin tingle as with a rising storm. This was not the gentle magic of suggestion, but something much more violent. It was the "bad" magic — the will bender. Her stomach clenched in fear.

"This is wrong, master!"

"Sleep," was all he said. One word in the old language. It was an evil thing to tamper with another so — a horrible abuse. Yet he had said it so softly, so lovingly, it made her want to curl herself in his arms forever in total trust.

"No!" she pushed herself away. Her body trembled. Her thoughts were drifting and even though she forced her eyes open, it was hard to make them see. She stumbled past him.

"Where are you going?" he asked her gently.

"There," she said, pointing toward the little house in the valley. "I must, Master. Please. I must."

"You must sleep."

He left her no way to fight him unless she dared strike to destroy him. They both knew she could not do that. Even if she had her shaman name, she could not have used it against her beloved master. He caught her in his arms again, and this time she could not resist.

Misa watched her sister, her strange, gentle, beautiful sister, so close to being a woman, now turned back into a sleeping baby, her will crushed, her voice silenced. Grief welled up in her at the sight of it. "Are we all so weak, so fragile," she wondered, "that one fool with only one word can so easily destroy us?"

Yaku Shaman looked down at the sleeping girl in his arms. He stroked her hair tenderly and smiled.

"You can't keep her a child forever," Misa told him, her voice soft to mask its grief. "You can only cripple the woman she is meant to be."

"She is not a woman, but a shaman. She will claim her adulthood this summer. That is the proper time for it. And she will take it like a shaman — not a woman. A shaman!"

Misa bowed her head and wept for her lost little sister.

———◆———

Jovai awoke back in her bed, wrapped carefully in furs. Her master was tending the fire. He did not look at her, but he knew she was awake.

She said nothing. She washed herself and dressed again in boy's clothes and spoke no word more than was necessary. From then on she kept her eyes lowered and would raise them to no man or woman or even child. Only once or twice did her master catch her eyes. He saw no reproach in them, only sadness. Otherwise, she was as dutiful as ever.

She took over Kotayu's lessons more and more as other duties called the shaman away. People no longer came to Jovai, not even as a healer.

"It's a bad business," they would say when they spoke of what had happened. The shaman's actions troubled them, especially the women. They did not know what to make of this person who was no longer a little girl, but not a woman either — a nothing, a wrong person, a witch — good only for evil — a walking curse. They refused her services. They barred their doors against her. Some would not look at her or say a word in her hearing, except the child's protection prayer. Even Misa avoided her. She sought another healer to tend the wounds the shaman had caused and would not take her tunic back.

When the Trintoa came, Jovai would not sing it.

"You must! Kotayu does not know it yet," Yaku Shaman insisted, but she only shook her head.

"You have brought us many good years," he told her gently.

She got up quickly and left the room. Some unnamable fear stopped Yaku from chasing her.

When the Trintoa came, only Yaku Shaman, old and tired Yaku Shaman, walked the dawn.

Chapter 19

Name of Power

During the spring the shaman spent more time with Jovai than with Kotayu, preparing her for her spiritual journey. It could be a dangerous thing, depending on the spirits, but it would be during this journey to the spirits themselves that Jovai would be given her shaman name. He knew she was worthy of a truly powerful name, perhaps one even more powerful than his own. But he had to be sure she was completely ready. Physically, mentally, spiritually, she had to be as strong as she could be. The spirits might choose to test her before giving her the name. The name itself might be one of such power its weight would fall heavily on her and stun her at a crucial moment when her wits were required to keep it secret. More than anything, he trained her how to carry her name with such secrecy that no one, not even Jovai, herself, would ever hear it uttered aloud after the spirits gave it to her. This was the most important thing, and the training had to be so deep that no trickery or evil magic could ever compel her to break it.

"The name the spirits will give you is everything you are," he repeated to her, over and over. "It is the very essence of you, and anyone with knowledge of it has absolute power over you. You cannot allow this. Every man is important, but a man with a shaman name is a channel of such tremendous power that his name can change the very shape of the world if he is not careful. Only those who are worthy of the responsibility are given such names, and to give it to someone else, to kill yourself, for, spiritually, that is what this means, and let someone, who has not been chosen, abuse your power, is the greatest evil you can do. It can mean the end of the world. It can mean the spirits abandoning us forever. It can mean something even worse than we can imagine. No one who has not been given a shaman name can possibly use such power rightly, no matter how well-intentioned such a person might be. And no one who has a shaman name can ever be forgiven for betraying it. To give up your name is to lose yourself, completely and forever. And whatever space in anyone's heart ever held love for you will be filled with pain until it shrinks into complete oblivion."

He tested her, by making up a secret name for her to guard, then bending his efforts to tricking it from her. He also had her choose a secret item that only she knew and tried to trick her into revealing what it was she had chosen. He could not get her to betray her secrets even when he declared the test finished.

He also tested her again on everything he had ever taught her. In all the tests she did well. Yaku was very proud of the shaman he had trained.

The people objected. Why did he spend so much time with her, now that he had a real apprentice? He told them:

"We have great reason to rejoice. Jovai is adult now. This summer she will be given her name and, if the spirits will it, I will mark her myself as a shaman. Our people will be rich with her."

"Our people will be well with her," was the ritual statement. He was saying more, bragging of her great power. The people were furious. They did not want a woman shaman, especially a cursed woman. And they had Kotayu. It was a dangerous thing to have two shamen in a village when one was not the master. The spirits could easily be split and the village could become a chaotic battle ground between them.

They would let Jovai serve her master if he insisted. They would even let her help train Kotayu if Yaku Shaman died, but once Kotayu was shaman, Jovai had to disappear. She could not even be a healer or a wife, not now that she was a cursed woman.

"You are lucky," Yaku Shaman told his people, "that your shaman is wiser than you." That was all he would say.

"Is it wise," Jovai asked him privately, "to make me a shaman when no one else will accept me as such?"

"I did not make you a shaman," her master told her. "That was the spirits. I trained you because you needed to be trained for the spirits' sake, for the people's sake, and for your own sake. You are a shaman. You will always be a shaman."

"Even if I had gotten married and had children?" she asked, but it was a foolish question. No man of her people would ever touch her. If she bore any children now, they would be killed or taken from her, for she was not a woman in the eyes of her people.

"Even so," the shaman replied. "It is much harder then to serve, and there may come a time when you will have to make a choice — your children's well-being or all your people's, the spirits' needs or your family's. The spirits can test you like that, and they can be very angry and dangerous if you disappoint them. It is much wiser for a shaman to keep that part of life away from him. If you let someone get too close, too distracting, the spirits can solve that problem in ways that could be very painful for everyone."

There was sadness in his expression that spoke of bitter memories. Jovai averted her eyes as he paused, lost for a moment in his own dark thoughts. She did not want to intrude.

"You will be a shaman, because you are a shaman," her master said at last. "I will send you to your naming and mark you so that the people will have to accept and honor you. You deserve that much."

The traders returned in the middle of spring. There were more of them this time, twelve or more. They did not initiate a meeting with the shaman's people but wandered through the mountains and hills which surrounded the village's valley.

"They are looking for the silver," Jovai guessed.

Her people rode forth in a large and well-armed group to meet them. They found that the strangers were not the same as had come before. Even the Gicok guide was different.

"Where is Bawlner?" asked Jovai.

The strange men glanced between themselves.

"He is dead," they answered. "He and his crew died shortly after they returned."

Jovai told her people. They saw it as a bad omen.

"Bawlner said there was a boy he had trained to speak our language. Is that you?" asked the long-haired man with black skin and a golden mustache who spoke for the new strangers.

Jovai nodded.

"I am called Aitouku."

"We'd be interested in having you come with us, back to our city. Our emperor is curious about your people. Your leader is invited too, of course. You can be the interpreter."

When she told her people this, Yaku Shaman frowned most ferociously.

"We could learn much from such a visit," commented Tapeten Winter Leader.

"She is my apprentice. I do not allow," said Yaku.

"It could be dangerous," warned Takan Elder. "Once they have you, Tapeten Leader, they might not want to let you return to us."

"Perhaps another could go," suggested Jovai. "There are now several in the village who speak well enough."

"But none so well as you," replied Jatoyen Elder with a sly grin.

"My master has spoken," Jovai dutifully replied.

The strangers watched the exchange carefully. Jovai did not enjoy the intensity of their gaze. These men still seemed friendly, but not as foolishly relaxed as the strangers before had been. She declined their offer for herself and told them her leaders would think on it.

The strangers claimed to be passing through toward other parts of the world. They said they would be back in the Fall to discuss trade when they had better horses and more things of interest.

The next day the traders made a grand show of leaving, but the shaman and his older apprentice knew that a few of their number stayed behind. They kept their distance, roaming the hills and mountains around their village, rather than attempting any direct contact with Jovai's people through her.

"Three or four are no threat," decided the council. "They are still friendly. As long as they don't come into the village, we will leave them alone."

Summer came with no intrusion from the strangers. Jovai prepared for her shaman's journey. She fasted and reached her mind toward the spirits, to let them know she was coming. She stressed her body, stretching every muscle, and pushing its energy to the limit with focused determination, to make sure it was sound and strong. She sat for days in strict discipline, listening. When the time arrived, she was ready.

Her master mixed the konis. He made it very strong — a stronger dose than she had ever had before or probably would ever have again. It was only one part "body" to four parts "mind." Yaku Shaman was extremely careful. The dose, if wrong, could kill Jovai or push her mind beyond its limits, past any point from which it could heal. If it were not strong enough it might not let her reach as far as she needed. He had to mix it well, using all the knowledge of her he had. He put it in a flask, to be sipped, not gulped. Then they started out together.

One sip. They walked through the village, calling to the village spirits, introducing her as the shaman-to-be-tried, encouraging their response, be it welcome or challenge. The village and house spirits watched with their families. The people were not happy, but many of the spirits bowed to Jovai as she passed.

Two sips. At the eastern hill, the place of beginnings. She bowed before the sacred tree and sang to the child within. She listened and heard the child singing back. The trunk of the old tree shifted before Jovai's eyes into the double face, the Mother/Father. It smiled at her and nodded, the branches waving in the wind. Yaku Shaman watched in wonder. He sensed the presence of the greatest of all gods and fear filled his heart. Such an honor for a human, it was almost too much. Things beyond his understanding were being connected to this girl. Jovai sang for the Mother/Father. She loved the great god and all its creation. She loved the child. She felt no fear, only happiness.

Three sips. To the western river, the place of wisdom and of power, they walked. Her master helped her drink the cool, sweet water that washed away the bitter taste of konis. He helped her bathe in the free-flowing waters. They filled a second flask for her, to hang on her belt beside the first. The spirits came splashing upon the bank, sparkling in the late afternoon sun. They talked to her with joyous babble, laughing as the dizziness shook her. The konis was very strong.

Four sips. Yaku Shaman led his apprentice to the northern plains, the place of ending, where a different life began. They sang to the ancestors, not asking them to come, but letting them know they were welcome if they wanted to greet the new shaman. Jovai was overjoyed to see her mother's parents and father's father come to greet her. Behind them followed a great, grand crowd, not just her ancestors, but all the village's people back beyond the time when they still roamed like nomads. They crowded around her silently, touching her cheeks and hair with their ghost-wind fingers, smiling. Then they parted, and before her stood her master's master, his master, his master before him, all the shaman the village had honored and some from before the village had even been.

"I am proud of him," said Cokru Shaman, smiling easily at his own apprentice, Jovai's master. "He is a great shaman."

Jovai nodded happily, her eyes shining with the brilliance of the konis.

"It was a bad business," said an old woman, coming up behind him.

Cokru Shaman bowed reverently to her and withdrew. Jovai looked curiously at the woman who claimed such respect. She was short and round with feather-shaped lines under her eyes from often smiling and often crying. Long hair flowed like a white stream around her stooped shoulders. Her lips held themselves on the verge of a smile, although her words were serious and her eyes intense. She did not look at Jovai, but beyond her, around her, at all the world.

"The Great Bear did wrong. He shall pay, and she shall suffer for it. I gave him more time with her than he could have expected, and he still would not let her come."

"He did not understand..." Jovai said quickly, in defense of her beloved master, but the lady didn't hear her.

"We will have to take her from him. No other way now."

Cokru nodded. They all nodded. Jovai watched, bemused by konis, not fully understanding what they meant.

"Your journey will be long," said Cokru to her, "and will take you very far. By seeking your name, you are seeking yourself, your soul. It is everything you are. Even if the spirits give it to you, it is still for you to understand. There is much my apprentice could not teach you, and there are important things he would not let you learn. You must learn these things."

The words of Cokru Shaman flowed over her in her konis induced haze. She did not fully understand but she would, she knew, in time.

"Thank you for your wisdom, Master," she replied, bowing with deep respect.

Five sips. In the southern woods, her solitary journey would begin. That was the place of maturing youth, of directing power, of coming to adulthood.

Her master helped her walk to the edge of the wood. She looked for the path she and Misa had taken, but she could not find it now. Already, the world was tilting around her, growing bigger and smaller wherever she looked. Nausea rose and fell in her as her heart beat too quickly and her body trembled.

From here she would go on alone, unarmed, as far as she could walk, and await the will of the spirits. If they came to her, if they gave her a shaman name, and therefore shaman power, that would be the sign of their approval. Her shaman name would be secret, and she would continue to be called by her child's name, but she would carry the mark and the title of shaman.

"You don't need to go far," said her master.

She nodded. It was a spiritual journey. She need only sit and wait.

"You will be alone from here," warned Yaku Shaman. "I will not listen tonight, but I will pray for you."

He kissed her gently, like a father. It was the first time he ever had.

She kissed him back and hugged him.

"I love you, Master," she said. "Don't worry."

She could feel her master's eyes watching her as she walked into the woods until she was out of sight.

Into the woods, through the glow of the setting sun, she walked. Branches and leaves split the light, spilling it into dancing pools at her feet. The early summer air was warm, and she felt hot, for her master had made her dress again as a boy, covered all but her head and hands. He was worried for her. He had warned her of snakes and wild animals and the befuddlement of konis, but she was in the spirit's hands, and she felt happy and safe.

She went as far as she could walk. The village was out of sight. She tried to listen for it, but her head was spinning, and her expanding spirit drained the last of the energy from her body. She sank to the ground, next to a tree.

In her disorientation, she could not tell where she was. Perhaps her spirit journeyed from her body, for it felt free, uninhibited, and as large as the whole world. At first, she thought she was on the eastern hill again, leaning against the holy tree. As she sat, the tree expanded and grew around her like a loving hug, pulling her into its heart. It was dark and warm there, and she felt safe and very happy.

Where was the child, she wondered. But she was the child, lying in the tree, waiting for her singer to come. She wanted to hear the stories of the wonderful people and things the world was full of, not for the stories themselves, but for the love with which her singer sang them.

With a jolt, Jovai was back in the southern woods, a gentle breeze caressing her cheek, cooling the sweat on her brow. She felt like one awakening from a beautiful dream, who does not really want to leave it but who has a new and eagerly anticipated day to greet. Time seemed to be racing around her, yet every moment was full of wonders she had not ever fully appreciated before. The smell of the leaves and grass and flowers, the warmth of the air, the shifting pattern of the shadows as they stretched toward her, the texture of the bark, the dirt, the plants, her clothes, everything delighted her. She could taste the konis still on her tongue. Even its bitterness pleased her. The sounds of the rustling bushes as animals scurried and darted around her, the fresh, young leaves shivering as the night air grew cooler, the wind singing its breathy chant — there was so much to hear, even when she couldn't concentrate enough to listen.

Through the shadows came a stranger, tall and slim, dressed as she, yet it didn't seem fully a man, nor fully a woman either. When the first ray of the rising moon struck the stranger's face, she saw that it was someone she knew, yet had never actually met. The face looked both masculine and feminine, not split into two as her charm had shown, but full and complete within itself. It was a perfection and therefore beautiful beyond comprehension.

She would have greeted the greatest of all gods with proper respect, but her body no longer obeyed her. Her tongue felt thick and heavy and would not move in her mouth. Even her jaw was locked shut. Or did it hang open? She wasn't sure. Her limbs felt numb, but her mind was extraordinarily sensitive.

The stranger sat down next to her and took her hand. Other spirits came, one by one, in the shape of animals, birds, reptiles, human-seeming shapes, strange, unidentifiable shapes, and some with no shape at all. A glowing giant, like no spirit or god that her people recognized, descended from the stars and, nodding politely to the one who held her hand, set itself among the others. Some of the spirits she recognized. Some were new. They crowded around her, filling the trees and bushes, the ground and the air. They watched and waited with her for something to happen. She could feel their support and love like a soothing lullaby and thanked them silently and fully.

The waxing moon filled the sky, shining like the sun. She watched as it rose, as it floated overhead, and as it started to drift toward the west. The Great Spirit's hand, which held hers, was warm and gentle. She listened for the spirit to give her an adult name — hopefully, something describing a great power — a shaman power. The spirits smiled at her but said nothing.

She trembled at her boldness before the greatest of all spirits but could wait no longer.

"Please, Great One, have I a name?"

Her tongue could barely form the words, but the spirits understood.

The Great Spirit picked up a small stone from the ground and handed it to her. It was a strange stone, a small black one, smoothed to a shiny polish and flattened on one side. It felt warm, nestled in her palm.

"Your name," whispered the Mother/Father.

Jovai looked closely at the stone. In the dark, she could not make out any markings on it. She ran her finger carefully over it, especially over the flattened side, but not the slightest scratch interrupted the flowing smoothness of the stone.

"What is it?" begged Jovai. "I can't see anything on it."

The spirits answered with only silence. Silence, smoothness, darkness, nothing.

"Not a shaman then?" she wondered. Shaman. It was something she knew, simple and real. A word she understood. Not shaman. All her life made meaningless to her, but still that she could understand. She could be "not shaman" if it must be. She would not fit the only life her master had left for her among her people, but she could make a new one, somehow.

But there was nothing here — no shaman name, promising great power, but no common name either. Slowly, through the konis, she realized what not having a name would mean. It was not a matter of position, but rather one of being. No one suffered a lack of name who reached the age for one. Sometimes a boy who tried for his adulthood too soon would have to wait, but he would eventually be named. If she were a boy she could try again next year, but she was a woman, and her adulthood was clear — only needing acknowledgment. Surely, the spirits would grant that.

"Is it because I'm like you?" she wanted to ask the greatest of all gods. "I'm not a man but not a woman either?"

As she looked up into the perfect face, however, she knew that she was not like the god at all. The god was whole. The god was both man and woman, everything, ageless and right, complete and balanced in inhuman purity. Jovai looked at herself in the darkness of her being and saw nothing, not a man but not a woman either — not a child, but not an adult. She was something wrong, something evil in the world. She felt shattered, fragmented, with all the little bits of herself working against each other. Even through the pleasant konis haze, she wanted to cry.

And the god held her gently, like a loving parent. All around, each of the crowd of spirits smiled or nodded encouragingly. The breeze stroked her hair. Even the trees, the plants, every blade of grass, and every speck of dust that formed with proud unison the solid-seeming earth, everything welcomed her with joy.

The konis muddled her into a pleasant contentment. Was she not here safe with the spirits? And the greatest of them held her hand. It would be all right...somehow.

The woods grew strangely quiet. All other sounds were stilled to let her hear the footsteps that disturbed the night. No one should be walking tonight, especially not so late. The shaman had forbidden his people to interfere with her passage. It was something out of place, and yet, so wrapped in konis bliss was she, that she could not be alarmed. The Great Spirit kissed her gently as the strangers approached.

A Gicok came first, dressed not as a warrior, but as one of the traders. He paused when he saw her and looked around as though sensing something strange. His eyes, which darted everywhere, were unreadable, but his face looked afraid. It was a look Jovai had never seen on a Gicok. She found it amusing.

"There he is," whispered the large, golden-haired stranger with a mustache, coming up behind the Gicok, "right where they said."

In his dark-skinned hand he held a sharp-tipped whip, readied to strike. Behind her, she could hear the footsteps of two other men. They had surrounded her.

The Gicok tried to back away, but the man pushed him forward instead.

"No," said the Gicok haltingly, in the foreign stranger's tongue, "Something not good here."

"It's all right," the golden-haired man insisted, though he approached her warily as he said it, his whip ever ready. "They said he'd be sleeping, that he wouldn't fight."

He paused when he got close enough to see Jovai's eyes were open and watching him.

"You're not going to fight me now, are you boy?" he asked.

Jovai could do nothing but calmly watch. The spirit held her. She trusted it completely.

"What's wrong with him?" asked one of the men coming up from behind her. He flashed a light from a shielded lamp into her eyes. The brightness pained her. She wanted to close her eyes, but even her eyelids would not obey her.

"Great Gorat, look at those eyes," he exclaimed, his voice as rough as his hairy chin. "They've got him drugged out of his druthers."

The golden-haired man took her hand from the spirit's and felt the pulse on her wrist. He shook his head.

"They sure made it easy...if he doesn't die." He smiled. "I think I'm going to like these people."

He searched her clothes briefly and found the two flasks on her hip belt which he sniffed.

"No weapons," he announced. From behind Jovai came the other man, more of a boy really, with no beard or mustache yet, but only long, golden hair framing his dark face. Still, he was large, and there were four of them. Only the spirits could help her escape now. She waited, wondering what they would do.

The golden-haired man called the Gicok to him. The Gicok approached with the look of a hunted animal. Everything around startled him, though nothing moved. He seemed ready to run at the slightest sound.

"Take him," the golden-haired man with a mustache ordered.

"He'll have to be carried."

When the Gicok seemed reluctant, the man flexed his whip and hit the Gicok. He doubled over, wincing in pain. It took several deep breaths for him to find the strength to stand again. When he did, there were three little needles imbedded in his belly which he had to pick out before he could move again.

"Do what I say," the man ordered. "Now!"

The Gicok obeyed. He heaved Jovai across his shoulders and carried her through the woods toward the southern mountains.

Jovai could not struggle. She felt aware of a vague fear that could have belonged to someone else. It didn't seem to be her own. The spirits watched as the strangers carried her away. She still felt their love and support, but not one interfered to save her.

Then the darkness came crashing down on her like an angry, meaningless shout. She felt herself engulfed in a wave of inexplicable hunger. It was more than hunger. It was a craving, a constant, endless pain. She felt it all around her. The air had grown thick with it and was crushing her, pressing in on her as though trying to eat her alive. She could not think. She could barely breathe. Finally, she passed out altogether.

Chapter 23

Killing Games

Darkness. Jovai could not open her eyes. She could not feel her body. Not at first. Voices in a language she had never heard rustled in her head and slowly took form in a space outside of her, at a distance. She remembered the ghost boy and shivered.

Gradually, feeling in her body returned. She felt a stiffness as if every muscle and joint were carved from wood. She tried to open her eyes. The struggle was great, but she managed to lift her lids half way. Blurriness around her slowly took the form of the Gicok sitting in the last light of day against a tall pole that supported some kind of large tent. He was watching her, his eyes dull and unnaturally still. Jovai tried to speak, but it was a while before her tongue and jaw obeyed her enough to form words. Meanwhile, the Gicok watched.

"Wh... what's... what's hap...pen...ing?" she finally managed to ask.

The Gicok continued to stare at her, so stilly she wondered if he were dead. Then, stiffly, he jerked his head away. Whatever had been used on her had been used on him as well, she realized. She sat quietly and waited. The wait was so long she thought he would not answer the question, then slowly, he started to speak.

"I take you to the... my people. See if you liar... thief. They... they all... dead... or... Now we... Kolvas... Kolvas kill us... eat us."

Jovai stared at him confused, not understanding.

"Who killed Gicoks?" she asked, her words still a struggle, but clearer now.

"Kolvas not kill like that before," he answered slowly. "Not hunt people like that before." Then he fell silent and would speak no more. She heard his stifled sobs when night's shadows had hidden his face from her. He had a family to grieve for, a whole people even. She did not intrude.

Through the night they waited. The Gicok finally slept. Jovai listened, her senses keen enough to hear the murmuring of voices, the sighing of sleepers and sometimes even the crying of a child at a distance and the soft shuffling of bare human feet outside the tent, nearby, on guard. In the corner of her eye, she saw movement, like flickering shadows, soundless. She could not move quickly enough to see them straight.

Sometime late at night, the guard fell asleep. It didn't matter. The prisoners were still partially paralyzed and tightly bound. There was no escape.

Early the next morning five very tall men appeared, of bronze skin and long brown-red hair, some with eyes of green, others blue and others tan. They untied the prisoners from the posts but kept their wrists and ankles bound as they carried them from the tent and through the forest, past the whispering, ghost filled Gicok camp and into a nearby clearing.

The prisoners were dropped at the feet of a man who, in dress and bearing seemed their leader. He was a well-fleshed but muscular man of middle years, draped in hides of the cunning, killer cats and patched with long braids of hair strung with beads and carved bones. His headpiece was enormous, forcing him to balance carefully each step. It was the wood-carved face of a grinning god with real human teeth and green feathers where his hair would have grown. He had four eyes, two on each side, all carved from bone. The man who wore this headdress had painted his face with two more eyes in imitation, but these were modestly darkened. He was seated on a wooden stool with a painted hide draped over it. Slowly he stood as the prisoners were set before him, and addressed the surrounding crowd of his people in a language Jovai had never heard before.

Jovai glanced at the Gicok, to see if he could translate or explain a little. He knelt where they had thrown him, even though the poison they had been subdued with had now worn off. His head was bowed in an attitude of defeat, accepting of his doom.

The crowd screamed wildly as their leader finished his speech. At his direction, the five men who had carried them before now picked them up again and dragged them to the center of the clearing where a tall pole had been erected. Around the pole swung a thick piece of wood that made two arms, opposite each other, holding two wooden collars, one at each end. They were fashioned to move but only in a very limited way. As one arm circled forward, the other was forced to circle backward to the same degree, and neither arm could move more than half a circle. Into these, Jovai and the Gicok were bound, backs to the pole and the collar fitting tightly around their chests. The collar piece came apart easily without anything inside it, but once the pieces had been put back to hold someone, the only way they could again be opened was by tearing the body of the person it held apart.

Once the collar was in place, the binding ropes were removed, and a sharp, stone long-blade was given to each of them. The Gicok immediately swung it toward the man who had armed him but the man, expecting that, jumped back out of reach quickly enough to avoid the blow. Jovai, on the other hand, immediately set her blade to work on the harness that held her, slowly dulling its edge as she awkwardly tried to saw through the wood. The Gicok's angry attacks moved the arm dangerously, causing her blade to bounce and barely miss slicing her face.

"They give us honorable death," shouted the Gicok to her.

Jovai looked up and saw a man approaching her, a blade of his own in his hands. She readied her weapon and calmed her mind and body as the weapon's master had taught her.

The man swung at her, a blow to decapitate. She tried to duck away, but the Gicok behind her was fighting his own battle and, being the taller of the two, had greater control over the arm. She found herself swinging toward the man's sword instead. The arm ducked just in time, the Gicok having jumped as high as his limited movement allowed, and this alone saved Jovai.

The arm suddenly swung her back toward her enemy. She quickly thrust with her own blade, but the man easily jumped out of her reach.

"That's enough!" she decided. Honorable death or not, she was not ready yet to die. She was not a shaman. She could not call on the spirits and trust that they would come, but her master's training had not left her completely defenseless.

Suddenly, a man behind her screamed. She could not tell if it were the Gicok or not. Her enemy startled and looked up. It was just the break she needed. She flashed her fingers in well-trained patterns in front of his distracted eyes and talked to him softly, in a special tone of voice, in the old language which he would not understand, but his spirit would know.

"Be afraid. Run away. This monster you fight cannot be defeated but will destroy you and all you love."

It was not the evil, will-bending magic but only a gentle suggestion. The arm whipped her away before she could be sure her spell had taken. At least she knew by the arm's movement that the Gicok still lived. The fighter was staring at her with confusion on his face. She readied her weapon and, as the arm swung her back, thrust it at him. As though something had suddenly snapped inside his head, the man started screaming. He dropped his weapon and fled, through the jeering crowd, away into the forest.

Jovai had only hacked away a few more chips from the collar

when another man rushed forward, at a signal from their leader, to take the previous one's place.

She managed to parry his first blow and caught him quickly with her patterning fingers but was pulled away from him before she could finish the spell. He stood, quietly, like a sleepwalker and waited until she could struggle back to finish her task. Then, like one awaking, he shook his head, looked toward her, screamed, and he too ran away.

Another man behind her screamed, not in terror but in death. She could tell by the lightness of the heavy wooden arm that it was not yet the Gicok. She worked quickly at chipping and sawing through the collar. So intent was she, that although she knew another fighter would follow the last, it was not until he brought his blade down like a club, barely missing her as the arm swung her away, that she became aware of him. This man was large, with mighty muscles declaring him a trained fighter. He stared at her challengingly, full of self-assurance.

"You are strong," she told him, in the spirit tongue, "but now you feel the thrill of fear for such a monster as this before you, is for the gods only to conquer. The greatest of men, before it, is helpless."

He laughed bravely, not understanding her words, yet feeling them. She saw him tremble, in spite of himself, but he readied his sword for another blow.

She prepared to parry and whispered again, "Run fool. If anyone loves you, if anyone needs you, for their sake and for your people who value such a brave, strong man, run."

He hesitated in his attack just enough for Jovai to strongly counter as the weapons master had taught. The man's grip, already weakened with uncertainty, gave way and his weapon fell harmlessly at her feet. He turned and ran.

She was almost through the collar, going slower now for fear of wounding herself, when two more men rushed upon her. They were nervous, sweating already. They knew she must be some kind of monster even before she suggested it. She spelled one easily and the other, seeing his partner suddenly stupefied, turned and ran before it could happen to him. His partner followed on his heels, in terror of the monster his own imagination had created in Jovai's place.

Four more men came toward her, though all of them held themselves back, out of her reach, too distant for them to attack her.

"*Agganna! Agganna!*" their leader shouted at them.

They looked at him, and amongst themselves and tentatively started forward. Jovai stopped her sawing and quickly looked up. She kept assurance shining from her eyes, although in her heart she despaired of spelling so many at once. The men, seeing her eyes focus on them, pulled back again. One needed no more to impel him to run away. Another followed with a feint of anger at his cowardly fellow. The other two yelled furiously at the two who had already disappeared, but they kept their distance and would not approach.

With a loud crack, Jovai managed to break off enough of the weakened collar to allow her to slip through. She grabbed a fresh blade from the few at her feet and started toward the two men who now yelled frantically at the crowd behind them. The crowd backed away, leaving them to face her alone. They trembled before her. The braver of the two approached her warily, sweat pouring down his face. Halfheartedly, almost apologetically he swung at her. She easily disarmed him and freed him to run away. The last man, seeing his only remaining ally flee, quickly followed.

"*Gicoook*" she heard the Gicok yell. It was the famous war cry that had earned them their name to her people, but he sounded it weakly. The wooden arm, without her weight balancing it, was a heavy burden for a battle-wearied warrior. Jovai rushed to aid him and found him bleeding badly, one man dead at his feet, another wounded, being carried away by women, and a third fighter readying his attack.

"Use your blade to break free as I have done" she instructed the Gicok. "I will hold this man off."

"Vohee not fight for piss!" shouted the Gicok.

"Then why could you never defeat us?" she challenged angrily, but her eyes were on the fighter.

He circled her warily, obviously nervous. He seemed not to want to fight her, but as he tried to move around her, she blocked him.

"*Gohennis fackist veb*," he said quickly, in what sounded like the Gicok language, pointing toward the Gicok.

"You will suffer at this monster's wrath, and all you love shall perish before you touch that man," she told him softly in the spirit's tongue.

He backed away, uncertain, her fingers dancing before his eyes, her voice soft, seductive in his ear.

"*Gohennis fackist veb*," he tried to insist.

Jovai raised her blade. The man before her quailed.

Behind him rose another, a boy on the edge of manhood. He held no blade but only a long wooden tube, like a whistle or a music pipe, which he aimed at Jovai. With one, quick blast of breath, a quill came flying out of it. She ducked, and it flew past, disappearing from sight.

"Keep your people from hurting this monster," she warned the fighter who still trembled before her, "or the wrath of its kind and all the spirits shall be visited upon you all."

The man stared at her in horror. His mind did not understand her words, but his spirit knew what he must do. He turned to his people, yelling frantically, issuing warnings of vile destruction if they did not let the prisoners free. The people started screaming. Mothers grabbed their children and scattered in no direction but just away.

At first angrily, then soothingly, then desperately, their leader shouted to them, but their terror resisted any order he could issue. Had they not seen their bravest and strongest warriors run in fright from this slip of a boy? Had they not heard the words of one who, with all the certainty of a true prophet, warned them of their doom? What could their leader possibly do to assuage their fears?

Meanwhile, Jovai frantically helped saw at the wooden collar around the Gicok until it was thin enough that both of them together could break him free. He tumbled to the ground, weak from exhaustion and loss of blood. A deep gash on the side of his head looked as if it might have cracked his skull. He had taken several blows to his legs, and one of his arms hung limply by his side. He shook his head like one who was dizzy, and when he tried to stand, he swayed.

"Lean on me," Jovai ordered, slipping her shoulder under his and pulling his weight onto her. He was very heavy and staggered still, even with her support.

"Vohee..." he struggled to say something, but his breath came weakly.

"Don't talk," she ordered. "Save your breath for walking."

"My people..." he whispered.

"Keep quiet Gicok," she answered, angrily.

He nodded slightly and, to Jovai's surprise, obeyed.

Their pace was slow, hobbled by the Gicok's weakness, but Jovai maintained a dignified air, still playing the all-powerful monster who need fear no one. People ran from them screaming, leaving their path free.

They had almost reached the forest, out of sight of the Kolvas, when a man suddenly stepped forward, appearing from nowhere. It was the Kolvas Leader, the man beneath the headdress which now no longer crowned him. He stood, glaring at them, blocking their path.

"For your people's sake, let us go," Jovai ordered him softly in the spirit's tongue.

"Such tricks do not work on me witch-boy," he answered her disdainfully, also in the spirit's tongue.

Chapter 24

Night of Terror

Jovai stared up at the leader, shocked. He laughed at her surprise.

"Shaman, you have no reason to keep us," she told him. "I mean you no harm, and this Gicok is too weak to avenge his people. Let us go peacefully on our way."

"We are at war with the Akarians," he answered her. "We have sworn to kill every one of them we can before we die."

"That means nothing to me. I do not know the Akarians."

"You lie!" he accused. He murmured softly under his breath and brought his arms from his side stiffly even with his chest.

The ground beneath Jovai and the Gicok suddenly grew soft. She scrambled to move away, but it had hold of her feet and, with strong suction, pulled her and the Gicok down into the earth, up to their chests.

"He demon man!" screamed the Gicok in the traders' language. He struggled frantically to swim out of the pool of earth, but no matter how he flailed his arms, there was nothing solid to grab. His struggles only sunk him deeper into the quicksand.

"Be still!" Jovai begged him, but his struggles continued.

"You speak Akarian," shouted the shaman accusingly. "He wears their clothes, and your horses carry their supplies. How can you deny you are Akarian?!"

"I speak the language of traders who stole me from my people," she answered. "This man was a slave among them who helped me escape."

"His kind are no slaves. They serve the evil ones gladly."

"I do not know the general truth of what you say except that this man escaped them with me."

"How can I believe you?" demanded the shaman.

"We speak the spirit's tongue," Jovai reminded him. "What lie could be sustained in such a holy language?"

"But he does not speak it," said the priest, pointing at the still flailing Gicok.

Jovai turned to him thoughtfully.

"Gicok, save your strength. We must use our heads now, not our arms."

"Demon man kill us!"

"Since when have the great warrior Gicoks feared death?"

"Not death, Demon-death. They eat us. Steal our spirits."

"Gicok, listen. I need to know what you are to the Akarians."

"It does not matter now," he said angrily.

"It does. Were you their slave, or did you help them willingly?"

"My people have peace-pact with Akarians. We allies. We share horses and guides for Akarian things and Akarian protection. We traders now, not warriors."

"You traded your horses, your power?" Jovai stared at him shocked. She had assumed the Gicoks had been conquered and taken as slaves. It never occurred to her that they would willingly give up their horses.

"Akarians very strong. They protect. Give many treasures, other power."

"Do you know why the Kolvas hate the Akarians?"

"Kolvas evil...savages...worship evil gods...they kill people and

180

eat them. It give them evil power. Akarians protect us from them."

"How? How do Akarians protect people from the Kolvas?"

"They battle Kolvas. Take many prisoners. Will conquer Kolvas soon and kill them all."

Jovai looked back at the shaman who was observing their exchange curiously.

"Shaman, what must we do to earn your friendship?"

"Witch-boy, you have frightened my people. You must let them vent their fear and anger on you freely. You must say nothing and do nothing — only die."

The image of the Gicok boy her people had tortured flashed into Jovai's mind. He was asking the same of her.

"If I do this, I will earn your friendship?"

The shaman nodded.

"As proof of your friendship will you agree to heal this Gicok, give him back his horses and supplies and let him free?"

"Why should we heal our enemy?" demanded the shaman.

"I am in his debt for my escape. Honor forbids me to seek your friendship if it means denying this debt. Also, two, maybe three Akarians are dead, so we could be free. Is that not worth the life of only one whom you consider an enemy?"

The shaman nodded slowly.

"I will allow this, if you die bravely and if he will leave us and cause no harm to us."

The Kolvas were probably going to kill them anyway. It might mean a more painful death for her, but at least this way her death could serve some purpose.

"Kill me then," she agreed.

She tried to speak bravely, but her voice shook and, beneath the watery earth, her heart was pounding with such a force it threatened to burst through her chest. She was a nothing, or worse, a witch. She had no place, no family, no people. There was nothing to live for. Even so, she didn't want to die, not yet. She didn't want to suffer...Jovai forced her hand slowly through the quicksand to touch the place on her tunic under which her bag of treasures was held. Somehow it seemed warm, as if the bag were glowing. She could see the star-bone in her mind shining as the Gicok warrior handed it to her. He had been sharing his destiny, perhaps more than he knew. She smiled, drawing comfort from his example. If he could be brave, so could she.

"Gicok," she said, turning to the frightened man, "I have made a deal with these people..."

"No deal with Kolvas! They evil! They not trust."

"We are not in a good position to argue..."

"How you talk to demon man, anyway?" he demanded, suspiciously. "How you know language?"

"He knows my language."

"He evil, Vohee. This one, demon man."

"He has agreed to heal your wounds, give you back the horses and supplies and set you free."

"What I give him?" demanded the Gicok, frowning.

"Just leave them alone, Gicok. Do what they tell you to while you're here and don't interfere with them."

"They kill my people!"

"This is not the time to avenge them. You may do as I tell you, Gicok, or you may die now."

He looked mistrustfully toward the demon man, then back in Jovai's direction, his eyes flickering furiously. With a deep frown to register his misgivings, he nodded his agreement.

"I am ready to submit to your people," Jovai told the shaman. Her voice shook slightly as she said it. She hoped he did not hear.

"Then push the White One away from you," he instructed.

Jovai obeyed, pushing the Gicok as far away as her arms could reach. He did not resist but only watched her, confused. As soon as he was well away, the shaman once again raised both his arms to his chest. Then, with a few murmured words, he lowered the arm that faced the Gicok back down to his side. As he did so, the earth pushed the Gicok back to its surface and hardened underneath him, leaving him standing, shakily, with caking mud all over his body.

The shaman then turned to Jovai and the arm that faced her slowly raised. She felt herself sinking deeper into the quicksand until it was just under her chin. Then the shaman fisted his hand and the quicksand turned to solid earth. She was trapped so tightly she could hardly breathe.

"You see, he lie!" exclaimed the Gicok, rushing angrily toward the shaman.

"Be still Gicok!" yelled Jovai, but he did not heed her. He rushed to topple the shaman and found the man suddenly not there. He had vanished as quickly as he had appeared.

"Demon man!" yelled the Gicok angrily. He turned back to Jovai and began pounding and scratching at the now solid ground around her, trying to dig her free. As hard as he tried, the ground would not loosen. Jovai let him struggle until the last of his energy gave and he collapsed, panting, on the ground next to her.

"This spirit man has not lied," she told him. "Not yet. He has agreed to heal you and let you go. If you don't trust him, then leave now while no one can stop you."

"And Dolkati Friend?" demanded the Gicok.

"I stay."

"They kill you?"

"They could easily have killed us both. It is generous of them to let you go."

The Gicok shook his head and struggled to rise.

"I not let them kill you," He declared. "They eat you. Steal your spirit. I not be dishonored."

"Why do you care, Gicok? I'm only a 'Vohee.' You don't even like me."

"I like you O.K., Vohee. You ride horse like bulky sack but you not so stupid otherwise. You Dolkati Friend. I believe you not steal. You earn."

"You cannot help me, Gicok. If you do not get healing, you will die yourself. Just don't fight them — at least not until you have a chance of winning."

Through the woods came the sound of the footsteps of several men. Jovai's heart leapt with fear as the shaman and two warriors stepped around to where she could see them. She forced a small smile for greeting. The shaman watched her closely.

"We have come to take the White One for healing," he told her.

He motioned for the two warriors to take the Gicok.

"No!" yelled the Gicok, pulling away. The shaman frowned and looked toward Jovai.

"They are taking you to heal you," Jovai told him as the warriors again tried to grab him. Again the Gicok pulled away.

"Wait," he said. "Talk to demon man for me. Tell him I make deal."

"The deal is made. What more could you want?"

"Tell him, Vohee!"

She spoke to the shaman, delivering the message.

"What deal will he make?" asked the shaman.

"He will listen to you," she told the Gicok. "What do you want?"

"Tell him I trade places with you."

Jovai glanced at him surprised.

"Tell him, Vohee," growled the Gicok, "or I kill you, myself, so they not steal your spirit."

"Don't interfere!" she ordered.

"You fight me about it?" he jeered.

"What does he want?" demanded the shaman.

"He offers to trade places with me."

The shaman turned thoughtfully to the Gicok.

184

"Does he know you are to die?" he asked.

"He expects you to kill me and steal my spirit."

"Tell him his bravery is admired but that we do not accept."

The Gicok's face darkened angrily as Jovai translated for the shaman.

"Tell demon man he dishonored killing boy," he insisted. "I am warrior. I am man."

Jovai reluctantly translated.

"My people want the witch-boy. The warrior is uninteresting," answered the shaman.

The Gicok saw the answer in the shaman's face. Before Jovai could speak, he had grabbed a heavy stone from the ground nearby in one hand and Jovai's head in the other.

"I give you better death!" he shouted, holding the stone ready to bash her skull.

Then suddenly the stone slipped from his grip to fall harmlessly to the ground. His arm dropped, and the Gicok fell face downward next to Jovai's head, several darts stuck in his back.

"Did you kill him?" asked Jovai, horrified.

"He's sleeping," answered the shaman as the warriors lifted the Gicok between them. "We can heal him better if he doesn't fight."

He signaled the warriors, and they carried the Gicok away.

The shaman glanced back once, over his shoulder as he left. Jovai heard his soft voice floating back toward her.

"Soon," he said. "Your death will begin soon."

Jovai waited through that day, heart leaping at every sound. Every twig snapping or tree rustling behind her made her want to scream. Through the ground that encased her worms wiggled by. She could not escape their slimy tickling against her skin. It led her imagination to burrowing snakes or animals that could feast on her helpless body.

Above ground, small animals scurried past, sometimes shy of her, often taking no notice. Ants and flies only bothered her, attracted perhaps by the scent of her sweat. The flies buzzed around in slowly increasing numbers, and a few ants explored annoyingly through her hair and over her face. She could not raise a hand to brush them away.

The shaman did not return until dusk, and when he came, he was alone. He stood before her, smiling, then pulled from his robes a flask with strange designs of skulls and glowing eyes around a bat painted on it. When he opened the flask, a stench flowed forth from it like the smell of rancid fat. He poured a little of the contents into his hand. It was a dark yellow powder. He mixed it with some liquid from another flask and turned it into a paste.

"When did you eat last?" he asked Jovai.

"The morning of the day you took us," she answered.

"Good."

He knelt before her and gently smeared the paste onto her face, around her eyes and a little down her cheeks. She did not resist.

"From now on, say nothing," he ordered as he finished painting her. "One word or sound and the White One dies."

He poured more powder into his hands and dropped it carefully in a circle pattern around her, singing softly as he did so.

In the gathering shadows, she could not see the design he drew, but she could feel its power. He was making her a focus of some strong energy. She felt the pressure build within the circle he had defined for her. She felt the heat rise against the cool of night and her blood pound in her ears.

The dark was complete, and the air thickening with mist, before the people of the shaman started to come. She could not see them through the shadows. She could barely hear them through the beating in her head, but she knew they were there. She could feel the growing presence of people, and also of spirits — some she knew, many she did not.

186

Cautiously, silently, she reached forth with all her senses to find any friend among them. All that was there was hostility and hatred aimed at her. They were eager to hurt her. They rejoiced at her death.

The shaman's song finished and left silence clinging heavily in the air. Everyone waited, people and spirits. The shaman moved away behind her. The people gathered around, outside of the circle, watching him intently. At some sign Jovai could not see, the silence suddenly exploded with frightful screams, and the crowd fell into a frenzy. They jumped up and around, brandishing weapons, screaming words at her, which she could not understand, yet they did not break the painted circle. They moved briskly around it, their steps falling into rhythm and the rhythm forming a dance, the dance somehow increasing their hatred and focusing it on her. She expected to feel the prick of darts in her skull, or the blow of a club, at every moment, and every moment brought both relief and greater anxiety.

Then behind her someone broke the circle. She could feel the presence in her space as tangibly as though it were a blow to her bones. The presence felt huge, monstrous. It could not be human. Somehow it seemed too grotesque. It circled around in front of her, but so close that even as she stretched her neck to look up at it, she could see no higher than his knees. A sudden stream of warm urine gushed onto her forehead and flowed down her face. She stifled a scream of surprise and closed her eyes.

When the man was done, he left, behind her where he had entered, and another person invaded her circle. This one was a woman who had brought a brush of leaves and thorns to prick up the dust and wave it deftly into Jovai's face as she screamed in a hideously shrill voice things Jovai could not understand.

She was followed by spitters and shitters, people who kicked earth at Jovai, others who pounded their weapons a hair's breath from her head, but none touched her directly. Jovai bowed her head and waited patiently for the blows she knew would soon come.

"You're going to die," a voice sounded, clear and loud within her head. She was not sure if it were a spirit or her own, frightened imagination. "All Yaku Shaman's work and this is the end of it. What a pitiful disappointment for such a great shaman."

She kept her silence even in her thoughts and did not answer.

"A less than worthless life," shouted another voice, not exactly inside her head, but not precisely outside of it either. "You have done nothing but make everyone hate you."

"No people stand with you, witch," screamed another voice. "They cast you out. They would be happy to know you were dead."

"Your own parents are ashamed of you..."

"Your leaders hate you..."

"Your people fear the evil that is in you..."

"You must die, witch. It will be the only good thing you've ever done..."

Jovai wanted to scream. She wanted to cry. She wanted to make the voices be silent and to tell them...but she could not think what she might say. Her head was pounding. The earth felt as though it were crushing her body. The people were screaming and banging weapons in a horrible cacophony all around her. They were throwing things at her, fouling her, and soon they would be killing her, or worse.

"Traitor! This is what a traitor deserves."

"The spirits have always hated you. They tricked you to make you suffer. They gave you to the slavers..."

"They gave you to the demon!"

"They gave you to the witch's death. You will never join your ancestors now."

Jovai bit her tongue to keep it still. So hard did she bite, that blood spurted into her mouth. She had to keep silent, although she couldn't remember why. She simply clung to her silence as though it were the last branch stopping her from falling to her death.

A dart shot so close to her that it scratched her cheek. It was followed by a long blade that took just a single layer of skin from the tip of her nose. Jovai wished with all her heart that it had struck her full through the skull and ended her torture.

Her heart was beating faster and faster. It beat with a soft, breathy sound like leather wings on the wind. A shrill sound, like a bell but so high-pitched as to be barely audible, pierced her mind. Shadows fluttered around her strangely like little spirits, dark and evil. Something swooshed past her ear. It was not a blade this time or a club or a stone, but something warm and living. She dared not look up to see.

"Can you be proud in death, looking like a dung heap, shit tangled in that hair that made you almost a girl?"

"Now you are uglier than ever."

"No man could ever have wanted you as wife."

"Your master was always ashamed of you. You were never what he wanted you to be."

"You are not good enough."

"All you've ever done was submit to those who wished you ill."

"You are helpless."

"They are taking more than your life. They are stealing your sanity and your spirit. If you were a shaman you would fight."

"But there is nothing in you to fight for."

"There is nothing about you worth keeping."

All her fears, all her doubts, all the darkness that was in her was engulfing her, beating at her, destroying her. She wanted to strike out at the voices with her fists and kill them all. Her body, cased in stone-hard dirt, refused to move. Her only weapon was her voice. She could scream at them. Scream and silence them or drown them out with her own cries...

Or submit. Let the voices cry what they would. Through silence she would face them, hear them, accept them. Through silence she would prove her courage. Her life had been meaningless. Silently she would let it go. If it was all she ever had, she would make her death something to be proud of.

The mist around her lightened gradually until the noonday sun finally burned it away. People still crowded around her, sometimes more and sometimes less as people came and went. Intruders in her circle were coming at her now in threes and fours. The stench of the piles of waste that surrounded her caused her eyes to burn and made every breath a misery. Heat beat down mercilessly upon her dark hair and painted skin, and the flies swarmed buzzing around her. Her jaw grew sore from being clenched tightly for so long, but it was locked into place, and Jovai could not have opened it now without much pain. She waited silently, with no hope left but that the anger of these people would soon exhaust itself so they could finally kill her and be done.

Still, they continued, on and on. People would stop and eat, watching as the others continued. Some napped against nearby trees. No one wanted to miss the spectacle, but their energy was gradually dying. By the time dusk had come again, only a hardy handful remained to torment her.

As the sun set, Jovai once again became aware of the shaman singing behind her. The last of the revelers finished their business and stepped respectfully away. Around her, the wind swirled, kicking up dust and flying away the last of the powder drawn designs. The earth softened its hold on her limbs and slowly squeezed her out, back to the surface. Her legs by this time were too weak to hold her. Hunger and exhaustion stole the last of her strength, but she forced herself to sit, surrounded by piles of stinking feces, and waited for what they would do with her now.

People were gathering their things and walking away, back toward their camp. She watched them, waiting for someone to grab her too. No one did. Dazedly she wondered if she should follow, but she dared not break her silence to ask the shaman. She turned to look at him, hoping he would give her some clue and saw that he, too, was walking away.

Soon she was completely alone, unguarded, unwatched. They had not killed her yet. If she wanted to escape, she could easily do so now. They would kill the Gicok, of course...but he had wanted to die, after all. All his family, his people, were dead. It was natural that he should want to follow. Yet, even as she thought this, she cringed in shame. She was still in the Gicok's debt. If he wanted to die, that was his choice. She could not make it for him. It was she who had offered herself to the Kolvas. She would wait patiently until they finished their business.

It was nearly dawn before the shaman returned. Exhaustion had overtaken Jovai, and she was deeply asleep, only a little away on a cleaner spot than where he had left her.

She awoke as the shaman lifted her in his arms. Half asleep she smiled up at him, dreaming it was her master, but he smiled back at her, and she knew it was not.

The shaman carried her to where a large cask of water was waiting. He set her down on a soft patch of earth at the roots of a great oak and pulled a blade from his clothes.

Jovai tensed when she saw it. She clenched her jaw and waited in silence for the death blow, her mind frantically wondering whether he would cut her throat or plunge it into her chest. It seemed, somehow, important to know.

The shaman watched her, a strange glint in his eyes. She might have thought him merry had he not been a shaman. He grabbed the collar of her tunic and pulled it away from her throat and lifted the blade high above her.

With sudden swiftness, the blade descended upon her. Her heart thudded. Her body went numb. She heard a horrifying sound like the tearing of thick flesh and expected death to follow. It did not.

She looked up at the shaman, who stared at her curiously, then down at her clothes. He had cut through her leather tunic so deftly that not a scratch marred the skin beneath. Two little breasts peeked shyly from beneath the hanging folds. Jovai frantically grabbed at the torn tunic, but the shaman pulled the leather from her hands and off her shoulders. He brought his blade to task again and cut until the tunic lay in pieces beside her. Then he started on the leggings and even removed her leather boots until, at last, Jovai sat before him, naked.

From the cask, he drew a cup of water and offered it to Jovai. Her eyes lit with hope at this unexpected gift, and she drank it greedily. When she had finished, she handed the cup back. She hoped the shaman would give her more, but did not ask when he did not offer.

Next, he drew forth a bowl of water and, with a wet cloth and a sudsing piece of root, wiped the grime from Jovai's body. His scrubbing was harsh, but no more than the filth required.

Only when she was sufficiently clean did he let her drink again. This time he let her drink her fill.

When she was finished the shaman handed her a white woven cloth to wrap around her waist and white woven vest with white fur designs. They were cut large, for a man, and adequately hid her young woman's figure.

"You looked like a boy, the way you were dressed before, so I brought man's clothes, and came myself instead of sending women."

Jovai blushed and looked away.

"Come," he ordered.

He stepped before her and started back toward the camp. Jovai obediently followed.

Chapter 25

Blood Feast

The camp was just behind the trees. It was formed of many wood and hide tents — obviously made quickly and not intended to be permanent. A larger tent had been erected where the fighting post had been. In fact, the fighting post now served as a central support with its arms raised higher to help lift the cloth and hide ceiling. Smoke rose up through it, filled with delicious scents. The sides, made of many tanned hides sewed together with sinew and pulled tightly around long poles, had door flaps tied open, inviting entrance. It was there that the shaman was leading her.

People watched Jovai as she passed. She looked around shyly, expecting to see hatred burning in their faces, but most were merely curious, and some even smiled. She noticed now, as she had not before, that these people were poorly dressed, their clothes torn and not yet mended as though there had not been time. They were tall, but thin, marks of hunger on their bodies, especially the children. Most went barefoot even though the ground was rocky. A few dogs gamboled in and around the large tent, attracted by the smells of food. They were bony. A boy walked by dragging a travois loaded with foods. Even though he was young, he had to bend low, for the travois had been made for a dog, not a human. She found herself wondering what had happened to the dog.

The shaman paused before the open flap of the tent.

"In here," he told Jovai. "Here we will finish this thing. Here I will release you, and when you are finished, our people will celebrate."

Jovai nodded grimly.

The shaman raised his voice, singing loudly in his language, calling to his people within the tent. As he did so, Jovai heard a scrambling from within, and the noises grew momentarily louder. The shaman paused, then repeated his call. The noises started lessening. He called a third time, then a fourth. By the time the last echo of his last call had faded, all was still in the tent.

They bent low to enter. When Jovai raised her head, she saw the space crowded with people, all of them watching her. In unison, they raised their voices in their strange, rhythmic language. They raised their arms, palms held open, facing her. They brought their arms in, across their breasts, before lowering them.

Jovai followed the shaman to a space cleared for them in the center of the tent. There he had her kneel, head bent, hair pulled forward, so the back of her neck was clear. Once again, he drew his knife. Jovai was almost past caring. She was numbed from exhaustion, confusion, and the aroma of the cooking food enraged her hunger. She only wished that the shaman might finish her quickly and let her die. These people were hungry for their feast. If she was to be the main course, she did not care to keep them waiting.

In spite of herself, she winced as the blade nicked her neck. She felt the stinging heat of her blood welling forth, but the cut was shallow, not meant to kill. Again, the shaman cut, across the first. This time deeper, but not nearly deep enough. Then the shaman knelt beside her, placed his mouth to the cross he had opened in her neck and began to suck. She nearly screamed when she realized — he was drinking her blood. They did not plan to wait until she was dead — they were going to consume her alive!

Her fists clenched against her sides and with all her effort she managed to hold herself still. No wonder the Gicok had been so afraid. Yet he had offered himself in her place. For that, she owed him her silence, that she might buy him his life.

The shaman sucked, pinching at her skin until the blood filled his mouth with three swallows. Jovai's head swam. Even kneeling, it was all she could do to keep from toppling over.

When he had finished, the shaman rubbed a powder in her wound that made it sting terribly.

"The cross will be red," he whispered to her, "and the mark will stay on your body forever."

To his people he turned and spoke as he positioned himself in front of Jovai, kneeling, so his head was equal to hers. Then he turned to face her. He lifted her limp arm and pressed a heavy object into it. It was the stone knife he had used on her, still smeared with her blood.

"We have killed our enemy. We honor your bravery through death by taking your blood into our bodies so you may live on as part of us and our children forever. May it bring us strong life and good hope. Now we wish to welcome the one we would be proud to call "friend." For the life we have taken, we give new life, and since all new life is first fed by the parent's blood, so we shall feed you."

He opened the thick skins of his vest, dropping them to his waist, and pulled away the cords and chains and beaded ornaments, leaving his chest bare to her.

"I offer myself for all my people. Here," he pointed toward his heart. "Our blood flows from here. This is where you cut."

He traced the cuts she should make, one down, one across. She stared at him dumbly, then down at the knife in her hand. It was so heavy — too heavy to lift, even if she could believe what he was asking her to do.

He took her hand with the knife up in both of his and lifted it to his chest. One cut, light, just the skin, the second cut, deeper but easily healed. His blood pumped forward, gathering on his skin. She watched, mesmerized, as it slowly started to trickle toward his wide belly.

"Now drink," he said.

She stared at him, eyes wide, and shook her head in horror.

"Drink," he insisted. "You must."

He cupped his hand behind her head and pulled it, forcing her lips to press against his wound. She tried to squirm away but did not have the strength.

Then she tasted it — warm, salty, thick — and her hunger overwhelmed her. She sucked, greedily devouring this almost-nourishment, until the blood from the small cuts stopped flowing.

The shaman gently pushed her away.

"That was the blood acceptance," he said smiling. "Now you are one of us."

As she wiped at her mouth with the back of her hand, she saw it come away red and sticky. She closed her eyes and shut her breath against the sickness that rose in her.

The shaman spoke again to his people, and the people around her cheered, not now in practiced song, but in wild whelps and cries. The tent became a madhouse of activity as people scrambled away in directions of their own.

"You may speak now," said the shaman, good-naturedly.

"Then you will not kill me?" she asked, still dazed.

Before them, mats had been spread and were being filled with food. She could hardly think for hunger. The shaman did not wait but eagerly grabbed at the pasty contents of the nearest bowl, passing it to Jovai only after he had filled his mouth with enormous portions. She tasted it eagerly. It did not have strong flavor but was delicately scented with herbs that made it pleasant to smell.

"Not again," the shaman answered her question as soon as he was able. "We have made you one of us — our daughter and sister.

Soon, we will decide among the families which of them will be enlarged by you."

"What if no one wants me?"

The shaman laughed.

"Everyone will want you," he said. "Your courage was much admired and your loyalty to your friend — and of course, the entrancement. Vakit, one of the warriors who ran away from you, has already requested you for his family since l told him l would not let you be of the warrior lodge. l know you will do better though. lf he wants you in his family, l think he will have to marry you to one of his brothers."

Jovai blushed deeply.

"Will l have a choice — of family?" she asked.

"Of course. But l will help you since you cannot speak to us yet."

"And who...what may l call you?"

He turned to her astonished, then laughed.

"You know, l can't remember even once in my lifetime that anyone whom l wanted to have my name did not already know it. l am called Difsat, of the Bat Clan, one of several shaman for my people and acting leader for this particular group."

"Are there other groups?"

He nodded, his mouth too full of food to answer with coherent words.

"But why have you split apart?"

He nodded again and forced a quick swallow.

"It is sad business — not good for the digestion," he answered, and stuffed more food in his mouth.

A young and very beautiful woman came by, offering up a bowl filled with chunks of spiced meat. Jovai grabbed at some hungrily, then stopped herself, suddenly remembering the Gicok's fear. She sniffed at the meat but could not identify it through the spices.

"Boshaia," Difsat thanked the woman politely.

She nodded to him, smiling, then stood expectantly before Jovai.

"Boshaia," Jovai said awkwardly.

The woman nodded, but still stared, smiling.

"Gilix awaits the compliment of your expression as you eat it," the shaman explained.

"It...it smells delicious," Jovai said, nervously, "but who...what is it?"

"An aged buck came among us this morning. He slowly walked through the center of camp. Many men tried to kill him, but no arrow or dart could touch him until he came before Gilix. She was sitting to eat her breakfast, but when the buck stopped before her, she set her bowl on the ground and let him eat it instead. People gathered as he ate. When he had done, he raised his head and nodded toward Gilix. Then he turned toward a bowman who was aiming his bow and let himself be shot. As was his wish, Gilix had the honor of preparing him for this feast."

Jovai nodded respectfully to the honored woman and politely tasted the meat as she watched. The juice of the meat came pouring into her mouth, filling her senses with waves of delight. She felt a shiver of pleasure down her spine, and her body tingled with the warmth of the mouthful.

Jovai looked up at Gilix, amazed.

"You are skilled beyond any cook I have known," she exclaimed.

Difsat happily translated. The woman, much pleased, set the bowl down before Jovai, holding eyes with her a little longer than was comfortable. She glanced back once as she left, smiling coyly.

As soon as the woman was out of sight, Difsat burst out laughing. Jovai stared at him, shocked, for she had never seen a shaman laugh.

"I think she likes you," he said when he could catch his breath.

"Then I was not rude?" asked Jovai, confused.

"Oh, you were. You waited much too long to taste her food and you never once smiled at her."

"I don't understand..."

"She thinks it is a brave, young, warrior man whom we are honoring today — someone new, who does not love her yet — has not played for her yet. I think we will let her continue believing that for a while. It will do her good."

"Then you have not told them...?"

"Not yet, and now I won't for a while. Can I trust you to not tell?"

"I will defer to your judgment," Jovai answered. She was not sure what she felt.

"And your friend — the White One?"

She shrugged. "He doesn't even speak the language." She was not sure if he knew her gender. She felt fairly certain that he wouldn't care.

She glanced around for the Gicok but was not surprised to find him absent.

"How is he?" she asked.

"His wounds were not as bad as they looked, no compliment to our warriors, but he is stubborn and won't let us help him. Last night our best healer attended him. This morning we found him collapsed and almost dead near his people's camp. He had torn his bandages off his body, and his wounds were ripped open again and made much worse. It will be all right, however. Our healer is certain that, if he lets us help him, he will soon be well. We'll take you to him as soon as we're finished here."

For all her hunger, Jovai ate slowly and with much restraint, in deference to the obvious time of starvation her hosts had been through. Difsat, however, feasted heavily, taking to excesses more food and drink than Jovai had ever witnessed before and eating with such obvious relish that Jovai began to wonder if he really was a shaman or just some half-educated pretender. Others of the Kolvas were eating heartily enough for her to believe that it might be a manner of these people. However none were quite as excessive as

Difsat.

His amazing voracity was checked only by his taste for gossip. He pointed out each person who passed and filled Jovai's ear with stories about the people of whom she was now a member. Through his chatter, she caught a glimpse of a people who had suffered much. He vaguely referred to the wars, the bad years, and mentioned the recent past as when they had been "escaping" but would not be pressed into explaining these allusions. He simply dismissed them saying, over and over, "we do not speak of sad things while we eat."

At last, the feast ended, more because the food was exhausted rather than the appetites. Much drinking still commenced, especially of a fermented berry juice that Jovai found too bitter and burning on the tongue to enjoy, but this activity did not require her presence.

She politely requested to be taken to her Gicok friend and the shaman, too intoxicated to stand, called a couple of boys to guide her.

CHAPTER 26

TENSION BOUND

They led Jovai to a tiny hut in which lay the Gicok stretched out on a thin sleeping mat, arms and legs bound to stakes driven into the earth floor.

He turned his head toward her as Jovai entered and his eyes flickered at her in unconcealed astonishment.

"You not dead?!" he exclaimed.

She shook her head, scanning the clean cloths that wrapped his wounds. Someone had done a good job of bandaging him.

"How are you, Gicok?"

For answer, he pulled his arm against the cords that bound him.

"I tell you not trust them. They lie. They not let me go."

"I asked them to heal you first," she said in defense of the Kolvas as she knelt beside him and untied his knots. "Here. Sit up and eat while I untie your ankles."

She handed him a large bowl of food she had brought for him from the feast.

"I not eat filthy Kolvas food," he said with a contemptuous shove at the proffered bowl.

"It will be filthy if you spill it in the dirt. Otherwise, it's fine. Everything there I have tasted myself. Some of it is very good."

"Man meat," he declared, disgusted, "Man flavor. Dolkati not eat man."

"It's deer," she explained, pointing to Gilix's meat cubes. "And very tasty."

"How you know?"

"They assured me."

"They lie. I killed two fighters — more maybe. That one."

"I would have liked to see you fight," Jovai told him, quickly changing the subject. "The Kolvas were very impressed with your skill."

The Gicok grunted, disdainfully. He obviously did not care what the Kolvas thought.

Jovai separated the vegetables from the meat and handed the bowl back to the Gicok. He ate a little, sniffing at each carrot or turnip suspiciously before he bit it. Meanwhile, Jovai untied his legs.

"It good thing you Dolkati Friend," he said as she worked on his bindings. "I protect you now. We escape together."

"The Kolvas have offered us friendship and acceptance here."

She glanced at his face to gauge his reaction, but his flickering eyes were inscrutable.

"Do not trust Kolvas," he growled softly.

"I earned their friendship. I trust it."

"What did they do to you?" he demanded.

She struggled for words to explain, but words did not come. It was not the foreign language they were using, but her own spirit, still confused, that held her dumb. At last, she gave up.

"I am alive. It is more than was promised and more than I expected. After...after everything...they bathed and fed me and welcomed me — us. They will heal you, or I will, if you prefer. As soon as you are well enough, you will be free to go."

"We go now. Kolvas evil. They kill people — my people. They steal souls. Maybe they steal yours already. Maybe that why you not see them evil."

"Maybe they are not evil."

"They eat man."

She shrugged. "So you tell me. But they won't kill or eat us. We're safe here as long as we choose to stay."

"Kolvas always Dolkati enemy."

"You need healing. I suggest we stay for a while."

"No!"

"Then you go," she said, too tired to argue, "but I'm going to rest here at least a couple of days. I need to heal too."

The Gicok swayed unsteadily to his feet, wincing in pain. When he tried to step, his wounded leg buckled underneath him, tumbling him back to the floor. He pushed himself up again and with great dignity lowered himself back to the mat."

"My people must protect you as long as you Dolkati Friend," he pointed to the medallion which Jovai had kept and hung around her neck. "I will honor it."

"Then you will stay?"

He nodded.

"Until Vohee get smart," He frowned, "But not forever."

Jovai smiled.

"I must thank you, Gicok...I don't know your name — you've never told me."

"Name is personal power. I not tell you. I not ask you yours."

Jovai accepted that with a nod. It was not so different with her people who would not share their real names, except that her people had social names for convenience.

"'Gicok' then. Thank you for freeing me from 'Master.' Thank you for leading me to safety. And thank you for offering your life in place of mine."

He grunted. "You Dolkati Friend," was all he answered.

Later that evening, after she had examined the Gicok's wounds closely and satisfied herself that they were healing well, Jovai was led to a Kolvas council. It was formed largely of women, many of the men were, apparently, too drunk to attend. It was woman's business anyway, they explained to her. It was women who brought new people into their lives. Difsat attended as her interpreter. He was less inebriated than when she had seen him last but still very merry.

"I told you I was the leader of these people," he said with a laugh, "but I lied. This one," he gestured to the round-faced, squat little woman sitting beside him, frowning at him, "my wife. She runs us all."

Jovai looked between the couple, confused.

"You are a shaman?" she asked.

"Of course. First requirement for a leader, be a shaman or be married to one," he doubled over laughing.

Jovai nodded respectfully to the woman. The woman smiled back at her, her face suddenly aglow with good-natured wrinkles and kind eyes.

The lady said something to her husband who stared at her a moment before he burst out laughing with renewed merriment.

"Milapo wants me to welcome you, as a brave warrior, to our council and explain that I am too drunk to be of any use, but I am the only one who speaks to you, so I must stay all the same."

Milapo spoke again. Difsat made a rude snort of unsuppressed laughter and continued his translation.

"She wishes to congratulate you on your sobriety, but hopes you will feel at ease with us in time."

They made a place for Jovai to sit between Difsat and an old woman who nodded sleepily in the warmth of the fire.

"Now she says...and she will keep me busy for she speaks a lot... she says you must have many questions about us. She plans to tell you everything without reservation. We are curious about you, too, but you must not feel pressured to tell us anything you don't want. Only, because of the trial we put you through, any shame or dishonor you've accrued is considered as belonging to the dead now and no longer a part of you."

He smiled broadly at her, his eyes glittering with delight.

"Tell them nothing," he advised. "It'll drive the old gossips crazy!"

In spite of herself, Jovai laughed. Milapo frowned and jabbed Difsat sharply in the ribs, her voice suddenly scolding. He responded indignantly and made a show of rising. Milapo pulled him back with the air of disciplining a child and cut their argument short. Then she turned to Jovai and commenced speaking.

She introduced the others in the council, all but one old woman who sat silently in the shadows away from the group watching. Then she began their story.

Although Milapo spoke solemnly, Difsat interpreted with a livelier air that suddenly reminded Jovai of her father's stories when she was small. He did not bring them alive with wild gestures and many voices, but she did suspect there was some exaggeration in his narrative.

She learned of the creation of the Kolvas and their basic history which was so similar to her people's that it seemed certain they were related in the distant past. When the ice that destroyed the Fourth World came, the people retreated underground. They built great cities and tunnels to connect them and learned to live in the womb of the earth. But after many generations, strange dreams began disturbing the sleep of many — dreams of a green ground beneath their feet, warmed and lit with a shining star.

Then the Great One emerged from the darkness — the void that is the origin of everything. He took human form and walked among the people. He talked to them about their dreams and inspired them to trust what seemed too wonderful to believe. The New World under a new sun was ready for them. It was time to climb toward light.

Many people rejoiced, but many more scoffed at the Great Spirit. People gathered to follow him, and others came to prevent them. A battle was fought, and the old world was destroyed.

Many died, staining large areas of the Earth red with their blood. The stones still shaped the faces and the deeds of the warriors of this battle. Nevertheless, many people escaped, all in small groups, through different tunnels leading different places. The Great Spirit sent different spirits to lead each group to their waiting world.

The Kolvas were led by the spirit of the bat through the deepest tunnels and even through the World of the Dead. They had to swim through the river of blood that fed the dead in the darkest plains. Only the wisest and best among them survived to find the surface of the living world again.

When they emerged, it was a moonless night, and a sorrow struck their hearts to find this world almost as dark as the other, but the bat promised them light, though he, himself, could not endure sun. When the sun rose, the people rejoiced until they saw their faithful guide fall dead at their feet. They mourned the bat and hung him, as was their custom at the time, from the nearest tree. All day they sung their loss to the Great Bat Spirit. They mourned and cried and tore their hair.

Then the sun sank, and the moon arose, and the bat stretched its wings and came alive again. He told them never to mourn for him, for even though he died each day, in every night, he would find new life.

The Kolvas grew in numbers and in strength through the years. Many spirits guided them and taught them their wisdom. Several times, groups of their people split apart, but those who remained became a great city, sure in its strength and proud of its beauty. They warred with very few, only the White Ones and, from time to time, some others. They always won, and their confidence grew.

When the Akarians first appeared, they came as traders with feathers, fabrics, foods, herbs and even tools never seen before and greatly prized. That was only seven years ago. They were graciously welcomed. The Kolvas eagerly made trading treaties, much pleased with the wealth they were offered. For three years the friendship grew until it seemed a natural thing to cement it with a joining of the peoples.

The Kolvas had a daughter of marriageable age, Faiel, a special person of considerable beauty and skill at weaving. The Emperor of the Akarians was a man with over two hundred wives and five sons of marriageable age who would be considered for emperor after him. The Kolvas woman was offered to the emperor for himself or his favorite son and the emperor gladly accepted.

The woman was sent ahead, and her family followed two weeks behind to attend the wedding. When they arrived, they were greeted royally and escorted to the temple, the center of the Akarian capital. In the open space before the temple a play honoring their god, Gorat, was performed. The Emperor's eldest son, the high priest, played the young woman sacrifice. His costume was the flayed skin of the Kolvas woman.

Her people, horrified and outraged, turned against the Akarians. Several men of great warrior skill fought to kill the Emperor, but were slain before they could succeed. Some others fled but only one, with the help of a kindly trader, ever managed to escape. That one was the woman's great-grandmother and a shaman of almost mythic power.

Alone she managed to return to her people and tell them all that happened. As she recounted her story, her heart broke, and with her dying breath, she begged her people to avenge this terrible wrong. The promise was made and sealed with the shaman's blood. The people mourned and armed for war, but the Akarians struck first.

They maintained that their god had been wronged by the Kolvas' incivility, that their crops were failing because of it and only Kolvas' blood sacrifice would appease their god. They came against the Kolvas with a mighty army which the Kolvas turned away, but they lost many brave warriors in the effort. The Akarians came again and again. Again and again, they lost, but each time the Kolvas were sorely weakened. Still, the Akarians came. They seemed to rise from the very blood of their slain warriors, three for every one that died. Their numbers were inexhaustible, and at last, they conquered the Kolvas.

They tore down the Kolvas' temples and statues — every sign of their spirits — and replaced them with the image of their own ugly gods. They took many prisoners, even children, and killed those too old to be of use in the fields or to survive the journey back to their empire. They killed all the shaman-trained that they could identify and many who were wrongly suspected. They killed the leaders who would not bow to them and took their sons away and married their daughters to their own people who came and settled in the Kolvas lands.

The Kolvas war king, who was not a shaman-trained but so particularly skilled that he was as highly honored, was taken as the highest leader of the Kolvas. He loyally named, as his sons, the sons of the Kolvas' shaman leader, to be protected in their place, and let several of his own children be taken captive as common people. The Akarians came and ruled with bloody hands. Any voice against them was quickly silenced. The people who still could, were forced to pay tribute to them regularly, others were used as slave labor, and any who seemed at all unreliable were sent to the empire.

"We lived through death once," Milapo explained through Difsat. "We remembered the bat and knew that we could die and live again. We let them kill us — became as nothing but breathing dead by day, and at night we made our plans. We took only what we could carry easily and run — food so we would not need to stop to hunt or gather and the few horses and dogs we could steal. We divided ourselves, and in the darkness of a moonless night we rose together and left the place of our birth, of our lives, to go, each group a different way.

Families are broken, and friends may never see each other again, but the Akarians could not catch us all and some of each family, each clan, will carry on to a new life."

She paused, tears in her eyes. Even Difsat now seemed sad — his laughing eyes distant in unhappy memory.

"The Akarians followed us but not with horses. They would rest at night, but we did not. They did not know the way of the desert as we did. We could get farther in the cool of the night than they could in the heat of the day. When they seemed to draw nearer we pressed on faster, by day and night, until they fell too far behind to hope to catch us. It has been almost a season, and we have not seen or heard any sign of those who chased us. We are hoping now that it is safe to rest and we have come to where we were told to wait."

"Here?" asked Jovai, amazed.

Difsat nodded.

"Kital, the greatest shaman who survived the massacre, dreamed of a place where the sun was not seen until noon. At such a place we were to blow a dart toward the eastern sky, where the morning sun would be breaking the horizon if we could see it, and food would fall at our feet. For four mornings we have done this, ever since we arrived. The first time a honeycomb fell full of honey but no bees. The second time we received a bird of brilliant feather and plump flesh. Yesterday a strange fruit fell and all who tasted it felt happy and full. One who was lame walked and a child, near death with hunger, rose laughing and played with the others. This morning, a bat fell, clutching more of that same fruit. We mourned the bat and hung him from the nearest tree, his fruit on the ground below, and in the evening, he rose again and flew away, and the fruit had multiplied and surrounded the tree, and some had even sprouted. Now we are sure we are home, and the spirits will provide for us here."

Milapo asked Difsat something. He answered soberly, then let her speak.

"My wife wants you to know that we wait here for the others who survived and for a great one — perhaps Kital herself. We know the spirits will lead them here and it is our task to be ready to welcome them."

"But why...I mean, the Gicok camp...it is very close isn't it?"

Difsat nodded, and at a jab from his wife translated for her. For once she sat quiet, with nothing to say.

"They are all dead!" exclaimed Jovai. "No one has prepared their bodies. No one has released their spirits. I would not wish to be so near, and I did not even kill them."

"We did not kill them," Difsat answered her implied accusation.

"Then who did?" demanded Jovai.

"We don't know. We did not discover them until we found you there. We thought...we hoped that you would tell us."

Jovai shook her head.

"The Gicok was helping me escape from the Akarians. He was taking me to his people. We had just arrived and found them all dead — his wife and children — everyone. Then you attacked us. It seemed natural to assume you had attacked them too."

Difsat translated for his wife and the others. For a solemn minute, all were quiet, absorbing what he said. Then a woman across from Jovai said something to Milapo, and another added something else, and soon all the women were talking.

Jovai looked to Difsat for translation. He just shook his head.

"They are sorry for your friend and are trying to plan what they can do to ease his grief," He shook his head in mock despair, but a tear was in his eye.

"I love women," he said. "If their husbands were here most of them would say we should be careful of the Gicok taking revenge for his family on us — but our wives...except for Bulih and Trafed and this time, Freni...most of them think only of him as a man in pain and want to help. It will be up to you to protect him from their good

210

intentions — or else he's in big trouble."

"Your people seem to have good hearts," said Jovai.

Difsat nodded.

"We wish to help your friend," Milapo said at last through her husband. "What can we do?"

"I will talk to him and let you know," Jovai promised.

"He will not hurt us will he?" asked Freni next.

"I will tell him what you told me. I don't know if he'll believe me, but he is weak from his injuries now and is only a threat if your people attack him."

"If we are kind to him, perhaps he will trust us."

"He has suffered greatly, especially these last days with you. It might take quite a lot of kindness to convince him that you are not as hostile as you seemed."

"Are you afraid of us?"

Jovai shook her head.

Milapo spoke to the others. Several raised their voices in angry protest — one at a time. Others seemed calmer, more rational.

"You can speak the shaman tongue. It helps you. Does your friend speak any other language besides the Dolkati and the Akarian?" Milapo asked Jovai.

"Not that I know," Jovai answered. "We speak to each other in Akarian."

"We all know a few words. Some of us know the language well, but we have agreed not to speak it since it is the language of our enemy."

"Then you knew what I and the Gicok were saying all along?" asked Jovai of Difsat.

He smiled with charming mischief and continued his translation.

"Perhaps this is cause to speak it, but we cannot decide this now. We will discuss it further among ourselves, and we will have people help you learn our language. Will this help you?"

"It will help me, but the Gicok might not be quick with languages. He does not speak Akarian well. I don't know if he would want to learn another." She shrugged.

"We will offer you both a teacher and let him learn what he would like."

Difsat turned to his wife and said something quickly. The only word Jovai caught was "Gilix." His wife nodded, and others agreed.

Jovai's eyes narrowed suspiciously. Difsat's expression back was full of innocence — too much innocence.

"Now they would like to know what you would like to tell us about yourself — your other life before this one we've given you."

"I am from people who dwell in a valley northeast of here. We call ourselves simply 'the people.' The Gicoks call us 'Vohee.' We have almost no contact with any other people — except the Gicoks who have made war on us almost every year since the oldest of our people can remember. Last year, the Gicoks led strangers — traders to us — hairy, smelly men with dark skins and golden hair. They traded us Gicok horses for metal trinkets and taught me to speak their language. I, in turn, taught some of our people. We are divided, some of us want trade with these strangers, others are afraid because our enemies brought them and because there have been terrible prophecies. My master was against contact with the strangers..."

"Your master was a shaman?" guessed Difsat.

Jovai nodded.

"And you?" he pressed.

Jovai paused, then slowly shook her head.

"What are you then?"

Jovai stopped and faced the uncomfortable silence, not knowing what to say.

"Are you a witch?" he pressed.

Was she? Was she one who twisted nature, misdirected spirits, and abused a gift that was not a shaman power but something dark and evil?

Milapo demanded translation from Difsat, and he gave it, as far as he had gotten.

"I have served my people as faithfully as I could," Jovai said softly, before he could ask any more questions, "as their teacher of the traders' language and also as a healer. But the people would not have me as a shaman and my master would not let me be anything else. It was...a bad business. When I went before the spirits, they did not give me a shaman name, or any name. So I am not a shaman, and I am not anything else."

Difsat finished his translation, then turned to her and spoke gently.

"You should know, the death we put you through, that is also a trial for a shaman sometimes. By our standards, you are a shaman, if you consider yourself so."

"I do not," she answered. Didn't he understand what it meant that she didn't have a name? He had seemed a very powerful shaman — how could he be so ignorant?

She felt his eyes searching her soul and turned away angrily.

"As a healer then," he acquiesced, "we are glad to welcome you."

CHAPTER 27

GHOSTS

The council seemed to have every intention of talking through the night about the various petitions they had already received from families wanting to adopt the new shaman/ warrior, but Jovai was exhausted and soon could not keep awake. One of the women kindly escorted her back to the shelter where the Gicok slept.

As they walked, a small boy, uncommonly pale with still, yellow eyes crossed her path and stopped to stare at her. Jovai nodded, too tired to pay much attention until the boy faded into the evening fog before her eyes.

That stopped her. Suddenly fully alert, she grabbed the arm of the woman beside her.

"Did you see that?" she demanded.

The woman turned to her, uncomprehending.

"There was a boy — a Gicok — a ghost." Jovai tried again, this time in Akarian. "He...he was there and then he vanished!"

The woman frowned at her, perhaps still not understanding. She said something softly in her language, in a tone meant to soothe, and took Jovai's arm to lead her on to where she could rest.

"You must tell your shaman that there are ghosts about," Jovai instructed the woman as she prepared her sleeping mat. "The living are not safe."

The woman ignored her, but hurried to her task and, with a few kind sounding but incomprehensible words, left Jovai to sleep.

"Gicok," called Jovai nervously through the dark. There was no answer except the muffled sounds of a sleeping man.

"The fools," she muttered aloud to herself, as though filling the air with sound would leave less room for ghosts. "What crazy man is this they call their shaman? What fool would let his people lie so close to restless dead?"

She had no ghost bane to shield the door — no herb at all nor paint nor colored sand nor any tool of strength, nor any spirit to call for aid, but she could not rest easily while being completely vulnerable.

She felt the floor until she found one of the spikes to which the Gicok had been tied. With many tugs, she finally managed to pull it from the floor and, wielding it like a knife, she carried it outside and began the tedious task of using it to dig a circle in the stony ground around the hut.

The air around her felt bitter cold and was thick with mist that clutched at her clothes with moist fingers and brushed through her hair. She could not see the other tents, which she knew to be nearby, nor could she hear any living being stir, except the whining of some dogs many huts away, but still she felt watched. Every breeze that sighed through the night roused the tiny hairs on the back of her neck and made her breath catch in fearful anticipation.

At last, the circle was drawn. She knelt at the eastern facing door where the circle had begun and finished, closed her eyes and lifted her voice against the heavy night to seal the simple sign of protection.

As her prayer rose, she felt the power gather through her. She was flush again with the thrill. She felt light, almost dizzy, and happy and safe, like a baby in her mother's arms. The seal was made and would hold as long as no one living crossed it.

When she opened her eyes again, she saw them, all gathered outside her circle, hovering about like moths to a flame. There were so many of them, the whole Gicok village perhaps, and they all watched her, blue, yellow and red eyes uncommonly still. Jovai had never seen so many up close. Tall and beautiful people they were, even though many bore the gashes of their death. The women, especially, were to be envied for the delicate strength of their features that made even the plainest among them worthy of a second look.

"What do you want?" Jovai demanded nervously. She had heard of the trapped dead. She had heard of them in stories told her first by her father, then by the shaman and the storytellers of their village, but never had she seen them or had to deal with them. Her master had taught her, of course, what to do if any of her own people somehow turned ghost, but these were not her people. Their customs were different, maybe even their spirit language. Who they had been and what their needs now were, both were beyond her understanding.

They made no gesture to respond to her question. They did not even seem to have heard it. They did nothing but press around the circle she had drawn and stare at her with still, expressionless eyes.

"I can't help you," she told them. "I don't know you. I don't know what to do. If you tell me, I can tell the shaman and he will help you."

No answer even in the slightest change in their expression.

"Please — go away. Leave me alone!"

She fled into the hut and tightened the door-flap against the chill night full of ghostly faces, but the sky was already lightening before she could at last fall asleep.

The next morning, Difsat awoke her by standing outside the circle at the door and shouting.

"What is this? Come out here. Tell me what you're doing. Do you hear? Wake up and explain this!"

With great effort, she pushed herself up from the sleeping mat and went to the door. The Gicok stirred in his sleep, coming awake and alert. She could feel him watching.

Jovai had to lean heavily against the door post to keep herself standing.

"Are they gone?" she asked the fuzzy forms that stood outside.

"What are you talking about?" demanded Difsat.

She squinted against the brightening morning haze, and slowly his features began to take familiar shape. He was not alone. Several people watched the exchange from behind him, and more were stopping to stare.

"Ghosts," she answered, "from the Gicok camp. They were all around here."

"What do you mean? Here?"

He looked around the ground and shook his head.

"I don't see any signs — no footprints..."

"Ghosts," she repeated. "They just stood outside the circle and stared. I...I ah, I didn't get much sleep."

A big yawn confirmed her statement.

"Well, are you done with the circle, or aren't you?" he demanded angrily.

She looked through the crowd of faces watching her this morning to make certain there were none from the night before. All these faces had burnt red skin and dark red hair — swimmers of the river of blood that separates the land of the dead from the land of the living. No Gicok, living or dead, stood among them.

"Come in Shaman and be welcome," she mumbled.

He crossed the circle, breaking its protection, and followed her back into the shadows.

"The healer was afraid to enter," he chided Jovai peevishly. "We were all wondering if it were us you feared."

"I told the woman last night to warn you of the ghosts. I guess she doesn't speak Akarian well enough to have understood, or else she thought me crazy..."

Difsat cut her off with an angry scowl.

"We do not speak the language of our enemies!"

She stared at him in surprise for a moment, unsure of her understanding.

"But...how else should I have told her? I don't speak your language."

"You will learn."

"But until I do...when there is something important..."

"There is nothing important about ghosts."

"I have heard that ghosts can do terrible things to the living. I have heard that they are jealous of the life they can no longer live and that they try to steal it from others. They are not like the spirits of our ancestors — free to come and go back to the dead lands. Ghosts are those who are trapped, and they grow angrier and more confused and resentful until they are freed."

"What you have heard are stories to scare children."

"I have seen them!"

She looked away, in the direction of the slaughter at the Gicok camp.

"All those people, whose bodies rot with no one of their own to attend them...their spirits are not free to go where they belong."

"I don't care, as long as they don't threaten us — and how can anything threaten us that hasn't enough presence to move dust under its feet?"

"But they suffer!"

"What do we care? They're not our people — they're our enemies. Let them suffer. Let their bodies rot and let their spirits wander forever in pain for what they helped the Akarians do to us. If anything, let us rejoice that we can witness it!"

Jovai turned away, sickened, from the shaman's enraged expression.

Difsat winced in pain at the effort of raising his voice and clasped his hands to his head to mute the echoes that still rang there.

"I am a leader for my people," he continued after a moment, his voice softer, "the only one we have right now and all my time and all my energy devoted to them are not enough to meet their needs."

He rose and gathered his robes to leave.

"We sent the healer for the White One this morning. He was afraid to cross your circle, so he made me come. Will this happen every morning?"

"You may give him my permission to break the circle after sunrise from now on, but this morning I would have welcomed the extra sleep."

"So would I," responded Difsat, coldly.

In the corner, the Gicok stirred. He tried to lift himself up and grunted at the pain that still held him down.

"Why you fight with magic man?" He demanded after Difsat had gone.

"It's nothing. He's sick from last night. The healer will come soon."

"You stupid. Don't let 'healer' come. Don't trust Kolvas — nothing Kolvas say or do. They filthy savages!"

"We have to trust them, for a while at least. You leave now, you die. And I have nowhere else to go."

"We stay here we die — and worse. They eat us, drink blood, steal spirit."

"They could have killed me, and they didn't. They could have killed you, easily enough..."

"Death means nothing to Kolvas. They want more! I tell you, fool Vohee. You know nothing. They tie me down. They force me take evil medicine — make me sleep. Make me dream. My wife's child come to me. *Quanorika co.* Warrior come. He take my hand. He take me to my wife, her baby. All my people, all well. Wife turn to me and smile, and blood fill her face — eat away flesh, burn hair. Only eyes stare — not in Gicok way but like you, like them, like dead. Still Eyes. She reach for me. I turn to run but she where I turn. Something bite my hand — her child. He eat me, like Kolvas. His hand is bone. It rip me. All come now — come to drink blood, eat flesh, like Kolvas. I push him away. My hand go through him while his hands, his teeth rip me. I fear. I run, run into, through family, friends, people. They chase me. When I fall..."

He shuddered. His breathing was rough. It was a moment before he could go on.

"I wake here. Tied up. Kolvas want me eat more medicine. I eat nothing."

Jovai stared at him in horror. The Gicok closed his eyes and lay back his head, as though exhausted in the telling of his story. Then, suddenly, every muscle of his body flexed, and he pushed himself shakily off the sleeping mat.

"I go."

"Where will you go?"

"I piss."

"Then?"

"I go to my people."

"You go to ghosts who will eat you?"

"Better people than enemies."

He pulled himself to standing, his face twisted in pain at the effort.

"Why they let you live?" he demanded.

Jovai shrugged. Her mind felt numb from so much weighing upon it and so little sleep. Ghosts in the night. Ghosts who drink blood and tear flesh. Ghosts to scare children. She didn't want to think about them.

"What they do?" insisted the Gicok. He wouldn't leave her alone.

"I saved your life!" she told him angrily. "Take it or throw it away, but I have nothing more to prove."

"They got you," he said softly. "You one of them now. You filthy Kolvas blood drinker, flesh eater. You not Dolkati Friend now. You not even Vohee..."

Anger flushed up in her, mixed with shame. It was too much to bear.

"I saved your life, Gicok. If that means I'm not your friend, so be it. I'm not Kolvas. I'm not Dolkati and I'm not Vohee anymore. You can hate me, you can help me. It doesn't matter, but maybe if you take my help you live."

The Gicok nodded sadly.

"They got you."

Just then the healer entered. He was a tall man, even for his people, and very gaunt. He might have seemed a walking skeleton had not dark burnt red flesh covered the whiteness of his bones. He was an older man with many wrinkles creasing his face and silver hair that fell unbound on his shoulders but did not climb high enough on his head to cover the top. He looked like a man who had carried so many illnesses for his patients that one more might kill him, yet he walked with a jerky kind of energy and his limbs moved with a strange grace that seemed always about to hit something but never did.

Jovai nodded deeply to him as he entered, showing great respect that she sensed, somehow, was due this man. He pulled back astonished and glanced nervously over his shoulders to see if anyone followed. Finding no one there, he avoided looking at Jovai again, but entered, moving around her, and muttering something she could not understand.

With quick movements, he tied open two flaps in the hut walls to let in light. Then he went to his patient, gently easing the weak

Gicok back into bed. He seemed not to expect the Gicok to resist and, surprisingly, the Gicok calmly obeyed him. Then he knelt beside his patient and stared at his bandages astonished.

"*Quaillic Sal soobirid, fildin morlik?*" he demanded.

The Gicok frowned at the unintelligible question and looked toward Jovai as if for translation. She shrugged.

The healer fingered the bandages, shaking his head, and muttering continuously. Jovai watched curiously as he unwrapped the clothes to inspect the wounds beneath. Again, he seemed surprised at what he found — surprised and obviously pleased. He treated the wound with a salve. The Gicok winced but did not resist.

The healer wrapped the wounds in fresh bandages and reached for some rope that was laying in the corner. Carefully he started tying long pieces to the stakes in the ground, in obvious preparation for restraining the Gicok again.

"Thank you for your help," said Jovai politely. "But my friend does not need to be tied."

The healer frowned, not comprehending.

"*Gohetic sa fer okaim brahami,*" said a light, cheerful voice from behind Jovai. She turned to see a very pretty girl, a few years older than she, standing in the entrance, smiling at her.

The healer immediately plunged into a string of words, obviously objections. The young woman stopped him politely with a graceful nod and turned back to Jovai.

"He wants tie White One again. He better tied," she said, her Akarian awkward and difficult to understand.

The healer exploded angrily in another stream of words, gesturing wildly at the girl and almost, but not quite, knocking Jovai aside.

The pretty girl flushed but waited politely until the healer's anger was vented. Then, in a gentle voice, she spoke to him slowly and calmly.

The healer sputtered, still upset, and started to push past Jovai.

Again, Jovai blocked his way.

"Do not tie the White One again," Jovai insisted, now directing her words to the young translator.

"He hurt us," she protested.

"No, he won't."

"He hurt him own."

Jovai shrugged, "If he wants to."

Once again, with great deference, the girl spoke to the healer. He objected. She sweetly argued. He gestured angrily toward the girl. She nodded toward Jovai. Her voice was always soft, always polite, but Jovai heard a note of threat underneath it. Finally, the healer threw down the ropes in disgust and, still muttering, left the tent.

"I Gilix," said the girl. Her eyes were now glued warily on the Gicok, and she hugged the entrance, ready to run. "I teach you speak us."

She tossed a basket into the room. The scent of fruit, meat, and heated grain rose from it.

The Gicok was standing again now. He was very weak, and his body trembled. In spite of himself, he turned toward the basket, kicked off the cloth that covered it and stared at the food, still steaming within it.

"Go then," Jovai told the Gicok.

The Gicok said nothing. He just stood, looking down at the food.

"You eat?" Gilix asked Jovai, her voice barely a whisper.

"I'll bathe first," answered Jovai, turning to her, "if you show me."

Gilix glanced uncertainly toward Jovai, then back again to the Gicok.

"He?" she asked.

"Come show me the baths," Jovai answered. She turned her back on the Gicok and left the tent, with Gilix hurrying after her.

CHAPTER 28

GRASP OF THE DEAD

The morning of this land was but a brighter version of the night. Mists rolled through the forests, around the towering trees, hiding all but their closest branches and chilling the skin with its cool, moist touch. It was alive with the movement of shadowy shapes that took human form only within the arm's reach and the cheerful noise of friendly people calling out greetings, chatting to each other, laughing, singing work songs, enjoying being alive another day. They were startled by a tremendous crash as one of the great, thick redwoods fell. For a moment, all was silent, reverent, then a loud cheer rose, all voices at once, in triumph, in celebration.

"One day and morning," Gilix explained. She led Jovai to the crowd of people. On the fallen trunk, the width of a standing horse, six or seven strong young men were resting, their clothes as wet as if they had been swimming in them, their red-brown faces bright from exertion and their eyes glowing with triumph. Already, the sound of chopping was heard from the shadowed distances where the branches lay, and children ran around, laughing, waving leaves and twigs.

"Home now," Gilix explained, although what she meant, Jovai was not sure.

They had no proper bathhouse built yet, so Gilix led Jovai to a nearby river where her people washed and drank. It was late in the morning, past the time for baths, although a few who had made themselves sick from the feast last night, stumbled to the edge and took a dive. There were some younger children splashing about near their mothers who laughed and chatted with each other while pounding clothes or gathering the seeds that grew on stalks in the shallows.

A woman nearby, tall with heavy eyebrows that grew long and low down on the sides of her head, greeted Gilix eagerly with questions. As Gilix answered, Jovai slipped away. Her own mood was brooding and heavy, like a sky full of storm, and the cheerfulness of these people oppressed her.

She followed the river upstream to a silent, lonely bank. There was only the sound of the water here, and she listened, listened deeply, listened to anything the spirit world might tell her. As she had expected, she heard nothing.

She took a stone in her hand and held it, feeling for its strength, its certainty of being. With her finger, she traced the blue, brown and white designs of it. It was a story. Every stone was a story, she knew, except the stone in her bag. There were no lines, no marks, no story. She examined the designs on the stone in her hand and watched as they slipped into the image of a face with a crooked smile and a single, sad eye. Who was he, she wondered. Why did the earth mark his memory?

"An offering," she whispered to the river. She tossed the stone and watched the silver flecks of fish and darting little frogs startle away from where it landed. There was so much life right here — brothers and sisters who shared this time this place with her, teachers if only they would teach, if only she could learn. Yet she felt isolated and alone.

"Why do you not talk to me anymore?" she asked. "Please, mighty spirits. I'm lost. I'm empty. Guide me. Help me to know what I should do now."

The river gurgled along, indifferent, unconcerned. The mist coiled around her but did not even whisper.

She sighed, stripped off the clothes Difsat had given her and plunged into the icy water. She came up gasping, shocked, although she had known it would be cold. It was painful, so bitingly frigid, and delightful. It woke her up as it washed her clean and she laughed at herself, at her own self-pity.

She emerged shivering and shook herself like a dog. There was no sun to dry her, so she dressed still wet. The clothes clung thickly to her skin, binding and chafing, the furs a heavy weight on her shoulders, but promising warmth.

Through the mist, she saw a dark figure approach — Gilix come looking for her. It was good, for the bath had enraged her appetite and Gilix would lead her to food. As the figure approached, however, it seemed to grow taller, until it was certainly too tall to be the young girl. As it stepped gracefully through the mist it seemed almost part of it, and it was before her, near enough to touch, before Jovai could see who it was.

The woman was tall and pale, with long flowing white hair and yellow eyes. A Gicok woman. She was very beautiful with exquisite, delicate features and a slim, though muscular, well-worked body. There was something familiar about her, although Jovai could not remember where she had seen the woman before. She stood before Jovai and stared, deep into her eyes. Jovai could feel the power of those eyes reach into her spirit like a vine, reaching to root a tendril in a new bit of earth.

The woman stretched forth her hand, it's slender, finely lined palm up, and long, slim fingers open toward Jovai. Instinctively, Jovai shrunk back. The woman stepped closer, still offering her hand.

"What do you want?" Jovai demanded. She had spoken, from

habit, in her own language so she asked again in Akarian.

The woman seemed not to hear, but stepped forward again and grabbed for Jovai's arm.

Jovai pulled away in panic but not before those long fingers had scratched her skin. She glanced again at the woman's hand, wondering at the sharpness of her nails. There were no nails, she saw. There was no flesh, just bone. The hand was bone, the arm was bone, the beautiful white shoulder — bone.

The face was still beautiful, the eyes entrancing, but as she watched, dark blotches, like bruises, welled up on the cheeks, the jaw, one patch over the brow of one of those still, yellow eyes. The bruises deepened and spread. Her face grew puffy and distorted. The flesh thinned as the bruises grew darker and the eyes glowed brighter. From the bruise on her cheek blood started to ooze, but it was not blood, not bright and red but thick and black and evil-smelling.

She grabbed for Jovai again, and Jovai pulled back screaming. From deep inside her, there welled a chant, a prayer for protection. Jovai was unaware that she sang. She didn't even hear the song. It was an instinct — a reflex to fear. She backed away as the Gicok ghost advanced, step by step toward the icy, flowing river.

The ghost grabbed at her again and caught her. The bone fingers gripped tighter and tighter, slowly pressing through the flesh of her arm. Jovai struggled and tried to push her away, but her arm went through the body as it would through mist. Only the grip was solid, and the fingers could not be pried. The ghost turned silently upstream and pointed. Jovai felt the pressure on her arm, pushing her that way, but the figure did not move to drag her. It only stood and pointed.

Through the mist, a voice was calling in a language Jovai could not understand. It was Gilix. It had to be. Jovai yelled back to her, calling for help in any language, in every language she could think of. The pressure on her arm tightened, and the push grew stronger, more insistent. She felt herself forced in the direction the ghost pointed, first one terrified step, then another.

Gilix's voice grew louder, more frantic in response to Jovai's yell. Jovai could hear her running through the forest, coming closer, almost there. The pressure on her arm was pain. She felt the sticky wetness of blood dripping down her flesh. She grabbed for the bone hand, but though it held her still, there was nothing for her to grab.

Then Gilix was there — a dark shadow growing darker, yelling in fright and concern. She crashed into Jovai before she saw her and they both went sprawling onto the soft, wet earth.

"Run!" yelled Jovai. She grabbed the girl and pulled her up with panic-driven strength. Gilix followed, unquestioningly, running after Jovai back to the village.

It wasn't until they were back among the cheerful crowd of voices and the sounds of people eagerly working, building a new life, that Jovai was able to halt her flight. Her lungs ached with every burning breath, and sweat poured over her body. She looked around for Gilix and saw the breathless girl tiredly trailing her. All the energy she had left was in her eyes, staring at Jovai with great concern.

They stood together silently for a moment, catching their breaths. People hurried past about their work although one or two called friendly greetings to Gilix and several glanced curiously at Jovai. Gilix took Jovai's arm and lightly touched where the ghost had grabbed. Jovai winced in pain. Large blue bruises were already welling up and five deep holes, four in a curved line and a fifth one on the other side of her arm, were bleeding.

"What?" her nod indicated Jovai's arm.

"Ghost — woman ghost of the white people," Jovai answered. "Did you see her?"

Gilix frowned, perhaps not understanding all Jovai was saying, and shook her head.

"Come," she instructed. She took Jovai's good arm and led her to the healer's tent.

Gilix stood at the entrance to the tent and called. The flap did not open. No one answered. She called again. Still no answer.

"Merha," she said. "Sit."

Jovai sat down outside the tent, glad to do so.

"I see he," she gestured vaguely, then pointing at Jovai repeated, "Sit."

"Merha," Jovai confirmed.

Gilix smiled, pleased, then ran off.

Gilix was gone a long time. People passed by but few seemed to notice Jovai and no one tried to speak to her. The sun started to brighten, or the haze to thin, but either way, the air grew warmer, and there was a feeling of contentment all around arising from a people tired of wandering, happy to be home again...

Jovai awoke confused by the strange brown-red faces staring down at her. One was a pretty girl with long, auburn hair and the other was an older man with a ring of silver hair around his head. They were talking to each other in an unknown language, talking about her.

"Merha," said Jovai, her memory returning. She had slept on her side in the dirt and leaves outside the healer's tent. Now she pushed herself up to sitting and nodded respectfully to the healer.

He was shirtless, with streaks of dirt and sweat decorating his thin torso. He wrung his hands nervously and wiped them on his dirty leggings, all the while muttering softly. He knelt beside Jovai and examined the wounds on her arm. Twice Gilix spoke to him as if answering a question. What she said the first time made him frown. What she said the second time made him blanche, and he hurriedly sent her away.

When she returned, it was with Difsat.

"Well, newborn," he greeted Jovai cheerfully, "it seems there's no

230

finish to the anxiety you cause."

The healer directed his attention toward her arm, twisting it gently so that he could see all the marks.

"What happened?" the shaman demanded of Jovai, ignoring the endless string of words from the healer.

"A ghost, by the river."

The shaman frowned at her, disbelieving.

"It was like a Gicok woman at first. It grabbed my arm. When I tried to push it away, it was as if no one was there, but its hand turned to bones I couldn't touch and held me harder. It was trying to push me along — up river. Then Gilix came, and I was free, so we ran back."

"A ghost did this?" He looked at Jovai as if she were crazy.

"A ghost," she insisted.

The shaman turned to Gilix and questioned her. She said something briefly. The shaman asked her another question and her eyes went big with wonder. She glanced at Jovai then back to the shaman and shook her head.

"Gilix saw nothing holding you," the shaman told her.

"There was thick mist..." Jovai explained.

"She saw no ghost."

"They are there, Difsat. The Gicok has seen them too. They are dangerous, and something must be done about them."

"Our people have put you through a lot. Many times a period of rest is needed after the night of death."

"You think I dreamed it? You think I dreamed this?" she held her arm up for him to see better.

"The healer will bandage that, then you can rest," he told her gently.

"And you will do nothing to protect your people?"

"I will talk to the Hawk Clan," he promised. "They will decide if there is action to be taken."

"They are your warriors?" asked Jovai.

Difsat nodded.

"And what can warriors do against ghosts?"

"If protection is needed, they will provide it. That is our way."

Jovai stared at him, wanting to argue, but with nothing to say.

"You rest," he encouraged her again. "You are newborn, our baby. Babies don't work. When the moon is full we will give you a name, a family will welcome you, and you may request consideration for a clan. Until then you have nothing to do but eat and sleep and learn our language from Gilix." He smiled at the pretty girl and chuckled. "No more talk about ghosts or people will think you're crazy. Since I welcomed you that will make me look bad. You understand?"

Jovai nodded, discouraged.

"Hmm," he grunted. He lightly patted her on the shoulder. "Good." Then he was gone.

It was already afternoon before Gilix led Jovai back to her tent. Through the confusion of the tents and the morning mist, now finally burned away, Jovai could not have found it on her own. They entered to find the Gicok, sleeping on his bedroll. The breakfast basket had been rifled through, and half the food was gone.

"Better hot," said Gilix as she offered the remaining food to Jovai.

"If it is from your hands, it will be good," responded Jovai. Gilix blushed and smiled.

They started the language lesson with the breakfast, Gilix pointing to each item of food, giving its name, then explaining verbs like "cut," "peel," "smell," "taste," and finally "eat". She was an attentive teacher and had a charming way about her that made the lesson like a game children play.

At some unknown point, the Gicok awoke. Jovai became aware of him only when he laughed at the silly gestures Gilix was making to try to explain a type of food gone bad. He startled both of them, but it was obvious he had been awake for some while and had not meant to interrupt.

"You should learn too," Jovai told him. At that, both he and Gilix frowned. Jovai smiled to see what she suspected was the first time a Gicok and a Kolvas were ever in agreement. The Gicok grunted and rolled over, his back toward them, pretending to go back to sleep. Gilix sighed with relief and continued with the lesson.

"I'm tired now," Jovai interrupted her. "Thank you Gilix, but now I need to sleep."

Jovai had to repeat herself more slowly, with gestures for sleeping before Gilix could understand.

"Ah!" she said at last, nodding. She gave Jovai the Kolvas words and left her for the day.

Once she had left, the Gicok turned back to Jovai and said, "I stay."

Jovai did not look up from her task of unrolling her sleeping mat. She merely nodded, saying nothing.

"I no leave Dolkati Friend."

Jovai threw herself down on the sleeping mat and sighed. She would awaken just before sunset to draw the protection circle again. Until then she had to sleep.

"What that?" asked the Gicok. Jovai did not need to open her eyes to know he had seen her bandaged arm. She felt him touch the bandage lightly. He was so close to her that she could feel the heat of his body and the stirring of his breath. "Enemy of my people," she thought, but she didn't fear him now. She opened her eyes and glanced up toward him.

"They hurt you?" he demanded angrily.

"No. Not Kolvas." She closed her eyes again with a deep, slow breath. "I'll tell you later," she promised. "Now I need to sleep."

CHAPTER 29

RIVER OF BLOOD

The moon had been swimming in the night for many hours before Jovai awoke. There was an odd tension in the air. The hair on her arms and the back of her neck were rising. Nothing moved through the darkness of the tent. There was no sound, not even of breath. Slowly, quietly she exhaled and inhaled carefully, her nostrils inspecting the air as it passed. Something was wrong.

She reached out quietly with her awareness toward the Gicok's mat. He was gone. It was already late at night. She had overslept, and now she was alone.

A thousand explanations passed through her mind: he had needed to relieve himself, or he was hungry, looking for food or their packs and horses which she had forgotten to ask about or simply exploring. He had slept much of the day — it was natural he would feel restless now. He was a grown man, a warrior. He could take care of himself. And yet he was still weak from his wounds, so he wouldn't be causing trouble...she hoped. Who knew what he would do? Who knew what the Kolvas might do to him if they thought he meant harm? And the ghosts — she knew even less about ghosts. But what could she do? A failed shaman, a failed adult — not quite a child but not a woman — a nothing. She couldn't even take care of herself. She had no spirits any longer to call on. All she could do was draw circles in the dirt and hope they would keep the evil away. It was late, but she could draw the circle now, and draw it again when the Gicok returned — if he returned.

She had a duty to this man. He was probably all right, but she could at least look and listen, to make sure.

She moved the tent flap aside and pushed herself out into the cold, clear night. She had expected mist, but there was none this night. Through the moonlight she could see the tents all around hers, filled with sleepers. Somewhere at her feet, there was still the circle she had drawn the night before. Even with the moonlight, she could not see it until she had knelt and put her hand close to where she knew it would be. It had already been broken with many crossings, she knew, but still she hesitated before crossing it again.

She listened to the breathing of sleepers in their tents. She listened for the sounds of people stirring and heard them, more than one. They were large, probably men from the way they moved, but not the Gicok. He would still be weakened. The shifting she heard had no sign of pain or hesitation. The people she heard watched, alert, but were not at all nervous as the Gicok probably would be. To them everything was normal, no danger expected. The Gicok, in a camp full of his declared enemies, would not be so relaxed.

Jovai forced her body into a practiced calm. She made her mind quieter, more open. He had to be somewhere. She just had to listen better, deeper. In all the many years of practicing this exercise, it had never been so hard. To listen deeply she had to leave herself open and, for the first time, she realized just how vulnerable that forced her to be.

She reached out with her awareness, let it expand into the night, like the moonlight, everywhere. As she was floating, she came up against a strange presence that would not let her awareness pass. It was something vaguely familiar, from some forgotten nightmare — something dark and hungry. She expanded along it to see how far it stretched. At first, it had seemed small, but it seemed to expand with her until it felt as if it were aware of her. Not just aware, but focused on her, surrounding her, closing in on her, and she found herself trapped within it. It was like a massive wall of hunger, pressing against her, trying to eat her alive...she remembered, suddenly, the darkness from the night of her failed shaman passage, when the traders had taken her, and fear rose within her.

"Help me," she prayed to her spirits. "How do l escape this thing?"

She tried to pull away from it by quieting herself into shaman silence, very small, unobtrusive, with no particular sense of intent that might be heard, and let the space move her as though she were a speck, floating on its sea.

The dark hunger seemed to sense her withdrawing and closed quickly, like a muscle contracting. She kept herself calm, almost unconcerned, and waited for the break in the wall of its power that she hoped she would find. Then she was there — a tiny chink, a space made by the very intensity with which the hunger was contracting to hold her. It was as if it had pulled tight in so many places that this place was, for a second only, open. She slipped quickly through and was free of the strange darkness.

She was herself again, eyes snapped open, body alert and ready for attack. Her hands dropped to the ground to help her up and met a sliminess all around her. She brought her hands to her face and saw them covered in blood. She was sitting in a pool of blood.

She jumped up and away from where the blood had gathered around her. The darkness of night quickly covered it, but a new pool formed as the blood flowed down her clothes, inside and out, to gather at her feet. She did a quick check of her body, searching for the wound. There were the scratches still on her arm. The bandage had come loose and they bled a little, but not enough to puddle at her feet. She felt no dizziness or weakness from loss of her own blood. Nowhere else was there any wound. She was not bleeding in the woman way. The blood was not her own.

Through the dirt trickled the blood in which she had been sitting. It was trailing her, like a living thing, seeking to join with the new pool forming at her feet. Again, she jumped away and the puddle she had just left quivered and reformed itself, before her eyes, as a little stream flowing toward her.

Her stomach heaved inside of her but time had left little to spill forth.

"I must wash," she thought. Could she find her way to the river? She had to. "I have to clean this off." The thought obsessed her.

She began to walk, leaving puddles of blood in every footprint — puddles that turned to little streams, joined by the other streams, following her. She began to run, and the streaming blood now chased her like a small river, growing all the time bigger, flowing faster, catching up.

The trees parted before her, and the river flowed through the night, dark and slow. It was not the river she remembered from that morning. There should be trees, thick and tall, holding the moon away from the earth but letting its light slip into the sweet, sparkling water. Where were the trees? They were on this side only, but they were gnarled now. They had hollows of dark ash and wood which was dry and splintered and the only leaves were at her feet where the blood was again pooling. These leaves were withered and dead, half-way to humus. That was on this side, where she could see. Across the river, there was nothing, only darkness. She might have thought the dark river was as wide as forever, but at some point, it no longer moved and all was still, an empty blackness.

The stream of blood that had chased her now surrounded her again until she was ankle deep in it. Then it reached out to the dark river. The dark river expanded toward it, and, when the waters touched and flowed together, she could see they were both the same. The river of blood! Where had she heard that before?

238

The blood swirled around her, up to her knees. Had the river moved or had she? For now she was within it. She looked back toward the bank where she had been standing. There were others standing there, pale skinned, pale eyes watching her with uncanny stillness. They seemed to be floating away, farther and farther.

"I can't go back. They'll kill me! But what is on the other bank?"

And the answer came, "Death."

A high-pitched cry, barely audible, shattered the silence. Jovai heard the flutter of wings around her. She had heard that before, in the night of terror.

"Why am I here?" she asked.

"An answer to your prayer," came the soundless voice through the rustle of invisible wings. "A way to be free of that which haunts you. Did you run from or to?"

"I was running away."

"From what?"

"From the blood. It was fouling me. It was everywhere. It chased me..."

"You ran from the river of blood to the river of blood." The voice was calm, passionless. It merely stated a fact.

"I wanted to wash myself — to be clean again."

The blood was now above her waist and rising quickly. Without moving she had been transported a great distance from either shore. The Gicok ghosts were little more than pale specks against a black cloth.

"This is life. This is death," said the whisper of wings. "To run from one is to run from the other. They are the same."

"I don't understand!"

"The beginning, the ending are only gestures to define the existence. The existence is all."

"And the existence is blood?" It didn't make any sense.

As she opened her mouth to speak, blood flowed in and filled it.

She tilted her head up, but the blood was too high. She breathed it in through her nose, in through her mouth. As her eyes watched, the darkness filled them, and she felt it rising to the top of her head.

"Help me," she prayed to the spirit of the bat. "You helped the Kolvas swim through this river to the new living world. Help me, please."

"Will you follow me?"

"Yes!" she promised.

"Then drop your burdens and swim."

Jovai flailed with her arms and kicked with her feet, forcing her head above the river.

"But I'm drowning!" She begged. "Please help me."

"Trust the river. It will carry you where you need to go," came the calm advice.

"Why me?" she thought, and with that thought, she grew heavier. The thick river pulled her down. Quickly, she abandoned her self-pity. She stopped struggling to understand and focused on struggling to survive. She concentrated only on kicking her legs and moving her arms as she had learned as a child.

"Where do I swim to?" she called.

"Trust the river. Trust yourself. You have the right way in you."

She struck out blindly, hoping the way she swam was to the nearest shore, but she could not be certain.

The current was strong, constantly threatening to pull her under. She worked against it to stay afloat. The harder she fought it, the stronger it pulled at her. She battled for a long time, but she could feel her strength fading as the blood closed in around her and cut off her air. Her breaths became gasps, grabbed further and further apart. Finally, exhaustion overcame her. She could fight no more. She gave herself up to the river and let it carry her. The current that she had expected to pull her under lifted her up instead and sped her away.

240

It did not take long to reach the shore. She couldn't believe she had been so close! But, perhaps it was a trick of this spirit — the Bat spirit. That was the one the Kolvas claimed had led them through the realm of the dead, across the river of blood and to the new world. Now it had led her...but what did that mean?

She stood silently, looking out over the river. It was now clear and clean, no longer blood — and the other bank, as well as this one, was alive with trees and bushes, with night birds and scurrying animals. She saw a small flying bat come swooping toward her carrying a strange fruit. Instinctively she ducked, but it had already veered away and was flying off, over the water.

Jovai turned to go and saw, beside her, sitting on the bank, a pale figure, his eyes flickering over the sparkling water. She had not heard him approach. Had he seen her climbing out of the water?

He acknowledged her with a silent gesture to sit beside him. She did so, shivering in the cool of the night. She wrapped her arms around her body and found her clothes dry, as if they had never been wet at all. Yet, they were fresh and clean.

Chapter 30

Escaping

Jovai and the Gicok sat together quietly as the time stretched on. There was a moment she thought the Gicok had fallen asleep, but his eyes were open, flickering. There was a moment she wondered if she had slept, although nothing had changed from when she had closed her eyes to when she had opened them again. It was a comforting stillness between them, the night wrapping them both in silent intimacy.

Jovai could feel the night turn to day, and she watched the mist rise from the stream to the morning. The Gicok stirred beside her and grunted as he stretched.

"Today I go to my people," he announced.

Jovai felt a chill rise through her, but she only nodded.

"You stay?" he asked.

"I'll help you."

His eyes shifted nervously, and he frowned.

"You Kolvas, you not Dolkati Friend. Dolkati Friend, not Kolvas."

She smiled slightly and shrugged. "Dolkati Friends aren't Vohees either."

"You not Vohee... now."

In the strengthening light, she saw that they were sitting near the place where the Gicok ghost had attacked her. For a moment, in the swirling mist, she thought she saw the shape of that ghost, standing a few feet away, pointing again up the river toward the Gicok camp. The scratches on her arm ached dully in a memory of their own.

"I'm Dolkati Friend," she answered, after a moment. "I'll help you."

They washed in the river and returned to the Kolvas camp to find food. Gilix was waiting for them outside their tent, another full basket on her lap. She jumped to her feet quickly as they approached.

"Where?" she asked.

"Bathing," answered Jovai, pantomiming washing.

Gilix seemed uncomfortable with that but said nothing further on the subject.

"I am pleased we meet in this world again, Gilix," said Jovai in her language. It was the formal greeting and wrong for the situation, yet, at that moment, it felt like the right thing to say.

Gilix looked at her surprised, then giggled.

The Gicok took half the breakfast, but he held himself apart as they ate. Jovai reviewed with Gilix what she had taught her the day before and gladly learned many new words. She was aware, however, of the growing impatience with which the Gicok watched her. As soon as the food was finished and Gilix was beginning to expand her Kolvas vocabulary with household words, Jovai stopped her.

"Gilix, there are many things I must do today."

She stared at Jovai, without understanding.

"The Gicoks, the White Ones...my friend and I will attend to them."

Gilix shook her head and held her hands open and away from her, in the gesture of one who believes she has misunderstood.

"The White Ones," repeated Jovai, pointing toward the Gicok.

Gilix nodded.

"His people...the camp...the dead ones," she gestured in the direction of the Gicok camp. Gilix frowned.

"You waste time," interrupted the Gicok. "Go now."

Gilix turned toward him as if to protest, then quickly turned away again, blushing. For the first time, Jovai realized that no one had spoken to the Gicok since the night of terror, and no one would. She might have found a measure of acceptance among these people, but Jovai now saw in Gilix's face that the Gicok had not and would not.

"No go," said Gilix to Jovai. "Bad." She searched for a better word but, not finding it, said again with stronger emphasis, "Bad. Bad."

"Why?"

A pained expression came to her face. She tried to speak but could only gesture with wild frustration and say again "bad!"

"I go now," said the Gicok rising. "You come now, or you stay."

Jovai also rose. Gilix grabbed at the hem of her tunic and tried to get her to sit back down, but Jovai pulled away.

"My people bury the dead. Your people eat them, so I hear. What his people do, I don't know, but no one leaves the dead to rot uncared for."

The Gicok moved as if to walk between them. Gilix shrank from him. Jovai nodded respectfully to the frightened girl and followed the Gicok out of the tent.

The mist seemed lighter this morning than it had before. Or perhaps it was Jovai's growing familiarity with the Kolvas camp that helped her distinguish shapes and people further away. She knew they saw her and the Gicok. No one greeted them cheerily as they greeted each other. People marked their passage with wary, suspicious silence and hurried away. She watched as the Gicok's hand moved of its own to where his knife would have hung. They had no weapons, she realized with a stab of panic. Then she forced herself to relax. These people claimed to be friends, at least to her. What need did she have of weapons?

Suddenly, two large Kolvas men stood before them. Their bare arms and legs were very muscular. Jovai recognized the many years of hard play these men had put into building such strength and agility. They must have been chosen from young boys. Their faces were painted lightly with red, and above the ragged pelts common to all their people, they wore a collar of net and hawk feathers. In their hands, which had also been painted, one held a long blade and the other a thick, carved stick with obsidian thorns imbedded all around it. They held these weapons lowered, but ready and their stance was balanced and on guard. Jovai felt the intensity of their gaze upon her and, even more so, upon the Gicok.

She also felt the Gicok gathering his strength. His body shifted slightly forward, and his breathing grew deeper, ready for attack.

She put her hand lightly on his arm and said, as gently as she could, "wait, friend."

To her surprise, he nodded and let go of some of his tension. Now the situation was her responsibility.

"Why do you stop us?" she asked the guards calmly in Akarian. They frowned and answered her with Kolvas words she could not understand.

"We do not harm or threaten your people. We ask only to pass."

She took a small step forward. Immediately the weapons rose.

From behind her sounded a woman's yell and Gilix came running up to them. She was breathless, but she managed to pant out many words to the guards.

"...bathe," the words were repeated in Akarian, and she looked to Jovai for confirmation, her eyes pleading with her to nod. Jovai nodded. Slowly the guards lowered their weapons. They spoke again to Gilix as if they blamed her for the "misunderstanding" and stood aside. Gilix smiled shyly and bowed her head in coy modesty. Only her eyes raised to meet first the one guard than the other with a sweet, sly look, as if they were sharing some very intimate secret. Suddenly the guards were smiling back at her, everything forgiven.

246

One even bowed slightly, with deference.

"Bathe," said Gilix lightly as they passed the guards. She said the word in Kolvas and conjugated it. Jovai repeated the conjugations until they were well out of hearing of the guards.

"Are we prisoners?" she asked. Gilix looked at her and shook her head, saying something in Kolvas that Jovai was beginning to guess meant "I don't understand."

"We must stay?" Jovai tried again.

"Stay," repeated Gilix. She nodded. She pointed to Jovai's arm. "Hurt," she said. She pointed back toward the guards, then at the Gicok.

"They would have hurt my friend?" asked Jovai.

Gilix shook her head.

"Friend hurt," she managed to say, and pointed back toward guards.

"No," said Jovai. "If he were going to hurt them he would have done so before you arrived."

Gilix shook her head again and fisted her hands in frustration.

"Friend hurt," she repeated.

Jovai turned to the Gicok in confusion "Did you hurt anyone last night?" she asked.

"No," he answered.

"Did you see anyone?"

Again he answered no.

"But there were guards. How was it they were unaware of you?"

He shrugged. "I saw no one."

Gilix pointed an accusing finger at the Gicok and said angrily to Jovai "Hurt! Filaph, Bokeen, bad hurt."

"By a Gicok? A White One?"

She nodded.

"You are very sure?"

Again she nodded.

"Not him," Jovai told her.

"Him," Gilix insisted.

"No."

The Gicok walked beside Jovai, his eyes flickering in every direction except toward Gilix. He did not attempt to defend himself, as if that would have wounded his honor. He could have taken out two guards, Jovai realized. Even though he was still weakened by his recent wounds, he was a trained warrior, and he could have surprised them.

"Maybe it was the ghosts," she said aloud. Both Gilix and the Gicok looked at her as if she were crazy, then quickly looked away. Jovai almost laughed to see these two enemies for a moment acting and thinking as one.

"Why did you help us?" Jovai asked the girl.

Gilix bit her lip and blushed, but she only shrugged in answer.

"She like you," the Gicok answered for her. "She betray her people to protect you."

Gilix turned on him in full anger, her fists raised. She attacked him before either he or Jovai realized she would. It was a match of one small female against one huge warrior. Her first fist slew his jaw, snapping it closed with such violence that blood erupted from it. The other stuck him in the ribs, knocking the breath out of him. His reflexes were trained to unthinking quickness. Even as he lunged forward with the pain of her second strike, he grabbed her, twisting her arms behind her back tightly and held her against him with his arm about her neck.

"*Leforcht ke! Leforcht ke!*" she hissed. Jovai did not need a translator to understand her meaning.

"Let her go," she ordered the Gicok.

Gilix struggled against him, but he held her firmly.

"She come," he told Jovai. "She see. My people, my family. Dead!" he was yelling in her ear. "Dead by Kolvas. Dead by her."

248

"*Leforcht ke!*" insisted Gilix, fright replacing anger.

"Ease your grip, Gicok. Even if her people killed yours, she didn't."

"She come," he repeated stubbornly.

"He won't hurt you, Gilix," Jovai told the girl, "or he will have to fight me."

The Gicok snorted as if that were no serious threat.

"But you will have to come with us," she continued to the girl. "Do you understand?"

Gilix lowered her eyes sullenly and answered in her language. Jovai didn't understand.

"He leforcht you. You come. No hurt. Now I know you understand."

"No," she answered.

"It's all right, Gilix," Jovai told her gently. She awkwardly touched the girl's face, forcing her chin up, hoping her eyes would follow. They did, and for a moment Jovai saw something of herself in them, her younger self, frightened of the giant man who was to be her master. "I won't let him hurt you," she told her, "but he's right. You should come now. There are things your people might need to know."

She watched as the frightened expression in the young girl's eyes turned into trust. Now Gilix was her responsibility too. She took a deep breath and accepted it.

"Will you come, Gilix?"

The girl nodded as much as the arm around her neck would let her.

"Let her go," Jovai instructed the Gicok. This time he did as she asked. As soon as she was free, Gilix ran to Jovai, putting her between the Gicok and herself.

"Told you she like you," he said, with a note of jealousy.

"Keep your mouth closed," Jovai warned him. "Every time you open it trouble comes spilling out."

She took Gilix's hand, like a mother might with her child. Gilix squeezed it softly and walked beside her.

They smelled the Gicok camp before they reached it. Gilix shied back, but Jovai squeezed her hand encouragingly and pulled her on.

"Teach," she told the girl, hoping it would ease the shock. "Give me words."

Gilix held her nose, made a face and said a word for the bad smell. Jovai repeated it, all her attention suddenly on the lesson. She realized it was her own fear she was trying to ease, even more than Gilix's.

"Word for that," said the Gicok, pointing to a fleeing wolf suddenly frightened from its feast. Gilix supplied it, softly. Jovai repeated it, almost unconsciously. A few more steps and they stood over the half-eaten corpses of what had been a beautiful woman and her two children.

"His wife," whispered Jovai to Gilix, "and their children."

The baby had been dragged several feet away from where Jovai remembered it lying. It was now at their feet. Gilix automatically reached her hand toward what was left of it, then in horror pulled it back again and hugged her arm against her chest.

"His family," Jovai repeated, wanting desperately for Gilix to understand.

"No Kolvas," she said softly, her eyes entreating Jovai to believe her.

"Not Kolvas," agreed the Gicok, angrily. "Kolvas not kill her. She die warrior. Children also — warrior brave."

Jovai remembered the way fallen Gicoks would kill themselves if they could not retreat. She remembered the way other warriors would kill their fallen companions if they could not get them away. She understood what he was saying.

"Gicoks will not be taken alive by an enemy if they can kill themselves first. They kill each other if they have to."

"No Kolvas," the girl repeated again. Tears were in her eyes. She did not try to hide them.

"What do we do?" Jovai asked the Gicok. He was standing over his wife, staring down at her. It was a while before he could answer.

"We burn," he said slowly.

"All together?"

He nodded.

"Where?"

He gestured toward the Gicok camp. "In center. In heart."

"And their "powers and loves?"

His head raised sharply, surprised or shocked, she could not tell.

"I do that," he answered.

"We'll go gather wood," Jovai told Gilix, leading her away. The girl looked back over her shoulder at the grieving Gicok.

"No Kolvas," she said to him gently, as if it could ease his pain. He ignored her.

CHAPTER 31

CURSES AND CLEANINGS

Gilix followed Jovai into the Gicok camp. Everywhere lay bodies where they had fallen. Wolves, wild dogs, carrion birds, rodents, ants, and flies had gotten to them, feasting on the bloated decay. It seemed to Jovai that there were more than she had remembered — many more.

She expected Gilix to scream or run away, but the Kolvas girl surveyed the scene with a face like stone. Death was nothing new to her people. They lived with death, built their lives upon its mystery. They were not without their own sufferings, and Jovai could not guess what horrors it was that they had fled.

"Difsat," Gilix said, cryptically, patting the air around her as if trying to hold its foulness down. "No come. Stay."

"He wants us to leave them alone, like this, to rot," Jovai guessed aloud.

Gilix nodded.

"I can't," Jovai told her.

Again she nodded. She seemed to understand. She stepped up to the corpse of an older man and pointed to the blade in his belly.

"No Kolvas," she said again. She pulled the blade out and offered it to Jovai. "Akarian."

"Are you sure?" Jovai demanded.

Gilix pointed to the knife "No Kolvas. Akarian."

"They traded with the Akarians. This could have been their own knife, turned against them."

Gilix pointed to other weapons, identifying them as Akarian. "No Kolvas," she explained again. It was true, there were no darts or long blades of the Kolvas style. There were no weapons of any kind that were similar to anything Jovai had seen in the Kolvas camp.

Gilix next found a corpse that was obviously not a Gicok. There were only a few shreds of torn flesh left on it, but the flesh was black, and the patches of hair on the left on the head were a bright gold.

"A trader?" suggested Jovai. But now she looked around and saw that several of the corpses were not Gicoks but Akarians. Enough still wore thick padded protection vests and heavy belts hung with many weapons. The Akarian traders had never appeared to her people so dressed.

"But they were friends," insisted Jovai. She pointed to the many signs of feasting and celebration scattered around. "It looks like they were feasting together, welcomed friends."

Gilix shrugged.

"No Kolvas," she said. It was the only point she had to make. There were no Kolvas bodies and no Kolvas weapons — nothing Kolvas at all. Jovai could only believe her.

Jovai grabbed an Akarian long blade and started toward the nearest tree. Time for her to gather wood. It would be at least one long day's hard work. She didn't look to see if Gilix followed. What the girl did now no longer concerned her. She had seen the carnage. That was all that mattered.

A short while later, Gilix joined her. Jovai smiled at her. Gilix did not meet her eyes but set into work on the trunk where Jovai had paused. She had found an ax she could wield and together she and Jovai felled the tree and chopped it into pieces.

When they reached the center of the camp with the first armload of wood, they found a large space cleared, with a pile of corpses stacked beside it, waiting. Tied to each of them, around their necks if they still had one, or tucked inside their wounds, was a reed plugged at one end and covered at the other with a piece of leather. The Gicok stood beside the pile. A reed was in his hand, from which he carefully removed a lock of yellow hair before he tied the reed to the one remaining leg of the topmost corpse.

Jovai stood silently beside him until he grunted to acknowledge her.

"Look, when you gather them, to find a sign of who killed them."

"Kolvas," he grunted.

"There is nothing here of the Kolvas — no bodies, no weapons..."

"They clear away."

"They haven't had that much time. The bodies were stiff when we first found them, but not decayed. They weren't long dead, maybe two days, or three. The Kolvas say they arrived just before they found us."

"They lie!"

"They would have missed something. There is too much chaos for every sign of the attackers to have been cleared away, yet the only signs that I have seen and recognized are of Gicok and Akarian. Just look," she suggested gently. "See what you can find."

By sunset the funeral pyre was piled high, the Gicok corpses nestled among the wood. The Gicok ghosts were all around. Jovai could feel them, although she didn't see them. There was an air of waiting, an expectation. She hoped fervently that the ghosts would go away once their bodies were ash and charred bone.

Next to the pyre was a small stack of bodies — Akarian. There were not many. The Akarians must have taken care of their own, accidentally missing only a few of their dead. It seemed unforgivably careless, but she had seen no Akarian ghosts so, perhaps, it did not matter so much to them.

"What do we do with them?" she asked the Gicok.

He shrugged. Then he pointed to one of several bodies that were lying separate.

"That one yours," he said.

"Mine?" she looked at it, confused, but in the growing mist and dying light, it was only a blurry lump.

"Vohee," he said. "Dead slave."

She stared up at him, shocked, and felt her face flush with horror.

"You kept one of my people slaves?" She demanded.

"His master honored him in death," replied the Gicok calmly.

"You mean you also killed him," she interpreted for herself.

"Honor," the Gicok stressed. "He burn with my people?"

She had to fight back her sudden renewal of anger and hatred of the Gicoks to realize the kindness he was offering.

"Stay. Wait," she said, gesturing him away. She knelt beside the corpse to which he had gestured and turned it so its face lay toward the sky. Fair skin, long brown hair, not pulled back now but hanging loose. The eyes had been pecked away, the body torn open and disemboweled, the throat cut with merciful precision and dried blood coated much of his nakedness, but she recognized the face. He was only a year or two older than herself. The thought struggled through the shocked numbness of her brain. He was practically as young as she, and a better warrior, and he was the only one to ever have said she was pretty.

"Litazu," she cried softly, "Berailen," that was his adult name — the bold fool. The one who had left his people to escape her. "Where is your spirit now?" she asked in spirit's tongue. "Are you trapped here too? What can I do to appease you? How can I set you free? Are you still waiting? Shall I call the ancestors here?" Would they come to this strange place? "Berailen," she prayed, "if you are here, help me know what to do."

256

"Do nothing, witch," came the answer from the swirling mist around her. She knew his voice from memory. "I would not have you touch me. I cursed you with my dying breath. Now your master can have his way. I prayed that no one will ever touch you in love or else he will suffer for it. Everyone you love will suffer because of you."

Jovai gasped in horror. For a moment, she felt she could not understand him. It was as if his words made no sense, then their meaning slowly sunk in.

"I love our people," she protested. "Have you then cursed them too?"

"I curse no one but you since no witch can love."

"Berailen, repeal your curse or everyone we have loved will suffer for it."

"I am dead. I can do nothing now."

"Berailen, you are a fool!" she cried. She buried her face in her hands, but they couldn't stop her tears. She felt the sudden pressure of a warm and living touch on her shoulder. The Gicok stood beside her, comrade in sorrow.

"How did you die?" she asked the corpse, with words his spirit would have to answer.

"The Akarians were welcomed as friends. When they started to attack, many of them were already inside and many others secretly surrounded. There was no escape. My master was kind. He offered me the honor of this death. Rather than feed Gorat, I accepted."

"Then it was the Akarians," she said softly to herself. She glanced up at the Gicok, but although his hand still rested on her shoulder, he gave her privacy by keeping his face turned away.

"Is your spirit restless still?"

"I am angry," it replied.

"What does it need to be calm and free?"

"What all the spirits here want — revenge."

"We are not a vengeful people," she argued, although she doubted her own words.

"Burn me with my people, those who accepted me after you made me an exile. But my spirit will not leave this world until Gorat is destroyed."

"I will sing you Soul's Ease," she told him.

"Then every sound will mock you," he answered.

She raised her voice in the sweet kindness of the song and the space around her echoed her words, casting them back distorted and foolish sounding. Never-the-less she finished her song and let the last echo die before she rose and addressed the Gicok.

"Let him burn with his master," she said. "I thank you for this honor to one of my people."

The Gicok solemnly added Berailen's body to the pyre.

"What about them?" asked Jovai, pointing to the two other slaves from foreign peoples and the pile of the Akarian warriors.

"*Vitka*," he said, pointing to the other slaves, "savages. Animals take care of animals."

"And the Akarians?"

He frowned, disgusted and turned away. "Animals take care of animals," he repeated.

"Then you know — it was they who killed your people?"

He nodded.

"Dolkati warrior people. Always ready for enemy. Always good to friend. Only way to kill Dolkati is come as friend. Akarians all die for betrayal."

"No Kolvas," whispered Gilix. She was hovering at a distance, so quiet that the others had forgotten she was there.

The Gicok flashed her an angry glance and turned away.

"We share a common enemy now," said Jovai. "The Akarians betrayed the Kolvas years ago. Now they have betrayed your people. Soon it will be my people."

"They will die!" he vowed.

"But now we are only two alone. The Kolvas are many people. They can help us. We need them."

"I no need filthy flesh-eaters. This only my Dolkati-ka. Many Dolkati-ka over world. I find others now."

"If the Akarians who came here maybe five, maybe six days ago, went immediately in search of other Dolkati-ka, would they find them before we could if we left now?"

The Gicok nodded bitterly.

"They know my people. They know Dolkati-ka all go."

"What chance is there that someone might have escaped to go warn the other Dolkati-ka?"

"No," answered the Gicok. "Dolkati-ka most women, children. Few men. Many men now help Akarian, make trade for winter goods."

"It would be stupid to kill only one Dolkati-ka and leave the others to make war because of it. They would eventually find out, wouldn't they?" The Gicok nodded.

"Then we must warn the other Dolkati. But we are only two, and there were many Akarian warriors who did this. Who knows where they went? They could still be near. They could kill us and nothing would be gained."

"Only two could hide. Dolkati know land. Akarian stranger here."

"If we do find other Dolkati-ka, will they be enough to help? Women, children, elders, can they be enough warriors to kill all Akarians?"

"They are Dolkati. Dolkati warriors all. All can fight."

"But are they enough? And if they are...if we can't find them, are we alone enough?"

"You speak evil," he growled at her.

"The Kolvas hate the Akarians. They have warred against the Akarians."

"They lost!"

"They might war again."

"They are few."

"They are more than we are now, and there are more Kolvas than we know here. Other Kolvas went other ways. If the Kolvas help us, we would have more people, more power. And maybe my people would help us too."

"You would get Vohee?"

"Some of my people might listen to me, but important others wouldn't. And you have been our enemy so they wouldn't listen to you. But they don't know the Kolvas. If the Kolvas would speak to them, warn them, then they might listen and believe."

"Vohee make pact with blood-drinkers!" He spat on the ground as if the taste of his words displeased him.

"It might save them if they did. It would help you if you would. They are a people of a different belief, but they are people, and their numbers can make us stronger."

"No!"

Gilix had eased her way to Jovai's side, again keeping Jovai between herself and the Gicok. She was quiet, unobtrusive. It was only when she took Jovai's hand that Jovai realized she was there. She pointed to the pyre waiting to be burned and then to the sky which had grown fully dark now and thick with cool mist.

"Dark now," said the Gicok, pretending to ignore her. "Time for fire."

"Kolvas come," whispered Gilix in Jovai's ear.

Jovai shrugged.

"Kolvas come," repeated Gilix, significantly. "Bad. Bad."

"Will they kill us?" asked Jovai.

Gilix frowned, not fully understanding, but she ventured a nod. "Difsat," she said. She pointed to the pyre. "Bad."

Jovai glanced toward the Gicok. He was busy sparking some kindling into a fire. Quickly she grabbed the girl's hand and led her toward the edge of the Gicok camp.

"Go back then," she told the girl. "Go quickly."

Gilix started running but stopped when she saw Jovai was not following.

"Come," she said. Jovai shook her head. The girl's eyes grew large and frightened. "Bad!" she insisted. "Come."

"Go," Jovai told the girl. "I'm staying."

"No." Gilix returned to Jovai's side and took her arm. "Bad. Kolvas come. Bad."

"Go to your people, Gilix," insisted Jovai, pushing her away. "Tell them the Akarians killed the White Ones. Tell them that the Akarians might still be near. Do you understand?" She used what she guessed was the Kolvas word for understand. Gilix shook her head.

Behind them, the crackling of a fire sounded, and the smell of smoke began to permeate the fog. Gently, a man's voice rose in rhythmic lament. It was a gruff sound but full of courage and strength. The hisses and pops of the fire grew louder, seeming to keep time with the song. As Jovai listened, she could feel her heart beat slower, also in time with the song. This was no shaman singer, just a simple man, but this song of his people drew her. She forgot about Gilix, about the angry Kolvas coming. She forgot everything except the beat of her heart, the rhythm of her steps, the glitter of the fire, and the song of the singer.

The words were simple. There were few and often repeated. She didn't know what they meant, but it didn't matter. Her voice sang them of its own accord. Her steps grew into a dancing pattern, circling the pyre. And it was a crowd of people she danced with — shapes appearing and fading as the mist swirled and the slow wind breathed life into the fire of the dead. Hands reached toward her that never touched, and lips moved in song that was only the whisper of the wind. Not all were human. Many were part or wholly beast, but great and strong in spirit power. Demon-like shapes played through the fire, devouring the bodies greedily — food for the spirits. And sometimes from the fire, arms would wave or faces would smile or grimace and seem so alive that it was hard to resist pulling them out into the safety of the cool night, but the dancers and the flames barred the way and laughed derisively at the humans so fooled. "Keep your place," they cried, "it's not your turn."

The flames climbed, and the dance quickened, and it was the song bending to the rhythm of the dead, letting them lead the way.

"The hero's glory!" screamed the Gicok.

"The hero's glory!" yelled Jovai.

"The hero's glory!" echoed Gilix, proud and defiant.

What language it was they saluted in, Jovai never knew. The words felt as if they were born from her soul and voiced in true intent, without the mediator of any words at all.

Others were crowding into the camp — men with weapons. At the sight of the fire, they stopped amazed and stared spell-bound at the Dolkati man, the Vohee youth, the Kolvas woman and the dancing ghosts.

One Kolvas man let out a high-pitched battle cry. Jovai laughed with an almost insane delight for, although she knew he was Kolvas, the cry she remembered from her own people in battle with the Gicok warriors.

The Kolvas men came alive at the sound of that cry. They raised their weapons and rushed forward into the crowd of dancing mist. They turned this way and that, attacking shapes that were nothing but empty air before their weapons could hit. They yelled, and they screamed in mad frustration, and their screams became a chant, and their attacks became a dance, and the fire grew higher as the night grew darker. The flames tore through the thick white air and reached up to a dazzling full moon.

"Great goddess," prayed Jovai, bowing to the moon, "bridge between the worlds. Half your light to all the world of the living and half your light to all the world of the dead. Your presence comforts us and eases our way. Thank you."

She felt the moonlight fall upon her, like a mother's kiss. The moon was shining in her valley now too, on her master's head as he sang the festival of the full moon. She could see his face, deeply lined with a lifetime of worry, reflected as if the moon were his mirror. His eyes met hers with surprise and joy. For one, miraculous moment they were together again. Then the smoke and fog rose to hide the moon from view.

By dawn, the fire was burning low, embers, ashes and charred bones. The dancers slumped, exhausted, and the few remaining singers, Kolvas, Gicok, and Vohee, pushed the last of the words through raw throats, over stiff tongues.

Gilix yawned, her head resting on Jovai's shoulder and sighed. She lifted her head, stretched like one awakening from a long, deep sleep and rubbed her eyes open. Then she stared around her amazed.

"Kolvas come!" she exclaimed.

Jovai let the last echo of the song die in the dawn before she came awake enough to see what Gilix meant. All around, the Kolvas people sat or lay — not just the men with their weapons, whom she vaguely remembered, but the women and the children too. All the people of the Kolvas were here gathered, sleeping or waking, exhausted from a long night of attending to the Gicok dead. A few at first, then others rose like sleepwalkers and made their way back to their tents.

"The Kolvas do your people honor," said Jovai to the Gicok. He sat slumped, head resting against his knees. He did not bother to raise his head but offered Jovai a tired grunt for acknowledgment.

"Are we finished? Can we rest now?" asked Jovai. Her whole body ached for sleep.

"Hmm." The Gicok pulled from his belt a cloth bag of his people and handed it to her to see. It was filled with the little locks of Gicok hair which he had pulled from the token-filled reeds. "This I do alone," he told her. "Even good Dolkati Friend no help."

She handed him back his bag and left with Gilix and the last of the Kolvas to return to the Kolvas village.

CHAPTER 32

BIRTH OF LATOHUA

Jovai slept dreamlessly for a long time. When she awoke, the sun was high and warm, the fog burned away. People were quietly attending to daily tasks and the smell of cooking food filled the air. Jovai felt starved and, somehow, deeply satisfied. She looked for her friend and saw the Gicok soundly asleep, with an odd expression, akin to peace, on his face.

"Now it's done," she thought, not quite knowing what "it" was. "It's done and well done."

She stepped out into the bright, sunny day. People who passed by her smiled and nodded, the ever-cheerful Kolvas.

"Food?" she asked one nearby lady, using the Kolvas word. The lady smiled and started talking, fifty words a second, and pointing all around the camp. She laughed and patted Jovai's arm, then she scurried away. A moment later Jovai saw her hurrying back with Difsat.

Jovai felt her stomach buckle. "It's just hunger," she told herself, but she knew she was afraid. She could not guess what the shaman might do to her for disobeying his orders. She pulled herself tall, forced a smile at the shaman, and greeted him politely with the proper Kolvas words.

"Well, a very good time," he told her in the spirit's tongue.

"What?" asked Jovai, taken aback.

The shaman laughed and hugged her with a hearty squeeze. "We'll make a Kolvas of you after all if you can have good fun like that."

"You mean the funeral?"

"Great power there," he told her as an answer. "It was just what we were needing."

He grabbed her by the arm and pulled her after him. "Come on," he told her, "My family will feed you. You and I, we need to talk."

He stopped, part way there, and pointed to a wide, deep pit dug into the ground and reinforced with wood around the sides.

"Do you know what that is?" he asked her.

Jovai shook her head.

"That will be my home. My home." He repeated the words with a solemn joy that warmed Jovai to hear.

"May it be a happy one," she wished him.

Difsat smiled and looked around him, at the giant trees, the root-gnarled earth, the sparkling of the river just visible in the distance.

"I do like it here," he confided. "The spirits led us well. It is a very good place."

He brought her to his current home — a tent, from the outside hardly distinguishable from any of the others. Inside it was carpeted with strange pelts and a thickly woven cloth of many vibrant colors. It was old and worn, but there was still a gayness about it. The sleeping palates were rolled and wrapped in pieces of woven cloth in bright, bold patterns and designs of animals and protection spirits. Along one wall a piece of wood hung suspended from hooks on two of the stays that supported the tent. From the board hung a couple knives, a pipe, and several various tools. On the floor in one corner was a box the size of a small child and carved in it were many magic symbols. Many were unfamiliar, but Jovai knew enough to recognize a few. That is where he would keep his magic tools, she guessed.

"The wife will be here soon," he told her. "She rations the food, so we eat last, but she's a good cook, so we eat well. Just one moment..." He took one of the knives and placed it before the door flap. "That will keep the children away until the food arrives. When food comes, they come, nothing you can do. There!" He threw himself on the soft floor pelts and leaned back comfortably against one of the bedrolls. He gestured for Jovai to do the same. "Now we can talk. Do you know what last night was?"

"It was many things," answered Jovai, puzzled.

"It was the night of the full moon. Do you know what that means?"

"My people honor the moon goddess every full moon..."

"It's the night we were supposed to name you," he answered for her, waving away her irrelevant words. "I told you, on the night of the full moon we would give you a name and find you a family and welcome you as one of us." He smiled, "It's not flattering that you forgot."

"Forgive the newborn," she solemnly begged. Difsat laughed.

"Since we didn't get around to it last night, what should we do? Do you want to be accepted as one of us?"

"Yes, shaman," she answered.

"Will you leave behind you your former people and your former friends?"

"No, shaman."

"Not even a moment's thought?" he asked, annoyed.

"I cannot leave behind my people because I am tied to them by birth and blood, and I cannot forsake my friends because I am tied to them by honor."

"But your friends are our enemies."

"The Gicoks have always been my own people's enemies."

"Then you do doubly wrong," he insisted.

"No. The Gicoks will not be our enemies much longer. Do you know what happened at the camp up the river? Do you know how they all died?"

"It is not interesting to me," he replied.

"The Akarians killed them with treachery. Now the Akarians are the enemies of the Gicoks and my friend has sworn to kill them all, or as many as he can."

Difsat laughed.

"One man against an empire," he mocked.

"I don't know how many the Akarians are, but I would not be one of them if they were a whole world full if it meant having such an enemy. The man is a warrior, brave, strong, and proud. There is no Akarian in this land who is now safe. And he is not one man alone."

"There are other White Ones?" demanded Difsat, suddenly alarmed.

"I don't know. What I meant is that he has me. What the Akarians did to your people, and now to his, they will soon be doing to my people."

"Those who cast you out." He was guessing. He watched her face for confirmation.

"And those who held me dear," she answered with a nod. "Everyone is in danger."

Difsat leaned forward, an anxious expression on his face.

"I will tell you something, newborn, and you must listen to me and understand. The Akarians are not just a few and not just many. They are multitudes. They are not a single race, but many races joined together under the dark-skinned ones. My people were many — a great empire covering many hills and wide, endless-seeming plains, but the Akarians were more. They are a whole world full. There are so many of them there is no more room for anyone else. That is why we had to flee, and even where we run they are there. Even in this land, given to us by the great spirits, they were here before us. How can you, a little woman, with no people, how can you even begin to be noticed by them, much less do them any significant harm?"

"It is true, Difsat," she answered, "your people are not safe from the Akarians here. Only a matter of a day or two before you came an Akarian army was here. They slaughtered a whole people, and there is nothing to stop them from coming back."

"That was not my question."

"But it is true. You cut down trees and build dwellings. You burn areas and make room for crops. You cut canals for irrigation. You start a life here, and no sooner will it begin to take shape than the Akarians will come and do to you what they did to the White Ones. If they don't kill you all, they'll send you fleeing again and you'll never be able to stop or rest...unless you stand and fight."

"Then we will fight," he told her, angrily. "We are not cowards. But we are weak now. We are tired and hungry and mourning the dead we know of and fearful for the friends and family separated from us. We need this rest before we can fight again."

"I too need rest," she told him, "and so does my friend. It is a difficult thing to lose everyone you love in one quick blow. But it is also horrible to know that your people are in danger. Even though you don't know what you can do, you know you must do something. The Akarians could come back at any time. Any morning you might wake to the sound of mothers screaming as their children are killed before their eyes. Are you ready for that?"

"How you speak!" he chided her. "You might make a good story teller. I could recommend you for that clan if you think you'll stay with us."

"The Gicok ghosts may still be restless. Do you believe me now?"

He nodded slowly. "I saw them dance," he told her.

"They wish their deaths to be avenged."

"But that means nothing to us. The White Ones and the Kolvas are not allies. We have been enemies since the beginning of this world. They are disgusting barbarians, living like animals without a home. They survive only by stealing what civilized people produce or, lately, by begging from Akarians. Such filthy beasts have no right to foul the earth."

"They are proud and honorable warriors. Difsat, they are excellent fighters. And they know the ways of the Akarians — probably even better than your people do."

"They did not know enough to save themselves," he pointed out.

"They did not suspect treachery from their allies because they would not have betrayed their allies. That alone should make them allies worth having."

"No," he told her. "There is too much hatred between our people. Let the White Ones go and fight the Akarians if they want. When they have done all they can, and we are healed from the wounds which their people helped inflict, then we will fight our own war."

"And you will fight it against a whole new generation of Akarians, young and strong where your people will be old and tired."

Difsat laughed as if at the foolishness of a child. "You are young still," he told her, "it will be many years before you can understand the art of war."

A woman's voice called from outside the door flap and the smell of freshly boiled meat and grain patties slipped through the tent to tease the people inside.

Difsat called his wife to come. She entered, brisk and cheerful, with two little boys and an older girl noisily following on her heels. The elder of the little boys immediately started talking, with animated gestures and excited eyes. He was telling the story, Jovai gathered, of adventures on the hunt. The little brother kept interrupting, wanting also to be part of the story. The older brother endured him with a patience Jovai found remarkable in one so young.

Meanwhile, the girl came beside Jovai. She touched her hair timidly, then quickly drew away. Her father turned on her angrily, and she answered him with words that were obviously not as meek as her manner would have suggested. Difsat laughed.

"Filani compliments you on your hair," he told Jovai. "She would very much like to play with it if you would let her."

"Play with hair?" asked Jovai, not sure that she understood.

"Braid things into it or shape it into styles. Our girls and women do that for each other. Don't yours?"

Jovai shrugged. "I don't know. Maybe." She thought back, of the girls she had seen giggling and laughing together. "I guess they do." She smiled at the little girl and nodded. "I would be pleased," she told her in Kolvas.

The girl's eyes lit, and again she reached out to stroke Jovai's long hair. Yes, Jovai thought to herself, it felt good to be touched so.

The meal was simple but tasty and the conversation light. The children dominated most of it. Jovai did not understand the words but found herself happy at the sound of their voices. She felt awkward and unsure of herself, ignorant of the Kolvas niceties as well as their language, but the family chatted away happily and let her feel as if she were one of the crowd.

"You like my family?" Difsat asked her, seeing how her eyes sparkled.

"Very much," she assured him.

"They are curious about you. I have told them I will bid with the other families to adopt you, but I've told them nothing else. They only know the general gossip."

"And what does the general gossip say?"

"Many crazy stories," he answered with a shrug. "There is one that you are a great warrior hero from our tales, returned to us now as he said he would return long ago. Some people say you are a spirit walking as a man to test us in our new home. There is even talk that you are a being from another world or a land farther away than we can imagine. But most people believe you are an escaped slave from the Akarians. We like crazy stories, but we believe the practical ones."

Jovai saw the family watch her as she and their father spoke in the spirit's tongue. Their gazes were frank. She met them with a smile and was answered by all with smiles. It felt very good.

After the meal, the family was ushered out again. Only the girl protested and argued to stay.

"She insists on braiding your hair now," Difsat informed Jovai.

"I would enjoy that, if it is all right with you."

"She promises not to listen, but she will," he shrugged and told his daughter she could stay.

The little girl, with great solemnity, drew from a bag that was hers alone a beautifully crafted comb. She showed it to Jovai, holding it before her as if it were the finest piece of art in the world. With her eyes, Jovai traced the patterns carved into the wooden base of the comb. Someone had crafted it with great care and love, and there was a rightness in the way Filani carried it. It was hers — made for her probably — or else given to her by someone who loved her very much.

"You were supposed to take your name last night," said Difsat to Jovai, "and so you have. Our people call you Latohva, Dancing Light, because of the way you wove the fire and the moonlight into your funeral dance. It is an honorable name. You can reject it if you choose, but then you must find your own name for yourself, and there will be many people who will still call you Latohva."

Jovai winced in pain. Filani was now pulling at tangles in her hair that might have been there from birth for all she knew.

"I suggest you keep it," Difsat continued. "Everything's easier that way."

"Yes. It's a beautiful name," said Jovai, wincing again. It was not a shaman name. There could be only small power in it at best. She was thankful for that.

"It is yours then, and you are ours, accepted by us as one of our own. The decision is yours if you want to stay or not. I'll give you until the next full moon to decide — maybe even longer if you need it. Meanwhile, you can learn our language and get to know us better. When it comes time to choose a family for you everyone will have a better idea of where you belong."

"Thank you, Difsat. And thank you for Gilix. She has been a very good teacher so far."

At that the shaman frowned.

"You forget Gilix. It was a stupid idea of mine. I'll find you someone better."

"I don't understand," said Jovai. "What was wrong with Gilix? Doesn't she want to teach us anymore?"

"She's just too silly..."

"Is it because of last night?"

"It is because she does not teach you as you should be taught. You must learn not only our language but our ways, our structure, our laws. Instead of teaching you our laws she helped you break them."

"How was she supposed to stop me?"

"She did not have to stop you, but she shouldn't have helped you."

"Then it is because of last night!"

"You could not know or understand, but she did."

"Is she in trouble?"

Difsat shrugged.

"Bad trouble?" pressed Jovai.

"With an unmarried woman, trouble is always bad trouble. There are men who might have been husbands who will not want her now, but the world is wide and full of men."

"What is her punishment?"

"It is not your concern."

"How do your people punish a girl who follows her conscience instead of your judgment?"

"The law is made to protect the people. One who breaks the law betrays her people. How would you punish a traitor?"

"But no harm came of it..."

"Who knew what harm might have come of it? I knew better than she and she ignored me. It is my right to execute her. I could have her tortured to death. In a generous mood, I could merely exile her."

"What did you do?" demanded Jovai.

"I like the girl. I have her shunned until the next full moon."

"What does that mean, 'shunned'?"

"It means no one will talk to her or hear anything she has to say or share food with her or touch her or help her or accept her help. It means that, although she can live among us still and claim her ration of food, in all other ways she no longer exists to us."

"That is cruel!"

"That is nothing! A month is nothing! You are willful, Latohva. Do you think I haven't seen? In times like these, a people need to stay together, to work together, to put the community first, before the self and to bow to the wisdom of those older and wiser. It doesn't matter if what she did caused harm or not. What matters is that it could have. What matters is that the next time one acts in selfish pride like that it could mean the destruction of all our people. She has only one month of her life taken away from her — just a little time to think about what danger she might have caused. And in that time no one will acknowledge her. You will not acknowledge her, or your punishment will be far worse. This is our law, Latohva. If you will be one of us, you will accept it!"

Jovai bit her lip and lowered her head. She felt swept by a sudden fury, followed by guilt that her actions had caused this punishment for Gilix. Then lastly her heart was filled with shame.

"You are right, Shaman," she said at last. "You are wiser than I, and I should accept your law. Please forgive my irrational anger."

274

"We will see," said Difsat, coolly. "I believe her punishment will be yours as well. I like you. I hope you can endure."

Filani stepped between them and lifted Jovai's chin to inspect her work with a critical eye. For a moment, she looked more like her mother than her father, but when she turned to Difsat and smiled, she was his child without a doubt. She said something to him in Kolvas, and suddenly he was laughing again.

"She says you are pretty enough to be a girl," he told Jovai. "We should be getting you proper clothes now. We should have done it from the first."

"I am comfortable in these clothes," responded Jovai. "May I keep them a while longer?"

"People will think you're a boy."

"Only for a little while."

Difsat seemed about to protest, but paused first and changed his mind. Reluctantly, he agreed. He stopped his daughter, who was busy undoing the braids she had made, and sent her away.

"One more thing," he told Jovai. "Your White One is almost completely healed. So what will he do now?"

"I don't know."

"Will he stay much longer?"

"I don't believe so. He has pledged himself against the Akarians. As soon as he is able, I believe he will seek out his people and keep his pledge. He will need the horses and packs with which we arrived."

"We will return to him what is left."

"You've used the supplies?"

"Only what was needed."

"Then the White One has been of service to you," Jovai said carefully. "I am glad."

"His people owe us much," Difsat answered.

"Are the horses well?"

"They are being tended by one of the Hawk Clan. I think he is very fond of them. They are much better than the few we managed to come away with. He asked to be your next teacher — I believe in the hopes that you might eventually give him one. Such generosity would be to your honor."

"They are not mine to give."

Filani spoke from outside the door, and her father called her in. She was followed by a man, young, strong, and very handsome. His long, straight auburn hair was pulled back from a noble face with a straight, long nose, intense, dark eyes, a wide brow, square chin and perfectly shaped lips that seemed just on the verge of a smile. He wore leggings but no furs or tunic. Only a simple string of hawk feathers worn around his neck and the naked, muscular chest and arms beneath it identified him as one of the Hawk Clan.

"*Koban issak.* This is Koban of the Hawk Clan," said Difsat.

"*Latohva issak*" he introduced Jovai to the man.

Koban smiled and said the polite words expected of him. Jovai just stared back, open-mouthed. She knew she should say something. She vaguely remembered learning what she should say, but her mind refused to find the words. All she could think of was how warm and strong his voice sounded and how pleasing his lips looked as they shaped the words.

"I offer you again some better clothes," said Difsat, teasingly.

Jovai blushed. She remembered Litazu/Berailen and her master's anger. If Yaku were here, watching her with this handsome man, he would insist even stronger that she dress like a boy. She could not bring herself to betray him.

"These will do for now," she said.

276

CHAPTER 33

KOBAN

"I am honored to be your teacher," Koban told Jovai in Akarian, as he walked her back to her tent.

"You speak the language well!" she exclaimed, smiling at him in surprise.

"I had occasion to learn it," he answered evenly. His face and voice told her it had not been a happy occasion.

The Gicok was awake and hungrily eating when they entered the tent. At the sight of Koban, he jumped to his feet, his eyes flickering around the man suspiciously.

"Who he?"

"*Koban issak,*" answered Jovai. "He is Koban of the Hawk Clan, our new teacher."

"Where Gilix?"

"She is being punished for breaking Kolvas law." Try as hard as she could, Jovai could not keep the bitterness out of her voice. Koban heard it and watched her, puzzled.

"Only good Kolvas," said the Gicok with a sour smile, "and Kolvas hate."

"She is not hated!" spoke Koban. "We only want her to learn to follow our laws. Every people must have laws, and everyone who would be of a people must follow those laws. Who here does not agree?"

The Gicok stared at Koban, surprised. Koban smiled.

"You see, I speak your language."

"Not my language," answered the Gicok with such vehemence that it was Koban's turn to be surprised.

"The language of your masters then," he said, after a pause.

The Gicok's face flushed with fury and his eyes flickered faster than Jovai had ever seen them before.

"Your horses have been under Koban's care," she said quickly, just before the Gicok lunged. It was the only thing she could think to say.

With impressive agility, Koban dodged the Gicok's blow. The Gicok swung around, then paused, caught suddenly immobile.

"Where my horses?" he demanded.

Koban was on guard, his body balanced and alert, all his concentration on the movements of his enemy. He did not bother to answer.

"Where horses?" demanded the Gicok again.

Koban rushed him, grabbing the Gicok low, beneath his center and hurling him to the ground. The Gicok brought him down with him and rolled on top, subduing Koban with a swift and painful blow to the gut and held him down with all his weight ready to crush the Kolvas warrior's throat.

"You eat horse, you die!" he exclaimed.

"Filthy dog...!"

"Where my horses?"

Jovai held her breath in fear, until finally, Koban answered.

"They are in a pasture, not far from here."

"You take me," he ordered the Kolvas man.

"Tomorrow..."

"Now!"

At last, he nodded.

"Now," Koban agreed, "and you can take them and go!"

He led them both out of the village. They walked down river a mile or two, over several hills, then, at last, descended into a golden clearing of very tall grass through the center of which ran a pretty little stream. As they entered the valley, they crossed the beginnings of a fence. Jovai looked up at Koban questioningly. He shrugged.

"Better than keeping them tied all the time."

The Gicok only grunted. He gave a sharp whistle as they came to the center of the clearing. From far away, toward the foot of the next hill, came back several loud whinnies. The Gicok took his direction and ran. Jovai and Koban followed more slowly.

"Will he take them all?" asked Koban.

"They are all his," answered Jovai.

"But he is only one rider. He doesn't need four horses," argued Koban, as if convincing Jovai might change the Gicok's mind.

"They are his power. He is now one man alone, against the whole Akarian Empire. He will need all the power he can get."

Koban snorted in disbelief.

"The White Ones are the Akarian's dogs!"

"Not anymore."

The Gicok was greeting his horses joyfully. He talked to them gently in their own language, like old friends sharing new memories. He stroked them lovingly, first one, then another, and inspected each one of them thoroughly from all sides.

"You see, I took care of them well," said Koban proudly.

"You lucky they alive," answered the Gicok, but he didn't seem displeased.

Koban patted the nearest horse possessively on the neck. The horse turned to him with a friendly snort, obviously pleased to see him. The Gicok glared.

"I ride now," he announced and suddenly he was flying on the horse through the tall, golden grass, the other horses running and prancing beside. They leapt lightly over the stream, circled the pasture and, in one surge of power, they were over the fence Koban had started to build. They climbed part way up the hill, then turned around and flew back down it, back over the fence, back into the open space of the meadow. At a signal from the Gicok, the horse he rode and another came along-side each other, matching their galloping stride for stride. As they did so, the Gicok jumped from the back of the one to the back of the other. Neither horse stopped or slowed, nor did they break from their matching gate until he signaled them to do so.

Jovai and Koban watched in astonishment.

The horses and rider took another turn around the meadow and another couple of passes defiantly over the partial fence before the Gicok finally dismounted."

"You ride?" he offered Jovai. She shook her head and smiled.

Koban stepped forward to take his turn, but before he could draw near, the Gicok slapped his horses and sent them running on their own. Koban watched them gallop away in obvious disappointment.

"I have never seen such riding before," he told the Gicok, his voice warm with admiration. The Gicok accepted his tribute with a stony expression. "I have never known such wonderful horses before either," Koban continued.

"Dolkati horse," explained the Gicok.

"Yes. The horses of your people are the best in the world. But these four, I think they are even better than the others."

At that, the Gicok smiled proudly.

"My woman. She know horse good. She get sire and dam and she choose when. That very good. Woman always know. We always have best horses."

"For horses like that, even I might marry a White One's woman," Koban whispered confidentially to Jovai.

"His wife was so beautiful, any man might marry her for no horse at all."

"Not a White One's woman," said Koban.

Jovai shrugged. "I only saw her dead, but even then she was at least as beautiful as the prettiest women I have seen alive."

"Maybe her face was pretty," he said, "but her spirit was still one of them."

The Gicok called for a brush to groom his horse. Koban pulled forth one of their bags from a hidden space between three boulders and dug out the brush from the collection of tools within it.

"I can do it," he volunteered.

"You watch," offered the Gicok. "Learn how."

Koban suppressed his annoyance and stood back with Jovai. Together they watched as the Gicok groomed his horses with smooth, loving strokes, singing, and talking to them gently as he did so. Jovai did not know his words, but it seemed as if the horses did. They snorted and huffed happily and conversed with him until the sun had set and the fog had gathered around the hills and was slowly creeping down into the clearing.

"What are you going to do now?" Jovai asked the Gicok as he replaced the brush in the bag and hid the bag again between the rocks.

"Sleep," he told her, and he led the way back to their tent in the Kolvas village.

The next morning the Gicok woke Jovai up. It was long before sunrise, and the fog-covered woods were silent and eerie.

"I go now," he told her. "Find other Dolkati-ka."

She groaned sleepily but forced herself awake. When the Gicok left the tent, she followed.

The Kolvas still slept. Even their animals stood with glazed eyes and drooping heads, and dogs lay curled before the door flaps of the tents. Jovai shivered in the cool air of morning, but it helped her come awake.

"We could eat first," she suggested, her hunger already awakening. The Gicok only quickened his pace as answer.

He was on guard, all his senses alert. When two of the guards of the dog clan stepped out to block their path, he was ready.

He had one disarmed before any of them knew what was happening. The other swung at him, from sheer reflex, and found himself suddenly face down in the dirt.

"Run," ordered the Gicok.

Jovai obeyed. It seemed the only thing to do.

They heard an alarm raised behind them and quickened their pace.

"They'll have darts," yelled Jovai.

"We get horses," the Gicok answered over his shoulder.

They scrambled up the hills and slid, more than ran, down them. The bushes rustled with animals fleeing from their path. A small bat screeched, startled from its tree, and flew at Jovai. She ducked just before it hit her face, causing her to trip and fall, tumbling down the slope of the last hill and into the fence that Koban had started to build. She heard a loud crack and didn't know if it was the fence or her forehead.

A man's voice yelled from ahead of her. It was not the Gicok. A man's voice answered from behind. They were surrounded then. She scrambled to her feet, but then a rush of darkness swept in through her eyes and forced her to the ground again. She was too dizzy to move, and the pain in her head was intense. She held it in her hands and waited for the men all around her to catch her.

"Why were you running?" she asked herself, realizing suddenly that it hadn't made any sense.

The yelling was right over her now. A pair of hands grabbed her roughly and pulled her to her feet. Her eyes squeezed shut with the pain. She tried to stand but found she couldn't, and another pair of arms caught her as she fell.

Voices, voices — all of them meaningless and loud, shaking the air around her with pointless noise. Then, from the sea of voices, one bit of meaning was somehow caught.

"Stay."

And then another voice, not so high-pitched but sounding human, like a man, "Are you all right?"

She floated on those words for a moment. They were something solid to hold on to. She didn't want to let go.

Firm, strong hands gently lifted up her head. She squinted and tried to see who it was, but the fog seemed thicker. Everything was very bright and very blurry.

"Can you hear me?" the man asked again, concerned.

"Yes," she answered the voice.

"Are you all right?"

"The bat," she answered. It was hard to talk, as though she were struggling against a weight and needed her energy for that instead. "I fell — hit my head. Let me rest. Just a moment. I'll be all right."

"Why were you running?"

She gathered her energy, but could think of no answer worth the effort of speaking, so she let it go.

"Do you know me?"

Maybe, she thought. She could probably identify him if she had to, but again it did not seem worth the trouble.

"I'm Koban. Do you understand?"

"Koban," she repeated the name, knowing that it would mean something to her when she thought about it. "You're angry."

"Yes. You break our laws. You make trouble. Now I might be blamed for this like Gilix was. Why?"

She sighed. The shock was lifting. Her mind was clearing, but she still didn't try to open her eyes.

"You wanted him to go, you said. Then you try to stop him. He has to get to his people before it's too late."

"You mean the White One?"

She tried to nod, but the effort hurt her head.

"The Akarians are killing them. He has to warn them, while there are still enough to fight."

Koban spoke quickly in his language and several voices, just overhead, answered. She heard many footsteps, men running off, running back. It was a swirl of activity just beyond her eyelids. The pain was receding from her head. Slowly she opened her eyes and blinked and squinted. It was still dark. She looked up at Koban. His attention was directed elsewhere, to the other men who stood, looking down at her, and to the younger men who took his orders and ran off. Yet he held her head gently and kept his body still in deference to her pain. She was struck once again by how handsome and strong his face and body were.

"Have you killed him?" she asked, afraid of the answer.

"He got away." He looked down at her, not bothering to hide his anger. It made his eyes flash in a powerful, brilliant way. "We let him get away. He took all of the horses."

This sunk in slowly. "All?"

"There is none left for you. He does not plan for you to follow?"

"Stay," said the high-pitched voice again. She glanced around for its source but could not find it.

"No," she answered, still confused. "I am to stay."

CHAPTER 34

THE BAT'S CHOICE

"**T**he moon has shown on us only six times since we found you and only four times since we welcomed you among us and already I am regretting it!" yelled Difsat. The little tent he had lent Jovai and the Gicok shook with the anger in his voice.

Jovai kept her head bowed and eyes lowered, hoping he would not see her squint in pain.

"Another of my people is hurt now, and the White One has gone to find his people and maybe bring them back to war on us..."

"He has gone to warn them of Akarian treachery and to raise a war party against the empire."

"Not against us?"

"Not against you."

"Are you sure?"

Jovai nodded.

"And you are sure that he will not come back for you and hurt or kill more of my people in the process?"

Jovai shrugged. "It wouldn't make sense..."

"Sense?" exploded Difsat, "Sense? When have our enemies ever made sense? The White Ones slink into our homes like thieving dogs and think themselves great warriors if they can steal a few trinkets!

285

The only thing they have of value is their horse stock which they'll trade with no one for any item of any real value, but they'll give away to people they can't trust and happily walk like slaves behind their mounted enemy. Is that the sense you talk of?"

"You are right, Shaman, I cannot answer for him, but I don't think he will come back for me. He has too many people to find, before it's too late, and too much to do to make good his vow. It is good that I stay here where I am safe and out of his way. I don't know the land, I don't ride well, and I'm no warrior or even a hunter. He has seen how kindly you have treated me and he knows I do not need rescuing."

"Does he still feel the bond of loyalty with you?"

"The Dolkati loyalty is constant — unless it is betrayed."

"Then that bond may be enough to cause him to attack us."

"No. Just the opposite, I think," or rather, she hoped. "He has brought me to a place where I could be safe and happy. He would not jeopardize that for me by hurting the friends who so generously welcomed me."

Difsat stared at her, suddenly thoughtful, and said, "then tell me, did you not mean to go with him?"

Jovai shrugged.

"I wasn't really thinking..."

"Of course you weren't thinking!" Difsat was suddenly yelling again. "In all the time you've been here, I've yet to see you think! But what were you doing?"

"I wanted to say goodbye. I didn't know your guards would try to stop us..."

"They stop everyone. It is their job to know where everyone who leaves the camp is going, so they can be found if there is an attack or sudden danger."

"No one told us that, and we didn't have the language to tell them where we were going anyway. Besides, would they have let the Gicok pass if they had known he was leaving?"

286

"They would have gotten me."

"And what would you have done?"

"Talked to you."

"Then what?"

"Then meet with the council, and we would have decided what to do next."

"The Akarian army may already have slaughtered all the Dolkati women and children, or they may be attacking them now as we speak. How long would you make the man wait for you to decide that he may do what he has vowed only death will stop him from doing?"

Difsat frowned in irritation. He stood up and paced, then plopped down on the Gicok's bedroll, then jumped up and started pacing again.

"It's not the White One I care about," he told Jovai, at last, "it's you. You are the one who must live among us. You are the one who must follow our laws and ways. You watched him attack two of our people, and you did nothing!"

"I ran. Forgive me, Shaman, I could think of nothing else to do."

"So now, what do I do with you?"

He tilted up her head gently and brushed the hair back out of her face. As he did, his eyes fell upon the purple bruise on her forehead. He frowned and lifted his finger to trace its shape. His frown deepened.

"Where did you get this?" he demanded.

"I fell."

He stared at her curiously then quickly left the tent. She could hear him outside issuing orders in Kolvas, his tone excited. She heard people come running and some ran off, apparently to get more people for soon a crowd had gathered outside her little tent. The door flap pushed aside. She expected Difsat to reenter, but it was Koban instead.

"What's happening?" she asked.

He stared at her thoughtfully and, like Difsat had, gently brushed the hair from her face. His touch was hesitant and light, as though he were afraid of getting too close to her skin.

"You're not in trouble, are you?" she asked him.

He startled slightly and blinked.

"No," he answered. "Not even my clan leader blames me for losing the horses and letting the White One escape."

"I am glad."

Koban shrugged.

"They are calling a council. We are to wait here until they want us."

He sat down, facing her, his back to the door. For a minute, no words passed between them, but his eyes never left her.

"How bad is the trouble I am in?" she asked at last, breaking the uncomfortable silence. He frowned at her.

"You sound like a little child," he answered. "It is time for you to act like a man."

"I'm not a man."

"To your people before, maybe not, but to our people, a boy of your age is a man and expected to act like one. What trouble you have earned will come to you, and you will carry it."

"You are mad at me?" she asked, hesitantly. Even to herself, she sounded very young.

He nodded.

She left it at that and was content to let him watch her in silence.

It seemed a long time before anyone came. A boy lifted the door flap and tapped Koban's shoulder, whispering in Kolvas. Koban signaled to Jovai, and together they followed the boy to the large gathering tent. At the door, Koban stood back to let Jovai enter first. He was about to follow, but a word from a badly scarred, older man, a member of the council, kept him out.

"Stand there, in the light, and pull your hair off your forehead,"

Difsat ordered. Jovai obeyed. The members of the council rose and crowded around her, taking turns to look more closely at her bruise. There were about twenty people, both men and women, of ages varying from young adulthood to very old. Each wore an outfit peculiar to his clan or family, and it was easy to tell which animal each held as his token, although not as easy to know what purpose that clan fulfilled. The Hawk Clan leader wore a collar of hawk feathers. A huge scar split the side of his face from his forehead through his mouth. The healer had brushed dye in the wound before stitching it, and he wore his hair back and his head high in pride as if the scar were a mark of great honor.

The council members muttered among themselves in Kolvas, and most of their comments seemed referred to Difsat. He said very little in response, but he listened well and seemed to be watching every individual there very closely at the same time. At last, they had finished their inspection and took their seats around the fire in the center of the tent. Jovai was dismissed to wait outside with Koban.

"What is it?" she asked, lightly touching the bruise on her forehead.

"They say it's shaped like a bat," Koban answered. "That means something to Difsat since, for now, he is head of the Bat Clan."

"But it's only a bruise."

Koban shrugged. It was not his place to question his superiors.

They called her back in an hour later.

"How did you get that mark?" asked Difsat, referring to the bruise on her forehead.

"I fell."

He watched her closely and waited for her to go on. When she didn't, he asked, "What do you know of Kaistai?"

She shrugged. The name was not familiar.

"The Bat," urged Difsat. "The spirit who most likes to take the form of the bat."

"The one who led your people out of the last world and into this one, through the land of the dead and across the river of blood?"

"And who helped to lead us here."

"I know very little more than you have told me."

"But you do know more," said Difsat, triumphant. "I thought so."

"I don't understand that spirit. It's trying to tell me something, but I don't know what."

"What does it say and do?"

"It made me swim in the river of blood. It said things I didn't understand about life and death being the same, to run from one is to run from the other. Then, I think it was a bat that flew in my face as I was running and made me lose my balance."

"It wants you to stay with us. That's what I thought. It wants you to be one of us."

"I will stay, Shaman, if your people will still have me."

Difsat spoke with the others. The discussion was not long.

"You will stay with us. Koban will continue to teach you our language and part of the day you will help us build our city and plant our fields. You will be of my family for now and, it is likely, you will be of my clan — the Clan of the Bat."

"A shaman?"

"A particular kind of shaman."

Jovai shook her head.

"No Difsat. I feel confused about many things right now but one thing, the only thing, I am sure of is that I am not meant to be a shaman."

"The spirits mark you with favor."

"And then they turn on me."

"We'll talk of this later. Now you go and sleep all today and tonight. Tomorrow your work begins.

CHAPTER 35

LESSONS AND LIES

The next day, Jovai moved her things into the tent of Difsat and his family. Milapo took Jovai with her in the morning to help distribute the food. The supplies were all kept in one large building, the only one finished so far. It was dug deep in the earth and had a sloping roof made of wood and mud and straw. The high part of the roof was tall enough above ground to allow the entrance of a full-grown man without stooping. Windows in the roof let in light. Although there was a shelf to access the windows and the chimney vent and to store things if desired, there was not a floor above ground. One immediately entered onto steps that led into the dark and warm single floor. It was filled with grains and fruits, both dried and fresh, and smoked meats and casks of various liquids. It also had lengths of tanned hides, weapons and weapon heads, ropes and cloth and tools and all the general supplies the Kolvas had managed to carry with them or make since their flight.

Milapo took Jovai through the room, giving her words for every item there. Then, with a collection of seeds, she gave her a quick counting lesson. They were often interrupted as people arrived to get their share of food and tools. Each person carried a band made of knotted strings which Milapo read to remember how much he was to get. She spoke aloud as she retrieved the goods, for Jovai's benefit. It was not long before Jovai knew enough Kolvas to retrieve any number of any item Milapo demanded.

It was almost the middle of the day before an older woman came to relieve Milapo and let her take her share of food home to her family. Koban was waiting for Jovai when they arrived at Difsat's tent. He greeted Milapo politely as she bustled about to prepare her family's food. She answered him cheerfully and chatted about the morning work, describing with flying hands and imitated voices the way Jovai had helped. Koban turned to her surprised.

"You have learned many words today, says Milapo."

"Enough to fetch like a well-trained dog," laughed Jovai. The work had made her feel useful and happy again.

"She says you learn quickly and are not lazy. Are you ready to learn more?"

Jovai nodded and let Koban take her around the tent and give her names for things. He showed her what Milapo was doing and gave her the verbs — lighting the fire, straining the beans, slicing the meat, boiling water in the water sack, etc. As the youngest boy came running by to check on breakfast, Koban stopped him and had him fetch his brother for a game. The game was played by Koban calling an object or an activity and the boys and Jovai either fetching the object or doing the activity. The game did not last long for the boys quickly got tired of it, but long enough for Jovai to prove that she remembered much of what she had just been taught.

After they ate, Koban took Jovai to where the Kolvas were building a bathhouse and introduced her to the Beaver Clan Leader who was in charge. He was a young man, not much older than twenty years, and uncomfortably new in his position. He was not a good leader of people, but he had the knowledge they needed to build, and the Kolvas managed to organize themselves around him.

Koban took her around the site and taught her the words she needed for the tools and the actions. As soon as he felt comfortable in doing so, he left her. His clan was hunting again today, and he had decided she could do well enough without him.

It was a hot day even in this cool place. The sun had burned through the morning fog early. Many of the men and women working on the bathhouse had stripped down to light cloth tunics or cloth skirts around their waists. Their bodies glistened with sweat, and their eyes glowed with a sense of joy. This was their place now, their home, and they were making it.

There was no one to tell Jovai what to do. She watched the many groups of people. There were some who crushed stones between harder stones and mixed the chalk-like sand with a kind of liquid she did not recognize, to make a paste of it. Another group measured and chiseled wood poles. Another group treated the poles with some kind of substance and burnt them hard with a carefully controlled flame. Another group worked in the pit, still digging. In one corner, they had dug a well, and they were piling stones and wood pieces around it to make a structure that would bring the water up when they wanted and keep it covered when they didn't. Another group hauled stones away from where they were expanding the pit, and yet another group worked on a wall to smooth and pack it. Also, along this wall, were people fitting the poles together, working at the joints so that they would be tight and solid.

Jovai grabbed a tool and joined the group who was firming the wall. People smiled in greeting to her, and one man corrected her, with gestures and demonstration, until she was using the proper techniques. To his surprise, Jovai thanked him in Kolvas, but she could not understand his reply.

She worked until sunset, switching jobs as the aches in her body demanded. By the end of the day there was not a muscle that didn't hurt in her and, overall, she felt wonderful.

The days slipped into weeks, and Jovai knew enough Kolvas to make her needs known and take instruction. She worked many different jobs — building, tilling soils and planting, digging the irrigation canals and wells, felling trees and chopping wood, working the hides and smoking the meat from the prey the hunters caught, and even gathering food and herbs with the women. People started talking to her more and more as she worked alongside of them. Some were doing it, they said, to help her learn to speak. Some, she suspected, were talking to her just to hear themselves talk. Many talked to her because she listened and, despite her handicap with the language, seemed to understand.

They told her of their capital city which they had loved — a city wider than this forest, than this valley even. A great expanse of fields and ponds and rivers that they had made or diverted — and buildings not only deep but tall and gilded with melted gold that shone like the sun. One old man managed to tell her that it was the beauty of their city that had caused its fall. He said the sun spirit was jealous and had made the Akarians – the children of the sun as they called themselves – to punish them for their pride. Jovai heard of the history gardens, where significant times had been immortalized in stone and metals. Each garden was dedicated to a different spirit, a different guardian of the people. In each garden there was a shrine, where people would bring things of beauty — weavings and bowls of food and wine and decorations of bead or glass or gems or shells — so that all who saw were forever impressed with the love the Kolvas had for their guardians.

In telling her of these gardens, they told her of their stories, their heroes, and their spirits. She heard again and again of the bat but also of the beaver who had shown them how to find and use water even in the desert and through the cruel drought. His garden was on floating mats laden with earth and anchored to the middle of a man-made pond. Children were taught to swim in his waters, and young and old would bathe there twice a year and be blessed by the spirit of the pond. She heard too of Stafe, a spirit who took no animal form but was the brother of the Bat. He had taught them to honor the dead by eating their flesh in a communal feast — returning the bones to the earth and offering the blood to Stafe who would keep the spirit well and happy and away from the living in exchange. It shocked Jovai to hear of such customs, yet the Kolvas spoke of them with warm pride and affection. Stafe was a spirit of great power. He was much loved and respected and seen as the protector of health and the giver of happiness.

The Kolvas also spoke of those they had lost. All the families had split, only the married couples and their youngest children usually staying together. There had been several groups, with representatives from all the families and all the clans, who had each gone in separate ways hoping that at least one group might survive to find the place the spirits had promised for them. Now this group had found the land, and they waited, hopeful that the spirits would guide the rest of their people to them. Meanwhile, they kept their loved ones alive in memory, sharing with Jovai stories of the parents, grandparents, brothers and sisters, and children with whom they were longing to be reunited.

Several times Jovai tried to ask about Gilix. Her shunning was serious, and many people would not even talk about her. Those who did had little to say.

"No one has seen her since the evening of the day she was shunned," Koban told her, at last.

"But it's been so long!" fretted Jovai. "What is she eating? Where is she sleeping? What if she's hurt?"

"She wasn't banished, just shunned. She could have stayed safely in the camp." He shrugged. "She chose to leave so she must take care of herself."

"She was probably upset and ashamed. She wasn't thinking..."

"She's an adult. Her choices are her responsibility."

Jovai's conscience still hurt over the young woman and she

waited impatiently for the month to end so that she might seek her out and find a way to make up to her for the pain she was suffering on behalf of Jovai, her Gicok friend, and his people.

As Jovai became more proficient in the language, the lessons with Koban changed in nature to socialization. The society was structured according to families and clans. Families were responsible for the farming and the supplying of their own every day needs. Although the state ensured that each family had enough land to farm and raw materials to use, it was the family's responsibility to ensure that each member had enough food and had all their needs met. Should any member of the family suffer deprivation, the individuals could appeal to the state for correction of the situation at whatever level it had failed. The clans were specialized labor — the craftsmen, the artists, the builders, the warriors, the healers, the ledger keepers, etc. Most people belonged to a clan at some time in their lives, and some even became clan masters. The clan served the needs of the families and states and were paid with support from the state land — the land worked by all the families for the benefit of the state to trade or keep in case of shortages. The family had absolute authority over its children, but once that child had chosen or been accepted into a clan, the clan, depending on which one, would become the primary law in the individual's life. Different clans made different demands on the individuals, some removing him from his family altogether, while others merely strengthened the family power. Different families and different clans had different internal laws, but all were subject to the civil laws and any conflict was brought before a counsel to arbitrate.

That was the way it had been. Now, although the counsel concept was still kept in theory, Difsat, as civil leader, had been acting in many cases as an absolute authority. The situation had demanded it, and Difsat had, in general, done a good job, but the clan and family leaders were looking forward to the nearby day when they could reestablish their own authority.

Koban taught Jovai politeness. One usually addressed the wife first, even if the husband were the civil leader, when visiting a couple's home — especially if it were a matriarchal family. When in a public meeting, however, one addressed the husband first. He taught her the forms of speech to use at different occasions and with different clans. There were also the kind of gifts that were expected to be made and when and how they were to be received. Also, looking forward to a more prosperous time, the kind of clothes and body decorations that were to be worn for different occasions.

"The Bat Clan organizes the festival of the Fresh Fruit Dropping and also the plea to Stafe for the winter solstice. Difsat may ask you to pledge to them at either festival."

Jovai shrugged.

"I have told him I do not want to be of the Bat Clan."

Koban stared at her, shocked.

"The Bat Clan chooses very few, and no one who is chosen has ever refused them. It is a very great honor and has more privileges than any other clan."

"I would rather be of some other clan — maybe of the Hawk Clan if they would take me."

Koban smiled in pride.

"You would have to pass many tests. You would have to be very strong and very brave and very fast. If they accepted you, you would have to live many years without a wife or family — only with the clan — until the master decides to release you. You would have to be obedient. I think that would be hard for you, Latohva."

"I've been very obedient lately," she protested.

Koban laughed.

"You do what you're told only because you have nothing better to do. I guess that the first time someone asks you to do something with which you disagree you will argue. In the Hawk Clan, you cannot argue. If you are not obedient, you could die in shame and others could die because of you. You would do better in the Bat Clan. They are more used to being obeyed than to having to obey."

"No. Difsat said once that the Hawk Clan wanted me, because of the way I fought and frightened all your warriors."

Koban flushed angrily. Jovai didn't remember who the warriors had been and it occurred to her, too late, that one of them might have been Koban.

"You didn't fight like a real warrior," he sneered at her. "You only cast little spells to frighten us. If we hadn't been so tired from many months of traveling, they wouldn't have worked, and you would be long dead now."

"Maybe so," she answered, "but it did work. It's easier to fight an enemy who's running away. Fewer people get hurt. Besides, it wasn't a very fair contest with me and the Gicok in the collar and the rest of you free to kill us at your leisure."

"The White One did well. He is a true warrior, even if he is a thieving, barbarian White One. But you..."

Jovai ducked and jumped back just barely avoiding Koban's unexpected blow. He pulled a knife from his belt and lunged at her with it. His attacking arm slid down hers, safely deflected, and his body followed to land, face down, in a tangle of nearby bushes.

"Is this a test or do you really mean to hurt me?" asked Jovai, watching Koban warily as he picked himself up.

"That's what I mean," he answered stiffly. "A warrior does not ask stupid questions. When someone attacks you, it doesn't matter why. Here..." he reached for her hand. She let him take it and found her arm suddenly twisted behind her back and a knife at her throat.

"Now you're dead," he told her, his breath tickling her ear.

She stood trembling in his arms. His body was pressed against her back, and his long hair brushed her cheek. She turned her head, letting herself inhale the salty smell of his sweat, letting herself

298

feel his heat, letting her gaze meet and hold his laughing eyes. She wanted to reach her lips to soften the firm line of his. He pushed her away quickly. When she turned back to him, he was staring at her in shock.

"What's wrong with you?" he demanded.

She was shaking so hard she didn't think she could move. Then she started running and couldn't stop until she found herself on the bank of the river.

She crouched behind a tree, half afraid, half hoping that he had followed her. He wasn't there. She tried to relax. She tried to listen deeply, to listen for him, then caught herself in shame as she recognized her madness. She sat, facing the river, away from Koban. She pushed her breath past the tightness in her throat and forced her heart to beat slower and softer until it no longer pounded against her ribs.

Chapter 36

Exposed

It was many hours after dark before Jovai felt ready to return to the camp. The family was already asleep, and she found her bedroll laid out and waiting. Milapo stirred partly awake as she entered but, recognizing the newest addition to her family, drifted back to sleep.

The next morning Jovai spent helping to clear bits of the forest for planting. It was bright, warm noon before Koban met up with her for her daily lesson. She looked up from the stump she was chopping and saw him watching her from across the field.

He signaled her to come to him. She started walking.

"Hurry" he yelled. "Run!"

She obeyed as he stood watching.

"It's a warm day," he remarked as she stopped in front of him. "Why do you wear so many clothes?" He reached for the fur pieces she still wore over a long, loose tunic. She pulled back alarmed.

He waved his hand at the rest of the people in the field.

"Everyone else has shed their clothes."

"I'm comfortable," she answered.

"You're strange, and you look over-hot. We will swim. That will cool you down."

"I don't want to swim," she told him.

"I'm the teacher. You obey me."

"No," she answered. "I've learned enough of the language now to learn the rest by listening. I don't need a teacher anymore."

"Listen, Latohva. I am your teacher until my clan leader or your family leader says otherwise. While I am your teacher, you must obey me. If I tell you we are going swimming, then we will swim. You're sweaty, and you stink."

"I will wash later. Now I have work to do — real work. If you want an excuse to be lazy, find someone else."

He glared at her, speechless with anger, his skin flushed a deeper shade of red, and his fist curled rigidly at his sides. Jovai left him glaring after her as she returned to work in the field. When she looked up again several minutes later, he was gone.

He had been right about her smell. She bathed every morning, in the custom of her people, but she worked hard during the day in heavy clothes. Difsat's tent was large enough for all that was left of his family to sleep and two or three more if everyone slept close, but still, it was likely her odor might discomfort them, especially if it were strong enough for Koban to smell even with normal space between them. She had bathed two or three times a day while she was bleeding. She decided to continue the practice even now that her bleeding was over.

She slipped away just as the sun was beginning to set and made her way to a hidden little cove she had discovered. It was off a fork of the main river between several large boulders and through some thick bushes. She stripped off the hides and furs and dived in, tunic and all. The water was a little warmer after a day of sun, but it was cool enough to refresh and send pleasant shivers through her skin.

As she came up, she thought she heard another splash. She looked around. The water was rippling everywhere, and little silver fish darted about just under the surface, but no one else was to be seen.

Then something grabbed her leg and pulled her under the water. She thrashed around in panic. The thing, she thought it was the same as had her leg, wrapped a strong limb around her waist. The water was too murky to see what it was. She kicked and struggled, but it wouldn't let go. It just dragged her deeper, then suddenly plunged toward the surface, pulling her up with it, and she could breathe again.

Water streamed into her eyes and mouth. She coughed and shook her head and kept struggling against the thing which wouldn't let her go. She felt something like a hand groping at her chest and working its way down her body and between her legs. If she could only break free enough to get her feet firmly on the bottom...

And he was laughing. It was a man. She managed to twist around and instantly, angrily, recognized him as Koban.

"I knew it!" he exclaimed. "You are a woman!"

"Let me go!" she yelled, furious. Her struggling increased, now that she knew what she was fighting and where to kick. He protected himself well as his hand glided over her hips, up into the curve of her waist and once again over the small bulges of her breasts. Then he let her go.

She scrambled out of the pool, her wet tunic clinging to her body, depriving her of any remaining shred of mystery.

Koban watched her, a broad and very satisfied grin on his face.

She shivered with cold in the cooling air and hastily threw her fur pieces over her wet clothes. Behind her, she could hear the water splashing as Koban climbed out of it.

"Stay away from me!"

"What are you afraid of?" he asked, his voice full of dare. He was closer than she had thought.

"Just stay away."

She grabbed what was left of her clothes, leapt over the rocks, and ran away.

"What's wrong?" asked Milapo, looking up from her ministrations over the outside cooking fire, as Jovai arrived at the tent red-faced and panting.

"Nothing," she said, forcing a smile to give truth to her lie, "I just felt like running. Didn't want to miss dinner again."

"You're early," said Milapo. She pointed to a bowl of fruit. "You can help by peeling those."

Out of the corner of her eye, Jovai saw Koban running toward them.

"I just remembered...I have to find Difsat. Be right back," and she ran away. Koban was stopped by Milapo and forced by politeness to exchange words. He didn't follow further.

"Difsat, I need to talk with you," said Jovai, accosting him as he left the tent of the Mirsant's dying family head.

He frowned at her rudeness.

"That's not the way to approach your family head. Hasn't Koban taught you anything?"

"Forgive me," she begged.

He silenced her apology with a wave of his hand.

"Good things or bad?" he asked.

"I...I don't know," she stumbled. "Personal things. I was just thinking..."

"Then it's probably bad and will have to wait until after dinner. Right now, I'm hungry."

The dinner progressed with pleasant chatter, as was the rule. As soon as it was over, Milapo claimed the attention of her husband. Jovai waited outside for her turn, at a distance where she would not hear their words, although their laughter was too loud to miss. Finally, Milapo came out and signaled Jovai to take her turn.

When she entered the tent, Difsat was still chuckling.

"Now you may tell me what you were thinking," he told her.

"Father of our family," she began with the correct address and polite bow. Difsat smiled in approval. "It is a time when our people must work very hard. Already we have missed the planting time of many of our crops and winter will come soon and may claim lives for lack of proper shelter..."

"I know all this," Difsat interrupted. "Now what's your problem?"

"I would like to be of more use to my new people," she answered. "I have learned the language enough to be a good worker, and now it is only a matter of my using it to perfect my ability to speak. At a time when every strong back is needed so badly, I feel like a thief to steal time for lessons, to steal my strength from where it serves my new people and to steal a strong and healthy man from pursuits that would benefit everyone more."

Difsat stared at her thoughtfully. There was a funny expression in his eyes, like a kind of slyness she did not understand.

"You think you've learned enough, do you?"

She answered carefully: "I think what more I have to learn can be taught me in the long, cold winter nights when there is nothing else to do."

"There's always something else to do. There will be tools to make and mend and clothes to sew and food to forage for. I'm sure we could trust you to keep yourself busy."

"Then I will be busy serving my new people."

"An honorable desire, but I wonder how much of it is honest. Milapo tells me Koban asked her to get you proper clothes for a woman."

Jovai stared at him open-mouthed in shock, then turned her face away to hide her blush of anger and shame.

"It is not his concern what I wear!" she exclaimed. "These clothes suit me very well."

"No. He is right. Your clothes are a lie, and it does not speak well of you that you would lie to us."

"But you know the truth."

"I know. Milapo knows. Our family knows. The clan heads know, but only because I told them when I claimed you for the Bat Clan. Others may guess. No one will say much. You are a stranger, and much is forgiven on that account, but Koban is right. If you want to be one of us, you must learn our ways and follow our customs and wear our clothes — the right clothes. And you must learn to speak. That is more than words. It's not just what you say but how and when. You've learned the words remarkably quickly, but you still don't know how to use them. That's what Koban is for."

"But those things I can learn later..."

"No!" snapped Difsat. "Don't argue. Now I'm speaking not only as your family head but also as your civil leader. The building and planting is important, yes, but being one people, a people who know how to work together, how to be together, is even more important. If I were to dismiss your teacher, then I would have to treat you like all the others. I would have to punish you for all the stupid, thoughtless things you do every day because you don't know any better. Now when you say or do something wrong, people let it go, knowing that Koban will teach you better soon. If there were no one to teach you, no hope anymore that you would learn, you would be intolerable. It is good that you help us work, but that means nothing much. There is no one so strong or so hard working that we would let him stay among us if he acted badly."

"I respect your wisdom, Family Father," said Jovai with as much politeness as she knew. "I will continue with a teacher and be thankful for your consideration, but perhaps someone older, someone weak who would not be so badly missed from the labor — an older woman perhaps who could teach me more of appearing like a woman in your society than a man could — would not someone like this make a better teacher for me?"

"Perhaps..." Difsat leaned forward and patted Jovai's knee affectionately, "But Koban requested the honor at a time when it seemed a warrior was what was needed to keep you under control. He was granted the honor and has done well by it. To dismiss him would be to dishonor him. Can you tell me anything he has done that would be reason to dishonor him?"

Jovai thought of his "attack" on her at the pool, but could think of no fair way to speak of it that would not make it sound like a harmless game. She knew herself there had been nothing more prompting it than his curiosity and possibly a bit of justified anger for the way she had spoken to him earlier.

"What about Gilix?" asked Jovai with sudden inspiration. "Her punishment is over, isn't it? She could come back anytime. She was my first teacher."

"She was dishonored. Besides, she has not come back. She hasn't even been seen. Her return is not expected."

"Has there been news?" asked Jovai, suddenly alarmed.

"That's not a question you should ask. She has nothing to do with you anymore."

"Forgive my impertinence. I know it is wrong, but I still feel responsible for getting her in trouble."

"No, Latohva. You're very childish about this matter." He sighed, looking suddenly like a frumpy, old wife. "All right. All we know is that she left the day she received her punishment. No one stopped her to ask where, since she was shunned. The Hawks say she went toward the White One's camp, but they didn't follow her to make sure. She hasn't been seen since. She is certainly nowhere nearby, or the hunting parties would have found some sign of her. I asked the Hawks and Dogs to find what they could about her, but by now there is no trace, not even a corpse."

"You think she's dead?"

"We probably won't ever know. It was foolish of her to leave the camp. It might have made the punishment harder to stay, but she would have been safe here. It's not a good world to be alone in." He shrugged. "If anything happened to her it happened far away. That's all we know. But if she were still alive why wouldn't she come back?"

He shrugged and sighed again.

"I liked the girl. She was too much of a flirt. Her family indulged her and wouldn't make her choose a husband, but they were changing their minds about that. Marriage would have settled her, and we need babies now — babies that might be strong men by the time the Akarians find us again. It hurts to lose such a promising young mother."

He turned to Jovai again, thoughtfully. She didn't like the look in his eyes.

"It's not your fault," he told her in conclusion. "It's not even mine. Everyone makes his own choices."

"Then I can choose to wear the clothes I want?" she asked, turning the subject away from the painful. It worked. Difsat startled at the question then laughed.

"Koban's your teacher. You do what he tells you."

"Everything?" asked Jovai, blushing deeply.

Difsat laughed again.

"He is of the Hawk Clan. They can be trusted to do only what's proper. If he orders you to do anything really bad, you can complain to me. Otherwise, he is your teacher and your authority. Do you understand?"

"Then where do my own choices come in?"

"If you don't like our laws you can leave our people, like Gilix did."

Jovai shifted uncomfortably. That wasn't the answer she had wanted, but she should have known it was the one she would get. She was trapped into submission by her own desire to stay in relative safety among people she was coming to like and admire very much.

"I accept your wisdom, Family Father."

She bowed low, to signal her submission.

"I'm glad," she heard Difsat say. "I like you very much."

Later that night she overheard Difsat in conversation with his wife as they returned from an evening walk.

"...an old woman!" Difsat was saying. Milapo shrieked with laughter. She said something Jovai could not catch about the Hawk Clan, and they laughed again. Jovai slipped back into the tent and pretended to be asleep with the others by the time they entered.

CHAPTER 37

FAIEL

The next morning, Jovai hid her clothes carefully and dived into the cove still wearing her tunic, although it no longer needed cleaning. She was sure Koban would try something. As she started to get out, she saw that she was right. People began appearing, some singly, some in small groups. They settled themselves under bushes or on top of the boulders and watched her as she bathed. She crouched down in the water, letting it cover her up to her neck and waited for them to go away. Those who had come stayed and more and more kept arriving until it seemed the whole camp of people were staring at her.

"Come out," yelled Koban. He and about four others were wading into the pool between her and the bush under which she thought she had so thoroughly hidden her clothes.

"I can sit here all day and night if I have to," she yelled back.

"So can we. Or I can get bored and come drag you out."

She was defeated, and she knew it.

"You win," she told him, "you can send the people away now. I'll come out."

"No one's leaving, Latohva."

"But Koban this is..." she looked for the word that meant embarrassing but couldn't find it. "This is cruel."

He smiled at her and waited.

People all around were staring, some snickering, some openly laughing. Difsat watched, so choked with laughter he could barely stand.

There was nothing else to do but take her public humiliation with as much good grace as was left to her.

She walked out of the water. Her wet tunic clung to every emerging curve of her body. Her arms hugged herself in protection against the eyes and the cool morning air.

"Arms down, Latohva," ordered Koban when she was in the shallows, "and turn around slowly so everyone can see."

She dutifully obeyed.

People cheered and hooted and hissed. People yelled things, both approving and not. Everyone was yelling together, and she could make nothing out of the jumble.

"That's enough," called Koban. "You can get dressed now."

He handed her a folded piece of white hide tanned so soft it was wonderful to touch. It was decorated with flowing designs of flowers and stars, patterned in bright, beautiful beads, and had panels of knotted threads so intricate it was as if the master craft's woman of the Spider Clan had begged the design from the spirits themselves. A spider could not have done more delicate work. She unfolded the dress with reverence. It was like nothing she had seen before — not in the style of her people, nor in the common style of the Kolvas. It was a dress of panels tied together with laces under the arms and down the sides. It was cut to conform to a woman's figure, to cover the breasts as the Kolvas women often did not, and yet to outline and draw attention to them. There was no belt at the waist or hips, nothing to hide the curves of the woman who wore it.

"You've given her the costume of Faiel!" exclaimed a nearby woman in surprise.

"It was the prettiest women's clothes I could find," Koban said.

"Put it on, Latohva."

She found some footing on dry land and carefully unfolded the dress, but when she tried to slip it on over her tunic, she found that she couldn't get her arms through the sleeves, or even her shoulders through the waist.

"I can't," she said, extricating herself.

"Of course you can. I've seen women much larger than you wearing that dress. You just don't want to."

"Stupid man!" exclaimed the woman with thick eyebrows. "She doesn't know how the costume works. You have to loosen all the laces, and she'll need someone to help her tighten them again once she gets it on."

"Motha Family Head," said Koban, addressing her with full politeness. "You are right about my ignorance. I would be pleased and honored if you would help my student learn what I cannot teach her."

"Oh no!" said Motha, trying to back away, "From what I see, it's not even proper that she wear such a dress. She doesn't even know who Faiel is!"

"You can tell her while you help dress her," called Difsat from across the pool. He said it as a pleasant suggestion, but it was an order, and Motha knew it. She turned away to hide her frown and held her tongue.

"We'll make a celebration of it!" Difsat announced merrily. "The changing of my daughter into a young woman. We'll have a feast, and the single men can bring their instruments and their songs, and she'll dance for us!"

"Dance!" repeated Jovai astonished. "I can't dance!"

"Of course you can," snapped Difsat, his good humor temporarily abated by her improper address. "All women can dance. That's what they do. And you will do what I tell you."

Jovai nodded in silent acquiescence. The day had hardly begun, and already it was awful.

Motha led Jovai to her family tent. She would not let Jovai carry the dress, for fear of her damaging it, but carried it herself with great respect.

"There are more parts than this to the costume," grumbled Motha. "There should also be two skirts and a pair of leggings and some shoes, but they went with the other groups, and if I know these fool men they won't notice if you go without. They never look below the waist when a woman wears this dress."

"Have you anything more appropriate that you could lend me, Family Head?" Jovai asked politely.

"They'd notice the change," Motha answered sourly.

Difsat sent his other daughter, Filani, over to dress Jovai's hair. She arrived just as Motha was helping Jovai out of her wet tunic and she began her work quietly as Motha tightened the laces. Meanwhile, Motha told them as quick and abbreviated a version of Faiel's story as she could.

"Faiel was the one who discovered the spirits."

"Discovered?" interrupted Jovai, "You mean, you didn't always have them?"

"Of course we did!" snapped Motha, "but we didn't always know. The Great Spirit made all the spirits that made all the worlds at his direction, and that made all the things living in them. But we didn't know. We were ignorant. The spirits stayed away and watched us, unsure if we were worthy to know them. Without the spirits, we had terrible times, sicknesses and famines. We didn't know to plant or even to hunt. We didn't know how to live together or with the other beings of the world. We didn't even know how to shelter our bodies from the cold.

"Among us was born Faiel. She was the most beautiful woman ever born, but we were so stupid we didn't even know what beauty was. The spirits did, however. They would come to see her and talk

314

with her and teach her, for each in his turn was astounded that his brothers and sisters had taught humans so little. They wooed her, one by one, and brought her clothes to keep the cold off her back and shelter from the blazing heat and freezing nights. They taught her what to eat and how to cook it and how to hunt and farm. One at a time they taught her how to live, and she taught her people. At first, they were too ignorant to even know they needed to learn from her. They laughed at her and teased her for her odd ways. They saw her only as a child. But then they saw the ease with which her family was living, they smelled the good food they had to eat, and while the others went dirty, she was clean, and her beauty was so bright because of it that even the ignorant humans could finally see it. At last, they bowed to her as a teacher and agreed to learn.

"From her, we learned tools and weapons and survival and comfort, but we also learned to help each other and to love each other for Faiel's example was as bright in this as in her outward beauty.

"When the spirits found out that she had shared with others all the gifts they had given her, they were angry. They stormed against the people, bringing famine and plagues and enemies of all kinds. Faiel pleaded with them, but they said she had chosen her own savage people above them and they would not listen to her. So she raised her voice to the Great Spirit, only he didn't notice her. She tried again and again. She saw him watching a little fish leaping over the waves, so she tried to leap for him, but he didn't see. She saw him watching a leaf spinning then falling from a tree branch, so she spun and fell to the ground, but he didn't see. She saw him watching a frog hopping and a bear pulling at a tree and smoke curling from a fire and all manner of other plants and animals and even elements moving, spinning. Finally, she decided that if she were going to get his attention, she couldn't do just one thing, but must do everything, so she danced. Then the Great Spirit noticed her. And he, like all the other spirits, was amazed at her beauty and grace. When she knew she had his attention, she began to tell him of her people's need and to beg him for his help. But she kept dancing as she spoke, so he would keep watching. And her words fit themselves to the rhythm of her dance and became a song. And it had power beyond its words, and it moved the Great Spirit to tears. And every tear that fell was a beautiful stone, of blue or green, the color of water, so, through Faiel, we also got the tearstone, which we found brings healing and prosperity. As the Great Spirit watched Faiel, he decided that he, too, wanted her as his wife. He stopped the cruelty of the other spirits against her people and asked her what gift she would take to become his wife. She cried at the thought of leaving her people, so the Great Spirit came down in the form of a handsome young man and agreed to live with her among her people for fifty years if she would spend the rest of forever after with him far away. He offered her many beautiful gifts, of which this dress is one, and promised to teach her people and guide them wisely and give them a happy place in this world. At last, she agreed.

"They lived among us, a happy couple for fifty years and had ten beautiful children – five girls and five boys. All of the girls and four of the boys stayed and married and founded the nine families of our people. Those founded by the girls were matriarchal families, like mine, and those founded by the boys were patriarchal, like Difsat's. One of their sons went away in search of his father's people. It is said he became a great hero and traveled far, to many lands unknown to us. It is said he spread his seed among many of the other peoples, so even you could be descendent from him. It is from his name that we have made our word "stranger" and strangers are considered to be, in a way, our tenth house.

"After the fifty years, Faiel and her husband left. They left their children and grandchildren behind, and Faiel wept to go as her family wept to see her go. The Great Spirit promised them that each generation would have its Faiel as long as we would honor her. She would walk with the spirit's grace and even the Great Spirit and his wife, themselves, would do her honor. Nine months after they left, a beautiful baby girl was born to Faiel's second daughter, and she was the second Faiel. From then on, the first girl child conceived after any Faiel dies is named Faiel, and everyone has always become the most beautiful woman among us and has brought her people honor."

"Who is the current Faiel?" asked Jovai.

"She is with another group. She is a daughter of the Komase. The one before her was the daughter of the Logartes. She was the one who was sent to the "Emperor" of the Akarians to be his wife."

"She was the one who was flayed?"

Motha nodded.

"She was dishonored, and so our empire fell."

While Motha finished adjusting the dress, Filani dressed Jovai's hair. She worked from the crown, making rows of little braids with Jovai's long, dark hair and bright colored ribbons. These she gathered at their ends into a hair buckle of intricately worked gold. On top, she placed a circlet of braided gold into which flowers had been woven.

"That's very good, Filani," said Motha, "But will it hold while she dances?"

Filani decided it wouldn't, so she redid it to hold it in place with the little braids.

"Will they really make me dance?" asked Jovai, nervously.

"They will. Your family head, your clan-head-to-be, and your civil leader have all three spoken with one voice. Besides, it is traditional at such celebrations. All new women dance for the men. It is our passage into womanhood."

"But I don't know how your people dance. I have never danced as a woman."

"You can walk, can't you? Then you can dance. The men just

want to see you. It doesn't matter so much what you do. Anyway, if you listen to the music, it'll tell you."

"Will I be all alone?"

Motha thought for a moment of all the young women. She glanced at Filani, but Filani was still a year or two away.

"When I danced there were five of us," she told Jovai, "and I thought that was terrible, to have so few. I was afraid everyone would look at me. But that is the point after all. We kept bumping into each other and then we started to try to outdo each other until it got so bad we weren't even really listening to the music or having any fun at all. By the end of it, I would have been happy if I could have had that space to myself. Just listen to the music. You don't have to think of them watching you if it bothers you. Just think of the music. Let yourself really hear it and try to hear the spirit of the musician in it. Here's a woman's secret for you, new woman: every unmarried man will play in his turn. When you find the music you like best, you will have found the man who will make for you the best husband."

"What if I don't like any of them?"

"Then you'll probably end up marrying someone your Family Father will choose."

"What if I like all of them?"

"Then you'll be another Gilix."

When their efforts on her were finished, Motha pulled out a little mirror for Jovai to see. Jovai had never seen a mirror before. It was very small, hardly as large as the palm of Motha's hand, but at the right distance, she could find her face in it.

"She is beautiful!" exclaimed Filani. "She's as beautiful as Faiel!"

"No," said Motha quickly, making a sign to ward off evil, but she turned an appraising eye on Jovai. "It's the dress," she said at last. "It is a beautiful dress, and it fits you well. Most girls are not so lucky to be shown in such a dress. You remember that now and wear it reverently. The Great Spirit, Himself, gave it to his bride — that very dress."

Jovai looked in the mirror and saw Katira's face, young and beautiful, only with darker hair and large, dark, serious eyes where Katira's had been smaller, green and laughing.

Suddenly Jovai was hit with a pang of homesickness so strong it brought her to the edge of tears. She wished she could run and show Misa and Katira. Her father would be as proud of her as he had been of her sisters, and her master...but he would be furious. If Yaku Shaman saw her now, he would rip the dress right off her back and cut her hair as short as a Gicok's and lock her away from men until there was nothing left of her youth. She was betraying him, and he knew it, her guilt whispered to her. Somehow, he would know it.

No serious work was done that day. The women cooked a feast while their husbands hunted for more and the unmarried men all practiced their music, eager for a chance to demonstrate their skill to all their people, especially the unmarried women.

No one thought much of Latohva. She was just an excuse for a party. She would dance, and they would politely play their songs and watch and afterward the real fun would begin.

Meanwhile, Milapo, as mother, finished the work Motha had started. She brought over some skirts and leggings but decided against them since Jovai would have to dance.

At Jovai's request, she told her more of the legend of Faiel and told her more of what would be expected from her. And for the rest of the day, Milapo, Motha, and even little Filani taught her how to dance, with Milapo singing the music until Jovai felt confident to take over. It was like having a party of their own, and they all ended up collapsed on the floor in exhaustion and merriment.

Finally, the feast was ready, the guests assembled, and it was time for the family head to lead forward the newest woman.

"Is Latohva ready?" called Difsat from outside Motha's tent.

"Come in and see for yourself," she invited.

They all watched, expectantly, as he entered and raised his eyes to view her. For over a full minute he stared in silence, his face expressionless. Jovai watched him, her tension rising. Filani held her breath, and even Milapo shuffled her feet, nervously.

"Say something Difsat," ordered Motha. "I can't take the suspense."

He answered slowly. "She's as beautiful as...beautiful enough to make a father proud."

He clapped his hands in sudden glee. "No one's expecting this! No one would even have guessed." He grabbed Jovai's hand and gave it a happy squeeze. "When they see you, they will thank the day you came among us."

It was still full daylight and, although turning toward winter, the days were summer warm. Difsat, lover of the dramatic, fetched for Jovai a long cloak with a hood and led her, thus shrouded, to the center of the circle of seated men, their instruments on the ground before them, ready. Difsat, as the father, took his place in the circle beside a large, deep-voiced drum.

He let the suspense of the moment gather, then, with great solemnity, gave one good pound on the drum. The man to his right started to play.

Difsat had instructed Jovai to throw off the cloak as soon as the dance started. She kept it on. The man played a pipe with gentle, slow rhythm. His music echoed the mystery of the hooded figure. Difsat tried to smile encouragingly. He gestured to Jovai to throw off the cape. She kept her eyes away from him and pretended she didn't see.

A deep-throated reed raised its song next. Briefly, it joined the first, and as the two played together, Jovai's movements grew broader and more complex. She pushed her hands from beneath the cloak and let them move as graceful storytellers, dancing with the music.

The pipe's song softened into silence, and the deep-throated reed welled, its sound falling into a steady rhythm that was picked up by a drummer next.

Once the rhythm was caught and the reed dismissed, the drummer changed the beat. No longer solemn, but playful. He was bored of the shrouded figure and wanted to encourage her to something more.

"Take off the cloak," Difsat hissed as Jovai pulled near. She hurriedly danced away.

The drum was beating merrily now, joined by another. She let her feet play with the beat, her legs working themselves free of the cloak, her arm pushing it back to give herself space as she swirled, hopped, and leapt with joy. Still, her face was covered. She liked it that way. It was she and the music dancing alone in the dark.

A flute picked up the beat, never echoing it but adding to it. Its voice was a challenge, playful and daring. It played in a subtle rhythm, sometimes with her, sometimes against her, seeing what she would do. It caressed her spirit and called her to come forth, daring her to be what he knew she was.

At first, she fought it, teasingly playing with her cloak, promising with movement to push it aside then pulling it closer around her. But the music grew more pulsing, more demanding, more yearning. It reached around her pride to her passion and promised to raise her to flight if she would only spread her wings.

She unclasped the cloak and pushed her arms wide, the fabric flowing down her arms and back. As she turned and leapt, the cloak swept up behind her, and she felt as though she were rising into the air. He was lifting her, with the power of his sound. She could almost feel his arms, reaching to embrace her. He was filling her with his courage. She raised her head high, freeing it from the hood, lifting her eyes to the sunset sky. She smiled, mesmerized, for the music was in her soul now, claiming her with its sure pride.

She let the cloak drop altogether and danced as free as the wind, as sweet as the light, passion and purpose filling every movement. Forgotten were the watching crowds. Only one watched her, with his burning eyes, his desire naked in his song, hers flashing like a dancing fire before him.

Suddenly Koban stopped playing. Jovai stopped dancing. Her chest heaved as it strained for breath. Bits of hair fell from Filani's beautiful braid-work and curled in the sweat of her brow. She stared at him in shock and wonder. He stared back — at first like a dreamer, his eyes still full of the visions he had seen. Then with shock, followed by anger and disgust.

Difsat stared, somewhat dazed. It took a moment before he came to himself enough to signal the next musician in the circle to play his turn. There were still many more men to hear.

The next man was singing, his voice making a beautiful, deep instrument. All the people stared at her now. All the men of the circle were watching her in a way she had never been watched before. Only Koban looked away and would not look at her again for the rest of the dance.

Jovai knelt, exhausted, head bowed and eyes lowered in submission to her weariness, while the last man of the circle finished his song. Then Difsat beat the drum three times and it was over. The musicians took their instruments and drifted off into the various congratulations of the crowd.

"Well done," said Difsat, helping her to her feet. The sun had already set. She had been dancing over two hours. The music had swept her through elation, and sorrow, triumph, and despair. "I named you well, Latohva, Dancing Light."

Jovai winced. "I had forgotten I had that to live up to."

"You did well," he assured her. "You should have seen the astonishment on the faces here when you finally took off that ugly cloak. The men, especially, could not stop staring."

"Koban could."

"Ah," said Difsat, smiling, "well. He is of the Hawk Clan. The young ones are like that sometimes. It can be taken as a compliment from them, if you want."

"It doesn't matter," she assured him. "May I change out of this dress now?"

"And into something ugly?" He laughed. "No one will ever believe it again."

Prizes from her family were given at the feast for the musicians who had played the best. To the favorite of the people, Difsat gave a beautiful coat of pelts. To the second favorite, he gave a newly sewn pair of new shoes. To the third, he gave a sharpened knife. The next got a blow tube for darts and on and on until all the men were adequately honored.

To Jovai's amazement Koban did not place among the top five. She had heard him as by far the best and could not even remember most of the music of the others, but the people did not agree.

She watched Koban as he came forward to claim his prize, a beautifully carved hilt for a long blade. He nodded to her, as custom demanded, but would not meet her eye or smile as the others did. Politeness required that he exchange words with her. She had heard praises of her beauty, of her dancing, and words of honor for her family. Koban stood, staring at her feet, dumbly.

Finally, he opened his mouth to say something, then shut it again as he changed his mind. His silence was painful for everyone. Difsat gave him his prize and let him go.

Chapter 38

Courting Danger

Jovai received many invitations that evening from family heads to take a meal with them.

"Since we're still on rations you take your share of food," Milapo whispered to her, "and you go early and help cook."

"I don't know how to cook anything more than you've shown me."

"It'll do. Cooking is all the same. The skill is in the seasoning, and I'll teach you a little more tomorrow."

After the meal, Milapo took Jovai for a walk, where they could speak with some privacy.

"You're a new woman," she said, "although you've probably been one for a while. I don't know what you know already, but I'm your mother now, and I will answer any questions you have." She smiled encouragingly, "Ask me anything."

The conversation lasted half the night as they walked or sat among the trees by the edge of the camp. Often, Jovai and Milapo saw fleeting shapes in the moonlight. The woods were full of people and the trees echoed with the sounds of pipes and flutes and songs.

"They're playing for you," whispered Milapo.

"For me?"

She nodded. "That's how our men attract their mates. They try to lure young women from their family homes at night."

"Do women ever go?"

"Of course. If you hear a song you like, you go to find out who the man is."

"Then what?"

Milapo smiled at the sweetness of her own memories. "That depends on how much you like the song and the man. Sometimes you try to sneak away without letting him know you were there. But they're looking for you, so that's hard. Sometimes you talk, and what you say is only between you two, and never goes any farther as long as both of you are honorable. Sometimes you kiss and play a little, but only if you really like him. If you think he is the one you probably want to marry, and you know he wants to marry you, then you can lie with him. You may do anything you like and, if the man is as a man should be, no one will ever know what you've done. Only, if you get pregnant, then your time for play is finished, and you must choose a husband — preferably before the men find out. Some men decide not to marry a woman if they think her child might not be theirs."

"What if you don't go out to see any of them."

"Then they give up. Men are usually very easily discouraged. But you shouldn't be so picky, or Difsat will end up choosing your husband for you. I honor my husband and his wisdom in all things, but, only between us, I advise you to choose your own husband and not let him get too much involved."

"Do I have to get married? Is there nothing I can do to avoid it?"

"Avoid it?" Milapo turned to her in surprise. "Of course, you can't avoid it. Especially now when so many of our young people have been killed or taken in the wars. We need every baby every one of our women can bear, even a tired old woman like me. It's the first and most important duty of every young person to get married. Even the ugliest and the most annoying, if they can't find anyone to marry them their family will buy or beg someone for them. You are very lucky. You don't know how lucky you are. We were afraid since you were a stranger and especially since you kept yourself so ugly, we were afraid the men would avoid you. Tonight, we thank all the spirits that you have made such a good impression. You now have your choice from all the very best men we have left. As you honor the people who have taken you in, as you honor the family who has worked so hard for you, you will use your choice wisely."

They talked as Jovai had never talked to a woman before on subjects that she had never dared even think about. In all things, Milapo was candid. She shared with the young girl all the knowledge she had learned not only from her own young womanhood and her many years as a wife and mother, but also from the experiences told to her by the other women she had known.

Jovai had never guessed that women would talk so easily about such intimate, and to her, very awkward subjects. She listened, amazed, as Milapo opened up to Jovai her history, her feelings, her frustrations and joys, her observations on men and women and their interaction and life in general. And she encouraged Jovai to express her fears, her worries.

Jovai found the courage to tell her things of her life before that she had not shared with anyone, ever. She told her of Litazu and her master, although she did not tell her of Litazu/Berailian's curse, for already she had forgotten it — it had faded away with the nightmare of the ghosts. She told her of Misa, who was not allowed to take her to the woman's place, and of her own mother who had been ashamed to even call her daughter, and of her father, who had been among those who had sold her as a slave to the traders.

Milapo took her in her arms, as a mother would hold a very young child, and stroked her hair comfortingly and helped her let go of all the shame and unhappiness that Jovai had not even known she was carrying. She cried as she told Milapo her stories, but with each story spoken, she felt lighter, until, by the end of the stories, she felt giddy and light enough to float.

"It was another life," Milapo told her comfortingly. "That's what it meant, that night of terror — the Initiation of the Bat. You can put it all away from you."

"I miss my family," confided Jovai. "I miss my sisters and my master most of all. I know he misses me. I know he's listening and maybe, somehow, he knows every time I betray him, and it breaks his heart."

"He's a good man, no doubt," said Milapo, although she did not sound as if she believed it. "But now you are an adult, and you must make your own life. He's not here to see what you need to do. I've let seven of my own children go already. Two directly to death but five I got to see married first. Every one of them made so many mistakes I often thought I must have failed as a parent. Most of the mistakes were things Difsat or I or our elders had warned them about, and they went out and did just what we had told them not to do. Every single mistake every one of them made I felt. I suffered from them, I think, more than they did. But after everything, they all made good lives for themselves. Even in these troubled times, as far as I know, every one of them had more happiness than not. Three of them may still be alive, if the spirits are willing, and if they are, they're still making mistakes and doing things I told them not to do. Well, after living almost forty years I'm still disobeying my own parents. It's wiser to listen. It's wiser to learn from the mistakes of your elders and not have to make them again. But eventually you find that you are not your elders, and the rules they made for their lives don't all apply to you. You compromise a little. You make yourself what they want you to be, and you make yourself what you want to be, and above all, you do what you have to do to survive and be happy. Among your people, that might have meant pretending you were a boy and never getting married, but here and now it means accepting that you are a woman, finding a good husband and having lots of beautiful, healthy babies."

"If I do that, then I can't go back. I can't see Yaku Shaman again. Not ever."

Milapo pulled her closer and gently kissed away a tear on her cheek.

"No one ever goes back. Childhood passes and is gone. It happens sometimes that people are born to the wrong family or even the wrong people. You are very lucky, and we are very lucky, that the spirits have been pleased to lead you here where you belong."

Jovai hugged her, grateful for her kindness and patience. She felt closer to Milapo than she ever had to any woman. She felt certain that she was in the arms of the best mother she could ever have.

It was almost morning before they returned. Both the women were exhausted and yet very pleased with the long night they had spent. Jovai worked at the dispensary with her that morning and took a cooking lesson from her for the breakfast and later for the dinner.

She had expected Koban to come as usual, for her lesson, but he did not come that day. Nor did he come the next day, although that evening, among the musicians in the trees, she heard one of such pure sweetness she thought it must be him.

"How go your lessons?" asked Difsat on the third day, catching up with her as she worked in the fields.

"I haven't seen my teacher since the feast."

"Not at all?"

"Not a sign. Perhaps he feels his work is finished."

Difsat frowned. "He hasn't been dismissed yet."

"He has probably just been busy."

"Too busy to do his duty? We'll see!" and he stormed off before Jovai could stop him.

Koban appeared a couple of hours later and signaled her away from work.

"I've talked to Difsat," he told her, leading her away from the camp.

"I'm sorry he was angry..."

"He was right to be," interrupted Koban. "I handled it badly. I told him that I have taught you as much as I could and I think, now, you should be taught by a woman."

"You liked me better as a boy, didn't you?"

"It has nothing to do with liking you," he told her sullenly. He kept his face turned away so she could not see his expression. "I just don't have anything more to teach you."

"You mean I know everything you know? I'm perfect in etiquette? I no longer say or do stupid things?"

"You're being stupid right now," he answered.

"So? Are you still my teacher or not?"

"Yes."

He picked up a stone at his feet and flung it as far as his strong arm could throw it.

"He said I was fortunate to have the rare opportunity to teach a woman how to be a woman that men would like, without too much interference from other women."

"You, of course, told him you thought it impossible that I would ever be a woman that men would like."

He shot a dark look at her but turned away before answering.

"I told him I didn't think I was capable."

"And he laughed."

"Were you listening?" he demanded angrily.

"No. But he could either laugh or be insulted, and he likes you too much to be insulted."

"You know him so well," said Koban, upset, "you tell me what I should say!"

"You think I haven't tried every argument I can think of? If I had any more, I'd already have used them."

"Why?" he demanded. He stopped walking, grabbed her arm, and roughly pulled her to face him. "I've been a good teacher to you!"

"You've been a horrible, arrogant bully. Ever since the Gicok left with his horses, you haven't had one good word to say to me. You've abused me, insulted me and humiliated me."

"You needed it!"

"Like I need a plague! You know nothing about me — nothing about who I am, where I come from or why I do the things I do. I have a whole life behind me that you can't even begin to imagine. I have to relearn everything I ever thought I knew and you haven't helped."

"If you thought there were things I should know why didn't you tell me?"

"Why didn't you ask?"

"I didn't think you'd tell me!"

"I didn't think you'd care!"

They stood, staring at each other in angry silence. Jovai was on guard, unsure of what the man might do. The tension between them was almost overwhelming. He jerked her closer then flushed and let her go.

"It's too late," he said. "You've already learned enough women's tricks to make any man crazy."

"How would you know? You're already crazy."

"I've noticed. I've watched the men who bring you water while you work and hang around your tent trying to find things to do for your family. They carve your name in their flutes and beg your brothers and sister for clippings of your nails or strands of your hair for love potions. They ask me to steal things for them or to speak well of them to you. Some even plant seeds in the dirt where you walked, hoping your love will grow as the plant does. Are you stupid enough to choose a husband who would do such foolish things?"

"Why is it foolish? A plant takes time to grow and so does love. I can admire a man who would wait. With enough time, maybe I could love him." She shrugged. "With enough time, I could even love you."

Koban turned to her, his brown-red face suddenly pale, his dark eyes holding hers with a terrible intensity.

"You can love me?" he demanded, his voice hardly a whisper but filled with the sound of suspicion and anger and something more Jovai could not recognize.

"Given enough time," she answered with a shrug, "I will probably be dead, and the mountains will be dust long before..."

He flushed again in hot anger, his expression grim and dark. She thought he would say something, but he clenched his jaw closed, turned, and walked away without looking back.

Chapter 39

Dangerous Game

That night, Jovai dreamed of flying on the wind. She was rushing someplace, only she didn't know where. She didn't care. She was galloping across open, endless plains, completely free. And she was one of the Gicok's magnificent horses, with the power to do anything. She raised her head and laughed. She stretched her neck and looked back over her shoulder and saw she had a rider. He was laughing, his handsome face beaming with joy, as open and innocent as a young boy's. She suddenly felt angry that he was there on her back.

"Get off," she cried, but he just laughed. He pulled out a flute and began to play the sweetest music she had ever heard.

She woke with a start. The night was full of the sounds of singers and instruments, but all she heard, somewhere in the distance, was the pure, sweet sound of a flute.

Her family was sleeping all around her. Very carefully, so as not to awaken any of them, she stepped over and around them and slipped out the door. She followed the sound of the flute like a sleepwalker, not fully aware of what she was doing. It drew her on, deeper and deeper into the woods, farther and farther away from the safety of the camp. Once she stopped, coming awake, and looked around wonderingly at the forest and the star-filled sky. She started to turn back and realized that she didn't know where she was or how to get home. Then the song of the flute began again and called to her. She remembered she had been following it, and now it was the only guide she had.

It led her deep into a part of the forest where she had never been. Then it stopped. She looked around for the player, but only trees stood near her.

"I knew you'd go chasing after men!" scolded a voice from above, and Koban dropped down from a branch, landing beside her. She frowned at him, surprised.

"You!" she exclaimed. She reached for the flute he still held, but he pulled it back, out of her reach.

"I wanted to see if you were yet running after a husband."

"I'm not," she answered.

"Then why are you here?" he challenged.

"I'm lost."

"You are stupid to come so far away from the camp, even after a man."

"Why did you call me?" she demanded.

"To teach you a lesson."

"What lesson?"

"That you're a fool to go so far away from safety in the middle of the night. You are nothing but a foolish woman."

"Thank you, teacher," she answered stiffly. "I'll remember that the next time I hear your flute."

She turned to go and realized that she didn't remember from what direction she had come.

"Who did you think I was?" he asked her, as she paused in confusion.

She shook her head, unhappily, and didn't answer.

"Who is it you like?" he insisted.

"No one. I don't know...anyone maybe. I didn't think it was you."

"Of course not. You wouldn't have come if you had."

She turned on him angrily.

"Why should I come so far just to be abused?"

"Why should you come so far anyway, unless you think you are meeting a lover! Were you going to kiss him? Were you going to lie with him?"

"Leave me alone!"

"You were hoping he'd take you in his arms and beg you to marry him, weren't you?"

"No!"

"Yes you were, woman. Don't lie to me."

She turned and angrily swung at him with both fists. He successfully blocked the first, but the second hit him in the stomach and blew the wind out of him. He doubled over in pain.

"I hate you, Koban of the Hawk Clan. You did it to me. I was fine as I was. I didn't want to get married, I didn't want to have children, I didn't even want anyone thinking of me as a woman, and no one was until you made them all look and see. Now everyone tells me I must get married as soon as possible and if I don't make a choice soon Difsat will make it for me, and it's all your fault!"

She swung at him again, but he caught her fist and flung her to the ground with her own angry momentum.

"All right then," he said, pinning her down with the weight of his knees, "Why?"

"Let me up!"

"You say I never ask you anything about you. Now I'm asking. Why did you dress like a boy? Why don't you want to get married? Why don't you want to have children? Why don't you want to be what you are?"

"Because I'm not a woman! You think my other clothes were a lie, but they weren't the lie. These are!"

"That doesn't make sense," he said.

"I knew you wouldn't understand." She struggled against him, but he wouldn't let her up.

"I'm listening." He continued to hold her pinned.

"If you let me up I'll tell you."

"Tell me something that makes sense, and I'll let you up."

"All right!" She calmed her anger with a deep breath. "Among my people, I was never meant to be a wife. I don't know how to do it, and I'm not supposed to even want to. From as early as I can remember I was told I could never have a husband, never have children, never do anything except serve the spirits and my people. I am untouchable. Do you understand? Even though I was born a woman, I was made to not be a woman. My master dressed me as a man because that was the right way for me to dress. Your people just don't understand. I want to do well and please my family here, but they're not just asking me to be something I've never been before. They're asking me to be something I was told over and over, for as long as I can remember, and for the sake of everyone I have ever loved, that I could and should never be. Now let me up!"

He sat on her harder, resisting her struggles. "If you're not a woman and you are obviously not a man then what are you supposed to be?"

"Nothing. I'm supposed to be a shaman but I'm not that either."

"You're supposed to be of the Bat Clan?"

"We don't have clans like that. And our shaman is different from yours. And I'm not a shaman anyway, so it doesn't matter."

"You're not a shaman and you're not a man but you are a woman." He was struggling to understand. He frowned in concentration as he tried to make sense of her words.

"But I don't feel like one," she tried to clarify. "I don't feel as if I can do what everyone now expects me to do. I'm trying. I really am, but they want everything now. Every day Milapo asks me why I didn't like any of the music the men play at night. Difsat has threatened to take away my bedroll and make me wander outside all night until I stop discouraging the men. Then, the first time I try to do what they want, I get you yelling at me and treating me as if I were doing something wrong. You're supposed to be teaching me to be what they want, but instead, you make me feel ashamed for even trying."

Koban unpinned her. He rose, staring at her thoughtfully, and helped her to her feet.

"So, no man has ever even kissed you?" he asked. She blushed.

"Only once. Twice. I was punished for a very long time because of it, and the boy ended up making an enemy of my master and leaving our people. It was a very bad business."

"Did you like it when he kissed you?"

She bowed her head in shame as her blush deepened.

"So, you like to be kissed?"

"I don't know. The kiss itself? I liked that part, but the shame and the punishment and the way it hurt my master and the way Litazu suffered — there was nothing good about that."

"But you like men?"

She balled her fists in frustration and pounded them against the air.

"I just don't want to be a wife! Can't you understand?"

He grabbed her wrists and held them still.

"So, since I am your teacher, what I need to teach you is to want to be a wife."

She broke his grip and pulled away.

"No wait!" he said, catching her before she could turn away. "I listened to you. Now you let me explain something."

"I don't like you holding me," she said, trying to break free.

"I know," he said. "But I have something to tell you that will make it all right. I'll let you go if you promise to stay and listen."

She agreed. He released her and gestured for her to sit at the base of a nearby tree. Then he sat beside her.

"You know I'm of the Hawk Clan," he said, "but I don't think you know what that means. When I became a man in the clan, I made a choice. I took an oath. All adults in the Hawk Clan take this oath. We agree not to take wives or even to lie with women without the permission of our clan leader. What this means is that I'm like you were. I will have no wife, no children until my clan leader decides that I am old and weakened enough to be of better service as a husband and father than as a warrior. By that time, you will have daughters of age and maybe even granddaughters who are women. When I am finally allowed to take a wife, I will probably choose from among them and women their age."

"You think that's the same way I was raised?"

"What I mean is that if you're afraid of men...all right. But you don't have to be afraid of me. I couldn't marry you even if I wanted to, so I'm safe for you. From now on you can...you can relax with me. You can practice, to a very safe limit, being a wife with me — being a woman. You can do what you need to get comfortable with the idea. I'll be the teacher you need, now. I'll be patient, and I won't make you feel bad."

"I don't understand," she said.

He slipped his arm gently around her waist. She stiffened and cringed away, startled, but not so far that he couldn't reach.

"You have to get used to being touched," he said in a voice of authority. "Now, if any other man were to touch you, it would frighten you, wouldn't it? You would know he was thinking of you possibly as his wife, and since you don't feel ready for that, all you would be able to think about was getting away. Am I right?"

She nodded, watching him warily.

"But you know I'm not thinking of you as a wife. I'm not going to marry you or even lie with you. So, if I touch you, it's only as a friend and a teacher."

He raised his hand slowly, letting her see it, and lightly stroked her hair. Still, she startled backward at his touch, but his hand only

338

followed, gently but firmly, until she closed her eyes and accepted it.

"That's good," he praised her. "And it feels good, doesn't it?"

"I guess so," she answered after a pause.

He let his finger trace her ear and draw a line down her neck to the base of her throat. Her breathing grew quicker.

"Yes. Very good," he encouraged.

She shivered as he brought his fingers up the back of her neck under and then through her long, thick hair.

"Are you cold?" he asked, drawing closer to warm her with the heat of his body.

"A little."

He drew her against his chest, opening his fur vest to cover her shoulders with half of it.

"Is that better?" he asked.

"It's warmer," she answered cautiously.

"If I were another man you would be uncomfortable being so close, wouldn't you?" His hands stroked her arms and back, gently sliding down along her legs.

"Yes," she answered, starting to enjoy this game.

"But I'm safe, and nothing bad will happen to you while you're with me."

"Are you sure?" she asked. Yaku Shaman's anger at her and Litazu flashed again in her mind. She could almost feel his presence, rushing toward her now...but, perhaps Koban was right. Perhaps even Yaku Shaman would not object to her being with a man so completely safe. It was only a harmless game, after all. Perhaps this really was something she should do...as long as it didn't go too far.

———◆———

Koban saw her eyes, those large, luminous eyes, turn to him full of fear and vulnerability. She was so young, so innocent. For a moment Koban's confidence melted and then was instantly rebuilt.

"I'm not going to hurt you," he vowed, pouring all himself into the words. "I could not live if I ever did."

He couldn't stand the uncertainty with which she watched him.

"I promise you." He begged her with his eyes and raised his fingers up to her temple, willing the touch to say everything his words couldn't. "I promise you. I promise."

With all his heart he made a promise. He couldn't say what it was that he promised, or even think it, but he made it to her with his most sacred intent. His spirit leapt with joy as he saw trust slowly creep into her beautiful face.

Before he realized quite what he was doing, he was kissing her, pressing his tongue gently through her parted lips. A feverish hunger overwhelmed him as her resistance slipped away. He could feel her heart beating wildly against his, and he trembled with her as she pressed herself deeper into his arms.

He buried his face in the crook of her neck, kissing her shoulder, her throat, her ear, while his hands glided over her soft, sweet body, under her skirts, down her legs and up again toward places he had never touched on a woman's body before.

———◆———

They heard a noise not far away and instantly jumped apart, both panting and red-faced. Jovai straightened her tunic and smoothed her skirts and stared out in the darkness toward the sound, waiting in terror for some kind of doom to approach.

A shadow emerged from behind a tree, large and looming and rushing toward them. Jovai froze in silent terror as she recognized Yaku Shaman, huge with anger, coming to tear her away.

"Who's there?" demanded the figure, pausing only a few feet away. It took Jovai almost a minute to find her breath again as she realized it was not her master's voice.

"Koban of the Hawk Clan," Koban answered, trying to hide his nervousness with the sound of anger. "Who are you?"

"Sofani of the Dog Clan," answered the man. "What are you doing here Koban and who is that with you?"

"This is Latohva, daughter of the Rifan family."

Sofani stepped forward cautiously, a long blade drawn, until he could confirm both their features with the moonlight. He looked between Jovai and Koban curiously, then smiled at Jovai. She recognized him as the musician who had won third prize at her dance. She shyly, awkwardly, smiled back.

"Latohva was out walking and lost her way," Koban said.

"So far from camp?" asked Sofani.

"I was thinking of other things and lost track of my feet," she explained.

"And you, Hawk Man?"

"I come here often," Koban answered lightly.

Sofani looked as though he didn't know whether to believe Koban or not. He looked around and spied something lying on the ground. He bent to pick it up and discovered it was a flute.

"Yours?" he asked with a curious smile, handing it to Koban. Koban glared at the wooden betrayer and refused to take it.

"Mine," Jovai said, stepping forward to claim it.

His eyes widened with surprise, and he examined the flute with more curiosity.

"Yes, I see," he said, "You have carved your name on it."

Koban's jaws clenched shut, and he squeezed his eyes closed.

"So if I lost it, I could recognize it again. Or if someone else found it, they could return it to me," Jovai explained. "Don't the Kolvas do that too?"

Sofani handed it to her with a disbelieving smile. "It's a good idea," he agreed. "Are you still lost? I'd be glad to guide you home."

"I'll take her," said Koban. "There's no need for you to leave your duty."

Sofani nodded, amusement in his face, and walked away.

CHAPTER 40

WATCHED BY HAWKS

K oban continued with Jovai's new lessons every chance they could find or make. He insisted that these lessons were completely in line with what Difsat intended, but neither of them felt the need to verify that with the reverend family head.

During the day, when too many people were about for any chance of privacy, they talked, walking or sitting together, or swam in the river or occasionally managed to sneak off to the woods, but all quite innocently. Had anyone been watching them they would have noticed nothing unusual, except, perhaps, for the occasional lapses in their conversations when it seemed as if they were suddenly, for no apparent reason, both thinking of something else, or the increasing frequency with which they would meet each other's eyes and blush or smile, conspirators in a shared secret.

Every night that Koban was not given a duty by his clan, he called to Jovai with the sweet voice of his flute. She begged him not to call so often, for their lack of sleep affected both of them badly during the day, yet, whenever he would call, she would come.

"Are you sure we are both...safe?" she asked him one night when he had caressed her to such a passion she could barely endure.

"Of course," he promised her. "I'm of the Hawk Clan. Remember?"

"But is your oath enough?"

He sighed into her kiss with a smile.

"We have excellent discipline," he assured her, with his next breath.

"So, you're not even tempted to betray your oath?"

"I don't feel anything, unless I let myself, and I won't let myself feel anything that will make me want to break my oath."

For some reason, his answer did not please her. The next day, she asked Milapo about it as she helped her fix the morning meal.

"Can a man kiss a woman and not feel anything?"

"What do you mean?" asked Milapo.

"Is it possible for a man to kiss a woman and not...not enjoy it?"

"That depends on the man and the woman," answered Milapo. "Whom do you have in mind?"

She had been burning with curiosity to know whom Jovai was meeting almost every night. Most of the musicians had gone away frustrated, now. Only the flute player was heard regularly and, with all her carefully restrained questions to everyone she hoped might know, she had still not been able to discover who he was.

"Well, if I'm the woman," said Jovai.

"And the man?"

"Does it matter?" she asked, blushing.

"How old is he?" amended Milapo, in deference to her daughter's modesty.

"Four, maybe at most five years older than me."

"And he kisses you and tells you he doesn't feel anything?"

Jovai nodded, unhappily.

"Does he then kiss you again?"

"Yes."

"Then he probably feels something."

"What if he were kissing me only because he thought he ought to?"

"He would only have that duty if he were already your husband.

Since he's not, if he doesn't enjoy kissing you then he wouldn't."

Jovai thought about it for a while, unsatisfied by Milapo's assurances.

"What if he were crazy?" she asked suddenly.

"Who?" asked Milapo, startled.

"The man who doesn't feel anything when he kisses me."

"If he's crazy then get rid of him."

She strained her imagination to find any young man who might by any stretch be considered crazy by Latohva.

"What if it's just a little craziness — just enough to make him think he has to kiss me even though he doesn't really want to?"

"If he keeps kissing you, but keeps saying he doesn't like kissing you..."

"He says he doesn't feel anything when he kisses me," corrected Jovai.

Milapo shrugged.

"Then he's either crazy, a fool or a liar. Anyway, go find a better man."

"But what if I like him — a lot."

"Has he said he wants to marry you?" asked Milapo, watching Jovai closely.

She shook her head, unhappily.

"Then go find another man. If he likes you as much as you like him, then he'll stop playing and ask you to marry him. If he doesn't, then you're better off without him."

That day, Jovai waited for Koban impatiently. When it seemed to her it must be late, although in truth he had never met with her so early, she left her work and sought him out.

She found him chopping wood, his muscles flexing as he worked, his well-formed chest and arms naked but for the gleam of his sweat.

"What's wrong?" he asked her, leaving his work.

"Nothing," she answered through her sudden embarrassment. "I just needed...wanted to talk with you."

He grabbed his tunic and led her toward the river where he could wash, but he left it for her to start the conversation.

"I...I was wondering...how do you think I'm doing in my lessons?"

"Very well!" he assured her with a smile.

Her heart leapt, but she tried very hard to keep any expression out of her face.

"So, when do you think I will be ready to be a wife?"

"I don't know," he answered. "It may take as many years to get you comfortable with the idea as it took to get you uncomfortable with it. Maybe even longer."

"I have a month," she told him.

"A month?" he laughed in astonishment. "That's ridiculous."

"Less than a month, actually. Difsat says I must make a decision by next full moon or he will make it for me."

"That's crazy!" argued Koban, suddenly upset. "You can't make a decision like that yet. He can't do that to you!"

"Can't he? He's my Family Head."

"I thought that they were all happy now that you were not staying home in the evenings."

"They were for a while, but now Difsat says I should make up my mind."

"Ask him for more time."

"I've begged him. Milapo has even talked to him for me. He is stubborn and says that this is no time to play. He says he has been patient, but I should be pregnant by now."

"I'll talk to him," Koban told her.

She looked up at him hopefully.

"Do you think you can change his mind?"

He thought about it a moment then slowly, sadly shook his head.

"So then, I must make a choice as soon as possible."

"Who will you choose?"

She shrugged. "I don't know. I haven't been thinking of any of them. You know these men better than I. Whom do you think I should marry?"

"I'm not the one who takes meals with different families every day!"

"But then they all try so hard to be so attractive that I don't know what they are really like. Besides, there aren't as many choices as I thought at first. Most of the men who played at the dance were Hawks, and you say they can't marry."

"Zocan could. He is the oldest, and our clan master would release him. He was the one who played for you first."

"He is old!" said Jovai, remembering.

"He likes you, though. He has asked me about you."

"What did you tell him?"

"I said you were stubborn and arrogant and impossible to tame. That you didn't know how to cook or sew or make good tools or anything and that you didn't like men."

Jovai turned on him in horror.

"I thought you didn't want a husband yet!" he defended himself. "Zocan has to marry right away before he's too old to make children or be any kind of a husband. He can't wait for you."

"Well, now I have to marry right away."

"So, marry Zocan," Koban told her, trying to sound indifferent.

"You really think he's the best?" asked Jovai, confused.

"He's of the Hawk Clan. We're all the best. He's proved his strength and courage many times over, and he's survived three wars and a very dangerous escape. Besides, it's a great honor for a woman to marry into the Hawk Clan."

"Would I have to live with the clan?"

Koban shrugged. "That would be a decision between the clan leader and your family head."

"Would it bother you if I did?"

"Why should I care?" he answered.

"All right then."

"All right, what?"

"I'll marry Zocan."

"Just like that?" he yelled at her with furious astonishment. Jovai blushed as two women carrying clothes and bedrolls to wash in the river turned to stare at them.

"You said I should," she reminded him softly.

"What do I know?" he hissed back. "I don't have to lie with him. I don't have to kiss his wrinkles and hug his fat and let him slobber and dribble all over me. Besides, he's ugly. You'd have ugly daughters."

"Then why did you suggest him?" asked Jovai, close to tears.

"I just meant you could meet him. Lofar, our clan leader, has invited you, a couple times I think. He is anxious to get Zocan married."

"Then I'll come and meet him," she decided.

Milapo frowned when Jovai asked her to accept the Hawk Clan's invitation for her.

"Why do you want to meet them?" she asked. "Only the old ones can marry you know."

"Koban says it's an honor to marry into the Hawk Clan."

"It's an honor you don't need. As soon as Difsat thinks you're ready he'll bring you into the Bat Clan. That's more honor, more privileges. You don't have to marry an old man. Find someone young and strong who can give you many healthy children and be around to help you raise them. Those old Hawk men, they die before a woman's breeding time is half over."

"Even so," said Jovai thoughtfully, "Since my teacher went so far to suggest Zocan to me, I should pay him the courtesy of at least visiting the man. It would be only polite."

Milapo sighed sadly.

"You're going to make your own mistakes, aren't you?"

Jovai hugged her mother.

"I'll listen to you before I ignore you," she promised.

Koban spent several days drilling Jovai on the proper etiquette for dining with his clan. He went over and over the proper addresses, the things she might talk about and the things to avoid, the way to sit and the way to eat and even, as far as he could know, the way to cook.

"So all these other meals I've been taking with families, I've been making a fool of myself?" she asked, distressed.

"Does it matter?" he asked, "You didn't like any of those men anyway."

"I don't like to be a fool."

He even found her skirts, prettier than those her family had yet made her. It was in the typical Kolvas style, to be worn topless except when cold demanded a shawl.

"I won't wear it without a tunic," she insisted.

"Why not?"

"I'm used to being more covered. I'll be too uncomfortable if I'm not."

"You won't do anyone a favor by hiding your breasts," Koban told her, staring at the bulges that pressed forward through her top. "It just makes them...mysterious. Men want to touch what they can't see." His hand reached forward to demonstrate, but he caught it, glancing guiltily at the people around, and pulled it away.

"I don't care," Jovai insisted. "I see some women wearing tunics over skirts."

"Only when it's cold."

"Then we'll pretend it's cold."

When the day came, she was ready. The clan was larger than a family and had many tents, so when they ate together, they gathered outside.

Zocan was sent to escort Latohva. He was greeted with politeness, but little more by her family. Jovai smiled graciously, especially when she realized that Zocan was much more nervous than she. He was many years older than Difsat but younger than Yaku Shaman, and he was still adequately strong and healthy. The lines on his face accentuated his thin lips, long, straight nose, and strong jaw. They betrayed his face as one more used to frowning than laughing, but her master had been like that and she could see no harm in it.

He barely spoke to her, and when he did, he mumbled and fumbled for words. He would only look at her out of the corner of his eye if at all and seemed unsure about whether he should take her arm to lead her or not.

At first, she made the decision for him by moving away, practically leading as they walked toward the Hawk Clan area. As they drew nearer, however, she changed her mind and offered Zocan her hand. He took it awkwardly, holding it as something so fragile the slightest pressure might break it. It was small in his palm. She tried to give his hand a reassuring squeeze, but that seemed only to make things worse.

Many eyes turned toward them curiously as they entered the clan area. Jovai looked for Koban and saw him glaring at her and Zocan. His humor seemed exceptionally bad. She decided she would have to ignore him.

It was a strange thing cooking with the women of the Hawk Clan. There were only a few, mostly the widows of the Hawks, only one or two were still wives. All of them were older, near Milapo's age. They still had some children, but there were no young people her age except some Hawk men who all kept their distance. The women spoke very little and kept their eyes submissively downcast when around the men. They treated Jovai with stiff politeness, reminding her with every gesture of the superiority of their positions, and making no effort beyond that to aid her comfort. There was none of the pleasant chatter she had enjoyed with the Kolvas families. These women made no conversation, and Jovai was too unsure to try to initiate any herself.

The dinner was almost equally as uncomfortable. The men stood as the women brought forward the food, but then the women all left to eat by themselves, and only Jovai was allowed to stay. She was seated between Lofar, the scarred clan leader, and Zocan, who still would not even look at her. The only other men near her were the older ones. The young men, including Koban, sat far away on the other side of the fire.

The food was passed around only once and whatever was left was taken by the children to where they and their mothers ate. No one talked during dinner. Instead, old and young all stared at her, watching her curiously while she ate. The silent attention was discomforting, and she felt sure she was embarrassing her teacher many times over. Milapo had been right. She should not have come.

At a signal from Lofar, the dinner finally ended and the men dispersed. The women came to clear the eating bowls. Jovai automatically rose to help them.

"No," said Lofar, rising beside her, "The other women can do that. You come walk with me."

Zocan looked up at his clan head questioningly. Lofar shook his head and signaled him to stay.

Lofar and Jovai walked a long way in silence. It was the clan leader's privilege to initiate conversation, but he didn't choose to until they had left the ears of the camp behind.

"What do you think of Zocan?" asked Lofar.

"He is a Hawk and therefore honorable," Jovai answered politely.

"Will you marry him?"

"I haven't decided."

"Then tell me honestly what makes you uncertain."

"He is old," she answered.

"Is that all?" asked Lofar, as though it were nothing.

"It is the worst, until I know him better. My family wants me to have as many children as I can. I should therefore take a husband who will live at least as long as I can breed."

"Humph," said Lofar. "It is a good thing to want many children, but the quality of child is also important. There are no better men anywhere than the Hawks, so there can be no better children than their children."

"True enough clan leader," she acquiesced. "You are right. We need both quantity and quality of children."

She slipped easily and naturally into the spirit tongue and suggested, *"You should let your young men marry."*

"Eh?" asked Lofar, not understanding her words. She continued in Kolvas as though she had never spoken any other.

"The best husband for me would naturally be one of the younger Hawks who could give me the best children for as long as I could bear them. But since they may not marry, I should look to the other young men, perhaps to the Dog Clan."

"The Dogs!" exclaimed Lofar disdainfully, "They are only the ones we wouldn't take."

"My teacher would make me the best husband," said Jovai in the spirit's tongue again.

Lofar shook his head, as if suspecting that something in his ears might be making him misunderstand her words.

"Even if the excellent reputation of your clan did not speak for you so loudly," continued Jovai in Kolvas, "the acquaintance I have with my teacher, Koban would have convinced me that you are certainly the bravest, strongest and most honorable of men. But one way or another it seems I must compromise. I will either not have enough children for my people, or I will not have the bravest and strongest to grow into proud warriors like their father."

"There are many reasons why our younger men don't marry," Lofar told her. "You must remember how they serve our people.

When they go into war, they must think only of fighting and not be distracted by concerns of wives and children. Also, very many get killed. There is no way to be sure that a young Hawk who still serves and fights will live any longer than an old Hawk whose fighting is, except in emergency, finished."

"If we were still at war…"

"We are still at war," Lofar interrupted. "It can surprise us any time. We need all our Hawk men who can serve to continue to serve."

"The more reason for healthy children to grow into brave warriors."

"Exactly!" Lofar smiled, pleased.

"But we also need as many as we can get. I am told the strength of the Akarians is not in the quality of their men but in the quantity. They never stop coming."

"I know, from more years of fighting than you have even lived, that two good men are of more value in a war than twenty weak ones."

"When the Akarians come, if they come, they will not be twenty, but more likely thousands, or so I'm told."

"If that is so then we will take every man, weak or strong."

"Then my husband, if he is a young, strong warrior, has a better chance of surviving than if he were only an untrained farmer or a dying old man."

"He has almost no chance at all if he's thinking of you instead of his enemy."

"You know your people best, of course," answered Jovai with a submissive nod.

"I know men," he answered. "I know how they work."

"Kolvas men certainly," she answered. "The people from whom I come have found that the men who are husbands and fathers make the most valiant warriors since they fight not only to kill the enemy but also to protect the families they love."

"To the Hawk men, all their people are their family. And their immortality comes from the stories that will be told of their courage at facing death."

"I defer to your wisdom," she answered politely, then quickly added in the spirits tongue, "*which would give me Koban as a husband.*"

"Eh?" he said. "You said something about Koban?"

"Only that he had told me of the greatness of your wisdom. He and others. Many speak glowingly of the way you freed the women Hawks to marry."

"I was never comfortable with women Hawks," Lofar admitted.

"They praise your wisdom in properly judging situations and bravely doing what needs to be done in them, even when it calls for defying custom. Since our people now need as many healthy, strong children as possible, it is only correct to free the young people to produce them. It is this wisdom, they say, that has made you so famous and admired as a leader in war."

Lofar smiled proudly at her words. Jovai watched, pleased, as the expression on his face grew distant. She guessed he was looking back over his life at all the accomplishments of which, indeed, his people did speak well. He was a proud man, she had been warned, but one who had every reason to be proud.

"Then you will trust my wisdom enough to marry Zocan?" he asked, after a while.

"I will marry a young man," she answered, as politely as possible, "one whom the spirits may be pleased to let grow old with me."

"And birth weak, scrawny little brats who will do no one any good?"

"These are hard times," she said softly. "The men who would make the best fathers may not be fathers without your approval, so I must choose as well as I can from those who are left."

"Then who will you choose if you will not choose Zocan who is the best?"

"My family will know my decision by the next full moon."

"We have Farmot. He is a little younger than Zocan."

"He is still too old."

"A brave warrior deserves a wife!" insisted Lofar.

Jovai shook her head and said no more.

"How was your dinner last night?" asked Difsat, during the early meal the next day.

"Not very pleasant," she answered, giving him warning. She knew all her family were curious, especially since Lofar had insisted on talking to Difsat privately for almost the whole morning. "You don't like to talk about unpleasant things while eating, but they don't speak at all. They just stare, as if they'd never seen a woman before."

She turned to her little sister and bulged her eyes in demonstration. Filani gasped in surprise, then squealed with laughter at Jovai's unexpected funny face.

As soon as the meal was finished, Difsat took her aside.

"What did you talk about with the Hawk Clan?" he asked.

"I only talked to Lofar. We discussed whether Zocan was too old for me or not."

"And what did you two decide?"

"I decided that Zocan was too old and Lofar decided that I was too stubborn and foolish."

"That isn't at all what he told me."

"What did he say?" asked Jovai, suddenly worried. She was sure Difsat would recognize her shaman's manipulations if Lofar remembered enough to describe them. It had been the impulse of a moment, and she had counted heavily on his dismissing her gentle spirit tongue suggestions as his own bad hearing.

"He liked you very much. He is very eager for you to marry into his clan. He wants me to put every pressure I can on you to do so."

Jovai took a deep breath and let it out slowly. She was not sure whether to be relieved or not.

"So, will you do as he asks?" she wanted to know.

"You understand that the Hawk Clan is very important to us, especially right now," he began. Jovai nodded. "We need them." He paused, watching Jovai. She waited, tensely. "But I do not think I need to buy them with my daughter. At least, not this one."

Jovai smiled with relief. "Thank you, Family Father."

"He is very anxious, though. Almost desperate. He even suggested, though I'm sure he wasn't serious, that he might release one of his younger men for you to marry."

"He did?" she stared at Difsat in open, eager astonishment. Her suggestions had worked. She had never used them like that before, and she could hardly believe that they had really worked!

Difsat was watching her so closely she was sure he could see her heart pounding in her chest. She blushed furiously and lowered her eyes.

"Of course, I discouraged him from that," Difsat continued. "If you want a young man, that's fine, but there are enough for you to choose from without sacrificing one of our warriors. You have enough trouble making up your mind without adding to the options."

"The Hawks are the best," she said slowly, keeping her eyes lowered.

"That's only what the Hawk Clan claims," said Difsat dismissively. "There are plenty men who could have been Hawks but chose not to. Not everyone needs the discipline. You go find someone else."

"Yes Difsat," she said, doing her best to hide her disappointment.

"I asked Lofar how you behaved. He said you were quiet at dinner, but otherwise very good. He was very impressed with you."

"Koban drilled me for days on every detail, but he said I shouldn't talk before the clan leader did."

"A Hawk would not, but a guest might."

"I'll remember from now on," she promised, halfheartedly.

"I think you've learned everything Koban can teach you. A little while ago he said you should have a woman as a teacher, to teach you woman things. Now I think he's right."

"It won't dishonor Koban, will it?" she asked. She was sure now what Difsat guessed.

"He hasn't broken his oath, has he?" asked Difsat, suddenly switching to the spirit's tongue.

Jovai stared at him in surprise and could not think to speak.

"He has told you of his oath, hasn't he?" pressed Difsat.

She nodded slowly.

"He told me," she answered. "No, he hasn't broken it. He is very honorable."

Difsat smiled with relief.

"People understand that women need to learn from women," he told her, once again in Kolvas, "It'll be all right."

CHAPTER 41

LATOHVA'S CHOICE

Koban called her away from the irrigation ditch she was digging that afternoon.

"Hasn't Difsat talked to you yet?" she asked as she approached.

"No. What?"

"You're not my teacher anymore."

He stared at her shocked.

"Why?" He asked at last, worry in his voice. "What have I done?"

"You taught me too well," she told him. "And you told Difsat I needed a woman teacher. Now he thinks you're right."

"Didn't you tell him the same thing?" he asked.

She looked away, guilty with sudden memory, "Yes."

"Come walk with me," he said. When she resisted, he took her arm. "They haven't dismissed me yet, so I'm still your teacher, at least for today."

"Did you tell him anything?" he asked when they were away from the people.

"He asked me if you had kept your oath. I told him you had."

"What does he think?"

"That I would do better staying with women and men I could

marry."

"Do you think that?"

"I know it!"

"So, if I...if I still played for you...would you still come?"

She hesitated. He slipped his arm around her waist. Even that was dangerous. Anyone could come by at any time. She should have pulled away, but she didn't.

"They'll know it's you," she said at last. "And it won't do any good."

"Don't my lessons still please you?" He nuzzled her ear, then lightly kissed the nape of her neck. She caught her breath and shivered.

"Then you'll come," he whispered.

She nodded.

There were footsteps in the forest, and a small group of people passed nearby, carrying tools to aid a clearing. They didn't see the couple, but both Koban and Jovai were painfully aware that they could have, easily. Koban let her go, but neither moved away.

"My family might stop me," said Jovai.

"Don't let them."

"But they're right!"

"Why? We're doing nothing wrong..."

"They why do we hide?"

It took him a moment to find a reason.

"So people don't think we're doing more," he answered at last.

"But you wouldn't, even if you could," she said.

"Would you?" he demanded.

"I'm going to have to, with someone I don't even know, by the next full moon. You know, that's only a matter of days..."

"You have a choice."

"What?"

"You can leave. No one can make you marry if you're not here."

"Leave!" She sat down, shocked, on the root of a tree.

"It's just an option," he said quickly.

"Do you want me to go?" She looked up at him, her eyes filled with tears.

"No. Of course not. But I don't want you to be unhappy." He knelt beside her and pulled her into his arms. "No. I don't want you to go. At least, not alone. You're happy here, aren't you?"

She nodded, although at the moment she wasn't too sure.

"No. Don't go then. I didn't mean it."

"I've left one people already. I don't want to leave another."

He held her in his arms and stroked her long hair.

"Don't go," he begged her, "I won't let you go."

"You're going to have to," she reminded him, "by the next full moon."

Every day Difsat asked her for her choice with increasing pressure. Every day she declined to answer, reminding him of the deadline he had allowed her.

"You just be sure to tell me first," he instructed, "before you tell anyone who might tell the Hawk Clan leader. I'll lose a lot of power over him as soon as he knows for sure you won't marry his man."

Koban called to her every night, but Difsat watched her with such angry suspicion the first time Jovai tried to sneak away, that when she met him that night, she begged Koban not to play for her anymore. She swore an oath as strong as his that she would not sneak out to see him again. He played even more sweetly after that, with such heartrending beauty that it took all her will, and Difsat sleeping across the door, to resist.

Latohva received several more invitations from the Hawk Clan. She politely turned every one of them down. Lofar even stopped by their tent one morning, in the hope of talking to Latohva. Politeness required that he talk with Milapo or Difsat first. Difsat was not there, and Milapo successfully wasted so much of his time that, when he was finished, Jovai had already gone to her new teacher and was tied up with her for the rest of the day learning to cut and stitch tanned hides into winter clothes.

Two days before the full moon, as Jovai helped Milapo in the dispensary, Koban came in. He needed an ax, he said. When Milapo turned her back to get it, he quickly leaned forward and whispered to Jovai, "Meet me tonight."

She shook her head.

"It's important!"

He pulled away just as Milapo was returning with the ax. Milapo looked between the two, curiously, but made no comment as she watched Koban leave. Once he was gone, she turned to Jovai and said, "He is crazy."

"Why?" asked Jovai, startled.

"The Hawks are supposed to be hunting today. So for what does he need an ax?"

Koban played that night, continuously. Jovai tried to ignore it. She tried to sleep, but sleep would not come. Long into the depths of the night Koban played without a pause. He wouldn't give up. He had promised himself to play all the way till sunrise if he had to. Just when he was thinking he'd really have to, she came.

"Latohva!" he exclaimed, joyfully pulling her into his arms.

"Koban, please," she said, pushing him away, "It just makes it harder."

"No, let me kiss you," he insisted. "Let me feel you! We don't have much time left."

"If you want to know who I'll marry I haven't decided yet. It's between three, maybe four. I don't know. I'll talk to Difsat and Milapo tomorrow and let them help me choose."

"Let me choose," he begged.

"No," she told him. "You'll only choose someone awful."

"I won't," he promised. "I'll choose someone wonderful. I'll choose someone strong and handsome and brave and young, who will live forever if you'll be his wife and who will love you for as long as he lives."

"Who?"

"Me."

She stared at him astonished.

"You?"

He smiled. "If I asked you to run away with me, would you?"

"Leave the Kolvas?"

He nodded, his smile broadening.

"We couldn't ever come back, could we?"

"No," he said, grinning like a fool.

"And we'd shame everyone. We'd shame ourselves, our families, that clan you're so proud of! It's my fault Gilix left, and now I'd be stealing another person from them. And you! How could you do it? You know how much your people need you now. How could you do that to them?"

"I don't plan to," he said with a laugh. "I just wanted to see if you'd consider it."

"Well I won't," she said angrily.

He beamed with triumph. "You already did."

"So, it's all a joke," she exclaimed, pulling away. "You call me out here in the middle of the night, you get me in trouble with my family, and you trick me and hurt me, just for a joke!"

"No," he said, still smiling, "I called you out here to see if you would marry me."

"I thought you didn't care."

"I couldn't," he said, trying to take her in his arms again. She raised her fists, warning him away. He only grinned. "But now I can."

"Are you drunk?" she demanded.

He laughed.

"I've been playing almost the whole night without a break. My throat's drier than my flute."

"Then what are you talking about?"

"I'll show you if you'll let me," he said, trying to draw closer. She raised her fists higher.

"No. You tell me. Now. No games or I'll hate you for as long as I live."

Koban laughed, with pure joy. "I'm released, Latohva! Lofar says he'll let me marry you. In fact, of all the Hawks, he chose me. He chose me. Me! He called me to him this morning and told me so himself."

"Are you still going to be a Hawk?" Jovai asked, unsure of what she was hearing.

"That's the best part! No, marrying you is the best part. But I can still be a warrior! He says he has been thinking that maybe, if a man has a family, he will fight all the harder because he has something real to protect. He says he's not sure. He's going to test this idea on me if I want. If you want."

"Can you marry anyone?" she asked.

"No," he answered, confused. "Why would I want to?"

"Why would you want to marry me?"

"Because you're...you're you. You're beautiful. You're...you're the woman I want."

"I thought I was stubborn and arrogant and untamable."

"I love you," he said, looking at her sternly, "but I hate your memory. Why bring that up now? You know I only said it to discourage Zocan."

"I think you want to marry me because that's the only way to get released from your oath."

"So why do you think I want to get released?"

"Do you really love me?"

He nodded, suddenly serious.

"I can't stop thinking about you, Latohva. All the time when I should be doing other things I'm thinking of your smile, your words, the way you laugh, how funny you look when you raise your fists." He took her fists in his hands, kissed them, and gently pulled her into his arms. "I'm remembering how you feel pressed against my body. Sometimes, it'll come to me when you're not even there — the way you smell, or the taste of your skin, or the sound of your voice, even when I know you're nowhere near me. I see you sometimes, across the camp, and I get so dizzy I can hardly stand. I dream about you every night, and in every dream, I break my oath over and over. Sometimes you're dancing, and I'm so hot I think I'm sitting in the fire. Sometimes we're swimming, and your tunic is clinging against your body. Sometimes we're even fighting, and you're dressed like a boy, then I get you in my arms, and you look at me, and you're trusting and beautiful! Sometimes I'm riding the White One's horse, only then it's not the horse, just the wind. Then the wind becomes you, all around me, dancing to my music as if I were master of the wind. Marry me, Latohva. I'll go crazy if you don't."

She kissed him, long and slow, rubbing her body against his, letting her arms and hands caress his strong back, his firm buttocks, his hard thighs. He responded ravenously. He kissed her as though he could never stop, his hands eagerly working their way up her tunic, under her skirts.

"So, you do feel something when I kiss you?" she asked as his mouth worked its way down her neck toward her breasts.

"I feel everything!"

"All right then," she sighed, "I'll think about it."

"No!" He let his hand continue where the tunic stopped his mouth. "What do you need to think about? You love me don't you?"

She kissed his ear and buried her face in the crook of his neck without answering. Her fingers lightly traced the stiff bulge under his tunic. He gasped in pleasure but would not be distracted.

"Say you love me, Latohva! Say you'll marry me or I'll stop this right now."

"Can you?" she asked. She slipped her hand up under his tunic and stroked him.

"Woman! Where did you learn that?"

She brought her lips almost to his.

"From you," she answered, smiling.

He plunged into the kiss, and she responded eagerly, but when she started to ease him toward the ground, he pulled away in panic.

"I'm still under my oath!" He exclaimed, panting for breath, his eyes wild. "Tell me you'll marry me, Latohva!"

"I'll make my decision tomorrow," she said, picking up her shawl, "and I promised Difsat he'd be the first to know."

"No!" cried Koban. "Tell me now!"

But she was already running back to her home.

She was too excited to even try to go to sleep. She considered building a fire, but she felt too restless to sit beside it. She had to dance. She had to sing! She hadn't felt like singing since she had been sold away from her people, but now the joy rushed to her throat, and she could not stop it. She slipped by the guards and ran down to the river. It was beautiful, sparkling under the almost full moon. There was no mist tonight. There had been none for a month. She raised her voice and sang the celebration of her life coming clear. She heard a baby cry, or maybe only a faraway bird, but she sang to it anyway. She sang to the new world sleeping in the tree. She sang to her own children to be. She sang to a life full of wonder and delight. She sang until her feelings overwhelmed her in a tearful laugh and then her laugh became a song.

Through the trees behind her, a figure approached. She knew someone was coming and she raised her voice in welcome.

"I've come to hear you sing," the figure said, stopping in the shadows.

Jovai didn't recognize the person. She was an old woman, her

366

silver hair glinting in the moonlight, with wise eyes twinkling like stars at Jovai. Jovai felt happy in the woman's presence. She sang and told the stranger of her reasons to be happy, of her feelings for a man who felt the same way for her, of her acceptance by a wonderful people, of her thrill that she would someday hold a baby of her own. All the things that she had been so afraid to even dream of before were suddenly coming true for her. She raised her voice in a prayer and wished for everyone in all existence to share in the joy she felt.

The stranger smiled.

"Be happy Jovai, Latohva," came the blessing in the spirit tongue, and then the stranger disappeared.

Jovai stared at the suddenly empty place, then slowly smiled.

"I will," she promised the old woman of the Vohees. "Thank you."

———◆———

Here ends "**Jovai: The Vohee Song**"
Book 1 of *The Shaman's Apprentice* series
by B. Muze

Special Scenes

The next book of *The Shaman's Apprentice* series, "**Latovah: Dancing Light of the Kolvas**" begins after Jovai is married. You can enjoy "Tying the Knots" - the description of Jovai's Kolvas wedding - for free by downloading it through:

https://BookHip.com/TGXNKNH

To subscribe to my newsletter please visit my website, **www.B-Muze.com** or **www.BAMuze.com**

Also, soon to be released, is the audiobook of "**Jovai: The Vohee Song.**"

Subscribe to my newsletter to know exactly when, and to take advantage of the early day's sale.

If you enjoyed this story, please post a review on Amazon.com, GoodReads.com,- and every other appropriate forum.

Who is B. Muze?

It seems odd to me that anyone cares about the personal details of the author of a work of fiction. A fair chunk of the world doesn't even believe that Shakespeare wrote his plays, but does that make them less enjoyable? So why drag me away from writing stories, which I love, and shatter my privacy, which I value far more than praise, wealth, or fame, to make me write this? I did it only because my editor insisted that people who enjoy my stories will enjoy them more if they know more about me.

So, here is me: I'm an American. Proudly! I'm mixed race, as most in the United States are. I have the blood of slaves, the blood of slave-masters, the blood of those who sacrificed and died to free the slaves, and the blood of many others who had no part in that mess at all, flowing through my veins. I am of the people who stood near the shore watching weird, white clouds moving across the ocean, attached to wooden ships full of pale, seasick strangers, and of the people who felt driven to cross the globe to make a home out of an unknown wilderness, in the hope that, with this fresh start, they would build a better world.

My ancestors each had their own, different, stories, traditions, and mythologies, which they passed down and shared with me. I loved it all, and now seek to share it with my children.

Some strive to keep all the people in the world divided from each other according to superficial qualities, but I am of a people who embraced all this variety and joined it together joyously, through love. There are some pockets of the world which are not yet be adequately represented in my personal lineage, but a few more generations and my descendants will likely have those as well. Meanwhile, I claim the right to explore and enjoy even those cultures.

I'm an American, and among all the God-given rights I treasure, is the right to love, honor, and celebrate anyone and everyone I choose!

To find out more about me, visit my website:
https://www.BAMuze.com. or
https://www.B-Muze.com
or contact me through my publisher:
https://www.WittilyWrit.com

Coming soon!

Book 2 of *The Shaman's Apprentice* series
Latohva: The Kolvas' Dancing Light
by B. Muze

The shaman's apprentice has betrayed her master to build a life with the man she loves. She no longer seeks the spirits, but still they are irresistibly drawn to her... as is something far more horrifying. Jovai is faced with a heartbreaking choice. Will she stay and watch her family and friends destroyed by a being of such immense evil that the entire world is gradually being annihilated by it, or should she try to draw it away by abandoning everyone she loves, never to return? The only other option is impossible. How can she, a failed shaman, dare to fight the insatiable demon-god who is hunting her? What chance could she have to conquer it, or even to survive?

Wittily Writ Publishing
https://www.WittilyWritPublishing.com
For more information sign up for B. Muze's Newsletter from her website:
https://www.B-Muze.com or
https://www.BAMuze.com

Sneak Preview

from Book 2 of
The Shaman's Apprentice Series -

Latovah: Dancing Light of the Kolvas

Chapter 1

The Fall of the Bat Clan House

Through the chase of shadows and light from her torch, Jovai stared at the carved and painted wooden panel covering the entrance into the Bat Clan House. Sweat prickled her brow, despite the pre-dawn, autumn chill, and her heart beat too quickly. With a deep breath, she commanded herself to be calm. Her self, willful as ever, refused to obey.

She had designed this panel to honor not only the Kolvas gods, but also the greatest of her Vohee spirits, so that they might aid the Kolvas in their new home. The figures depicted in it, both carved by a master woodworker at her direction and painted, seemed to come alive and dance to the soft crackle of the torch's fire.

On their own, Jovai's fingers stretched forward to trace the double-sided face of the greatest of her Vohee gods, the Mother/ Father, Creater of All. The face, half-male and half-female, was its common image, but not how the god had appeared to her. The god had shown her only one face – flawless, ageless and whole – too perfect to capture in the wood.

Now that this panel was in place and the house dedicated to the Kolvas' shamen, her own work felt like a barrier against her. Only real shamen and their apprentices should now enter here. The symbols of her own gods and spirits reminded Jovai that she was not a shaman. She was only a nameless nothing..

"Why won't you believe me?" Jovai asked Difsat, the father of her new family, civil leader of the Kolvas, and the head of the Bat Clan shamen.

Difsat was a large man – not nearly as tall as Jovai's Vohee master, Yaku Shaman, but still at least a head taller than the average man of her Vohee people . He towered over her. In this land, which had provided abundant game and forage all summer, Difsat was quickly growing wider as well. He had the red-brown skin and dark-auburn hair typical of his people, with a broad brow, wide nose, and thick lips. Today, instead of his normal leggings, he wore a colorful cloth wrapped around his hips that covered him to below his knees. He had put aside his common tunic, in favor of a more finely woven one, and a long, ceremonial, woven vest, both newly made. His long hair was pulled into a knot on top of his head, marking this as a formal occasion.

Difsat murmured a quick prayer as he untied the rope, holding the panel in place, and pulled it aside along the pole from which it hung, revealing a hanging tapestry behind.

"We'll talk inside," he murmured, taking the torch from Jovai.

Jovai shook her head. "I won't join the Bat Clan..."

"Inside, Latohva!"

Difsat lifted the tapestry and passed through easily, but Jovai felt a pressure pushing against her as she tried to follow.

Do you belong? it challenged.

Will you keep me out? she asked.

The barrier dissipated, allowing her to enter.

As she passed through the tapestry, an image of a large group of strange men with many weapons, forcing their way into this sanctuary, assaulted her mind. A rapacious spirit, like a dark mist, cloaked them. It rushed them to destruction – not only of others but of themselves as well. She heard crashes, the yells of warriors, cries of children cut suddenly short, and screams of terror and agony all around her. The smoke of the burning city seared her nose and lungs. Everything they had worked so hard to build was being destroyed!

"Come!" Difsat's impatience dispelled the vision, leaving Jovai momentarily reeling. Had that been a Kolvas memory, she wondered, or a prophesy? It was certainly from a Kolvas spirit, but which one and what it meant, she did not know.

Unlike other houses, which entered onto a ledge with a ladder to climb down to the open, main space, the Bat Clan House stepped up onto a wooden floor, coated lightly with clay and eventually to be covered with rugs. They had to pass over the full length of this floor to get to the ladder on the far side of the house. Even though she knew it was well supported by many wooden beams, the thought of this heavy floor suspended over so much space made Jovai nervous.

"Here," Difsat said. He held his torch up with one hand while his other pointed to the ladder, disappearing into the darkness below them. "You go first."

The next level down was another wooden floor. It was a place for training, storage, and some of the simpler rituals.

"Keep going," Difsat told her as she stepped off the ladder onto the second floor.

"But..."

"Don't argue, Latohva!"

The bottom level was the holiest. Now that it had been dedicated, it was reserved for only the fully initiated Kolvas shamen. It was the place of their most important rituals. Even if Difsat succeeded in forcing her to join the Bat Clan, Jovai expected this area would be forbidden to her for many years, until her training was complete.

"Take off your sandals," Difsat said as she neared the stone and clay floor, "and put them in there." He nodded toward a large basket hanging from the wall beside the ladder. Then he fixed his torch in a hanger on the other side of the ladder, so he could remove his own shoes.

In the meager torchlight, the room was still too dark to clearly see. Jovai could feel under her bare feet the cool clay she had helped to smooth during the summer. She remembered, rather than saw, the sand pit where bowls, fed by a series of troughs from the large table in the center of the room, were set to catch the blood that would be...that had already been made to flow here. A faint wisp of the odor of that blood mixed with the remnant of incense still clung to the air. Jovai knew, too, that the well for water was dug in the northwest corner. Against the northern wall, between the well and the ladder, were shelves and tables holding various sized bowls and tools for ritual use. Rows of massive wooden beams, imbedded in the stone floor, supported many smaller wooden arms that rose like branches of trees to support the wooden floors above. They had been treated to make them hard and strong, then coated in clay. She had helped paint them with designs that were now hidden in the darkness, and had watched as Difsat carved the figures of his gods and spirits in them.

Difsat headed directly toward the stone fireplace under the high, vented southwest corner across the room. At his instruction, Jovai drew water from the well to fill a bowl, which he placed beside the hearth. Once Difsat had set the wood and tinder in the fireplace, she brought him the torch to light it.

Difsat paused before touching the flame to the wood. With eyes closed, in a sing-song, he chanted a prayer of invocation honoring the gods, especially Kaistai, the Bat spirit. He called to them seeking their direction and protection. Jovai could feel the power gathering. She could sense that the Bat and two other spirits, whom she did not recognize, had responded to Difsat's call, but not any Vohee spirits. Difsat continued his prayer as he lit the fire. Once the fire was well caught, he took a handful of dried herbs from a bowl next to the hearth and threw them onto the flames, then sprinkled them with water to make them steam. A strange scent filled the air, green like grass but with a bitter edge and a cloying feel.

"Breathe deeply," Difsat told Jovai, drawing her near the flames. "Five deep breaths at least. Hold each breath as long as you can before exhaling slowly."

The first deep breath made Jovai cough. The second breath she took was shallower, but she managed to hold it longer. She felt her muscles relaxing and her awareness opening. It was a little like the effect of konis, the Vohee holy drink, she realized during the third breath, only not so overwhelming. With the fourth breath her skin was tingling all over her body and she started to feel dizzy.

As she took the fifth breath, Difsat took hold of her arm and guided her to sit against the southern wall beside the fire. The flames' heat warmed her left cheek and side, but the wall at her back felt cool.

Difsat's touch, however, was a power in itself, flowing into her, steadying her, stone solid and trustworthy, but warm and alive. She could feel that he was a shaman of great power. She forgot that sometimes, with his often playful, laughing manner, especially when she watched him with his wife and children, but now she remembered how he had made the solid earth turn liquid and swallow her once, instantly harding again to hold her trapped with only her head above ground. She remembered how he called on his spirits, strange to her, and Vohee spirits, whom he had not known before, had obeyed his call as well. She remembered moments she had never experienced, in which Difsat had led his people's escape against impossible odds, hiding them in the open, cloaking even the wailing babies in dense silence, calling water to parched desert stones, and creating food from air to allay the hunger of starving, if only in illusion. He had never told her of those things, but the memories flowed through his touch into her.

She opened her eyes to look at him. Instead, she found herself looking through his eyes at herself. She looked young and vulnerable through Difsat's vision, as if she were closer to ten years old than to sixteen. He had pushed her to marry and officiated at the wedding ceremony, only 25 days before, yet she suddenly realized Difsat thought her in many ways still a child. She saw her pale skin glowing with a light of its own, brighter than the torch or even the fire, illuminating all the space around her. Difsat saw her as pulsing with power. No wonder he refused to believe she was not a shaman! If what he saw was real, then it was a trick of the spirits, for whatever power she might have was nothing she could use. She had no shaman name to unlock it.

She had pulled her dark brown hair into a bun behind her head, but Difsat loosed it, letting it flow down her back. Then he stared into her large, brown eyes, now dilated wide in the darkness.

"You are ready," he whispered. His words reverberated through her body and echoed several times in her mind, changing its voice with each repetition to that of a different Kolvas spirit, until it was the high-pitched ring of Kaistai, the Bat. So, they all agreed she was ready, but these were Kolvas spirits whom she still barely knew. What did they know of her or of the evil that haunted her?

Already she could feel her spirit pulling away from her body. She struggled to keep it reigned.

"You put me in danger!" She heard her voice as if from a distance.

380

"The evil spirit..."

"When the last world ended, we sheltered deep in the earth. The earth protected us. Healed us. Strengthened us. It kept us in its womb until the new world was ready for us to come forth. Earth surrounds you here, Latohva. It's why I brought you to the deepest place we have. Earth protects you, heals you, and strengthens you. You do not need to go far, but it is time for you to emerge."

She pondered Difsat's words, wanting them to be true. To be free, to listen deeply, to let her awareness expand again as she once had, was her greatest desire. Difsat didn't need his strange herbs to make her want that. Her lifetime of training had also made her capable of doing it unaided. She could never go home, she knew, but there were those she loved whom she longed to assure herself were well. If she were free, she could see them again and, perhaps, even talk with her master one more time. The blockage was not in her, as Difsat clearly believed, but in the demon that attacked her every time she tried.

"The earth will protect you," Difsat promised, as though reading her thoughts. "And I'm here to guard your body. Let your spirit be free."

"The evil one is too powerful. My master, Yaku Shaman, could not protect me. The spirits would not..." but even as she spoke, she was slipping away, out of her body.

No! Panic engulfed her. Not out. She didn't dare! In desperation she turned her awareness in, instead. She had never done that before. It felt strange to be disconnected from her body and yet inside it. Something as normal as the tide of her breath became a new sensation. She both felt and watched the rocking of her heart, the surging of her blood through her veins...then something surprising. Deep, in the center of her being was something that was not her. It was a spark of life belonging to another person.

Oh! The realization of what it was burst inside her with joy. A baby! So new, so tiny. Delight engulfed her, leaving no room for fear. Koban! She had to tell her husband.

She had barely formed the thought and she was there, next to Koban as he crouched, hiding, in the brush, focused on a buck drinking from the river, easily within an arrow's flight of him. The sun had fully risen now, sparkling on the water and piercing the canopy of the forest with shafts of light. She paused a moment to marvel, yet again, at Koban's handsome, red-brown face, with his straight nose, firm jaw, and sensuous lips. The sight of his strong, muscular body stirred delightful memories of times she had recently spent in his arms. She marveled at the intensity in his brown eyes as he targeted his prey. He was not a shaman. His power was different, but strong in its own way and, at this moment, fully channeled into the hunt. She knew, without doubt, that if he took the shot, he would fell the buck with a single arrow, but he decided against it. He turned slowly and, looking through her, made a hand gesture to the boy behind her. She turned and saw Ainset, the youngest of the Hawk Clan, cautiously raise his blow pipe as he crept, ever so slowly, forward.

She should wait for him to take his shot, she thought, but the boy was wasting so much time she imagined her baby might be born by then. Anyway, she didn't need to bother him. It was her husband she wanted.

"Koban!" she whispered in his ear.

Koban startled, falling backward in surprise. At the sound of the bushes rustling, the buck bounded away.

"What is the matter with you?" Ainset started yelling.

"You're a father!" Jovai told Koban at the same moment. "We've made a baby!"

Koban looked confused.

"I'm a father?" he said to Ainset. "What are you talking about?"

"I said..."

Suddenly everything went dark and silent. Only a sense of craving – not her own – remained. Jovai felt a pressure smothering her, blocking not only light but also space and air. She was no longer with Koban and Ainset, or Difsat, or, for all she could tell, anywhere in the world. The hunger was huge and growing, consuming everything. It was insatiable. It wanted more than her life. It wanted her spirit. Her baby...

In panic she screamed and fought against its tightening grip. She kicked and flailed, as though the spirit had a body. There was nothing to hit or kick or bite. This was not what she should do, she knew. She had to calm herself. She had to become silent, shrink, and wait for an opening. So far there had always been a way to escape if she stayed quiet enough, long enough, but this time, unlike before, she felt unable to breathe.

A silent prayer was all she could manage: "Earth! You protected the Kolvas. Protect me now!"

She was losing consciousness.

"Think!" she commanded herself, but her awareness was dimming too quickly. When it was gone, she would be gone too.

Suddenly, the world lurched. Earth, as if it were a wave of water instead of solid ground, lifted her and the demon, tossing them both, then slamming them down again. In shock, the evil spirit lost his grip on Jovai and she tumbled away, with no sense of up or down. It was her only chance, so she fled, not knowing or caring where she was going.

Jovai felt the demon gathering its power again. Curiousity overwhelmed her fear. Looking back, she got her first view of this thing that had been hunting her since her people and spirits had cast her out. She saw the back of an impossibly large, black wolf, scarred by marks that look like it had survived being savaged by a bear. It slowly rose to stand on its hind legs like a man. As it drew itself up, it also seemed to grow, until it was so massive she could not see around it. There was nothing but an eternal darkness. When it turned toward her, however, she could clearly see that it did not have a wolf's head but something more like a boar's, with huge tusks and a quivering snout. It's eyes, burning red, fixed on her.

"They gave you to me!" it growled in fury. "You're mine!"

Jovai felt, rather than saw, it reach for her again. It didn't mean to grab her this time, but instead to smash her.

"Latohva!" she heard Difsat call.

"Difsat!" she thought, and in the space of that thought she was back with him, in the safety of the Bat Clan House's holy place.

Then the monster's fist crashed down upon her.

———◆———

To read more chapters of "**Latohva: Dancing Light of the Kolvas**" on line please go to

https://BookHip.com/BMKNAJN

To read all of the story, please watch for the release of
"**Latohva: Dancing Light of the Kolvas**"
on Amazon.com or on the author's website at
https://www.B-Muze.com or https://www.BAMuze.com

If you are interested in becoming an advanced reader for B. Muze, contact the author through her website (above) and let her know of your interest. Advanced Readers receive a free Advanced Reader Copy version of the ebook, in exchange for which they are encouraged to note any remaining typos, comment on any inconsistencies or problem areas in the text, offer suggestions for improvement, and, hopefully, leave reviews on Amazon.com and other forums as soon as the book is released.